CRITICS AND READERS PRAISE

DEADLOCK

"Intricate . . . Coulter expertly weaves all the plot threads together. Fans of extravagant thrillers with a paranormal tinge will be satisfied."

—*Publishers Weekly*

"*Deadlock* was a thriller from start to finish . . . an enjoyable ride, especially with our terrific, marvelous heroes. Catherine Coulter once again gives us . . . a fast-paced, exciting, intriguing, suspenseful mystery. If you like suspense, mysteries, espionage, especially in the world of CIA/FBI, I wholly suggest you read *Deadlock*."

—*The Reading Cafe*

"The story line gripped me from the first page, and the twists and turns kept me on the edge of my seat! Looking forward to the next book!"

—R. Shelton

"Just finished reading *Deadlock*. As with all Catherine's books, I loved it."

—A. Lynds

"*Deadlock* is another wonderfully written book that I thoroughly enjoyed. Thank you for always providing such an entertaining read. Can't wait for the next one!"

—S. Burian

"I just finished reading *Deadlock* and loved it as I have all the others. I can't wait for the next one to come out! Thank you so much for all the hours of pleasure your books have given me over the years."

—P. Schaefer

"*Deadlock* has such a great story line that I read it in two sittings! Savich and Sherlock are two of my favorite characters."

—S. Hammontree

LABYRINTH

"Readers will cheer kick-butt Sherlock all the way to the action-packed finale."

—*Publishers Weekly*

"The twenty-third installment in Catherine Coulter's FBI Thriller series comes out this summer, and you're going to want to grab a copy."

—*Bustle*

"Catherine Coulter is one of the bona fide rock stars of the thriller genre, and her last book, *Paradox*, was as good as anything she's written. *Labyrinth* promises to be another 'white-knuckled' thriller, which means Coulter's fans better get their preordering on nice and early."

—*The Real Book Spy*

"The things you can count on in a Catherine Coulter book are a complex story line with plenty of action, intrigue, and unexpected twists and turns. *Labyrinth* has all that and more. . . . With white-knuckled pacing and shocking twists and turns, this is another electrifying novel that will sink its teeth in you."

—*Fresh Fiction*

"Great characters with an interesting story make for a really enjoyable read. . . . I couldn't put this book down it was so good."

—*Red Carpet Crash*

"I began *Labyrinth* Wednesday afternoon and finished it Thursday night! I loved it. I was riveted until the end. Can't wait for the next one!"

—S. Campbell

"*Labyrinth* is a thrill ride from start to finish. Coulter will not disappoint. The interwoven twists and unexpected turns of this fascinating book kept me on the edge of my seat. I couldn't put the book down and finished reading it in two days!"

—M. Gagne

PARADOX

"Pulse-pounding . . . Coulter fans will have a tough time putting this one down."

—*Publishers Weekly*

"Action is nonstop. . . . Perfect reading for the beach and beyond."

—*Booklist*

"Catherine Coulter remains one of the very best at what she does, and *Paradox* is some of her very finest work yet. . . . Eerie, unsettling, and breathlessly terrifying."

—*The Real Book Spy*

THE FBI THRILLERS

A BRIT IN THE FBI THRILLERS (WITH J.T. ELLISON)

CATHERINE COULTER

POCKET BOOKS

NEW YORK   LONDON   TORONTO   SYDNEY   NEW DELHI

Pocket Books
An Imprint of Simon & Schuster, Inc.
1230 Avenue of the Americas
New York, NY 10020

This book is a work of fiction. Any references to historical events, real people, or real places are used fictitiously. Other names, characters, places, and events are products of the author's imagination, and any resemblance to actual events or places or persons, living or dead, is entirely coincidental.

First Pocket Books paperback edition July 2021

POCKET and colophon are registered trademarks of Simon & Schuster, Inc.

For information about special discounts for bulk purchases, please contact Simon & Schuster Special Sales at 1-866-506-1949 or business@simonandschuster.com.

The Simon & Schuster Speakers Bureau can bring authors to your live event. For more information or to book an event, contact the Simon & Schuster Speakers Bureau at 1-866-248-3049 or visit our website at www.simonspeakers.com.

Manufactured in the United States of America

10 9 8 7 6 5 4 3 2 1

ISBN 978-1-5011-9370-5
ISBN 978-1-5011-9372-9 (ebook)

*To my amazing, editorially talented other half,
who never fails to make my work better.*

—Catherine

1

Marsia Gay would be living like a queen, not like an animal locked in a cell, if it weren't for FBI agent Dillon Savich. He was the one who'd screwed her perfect plan sideways, the man responsible for her being locked in this soulless circle of hell. Of course, that bitch Veronica would pay for her betrayal, too, no doubt about that, but he was the one who'd rained this misery down on her, the one she wanted most.

Savich was a dead man walking—but not yet, not just yet. She wanted to savor his downfall. He would die only after she killed the two people closest to him, the two people whose deaths would hurt him most.

She knew she had to snag his interest with something unique, begin with only an oblique threat, nothing too over-the-top, but something enigmatic and bizarre enough that Savich wouldn't be able to resist. And suck him in. She wouldn't underestimate him, not this time. He'd proven he was smart, but she was just as smart—no, she was smarter, and she was going to prove it. She'd make sure Savich knew it was Marsia Gay who'd set everything in motion, who'd had her final revenge. Halloween was coming up. It was the perfect time.

She heard her mother's vodka-slurred voice whisper, *Even as a child, when you wanted something, you grabbed for it, didn't think. Didn't work out for you this time, did it?*

"I won't fail this time!" She didn't realize she'd screamed the words until the guard, a big lummox named Maxie, appeared at the bars and stared at her. Marsia wished she could tear her face off. "A nightmare, sorry."

Maxie didn't point out it wasn't dark yet, too early to sleep. She only shrugged and walked away. Marsia went over to the narrow window that looked out over the desolate exercise yard with its scarred, ancient wooden tables and benches, the pathetic torn basketball hoop where she usually won playing Horse—cigarettes, a small bar of soap from a Holiday Inn, an offer of a prison tattoo made from soot and shampoo or melted Styrofoam, no thank you. She saw Angela lounging against a wall, probably giving orders to her minions. What a sweet name for a mean-as-a-snake muscled gang leader awaiting trial for the murder of her boyfriend and his lover. It hadn't been difficult to seduce Angela into her orbit. She'd been even easier to manipulate than Veronica. Angela had taken to Marsia right away, told her she'd see to it no one would harm her, if Marsia was nice to her. Marsia had shuddered when Angela lightly touched her arm, but, well, Marsia had been nice. Angela always stayed in sight and took care of whatever Marsia wanted. She kept the other bullies away from the pretty artist girl who spoke so beautifully and was always so polite, so of course they hated her instinctively. Angela never tired of hearing about Marsia's sculptures, how she worked with this metal and that. Marsia missed her sculpting, of course, but now she looked forward to returning to her studio once she was found not guilty at her trial, and of course her studio would still be waiting for her. After all, she owned the building.

The wind had stiffened, whipping up the dirt into dust devils. She saw a dozen women wandering around the yard, doing nothing in particular, and one lone prisoner, head down, pacing back and forth, apart from the others. It was Veronica. She'd rarely seen her here. The guards made sure they were kept apart, but soon that wouldn't matter. Marsia knew Veronica well enough to know she felt guilt, awful guilt, about striking the deal as the prosecution's star witness against Marsia in exchange for the safety they'd promised her. *Sorry, Veronica, that isn't going to happen; it's going to get you killed*. With no witness to testify against Marsia, the evidence would be more circumstantial than not. No, not enough to convict her.

Veronica, I'm going to choreograph a special dance for you to mark your exit from the planet. Thank you.

Later, on the edge of sleep, she heard her dead lush of a mother speaking in her ear. *I could tell you things you haven't thought of yet, wormy things you could do. I could help you.*

She didn't scream out this time. She lay there and whispered, "Okay, Mom, talk to me."

2

The last place Rebekah ever expected to find herself was in the home of a medium. Zoltan the Medium was how the woman had introduced herself when she'd called Rebekah. But how do you say no when a medium tells you your grandfather who died only a month ago wants to speak to you? Wants you to forget he's dead and calling from the afterlife? Rebekah almost hung up, almost said, if he's in his afterlife, doesn't that mean his life here on earth is over? As in he's dead? But Zoltan had said her grandfather wanted to speak to his Pumpkin, maybe to warn her about something. Zoltan wasn't sure. Rebekah hadn't wanted to believe any of it, but Pumpkin had been his favorite nickname for her, and how could this self-proclaimed medium possibly know that? She'd felt gooseflesh rise on her arms. She'd had no choice, not really. She knew she had to find out what this was all about, and so here she was, walking behind Zoltan, a woman not that much older than her own twenty-eight years, into her living room. Rebekah had expected to see a table with a long red tablecloth covering it, primed to levitate on command, but there was no table everyone would sit around, only a small coffee table. She saw a long, narrow, high-ceilinged room lit only by one standing lamp in the far corner and draperies rippling in the breeze given off by a low-humming portable fan beside the large front window. Curiously, not far from the fan, a fire burned in the fireplace, low and sullen. However strange the mix, the room was pleasantly warm.

Zoltan wasn't wearing a flowing caftan and matching turban or big shiny hoop earrings in her ears. She was wearing a dark blue silk blouse, black pants, and low-heeled black shoes. Her hair was dark, pulled back in a sleek chignon. Her eyes were so dark a blue they appeared nearly black. She'd looked and seemed perfectly normal when she'd greeted Rebekah. She asked her to be seated on the sofa and offered her a cup of tea.

The tea was excellent: hot, plain, no sugar, the way she liked it. Zoltan smiled at her, sipped her own tea. "I know you don't believe one can speak to the Departed, Mrs. Manvers. Actually, I far prefer a skeptic to blind acceptance. I'm pleased you decided to come. I will tell you what happened. As I said when I called you, your maternal grandfather came to me very unexpectedly while I was trying to contact another Departed for his son. Your grandfather was anxious to speak to you. He called you Pumpkin, which you recognized. Do you wish to proceed?"

Rebekah nodded, drank more tea, and kept any snarky comments to herself.

Zoltan nodded. "Good. Let us begin. I want you to relax, Mrs. Manvers—may I call you Rebekah?"

Rebekah nodded.

"And you may call me Zoltan. I know this is difficult for you, but I need you to try to keep an open mind and suspend judgment. Empty your mind, simply let everything go. Begin by relaxing your neck, your shoulders, that's right. Breathe slowly and deeply. Good."

They sat in silence for a minute or so before Zoltan spoke again, her voice low and soothing. "Rebekah, when your grandfather crashed my party, so to speak, all he told me was he had to speak to you. I don't know why he was so anxious, he didn't say. On his third visit, three nights ago, he finally identified himself and you by your married name so I could contact you. He always came when other clients were here. Why? I don't know. Maybe it was easier for him to reach me with the pathway already open. His message was always, 'Rebekah, I want

Rebekah, I want my Pumpkin. I must tell her—'
A warning? That's what I thought, but I really don't
know. I asked you to bring something personal of
his with you."

Rebekah opened her handbag and pulled out a
letter and a photograph of her and her grandfather
standing on the steps of the Capitol building, people flowing around them. He was smiling, eager to
get on with his life, and beside him Rebekah, just
turned eleven, was clutching his hand and looking
as happy as he was. He had no way of knowing
what would happen to him, but of course, no one
did. The photograph had been taken a year before
the series of strokes happened and effectively ended
his life, leaving him in a coma for sixteen years.
He'd finally died last month and been buried in
Arlington National Cemetery with all due pomp,
with Rebekah's husband standing next to her, his
arm around her. Rebekah felt tears swim in her
eyes as she handed Zoltan the photograph and the
letter.

Zoltan took the letter, didn't read it, but seemed
to weigh it in her hand. She took the photograph,
glanced at it, then placed it faceup over the letter, in
front of Rebekah.

"Rebekah, please place your left hand over the
letter and the photograph and give me your right
hand."

Rebekah did as she was asked. She no longer
felt like she'd fallen down the rabbit hole. She was

beginning to feel calmer, more settled, perhaps even receptive. She let her hand relax in Zoltan's. "Why my right hand? Why not my left?"

Zoltan said, "I've learned the right hand carries more latent energy than the left. Odd but true, at least in my experience. Good. I want you to think about what your grandfather said to you that day the photograph was taken, think about what you were feeling in that moment. Now picture the man in the photograph. Tell me about him."

"Before the strokes and the coma, he was in Congress, always on the go, always busy with his political maneuvering against the incumbent majority. I remember that day he was happy. A bill I think he'd authored had passed." She paused a moment. "As for the letter, it's the last one he wrote me. It was chatty, nothing serious. Grandfather rarely emailed me; he preferred to write his letters to me in longhand."

"Now, lightly touch the fingers of your left hand to the photograph. Let them rest on your grandfather's face. Excellent. Close your eyes, picture his face in your mind, and simply speak to him as if he were sitting beside you on the sofa. It's all right if you think this is nothing more than a silly exercise, but indulge me, please."

Rebekah didn't resist. She was feeling too relaxed. Zoltan poured her another cup of tea from the carafe on the coffee table. Rebekah drank, savored the rich, smooth taste, and did as Zoltan said. Oddly, she saw her grandmother's face, cold and aloof, not her grandfather's. Gemma had been a séance junkie all her life, something that made Rebekah's mom roll her eyes. Grandmother was talking to dead people? No, her mother had said, talking to the dead was crazy, meant for the gullible. Rebekah wondered if her grandmother had tried to contact her husband since his death. Why would she? To gloat that he was dead and she wasn't?

Zoltan said again, "Rebekah? Please speak to your grandfather. Picture him here with you. Speak what's in your heart. Be welcoming."

Rebekah said, her voice clear, "Grandfather, I remember you when you were well and happy before you fell into a coma. I loved you so much and I knew you loved me. Everyone called me your little confidante, and it was true. You trusted me with all the stories you called your secret adventures, even when I was a kid. Do you know I kept my promise to you never to tell anyone the stories, not even my mother, certainly not my grandmother? They were always only between us. You made me feel very special." Her voice caught. "I miss you, Grandfather. I think of you every day and pray you're at peace." She knew, objectively, when he'd fallen into the coma, his life was over, though his body held on. She knew she should have been relieved when his body finally let go, but the reality of his actual death still broke her. She swiped away a tear, swallowed. "Zoltan said you want to speak to me. If you can hear me, I hope you can come—through." Her voice fell off. She felt a bit silly, but oddly, it didn't overly concern her.

The draperies continued to flutter in the breeze, the fire stayed sullen. The lamplight, however, seemed to dim, then brighten, and dim again. Zoltan's face was now in shadow. She said in the same gentle voice, each word slow and smooth, "Keep talking to him, Rebekah. I can feel a presence hovering close, and it's familiar."

Rebekah didn't feel anything different. Well, except for the dimmed lamplight. Zoltan's right hand held Rebekah's, and her left hand lay palm up on her lap. Rebekah knew she should feel like an idiot, but she didn't. She felt relaxed, curious to see what would happen. "Perhaps it isn't really Grandfather you're feeling, Zoltan—"

Zoltan suddenly raised her left hand, and Rebekah stopped talking. "Is that you, Congressman Clarkson? Are you here?"

The draperies grew still, though the fan continued to churn the air. The fire suddenly sparked, shooting up an orange flame, then the burning wood crumbled, making a soft thudding sound. The lamplight grew brighter, then flickered and went completely dark.

Only the dying fire lit the room.

All tricks, she's pressing some magic buttons with her foot—

She felt Zoltan's hand tighten ever so slightly around hers. "Someone is here, Rebekah," Zoltan said calmly in her soft, even voice. "I can't be certain until the Departed talks to me, but the feeling of his presence is, as I said, familiar. Do you know of a nickname your grandfather was called? Or did you yourself have a special name for him as he did for you?"

She remembered her grandfather's face, clear as day, saw him throw back his head and laugh at something she'd said. She whispered, "Methodist, that was his nickname. He told me his cohorts in Congress called him Methodist, too. The name got out, and even his own staff began calling him that—'Methodist believes this, Methodist said that.'" She swallowed tears again, hating they were so close to the surface. "I remember hearing Grandmother say he'd made up the name himself. When I asked him, he admitted it, said he didn't want anyone else making up a name for him, particularly the opposition, and Methodist practically made him a poster boy for God, full of probity and sheer boring honesty. A lot of people called him that before his first stroke."

"Call him by his nickname."

Very well, play along, why not? At best, it's entertainment, but you're here, so why not go along with it? But is it only entertainment? Grandmother would believe it, maybe, but not me.

She felt foolish, but she cleared her throat. "Grandfather—Methodist?—it's Rebekah, your granddaughter. If you are here, tell me what's so important."

A puff of dense black smoke plumed up from the fireplace embers, making an odd sucking sound. The lamp brightened, then darkened again.

Rebekah's throat was dry, and she drank some more tea, then placed her right hand back into Zoltan's. She knew the lamp, the fire, the billowing draperies were simple stage props, but she didn't really care, it wasn't important. She had to know what her grandfather wanted to tell her or what this woman wanted her to believe he did. Rebekah was surprised how calm she felt, her body and mind relaxed. Still, how could any of this be true?

Zoltan said, "I'm not sure if it's your grandfather I feel. Is your grandmother alive, Rebekah?"

"Yes, she is. Her name is Gemma Clarkson. She's in her late seventies. She continues to run all of Grandfather's businesses in Clairemont, Virginia, west of Richmond, where she and my grandfather lived all their lives. Clairemont was in his district."

"Did your grandfather and grandmother have a strong bond? Would speaking about her to him perhaps make him come through the Verge? That's what I call the threshold the spirits have to cross back over into our reality."

"No," Rebekah said, nothing more. It was none of Zoltan's business. Even Rebekah couldn't remember a time when her grandparents had shown any affection for each other, and her memories went back a very long way. She'd never seen her grandmother at the Mayfield Sanitarium during those sixteen long years her grandfather had lain there helpless, his only sign of life his still-beating heart. She'd asked her grandmother once, back in the beginning when she'd been young, why she didn't visit Grandfather. Her grandmother had merely said, "Perhaps I will." But Rebekah didn't think she had.

"I think my grandmother was glad when he died. She did go to his funeral, but she had to, didn't she? I doubt she'd want to be here in my place if she thought her husband would show up. Even though she'd believe it."

"Your grandmother is a believer, then?"

"Yes, but she's always careful because she thinks most mediums are frauds. That's what I heard her tell my mother."

She wanted to ask Zoltan if she was a fraud, but when she looked into Zoltan's eyes, darker now in the dim light, and felt her intensity, she let the thought go.

"Your grandmother is perfectly correct. There are many frauds." Zoltan began to hum softly, then she said, her voice barely above a whisper, "Congressman Clarkson? Methodist? Are you having trouble coming through this time? If you are, reach out to me, and I will speak for you to Rebekah. Come, I am open to you. I am your conduit. You've already connected with me, you know you can trust me. Your granddaughter is here. You must try again."

The lamp bulb burst into brightness that reached the far corners of the living room. Thick black smoke erupted upward from the fireplace embers, and the draperies began to move again. Rebekah held perfectly still. She heard her own voice whisper, "Grandfather, is that you?"

Zoltan said in the same soft chant, "Come in through me, Congressman. Let me speak for you. Give me your words so I can tell Rebekah what concerns you so greatly. Come through me."

Nothing happened. Rebekah took another drink of her tea, realized she was perfectly content to wait. The air was warm, and she felt calm, open, expectant, which she should realize was silly, but it didn't seem to matter.

Suddenly, Zoltan whooshed out a breath and stiffened. Her eyes closed, and her hand tightened around Rebekah's again, then eased. Rebekah felt a fluttering of movement, a brush against her cheek, and jumped. *What was that?* The hair lifted off the back of her neck as if there were electricity in the air. She whispered, "Grandfather?"

The room grew dim again, the embers quieted. Zoltan's lips began to move, and out came a flat, low voice, not quite like Zoltan's own voice, but deeper, sounding somehow distant, and older—like her grandfather's voice. "My dearest Rebekah. To speak to you again, even through this woman, it brings me great joy. You visited me when I still breathed earthly air. I knew it was you, always, and I understood you when you spoke to me. You came nearly every day, and I loved you for it. You held my hand, talked to me, and I savored each of your words, your loving presence. Everyone believed I was gone, even the doctors believed I was locked helpless into my brain, nothing left of my reason, nothing left of me, no awareness, no consciousness, and some of that was true. But even though I was unable to speak to you, unable to respond to you, I heard, yes, I heard everything, heard everyone. Do you know, I remember when Gemma came, only once, at the beginning, and she whispered in my ear she wished I'd just hang it up once and for all and stop wasting everyone's time. She punched my arm; I felt it. But your visits were the highlights of my day, and you came to me throughout the long years I lay there like the dead, which, thankfully, I finally am. It was only a month ago, wasn't it?"

Zoltan paused, her eyes flew open, and she stared at Rebekah. Time froze. Then Zoltan spoke again, her voice still deep, another's voice, still blurred, still distant. "Look at you, so beautiful, like your mother. I remember how proud you were when you told me you had earned your master's degree in art history at George Washington, that you knew you had the 'eye,' you called it, and you had decided to make yourself an expert on fraudulent art. You couldn't wait to start consulting with museums and collectors. You'd already begun your search to find a partner, someone who could work with you to identify stolen originals. And you told me you found the perfect person."

Yes, yes, my new partner, Kit Jarrett, now my best friend, a perfect fit, my lucky day. But wait, finding out about Kit Jarrett was easy enough. It wasn't a secret.

"Your excitement made me want to smile, on the inside, of course, and you couldn't see it. And now you are married, to another congressman. Manvers interned for me a very long time ago. I always found him a real go-getter. I think he was born knowing how to play the game. He's playing it well. Other than being a politician, Rich Manvers is a fine man, but isn't he a bit old for you, Pumpkin?"

"Perhaps, but what's important is he understands me, and he loves me." Rebekah licked her lips, drank more tea to get spit in her mouth, and managed to say, "Pumpkin—that was the nickname you gave me when I was six years old. Not many people know that."

Zoltan's brilliant dark eyes opened and fastened onto something beyond Rebekah. Rebekah turned but didn't see anything. Zoltan's lips moved, but no sound came out. There was no expression on Zoltan's face, only smooth blankness. Then her grandfather's voice again. "Yes, I remember the Halloween you carved a pumpkin to look like me. You nearly burned the house down."

Rebekah heard herself say, "Yes. I still have a picture of the pumpkin, and you're standing behind me, your hands on my shoulders. I have so many photos of us together over the years. Of course, I came to see you as often as I could in the sanitarium. I loved you. Grandfather, I will love you until I die. I know this sounds strange, but are you well now?"

The distant deep voice seemed to laugh. "Yes, Pumpkin, of course I'm well. I'm always well now. There is no more pain since I died—well, there was hardly any even before I died. I remember you were such a brave girl, never left my side during those long, final earthbound hours. You held my hand until I was able to depart my tedious life."

She remembered, too clearly, the shock, the pain, and the relief, too, when he drew his last breath. Dr. Lassiter, a kind, attentive man, had stood beside her, touching her grandfather's other hand. "John is at peace now," he'd said when it was over, and she'd finally known what that old chestnut really meant.

Rebekah said, "Yes, I remember. What is it you want to tell me, Grandfather?"

3

A pool of deep silence filled the still air. Suddenly, there was a touch, feathery soft against Rebekah's skin. She heard Zoltan's voice, lower now, almost a whisper. "Do you remember me telling you stories about my best friend, Nate, the adventures we had as boys, the stunts we pulled, how we were always getting the strap from our dads?"

"Yes, of course I remember. I grew up on your stories. I was always thrilled. I repeated many of them over and over to you in the hospital, hoping maybe they'd help you wake up, but you couldn't. I hoped you would at least hear them and know you weren't alone."

"Yes, I heard you, Pumpkin, and I thank you

now. As you know, Nate was smart, but like I told you, he wasn't so smart there at the end. Ah, what a long time ago that was. I don't think Nate's here, and I have looked for him."

She wanted to ask him where he was, but instead said, "Nate Elderby—yes, I remember, he was a big-time lawyer. I heard Grandmother tell one of her friends his second wife was a sexpot who married him for his money, a good thing since the sexpot, Miranda, had the IQ of lettuce. I remember she laughed about him and his wife, but you never said a word. But why are you asking me about him, Grandfather?"

"Did you know Nate never called me Methodist until nearly the very end, right before he went out fishing on Dawg Creek and got himself drowned? I remember what he said the last time I saw him: 'Methodist, it's no good any longer, you know it. I have to get out, or it's over for me.' Three days later he was stone-cold dead."

"Why are you telling me this, Grandfather?"

"It's important, Pumpkin. He failed with the wrong client and knew they would try to get back at him. He wanted to leave the country, wanted to leave as a rich man, very rich. He wanted his share."

Rebekah said, "His share of what?"

"His share of the treasure from that story I told you, the story we called the Big Take."

How did Zoltan know about the Big Take?

Rebekah waited, but he said nothing more. "You mean that adventure story you kept telling me about the treasure you and Nate managed to steal from the evil sheikh's caravan because he was going to use it to make war against his people? I remember you changed it, embellished it, every time you told it to me so I wouldn't forget. Are you saying it's true, Grandfather? The Big Take really happened?"

"Yes, the gist of it was true. I knew at the time you didn't believe what I told you was real, only another story to entertain you. But remember how I swore you to secrecy? Of course you do, you've kept all my secrets ever since you were a little girl. I wondered if I shouldn't have told you, you were so young. It was my legacy to you, yours alone, and there was time enough, I thought, to let you know it was true. Ah, the best-laid plans. I remember you talked to me many times about the Big Take story when you visited me in the sanitarium, and I know you had no way to know it was real. You'd joke, say instead of a sheikh's treasure, maybe it was a cask of ancient Spanish doubloons or maybe trunks of Nazi gold. I couldn't tell you what it was, that it was all too real, since I couldn't move, couldn't talk, could only lie there. Ah, but I'd already told you where it was."

"You mean the poem from the story? That was real, too?"

A long moment of silence, then, "Ah, yes, the poem. Do you remember it?"

"You had me repeat it so often when we were alone. It was one of our special secrets, for only you and me, but you never told me what it means, Grandfather. Is that why you gave me the poem, had me memorize it? You thought someday I'd understand?"

"Yes, it is my gift to you, Rebekah. It's time for you to have it. It's been over twenty years, enough time has passed so there will be no questions. And what is the treasure, you're wondering? No, it's nothing ancient from a faraway land, but trust me, you won't be disappointed. When you fetch it, you'll know why I kept it secret, and how much I love you. But you will need someone to help you, someone you trust, someone who will believe the Big Take is real. Do you really remember the poem? Tell me, Rebekah."

Rebekah opened her mouth to recite the poem, looked at Zoltan's face. And stopped. She wanted to believe her grandfather was speaking to her, but she couldn't. She'd promised her grandfather never to say the poem to another soul. Why would he want her to now that he was dead? Slowly, she shook her head. "No, Grandfather, I won't, I can't. If it's really you, you say the poem to me."

The air felt chilly suddenly, enough to make gooseflesh rise on Rebekah's arms.

An old, distant voice said, "Be careful, Pumpkin. I feel a wolf in the fold, close to you. Be careful."

The fan went still. There was only silence and the dim light of the lamp.

"He's gone," Zoltan said, her voice hoarse, but now her own again. "Give me a moment." She closed her eyes. Her breathing slowed.

"Are you all right?"

"Yes, I suppose so."

"I'll be right back," Zoltan said, and rose. Rebekah heard her soft tread, then the overhead light came on and flooded the room.

Zoltan walked back to the sofa, leaned down, lightly touched her fingertips to Rebekah's cheek. "Your grandfather, he was strong this time, Rebekah. He was here, and all that he was in life came through. Why couldn't he speak directly to you? I don't know. Amazing you already knew about this Big Take and you remember the poem you memorized as a child."

"Yes, and as you heard, he never told me what the Big Take was, and still didn't, for whatever reason. I don't even know if it's real."

"Interesting. Fascinating, actually." Zoltan straightened and looked around the living room, a question in her eyes. She said as she turned back to Rebekah, "Perhaps tonight was a breakthrough. Your grandfather came to us so clearly. I suppose you could say I felt what he was feeling, felt his concern for you, his excitement to tell you about your legacy, that it was real after all. You really have no idea where this Big Take is hidden? What it is?"

Rebekah looked into Zoltan's sympathetic face

and sighed. "He first told me the Big Take story when I was a little girl. The story didn't say where he and Nate hid the treasure." Rebekah shrugged. "There were so many of his other adventure stories I repeated back to him in the sanitarium when I ran out of news to tell him. That story was only one of them." She shook her head and sat silently wondering what all this was supposed to mean, whether she should believe anything that had happened here, anything she'd been told.

Zoltan took her hands again, squeezed. "I believe the Big Take, whatever it is, is real. You see, it's very difficult for most Departed to come through the Verge. Why come through if he was only going to tell you a lie? There'd be no point. I believe he wants you to have whatever it is he and Nate Elderby stole and hid all those years ago. And he wrote you the poem thinking you would figure it all out when you grew up, or perhaps he hoped you and I could figure it out together."

Rebekah shrugged. "I can't imagine the grandfather I knew and loved would want to make me a criminal, even if he and Nate Elderby were. I think if he loved me as much as he now claims, he wouldn't want me tainted by whatever he did, make me an accomplice to his crime."

She searched Zoltan's face, shrugged again. "Whatever it is you're trying to accomplish, Zoltan, you should know I don't want anything to do with it. Let the Big Take stay buried, if it's real. Let it stay forgotten. It all stops right here in this room. The last thing I want is for my grandfather to go down in history as a thief—even if I really was hearing his voice rather than your own." As she spoke, Rebekah rose. She felt a brief moment of dizziness.

Zoltan stood, too, lightly touched her hand to Rebekah's arm. "I'm sorry you're still unsure if your grandfather was actually here, and you still doubt me. He was here, Rebekah. I find it interesting, though, that he never told you exactly what the Big Take was. But maybe he didn't have time, maybe he had to leave before he could tell you everything."

But he'd told her there was a wolf in the fold, and what did that mean? It sounded ridiculous to Rebekah. She stared down at Zoltan's hand. Zoltan pulled her hand away, took a step back, but her voice remained calm. "Fact is, I've come to believe there's a time limit to how long the Departed can stay with us once they come through the Verge. Perhaps they need to wait their turn before they connect to us again."

Rebekah looked toward the fire in the grate, only embers now. "To be truthful, Zoltan, I don't know for certain whether to thank you for contacting my grandfather or compliment you on the quality of the research you must have done to convince me with your brilliant performance. More likely the latter, I think. Was my grandfather really involved in some kind of major theft with his friend? I don't believe it.

No, the Big Take was only one of the wonderful stories he told me. But as I said, it doesn't matter." She paused, leaned down to pick up her cup, and took a last sip of tea. "To pretend you're actually speaking to a dead person—well, thank you for the unexpected evening and the tea."

"Rebekah, I had an idea. Perhaps we could locate the Big Take and give it back to the original owner. What do you think?"

Rebekah said again, "As I said, Zoltan, this is over. I will not be coming back."

"You are free to do as you wish, of course, Rebekah. But if you do come back, perhaps your grandfather will tell you more about the Big Take, explain his motives, and you can question him. You can tell him you don't want it because you want to protect him. I know he can come back, his presence was strong tonight. He wants this desperately, Rebekah. Give him another chance to convince you."

Rebekah started to shake her head, but she stayed silent until Zoltan walked her to the front door. "I hope you will reconsider. But whatever you decide, Rebekah, you have provided me with an intriguing evening, you and your grandfather both. Perhaps you will come again on Friday night?"

Rebekah shook her head. "I've made up my mind. I won't be coming back."

As Rebekah walked to her car, she realized she still felt unusually calm, smooth as the flow of a placid river, and wasn't that odd? She carefully backed out of Zoltan's driveway, her hands a bit unsteady on the steering wheel, and wondered if she'd ever actually believed she was speaking to her grandfather. *He knew your nickname, Pumpkin. He knew about the Big Take story.* Zoltan couldn't have known about it, could she?

How could Zoltan have possibly found out Rebekah's nickname and all the rest of it? She realized in that moment she wished she could believe her. She, Rebekah Clarkson Manvers, wanted to believe what had happened tonight was real. But of course it wasn't. It was all smoke and mirrors. She had no intention of coming back on Friday, no matter what Zoltan wanted. Nothing good could come of it.

Was there a wolf in the fold? Why would Zoltan—or her grandfather—give her that bizarre warning? No, it was ridiculous, her grandfather was dead, gone. Still, why the warning? Who wasn't she to trust? Rich? No, it couldn't be Rich, her husband of six months, a four-term congressman from Talbot County, Maryland. She remembered he'd told her after his first wife died, he didn't think he'd ever find another woman he would love. But he'd chanced upon her at Lincoln Center at a Lucien Balfour piano concert nine months earlier. For the first time in years, he fell in love, with her, and now he told her he was proud of her every single day. They were still discovering how much they had in common, and always enjoyed each other's company. He dealt well with Kit, her business partner and friend, and he approved of her.

Rebekah turned into light traffic on Hazelton Avenue, only twenty minutes from Kalorama Heights and home. She thought of Rich's younger son, Beck. He was more a gold-plated prick than a wolf. He was a health insurance lobbyist, a job arranged for him, of course, by his powerful father, her husband. He was thirty-three, five years older than she, and he made it a habit to come out of his bedroom wearing only his boxer shorts when he knew she was close by, as if he'd been waiting for her. He'd quickly graduated to coming out of the bathroom with just a towel wrapped around his waist. Beck had moved back to his father's house in Chevy Chase the year before, after a nasty breakup with his then-fiancée, an investment banker's daughter out of New York. Rebekah's mantra to herself was: *Beck, find another girlfriend soon, and leave.*

Could Tucker be the wolf? Rich's eldest son was perfectly pleasant to her, though he ignored her for the most part, regarded her as his father's newest toy, a temporary diversion at best. That was fine with her. He seemed happy enough with his wife, Celeste, and their three sons. Celeste didn't like Rebekah, but did she hate her enough to wish her ill? Was she the wolf? Well, speculating about it hardly mattered. She was only taking the bait Zoltan had tossed out to her, the hints and warning she'd left her with to get her to come back for another grand-father show. She thought cynically she'd probably be billed five hundred dollars for the entertainment.

Rebekah felt a wave of fatigue, and drummed her fingers on the steering wheel. She forced herself to focus on the meeting she had scheduled with Mr. Clement Herriot, a wealthy collector of impressionist paintings. Alas, she had bad news for him. The Berthe Morisot he'd bought at auction seventeen years before was a fake. He wouldn't be happy, though Rebekah knew he must have suspected or he wouldn't have contacted her to authenticate the painting. Kit had ferreted out the painter most likely to have executed Morisot's style so beautifully—Carlos Bizet, who lived in Andalusia and was now ninety years old. Thankfully, he'd stopped his forgeries ten years before, but that didn't help Mr. Herriot. It would certainly get his insurance company's attention, since they'd doubtless hired an expert to authenticate the painting as well before insuring it. "No one else could have painted it," Kit had told Rebekah. "And now Bizet's so old, he spends his time bragging about his work hanging in museums all over the world, and, of course, in big muckety-mucks' collections, like Mr. Herriot's." Rebekah thought about the wages of dishonesty, how if malfeasance went undiscovered long enough, there weren't any wages to be paid here on earth. She'd decided long ago karma was only an inviting construct weak people used to

make themselves feel better about not doing something when they should.

She planned to forget about the Big Take and
the poem and the wolf in her fold. If Zoltan called,
Rebekah would tell her again she wouldn't be going
back.

4

Rebekah parked her silver Beemer on a side street, pulled the strap of her handbag over her shoulder, and stepped into the bright October sunlight. She gave the hood a quick pat. She loved her Beemer, her twenty-eighth birthday present from her husband. She sighed. She had to hurry or she'd be late to her daughter-in-law's whoop-de-do planning luncheon. Celeste wouldn't like that at all. But her meeting with her client, Mr. Herriot, had taken longer than expected. The news she'd had to give him hadn't made him at all happy. She didn't blame him. Mr. Herriot had even heard of Carlos Bizet, and when she'd pointed out the details that were his trademarks, he couldn't argue with her. He'd even grudgingly thanked her, after he'd calmed down.

Delivering bad news was never her idea of fun. She'd much rather be toasting the client with champagne. Well, now she'd taken on the best of clients, Mrs. Venus Rasmussen, a venerable icon of Washington, D.C., society, and still the active CEO of Rasmussen Industries. She'd hired Rebekah to authenticate a group of six paintings she wanted to purchase for the newly remodeled executive reception area in her headquarters. Better to hire Rebekah up front than to buy the paintings and find out she'd been had, Mrs. Rasmussen had told Rebekah.

Rebekah forced herself to slow down, to breathe in deeply, to reboot. She wasn't all that late, and no one would care anyway if she missed the soup course. So why not enjoy the perfect fall day, feel the cool breeze stirring the fallen leaves in nearby yards? She decided to relish her block-long walk to Celeste's house in this quiet, elegant neighborhood in Chevy Chase. When she'd driven by Tucker and Celeste's house a few minutes earlier, she'd seen the big circular driveway bulging with the cars of all Celeste's cronies and heaven knew who else, and continued on to park next to a nice shaded curb a block away.

She'd told Rich that Celeste had only invited her to this planning luncheon because she didn't see a way out of it. The last thing Celeste wanted was for Rebekah to complain to her husband. Rebekah knew Celeste would just as soon see her on the next transport pad to Timbuktu, considered her only a trophy wife of a rich man suffering a midlife crisis. Rebekah wouldn't be surprised to learn Celeste offered that opinion to anyone willing to listen, and that most people Celeste knew would listen happily.

Her husband had patted her cheek, told her to suck it up because Celeste was important to him. Of course, he meant her family—with their huge donations, the power they wielded was important to keeping his seat in Congress for another term. "She also has an excellent cook, so you'll eat well. As for all the other people there, they'll be pleasant and, of course, talk about you behind your back when you're out of hearing. At least it's for a good cause." He'd tapped his hand over his heart. She still didn't want to go, but obligation was the engine that ran most everyone's life, particularly if you were a politician's wife. You were gracious even when you wanted to punch the mouth trying to manipulate you.

Even though Celeste was holding the planning luncheon at her own home, she wanted the main event, a huge formal charity function, to be held at her father-in-law's magnificent house in Kalorama Heights. Rebekah had wondered aloud to Rich why Celeste wouldn't want to hold the charity function in her own lovely old Georgian house on Hempstead Road.

"Because," Rich had told her patiently, "Celeste considers me a power in Congress, thus a draw to the big spenders." And he'd rolled his eyes and grinned.

One of her husband's best qualities was that he never took himself too seriously. She'd said, "I wonder how it makes Tucker feel to know he's not important enough or his house grand enough to host this shindig?"

"Were I my son, I would be royally pissed." He'd shrugged. "It's not my problem. If Tuck doesn't like it, it's up to him to stop it."

Her thoughts went back again to the events of last night, her memories of Zoltan tumbling into her brain. In the bright sunlight on this crisp October day, what had happened now seemed preposterous, unbelievable. When Rich had met her at the door last night, he had drawn her in and kissed her deeply. She'd settled willingly against him, breathed in his seductive Armani scent. Had he worn the same scent for his first wife? She felt ashamed and hugged him tighter.

"So tell me, my beauty, about this Zoltan. Did you find out what your grandfather wanted to talk to you about?"

She heard no mocking in his voice, no barely hidden sneer, even though she knew he didn't believe the dead had a working voice any more than she did. But he knew her grandmother believed and Rebekah was curious, so he'd encouraged her to go if she wished. She raised her face. "Grandfather called me Pumpkin again—through Zoltan.

But of course he didn't really because he's dead, so how did she know? She invited me to come back, but I'm not going. All of it was really absurd." She paused a moment. "She's a charlatan. I didn't even wait to find out what she hoped to gain from it all." She shook her head. She felt the beginnings of a headache.

"So John, your grandfather, didn't speak to you, he spoke to you through her? Did you recognize his voice?"

"Not really. *He* wanted to talk about a story he'd told me as a child."

"A story? Oh sure, you told me several of them he entertained you with when you were young. But one particular story?"

She nodded. "Actually, one I never told you, a secret story, only between us, only for me." Her head began to pound. She drew a deep breath, held his dear face between her two hands, and smiled up at him. "I'm not going back."

Bless Rich, he'd only patted her face and led her into his study. He knew she loved this large room, all dark wood, rich burgundy leather sofas and chairs, and built-in bookshelves that reached the ceiling.

Her husband had sat beside her on the soft leather sofa, lightly stroked his hand over her cheek. "Tell me, was Zoltan at all convincing?"

"Well, she's remarkably talented and has all the bells and whistles, like dimming lights, fire leaping up in the fireplace, that sort of thing." She sighed. "Rich, I really want to forget it."

He took her hands between his, kissed her fingers. "Let it stay between you and the Departed, at least for now." He grinned as he spoke. Again, there was no judgment, no sarcasm in his voice.

Rebekah tucked her legs beneath her and leaned into her husband. "Enough about mediums. Tell me about your day."

"I arranged a meeting with Jacqueline tomorrow, and I know she'll want my support about her most recent skirmish with the president over his tax-cut proposal. Trust me, most everyone is afraid she could blow up the party's re-election chances if she oversteps." He sighed, sat back, and sipped his brandy.

"If she persists, smile at her and tell her the last thing she wants is to lose her own position as Speaker of the House."

He laughed and kissed her forehead next to where her headache still brewed.

That's not important right now. Put it away. Focus on Celeste and this blasted lunch, maybe practice a sincere smile.

Rebekah looked to the left, then to the right. Except for her Beemer, Hempstead Road was practically empty of cars this time of day. Well, it was never jammed with traffic any time of day, actually. She was about to step off the curb when she heard a car engine coming up from her left, closing fast, terrifyingly fast. She whirled about as a white SUV screeched to a stop beside her. A big man dressed in black, wearing a mask, a hoodie pulled over his head, jumped out and grabbed her. Rebekah screamed and kicked up at his groin, but he turned in time and her knee struck him hard on his thigh. He cursed, jerked her arm up high behind her, and raised a syringe.

5

Rebekah fought back, kicking and hitting whatever part of him she could reach. She felt him rip the sleeve of her blazer as he twisted her arm back, but she was too flooded with adrenaline for the pain to overwhelm her. He was cursing her, telling her to stop or he'd break her arm. When she knew her arm was about to snap, he was suddenly jerked away from her, spun around, and someone struck his neck with a fist. He went down hard, struggling to breathe, his hands clawing at his throat. A big man in a black leather jacket dropped beside her attacker. He was still choking, thrashing on the ground, trying to get away. His hoodie fell back behind his mask, and she could see he was bald—not naturally, he shaved his head. She could see the sheen of dark stubble. A second man, also in a mask and hoodie, jumped out of the SUV, a gun in his hand. Her rescuer jerked around, but he wasn't fast enough. The second man struck him in the head with the gun. He went down on his knees, dazed. The second man hauled his partner to his feet and shoved him into the open back of the SUV. He jumped in the driver's seat, and the SUV roared off, tires screeching. Her rescuer pulled a gun from a clip at his waist, fell onto his stomach, and fired off six fast shots. She saw the left rear tire explode, but the SUV kept going.

An older woman yelled out from a neighboring yard, clutching a hose still gushing water in her hand, "I called 911! The police are coming!"

Her savior started to rise, then stayed on his knees. He looked up at her. "I'm Agent Dillon Savich, FBI. Please don't move." Savich quickly pulled out his cell and punched in Detective Ben Raven's number. "Ben? Got a problem here." Savich told him exactly what had happened, how he'd shot out the back tire on the SUV, and gave him the address on Hempstead and a description of the two men. "They'll probably abandon it fast, a Ford Expedition, white, a year old, maybe. The license plate was muddied over. Yes, we'll be here. Thank you, Ben."

"Agent Savich, are you okay? He really hit you hard."

Savich nodded. "Yes. And you?"

"I'm alive, can't ask for more than that. The woman over in that yard clutching that hose like it's her lifeline, she called 911." She gave him a manic, adrenaline-fueled laugh.

He touched his fingers to the back of his head. "Give me a moment to unscramble my brain. I should have been faster."

"I think you're awesome, the way you hit that man in the neck—I've never seen anyone do that. And you shot out that back tire." Rebekah realized she was losing it and took a deep breath. Yes, she had to breathe and calm down. She said, "Okay, hold still. Let me look at your head."

Savich felt her fingers lightly touch behind his left temple. He smelled her perfume, a light rose scent, not unlike Sherlock's. "There's a bump and a bruise, but no bleeding. You might have a concussion, though. We should call an ambulance."

"No, I'm fine."

Men, did they always want to be invincible? She helped him to his feet and winced because she'd used the arm the bald man had nearly broken. But the pain wasn't important, and her arm worked. After a moment, he seemed steady on his feet. Rebekah realized she came only to his nose, and she was tall. He was well-built, wearing a black leather jacket over a white shirt and black wool pants. Kit would declare him seriously hot. Actually, Rebekah would agree with her. He was dark, eyes and hair, and he looked tough. His eyes were clear, and that was a relief.

Rebekah stuck out her hand. "My name's Rebekah Manvers, Agent Savich. Thank you for saving me. If not for you, I wouldn't have had a chance."

"You're welcome. I wish I had them in cuffs, but at least you're not in that SUV with them."

Savich saw she was very pretty, but her face was still too pale. She was a bit younger than Sherlock, her hair a beautiful dark mahogany, like his desk at home. She had light gray eyes, a shade he'd never seen before. Her hair had come loose to straggle around her face. Both of them probably looked like they'd gone twelve rounds. He smiled at her. "I'm glad I happened to be in the right place at the right time." He shook her hand. "It's a pleasure to meet you, Ms. Manvers."

Savich still couldn't believe he'd actually come across a kidnapping on the street. What were the odds? He'd been on his way to Ambassador Natalie Black's house a half mile away for lunch to celebrate the upcoming wedding between Agent Davis Sullivan, one of his agents in the CAU, and Black's daughter, Perry. He'd been less than a block away when he'd seen the SUV swerve off a side street onto Hempstead.

"How's your arm?"

Rebekah stuck out her right arm, flexed her hand. "It's still sore, but I don't think anything's broken. He ripped off my sleeve so he could shoot me up with a syringe. Look, there it is. It flew out of his hand when you hit him."

Savich leaned down and picked up the syringe. He pulled a small plastic bag from his jacket pocket and slipped it inside. "We'll find out what he was going to give you." He felt a moment of dizziness, then it passed. He ignored the low throbbing where the gun had struck him on the head. It could be worse—he could be dead. "They wore masks, but was there anything about them familiar to you, Ms. Manvers?"

She shook her head, then she gave him a grin. "Agent Savich, you saved my life. Please call me Rebekah. Let me say it again, you were awesome. Thank you."

Savich liked the sound of that. "You never gave up, you kept fighting. Well done."

An older gent appeared at Savich's elbow, a cane in one hand, a long leash attached to a bulldog in the other. The bulldog didn't bark, merely stared up at Savich, his tongue lolling.

"Name's Luther Frye. I was watching Mongo piddle against that maple tree when those goons roared to a stop, jumped out of that SUV, and grabbed this pretty little girl. Bad business, but what you did, boy, it was a job well done. And you," he said to Rebekah, grinning to show a mouth sporting a full complement of shining false teeth, "you've got an excellent set of lungs for sure. Nice and loud, sort of like my late wife."

Savich introduced himself to Mr. Frye, who dropped Mongo's leash and shook his hand.

"Figures you're a lawman. You shot that rear tire right out. You want me to stick around, talk to the police? I hear them coming."

Savich settled for the old man's phone number, typed it into his cell.

Mr. Frye saluted him and walked slowly away, Mongo trotting beside him, carrying his leash in his mouth.

Rebekah realized she'd started shaking. She tried to calm herself, swallowed to get spit in her mouth. "I don't understand any of this. Why me? Who were they?"

"We'll figure it out. Come sit in my car, and we'll both get ourselves together. I hear the sirens getting closer."

His car was a gorgeous fire-engine-red Porsche.

A woman's voice called out from down the street, "Rebekah, is that you? Charles came out after we all heard gunshots to see what was going on, and he said he recognized you. What happened?"

Rebekah drew in a deep breath and said to Savich, "That's my daughter-in-law, Celeste. Believe me, we do not need her here. I had a lunch date at her house, just up the block." She said with a sigh, "Charles is her butler and a very nice man." She called out, "Celeste, I'm all right. Someone tried to kidnap me, but it's all over and I'm fine. I don't suppose I'm up for having lunch with you now, though. I'll call you later, fill you in. Please, don't bother

Rich. I'll talk to him myself. And, Celeste, give your guests my apologies."

Celeste stopped in her tracks, still half a block away. She looked uncertain. "If you're sure, darling. But someone tried to kidnap you? That's crazy. I mean, who would do something like that in this neighborhood? I don't understand."

"It's all right, Celeste. Please go back to your luncheon."

She wondered for a moment what exactly Celeste would tell everyone. She watched her daughter-in-law slowly turn and retrace her steps, a half dozen people coming from the house to meet her. She sent one last furtive look back at Rebekah. She looked excited. Rebekah couldn't imagine anyone would be bored at the luncheon now, not with this delicious news. She said to Savich, "Sorry, but what happened will be all over Washington within an hour."

A Metro cop car pulled up, and two officers, one of whom Savich knew, asked them questions until Ben pulled his new silver Chevy Malibu in behind Savich's Porsche. Detective Ben Raven ushered both Savich and Rebekah to his car, and they went over everything once again.

Ben Raven said finally, "Seems obvious to me it must have to do with your being Congressman Manvers's wife. Your husband's also quite rich, right?"

Rebekah was feeling the aftermath, recognized it for what it was—her adrenaline taking a nosedive. Fatigue rolled over her like a tsunami. She felt scared, too, more than she had during the attack. She was thinking about it now, not only reacting. She knew the man in the hoodie would have injected her with whatever was in the syringe. Probably not to kill her, but they'd have taken her. Where? What would they have done to her? Ransomed her? She didn't want to talk anymore, didn't want to think about it. It was too scary. All she wanted to do was curl up into the fetal position and keep Agent Savich very close.

Savich took her shoulders in his hands and shook her. "You've made it through this, Rebekah. Everything's all right now, you're all right. Back away from all the what-ifs. That's right, breathe slow and easy. Try to relax."

Finally, Rebekah was able to dial up a smile for him. She reached up and took his hand, held on tight. "Yes, Rich is wealthy, it's no secret. Still, why me? This town is filled with wealth. I don't understand any of this, and that's the truth."

Ben tried to press her, but Savich recognized she was at the end of her tether. He didn't suggest going to the hospital. What she needed was to get away from this place to somewhere she felt safe. What she needed was her husband and her home.

Ben's cell rang out with the theme from the old

Hawaii Five-O. When he punched off, he said, "They found the SUV, parked on Hiller, about ten minutes from here. Forensics will go over it. Now, about the syringe."

Savich said, "Let me take it to our lab." He saw Ben was about to protest and added, "The two men attacked a federal employee, and don't forget attempted kidnapping. Sorry, Ben, that makes it FBI."

"Yeah, okay. Why don't you take Mrs. Manvers home? Keep me in the loop, Savich, all right?"

"Thank you, Ben."

Ben said to Rebekah, "Officer Hill will follow Agent Savich in your car, Mrs. Manvers. I hope I'll be seeing you again, but just in case." He handed her his card and walked back to his Malibu.

Savich said, "Mrs. Manvers, please call your husband. He needs to know what happened, and I'd like to speak with him."

"You already agreed to call me Rebekah." She managed a smile. "Actually, you can call me anything."

"I'll stick with Rebekah. Call your husband now."

When she punched off, she said, "Joy, his secretary, said she'd get him right away."

"Good." Savich had also called to give his regrets to Ambassador Black and Davis. He kept a close eye on Rebekah as he drove her home to Kalorama Heights. He said, "Who knew you were meeting your daughter-in-law at her house for lunch?"

Rebekah turned her head to face him. "Most everyone who was invited, I guess, and my partner, Kit Jarrett, not to mention my husband, his senior aide, Daniel Drake, and most of the people in his family. Not good, I know. It seems everyone knew where I was going to be." She sighed, leaned her head back, and closed her eyes. "I didn't park at Celeste's house. I parked a block away because there were so many cars. I guess that decision didn't work out so well."

"You're right, of course. The two men were following you. Your parking on the street gave them their chance, and they took it."

Surprisingly, she gave him a small grin. "It's got to be the only time in my married life I wish I'd been parked at my daughter-in-law's house." Then, "I think I know who you are. You're Sarah Elliott's grandson. I've seen your amazing whittled pieces in the Raleigh Gallery in Georgetown. Your grandmother—her painting *The Flanders Market Place* has been one of my favorites for as long as I can remember."

"Thank you. I have my favorite painting of hers hanging over my fireplace." Because the insurance company didn't want him to give away which painting it was, he didn't say more.

By the time Savich drove into the Manverses' driveway on Belmont Road NW, she'd told him, somewhat unwillingly, he'd thought, about her visit the previous night to a medium named Zoltan who'd tried to convince her she'd spoken with her dead grandfather. She didn't give him any details, said only the medium had to be a fake, and shook her head. He wondered if she'd told her husband any more. And why hadn't she wanted to tell him? Perhaps the medium visit was a coincidence, but he would look into it.

He met with Congressman Manvers, went through what had happened one more time as Rebekah added details, and listened to the congressman's shock, then his outrage and demands the FBI make this their top priority. Since Manvers was a politician, he was naturally concerned about the media and what would happen if news of Rebekah's attempted kidnapping got out, as of course it would. It was doubtless the main topic of conversation at Celeste Manvers's luncheon. "Agent Savich, what would you suggest we do?"

"I'd make a statement immediately, sir, explain what happened, and ask anyone with any information to call the FBI hotline."

Later that afternoon, Rebekah answered the door to the most beautiful man she'd ever seen. From behind her, Kit whistled. "I don't care what you're selling, I want a dozen. Maybe two dozen. Please come in."

He gave them a gorgeous white-toothed smile. "Actually, I'm not selling anything today. I'm

Special Agent Griffin Hammersmith. Agent Savich asked me to come over and keep an eye on you, Mrs. Manvers. And he wants to know if you've thought of anything more to help us find whoever's responsible for what happened to you."

6

Denny Roper from Security appeared in Savich's office with a large box in his hands. "Good day, Savich. This box just came over from Facilities and Logistics, cleared for delivery to you. It looked more than a little interesting, as it's addressed to you as 'PERSONAL' in big black letters, so I offered to bring it to you myself. You never know what some fruitcake might have sent you. I had to bring those two guys from Security with me. They want to see what's inside, too."

The four CAU agents working in the office today were just as interested in what had come in the package addressed to Savich personally, and followed Savich, Roper, and the men from Security into the conference room. Sherlock and Ruth weren't due back from Norfolk until later. Savich set the plain brown paper–wrapped box on the conference room table, Denny at his elbow. He pointed. "You can see it was mailed here in Washington three days ago, got diverted to our Cheverly facility to be checked out, and then delivered here. Funny size, about a foot square." He turned to Ollie Hamish, Savich's second-in-command. "Any bets on what's inside?"

"Maybe it's a baby gift you ordered for me, Dillon," Agent Lucy McKnight said. "A monitor to sing lullabies?"

There was laughter as Savich took the knife Denny handed him, slit through the tape, and peeled away the paper wrapper. They stared at a blood-red box inside. *Blood-red?* If someone wanted to make a statement, it was exactly the right shade of red. And addressed to him personally. He wondered if maybe the techs at Cheverly had missed something dangerous, but as far as he knew, nothing had ever gotten past them. He lifted the lid.

Matching red wrapping paper was folded around what was inside. Savich carefully lifted it all out and laid it on the table. The box didn't weigh much and the contents were solid but thin, like cardboard. Shirley, the unit secretary, all-purpose confidante, and logistics expert, joined them and looked with interest at the red wrapping paper so neatly folded in front of them.

Agent Davis Sullivan said, "I was hoping for a severed finger or a kneecap, disguised to fool the X-ray."

"Disguised how?" Shirley asked, an eyebrow arched. "You mean like dipped in French's mustard?"

There was laughter again, but then everyone's attention returned to the red wrapping paper. Denny rubbed his hands together. Savich didn't think there were any people on earth more naturally curious—or nosy, depending on your point of view—than cops: federal, state, local, didn't matter, it was a job requirement.

He opened the paper and saw an eight-by-eleven piece of thick blank cardboard, puzzle pieces scattered over it.

Savich started to fit the pieces together. With so many hands eager to help, the puzzle pieces soon formed the beginnings of a photograph—water lapping against pilings, a long, ancient wooden pier with spindly wooden legs sticking out of the water to hold its banged-up slats. There was a sidewalk, a rather narrow street, and the hint of buildings, some wood, some stone, some brick. There were no people, no signs, no animals, nothing to identify the location, no shadows to indicate the time of day. Savich moved the grouped pieces over to cover the bottom third or so of the cardboard.

Lucy McKnight elbowed herself closer without a problem. She was six months pregnant, though at first glance you'd guess maybe three months, so no one got in her way. "A town on the water. What town? What is that body of water? It gives the impression of being old, well-established. Look at that rickety pier. Does it look familiar to anyone?" She drew a big breath and stared at the assembled agents around the table. "It's kind of hard to miss the line of dead seagulls on the pier, and aren't those human bones on the sidewalk?"

Davis Sullivan said, "Maybe it's some kind of warning, or threat. And the box was addressed directly to Savich, marked 'personal.'"

Denny said, "I don't like this, Savich. A bunch of dead birds and bones. What do you think it means?"

Mr. Maitland's deep voice sounded behind Lucy. "What's this all about, Savich? Some goofball's sending you a freaking puzzle? And it's taking this whole roomful of brains to fit the pieces together?"

Savich nodded to Mr. Maitland, his boss, now standing beside Lucy, both of them bent over to see the puzzle better. Like with pregnant Lucy, no one got in his way, either. Not even when he cut the taco line in the cafeteria, claiming an urgent meeting, and no one believed him.

"Yes, they helped, and the 'freaking puzzle' shows the bottom third of a town. And dead birds and bones. Nothing obvious yet. No one knows what town it is."

Savich shook out the red wrapping paper. It

looked new, as did the red box. There was nothing else, no identifying marks on the box.

Mr. Maitland pointed. "I'll bet people have fished off that old pier for more years than we've been on this earth. It looks like those dead gulls were carefully lined up along that pier and the human bones arranged just so on the sidewalk. And no one's around. That's odd, too."

Savich said to the group, "A third of a puzzle, meant to be a teaser. We can shortly expect another red box with more puzzle pieces for us to fit together. I hope there aren't any more human remains—"

"Or whole bodies," Lucy said.

"Take photos and show them on our network. See if anyone in the building knows this waterside town. When the next box arrives—and it will come soon—Denny, would you please bring it to us yourself?"

"I'll keep an eye out," Denny said.

Mr. Maitland stepped back to let agents snap photos with their phones. He said to Savich, "Always something interesting going on in your unit, but this isn't why I'm here. Come with me. There's something we need to discuss."

When he and Mr. Maitland were alone in his office, Savich said, "That red box, I expected something horrific right off the bat, but this has some subtlety to it." He paused. "Well, subtle for now, anyway. I'll bet you when Denny arrives with the second red box, he'll have agents from all over the building with him."

"You'd win that bet," Maitland said. "Let's hope it's only a crazy and not a real threat to you."

Savich shrugged. "Whoever it is, this is his show for now. He wants to preen, show me how clever he is. Bones and dead birds?"

Mr. Maitland said, "Trouble is, the finale of his show might be to drop a hammer on your head. You know that, right?"

Savich nodded. Yes, he knew it was very possible.

Mr. Maitland stretched out his legs and studied Savich's face. "Whoever this is, he went to a lot of trouble. If he escalates, you'll find out soon enough why you're in his crosshairs. Use all the resources you need to get on top of this. We don't know if this wacko is serious."

Savich nodded again.

"Hey, Goldy told me Sherlock's memory is one hundred percent intact again. That's a huge relief."

Savich smiled and heaved a big breath. "An understatement. There are no more holes, no more questions or uncertainties. Her very fine brain and all her memories are once again with us." He paused. "It took nearly two months for all the empty pockets to fill in. Sean never realized his mother couldn't remember him, and for that we're profoundly grateful."

Mr. Maitland sat back in his chair and folded his hands over his belly. He said, "Halloween's right around the corner. I remember some years ago now, my four boys got all dressed up like Freddy Krueger and scared the crap out of most of our neighbors when they opened their doors. June and I tried not to be amused. The four Freddy Kruegers came home loaded with candy, doubtless from extortion. What's Sean going to be this year?"

"Captain Corbin. Astro will be his sidekick, Orkett." At Mr. Maitland's blank look, Savich grinned. "A children's series. Corbin hunts down crooks in the galaxy, and Orkett, his dog, eats oatmeal cookies and gets him out of tight spots. Now, sir, I presume you're here to talk more about Mrs. Manvers's attempted kidnapping today?"

"I guess you didn't see Congressman Manvers on TV this afternoon. He gave an account of his wife's attack and asked for information. I was impressed. He acted quickly, he was straightforward, and he delivered a clear message. Viewers will empathize with him since they could see he was quite upset by what happened." Mr. Maitland began to drum his fingertips on his chair arm.

"All right, sir. So there's more. Talk to me."

7

Mr. Maitland sat forward, clasped his hands between his knees. "Yes, I have something more to tell you. Turns out Arlan Burger, President Gilbert's new chief of staff, has been one of Congressman Manvers's best friends since their Loyola days back in the eighties. Manvers happened to tell Burger about his wife going to a séance to speak to her dead grandfather last night, and now Burger knows about her attempted kidnapping, too. Have the lab and forensics reported in yet?"

"Ben Raven told me they found the SUV with the exploded back tire, parked on a side street in Chevy Chase, not far from where the two men tried to take her. As of yet our FBI forensic team hasn't reported finding anything useful in the SUV. It was stolen, as we thought. The lab just got back to me about the syringe. It was ketamine. It would have knocked her out almost immediately. They didn't want to kill her, only take her fast, with little fuss. I've assigned Griffin to babysit Mrs. Manvers until we get a handle on motive, and the congressman plans to stay close to her."

Mr. Maitland nodded. "It could be a kidnapping for ransom of a rich young wife, but a congressman's wife? Oh yes, Burger told me the wife has a healthy bank account herself, thanks to a legacy from her grandfather, John Clarkson. So there's money on both sides. You're too young to remember John Clarkson. He was also a congressman, Clarkson from the Richmond area. He was quite a bigwig back in the day, had the nickname of Methodist, didn't hang it up until after the turn of the century."

"How did he die?"

"All I know for sure is he was in a coma for years before his body finally shut down only about a month ago. His funeral was very well attended." Mr. Maitland sat forward. "Tell me about this medium last night."

Savich said, "As I told you, Mrs. Manvers did tell me she went to a séance, but she went tight-lipped when I wanted to know more about it, and for no reason I can think of."

Mr. Maitland said, "I know this business of talking to dead folks is claptrap, but still, I'd have liked to be a fly on the wall at that séance last night."

"Actually, I would have, too," Savich said.

"Tell me, how did Congressman Manvers react to the news of his wife's attempted kidnapping?"

"He expressed shock, disbelief, and finally gratitude." Savich grinned. "He promised never to bad-mouth the FBI again."

Mr. Maitland laughed. "I don't suppose it's possible Manvers hired the kidnappers, despite his excellent plea for help on TV? I mean, did you see anything off between them?"

Savich shook his head. "No, only affection. He kept her very close throughout the retelling. Well, he is a politician, practiced in dissembling, but he seemed legitimately upset at what had happened." He shrugged. "It's early. Maybe I'm wrong about him. We'll see. As I said, Griffin is keeping an eye on her and, of course, interrogating the household." He rubbed his thumb over his chin. "My gut tells me her attempted kidnapping is connected to the séance last night, maybe even as a direct result. I'm wondering if I should talk to Rebekah Manvers again, urge her to tell me exactly what Zoltan had to say to her last night, or see Zoltan first?"

"I know you, you'll see the medium first."

"Yes, you're right."

Mr. Maitland gave Savich a fat smile. "I'm sure you'll do both, boy-o. Chief of Staff Burger is counting on you." He was pleased, Savich knew, to take the matter off his own hands and put it firmly in his.

Mr. Maitland rose. "Lots of moving parts here, Savich, maybe unrelated, who knows? Keep me informed."

Savich watched his boss make his way through the unit, pausing here and there to touch base with the agents. He saw Mr. Maitland speak to Sherlock, who had just arrived, more than likely about the Beach Killer case she was working on with Ruth in Norfolk, Virginia. The Beach Killer was the moniker the media had tagged to the man who'd murdered several young women and left their bodies on the beach near the high tide mark, covering them in sand, with only their faces visible. Sherlock gave Savich a wave and started speaking with Ollie, no doubt to fill him in on the new information they'd brought back from the Norfolk police. They'd update him about the Norfolk case soon enough.

Savich turned to MAX. There were thousands of hits about Rebekah's grandfather, Congressman John "Methodist" Clarkson from Clairemont, Virginia. Savich scrolled through them quickly until he found an odd news story and stopped. It was a story about Clarkson's close friend Nate Elderby, a criminal defense attorney who'd drowned in 1995 while out fishing alone on Dawg Creek, the local fishing hole where the two men often spent lazy afternoons together. He read the rumors about how Nate had drowned—speculation about a marriage gone sour, bad feelings between the good friends. Police investigated and concluded Nate Elderby drank too many Buds, fell overboard, and drowned. The locals said Clarkson was usually with him, but he claimed he wasn't that day. He was a powerful congressman, so surely he couldn't have been involved, said the police, much less murdered his best friend. But it appeared the gossip didn't go away. Savich sat back, his gut doing the rumba. Could this Nate Elderby, long dead, have anything to do with what was happening now?

Had Rebekah's grandfather actually been with his best friend fishing that long-ago afternoon? Had they argued? What about? Had Clarkson slammed him on the head, dumped him out of the fishing boat, and swum back to shore? It was so many years ago, but murder always left a stain and survivors who might want revenge or to get back what was theirs. Was that the reason Rebekah didn't want to talk? Did she know something about Elderby's murder and fear he'd find out?

8

If Zoltan was the key, the catalyst, perhaps the instigator, then to what end?

Savich wanted to meet this medium, Zoltan, a name both mysterious and exotic. He'd never really thought about mediums beyond the fact they made their living feeding off the desperate grief of others. Savich had dealt with gifted people over the years, and he thought he'd seen it all, but no, there was always something more, something beyond.

He turned to MAX and typed her name into his background search program. While he waited, he gave MAX another task: searching online images of coastal towns within a hundred-mile radius of Washington, D.C., that would match the partial puzzle picture. Had to be lots of possible towns, but maybe MAX could find it. While MAX worked, Savich studied the photos of the red box Lucy had forwarded to him. *Why a red box? Does it have some symbolic meaning to the person who sent it?*

MAX gave his sharp beep, and Savich saw a photo of Zoltan on the screen. Her birth name was Lorralynn Weatherspoon, born thirty-eight years ago in Willicott, Maryland. He drew back in surprise. Willicott was Chief Ty Christie's town and home to Gatewood mansion, where he'd found Agent Sala Porto tied up and left to die in an upstairs closet. He and Sherlock and Sean had visited Ty and Sala in Willicott the previous month for a barbecue at Ty's lake cottage. Sala had recently transferred to the Baltimore Field Office, much less of a daily commute for him since he was now living with Ty. And where would that lead? Life never ceased to amaze.

Weatherspoon had changed her name legally to Zoltan six years ago, a Hungarian man's given name she'd adopted as her mononym. A good choice, he thought again, mysterious and mystical, more of a draw than Weatherspoon. He scanned the rest, made notes, and left MAX to his second task.

He saw Sherlock peel away from Ruth and Ollie and come over to him, grinning. He wanted to hug her, but didn't, not here in his office in the CAU. She said, "I'm starving, didn't have time for lunch. You?"

Savich realized he hadn't eaten, either. They went to the seventh floor to have Indian food—dal, a lentil soup, was the touted dish of the day. Shirley warned them to beware of the peppers, the suckers would burn your tonsils.

When they snagged a table in a quiet corner and sat down with their dal and naan, Sherlock said, "Sorry to say we'll probably have to go back to Norfolk again soon. I wish I could stay here with you after all that's happened today. Tell me more about it. I'll eat, you talk."

Savich went through what had happened to Rebekah Manvers, beginning with the séance.

She whistled when he finished. "It never stops, does it?" She waved him back to his lentil soup. He wasn't paying attention and bit into a pepper. Two glasses of water later, Sherlock still laughing, he decided he would survive. He chewed on a piece of warm naan to soothe his throat and told her about Chief of Staff Arlan Burger's calling Mr. Maitland.

Sherlock listened closely as she dipped her own naan into the rich, thick soup and chewed slowly. She said at last, "Imagine, this medium, Zoltan, is from Willicott. You want me to give Ty a call, have her find out about her and her family? Get a feel for this woman before we go see her?"

"Good idea. Yes, check her out. MAX can give us the facts of her life, but not what she was all about growing up, what people thought of her and her family."

She smiled at him. "So much has happened today, so many threads to follow, not even counting the red box and the puzzle. What I can't understand is why Rebekah Manvers isn't telling you everything, whether she thinks it's important or not. That's got to mean she's hiding something."

She sat back in her chair and patted her stomach. "But you're not going to interview Rebekah Manvers again and try to convince her to talk to you, are you? You're going to visit that medium, Zoltan, first. I can't see a way she's not involved, Dillon."

He put his soup spoon down and smiled at her. Sherlock laughed. "At the very least, this Zoltan is bound to be entertaining."

He spotted another hot pepper and gently spooned it onto the bread plate. "I haven't done a deep run on Rebekah or Congressman Manvers, either. Do you know anything about her?"

"I know she's much younger than her husband, late twenties to his mid-fifties. No kids together, but they haven't been married long. I believe I heard he has two sons by his first wife, both older than his new wife." She paused a moment, studied his face. "Makes you wonder if maybe there's bad blood between the sons and their new stepmama."

"That's possible. Do you have any doubts Zoltan is a fake?"

"Now, there's a strange question for a man with your gifts to ask." She sat forward, took his hand. "All I've ever been certain of is there are things I don't understand, that no one is able to understand, not really. If Zoltan is a charlatan, you'll expose her.

Can the chief of staff count on you figuring it all out by close of business today?"

Such faith she had in him. He managed to avoid another pepper. "We'll see. At this point nothing would surprise me."

"You're planning to see Zoltan tonight?"

"You want to come with me? I'll bet my sister and Simon would love to babysit Sean."

Sherlock shook her head. "I'd be a third thumb." She leaned across the table, took his hand, and squeezed it. "Listen to me, Dillon. You be careful. We have no idea what to expect."

Back in his office, Savich called Zoltan's private number and spoke to her secretary, Candy. Was that a punch of nerves in her voice when he identified himself? What did Candy know about any of this? She told him Zoltan's last client would be gone by eight o'clock that evening.

9

**HOME OF ZOLTAN
THURSDAY EVENING**

Savich drove his Porsche to Cleveland Park, an old, established neighborhood in northwest Washington both he and Sherlock enjoyed driving through, especially when the fall leaves were at their most dramatic. There were beautifully kept older houses surrounded by mature oaks and maples, and it was quiet, not a single kid's bike to be seen in the neighborhood. Zoltan lived in a hundred-year-old house with a wraparound porch, surrounded by a well-maintained yard. There was a porch light on, and both downstairs and upstairs lights were on. Savich could see the pale brown paint and sharp white trim were fresh. Fall flowers still bloomed from baskets hanging from overhead porch beams, and piles of fallen leaves had been swept up. He paused a moment in front of the dark-brown-painted front door. The neighborhood, the house, even the planted fall flowers seemed so normal, so expected. Who would guess a medium was holding séances in her living room? Why, he wondered again, hadn't Rebekah wanted to talk about what happened here last night?

He fully intended to find out.

He pressed a button by the front door and heard chimes sounding a lovely deep Gregorian chant. He heard light footsteps, and Zoltan herself answered the front door. She'd looked formal in the photo MAX had shown him of her attending a conference in New York. Now she looked completely normal, wearing black leggings, whimsical moose-head slippers on her long, narrow feet, and a burgundy Redskins sweatshirt. Her thick black hair was pulled up and back in a ponytail, showcasing a face with sharp bone structure and a strong chin. She looked Black Irish with the dark hair, dark blue eyes, and very white complexion. She wore minimal makeup and small diamond studs in her ears. She did not look like anyone's idea of a person who spoke to the dead and called herself Zoltan.

"Ms. Zoltan? I'm Special Agent Dillon Savich." He automatically held out his creds, but she didn't take them. Instead she looked at his face and stilled. He raised an eyebrow but didn't say anything. What did she think she saw?

Zoltan said in a deep, cream-smooth voice, like

coffee with a dollop of Baileys, "Just Zoltan. Now, I have to admit I'm surprised. I find it hard to believe you're an FBI special agent. Candy—she's my secretary—told me your voice was dark and sexy, and she wished she could think of a bad deed she could confess to you."

Savich said nothing, kept holding out his creds. Finally, she took them, gave a cursory look, and handed them back, all the while continuing to stare at his face. She stepped away and waved him in. "It's fortunate for you I saw my last client an hour ago. I assume you wish to speak about Rebekah Manvers's conversation with her grandfather last night?"

"Yes."

"I am wondering why an FBI agent would have any interest whatsoever in a communication between a young woman and her dead grandfather. I do hope her husband, the congressman, didn't send you to harass me." She turned as she spoke and led him into a lovely high-ceilinged living room, long and narrow, with windows at either end covered in dark blue brocade draperies. A fire burned sluggishly in the fireplace, sending up an occasional spark. It was dim and cozy, the air soft with a light scent of night jasmine. It was a place to read a good book or maybe speak to a spirit. Savich said, "The Carrara marble looks original."

"It is. When I bought the house three years ago, it was because of the eight fireplaces, all working and all Carrara marble. Luckily, it's a chilly night, perfect for a fire. Do sit down, Agent Savich." She gave him a look over her shoulder. "Candy has quite the ear—you do have a marvelous voice. Alas, from your wedding ring, I will have to tell Candy you're unavailable."

"Yes, I am."

"At least for the moment."

Savich merely smiled. He looked again around the living room. "You hold your séances in this room?"

"Yes. Another reason I bought the house. I've found calling to the Departed more natural when a house is older, when it's lived through years of life and death and drama, of exquisite pain and flashes of joy. I find all that living human experience permeates the walls themselves." She cocked her head at him. "If you're wondering where my levitating table is, I'm afraid I don't use one. I simply arrange the chairs in a circle when I have a small group, and yes, everyone holds hands. It's not theater, although it certainly could be. No, it's to pool everyone's energy. May I get you tea, a nice Earl Grey, black?"

Savich raised a brow.

Zoltan said matter-of-factly, "The Earl Grey is nice and hot. No sugar or cream or lemon, straight-up black tea." She poured him a cup from a bright red thermos on a side table, handed it to him, then poured herself a cup, added milk and two packets of fake sugar.

"How do you know I don't care for anything in my tea, Ms. Zoltan? How do you even know I prefer tea? Did a visiting spirit mention it to you?"

She shrugged and looked away from him, toward the fireplace, and her eyes went vague and distant. He sipped his tea and enjoyed the performance. Had she read up on him already, in the few hours since he'd called?

The tea was delicious, the flavors deep and rich, better than his own, actually, and that surprised him. There was something else in the tea, some darker flavor. He let the thought go and studied Zoltan. "May I ask why you chose a Hungarian man's name?"

She shrugged, the movement strangely compelling and graceful. She smiled at him. "Do you like your tea, Agent Savich?"

He nodded. "You didn't answer my question."

"Should I satisfy your curiosity?" She paused, then nodded. "Zoltan was a man I met in the Village in New York. He played chess in Washington Square, played the violin in a sidewalk café, and made love to me like I was a Stradivarius. He taught me things, Agent Savich, so many things before he died from a curse he knew was coming for him. He awakened his powers in me before he died, in what he told me was an ancient ritual. His family was originally from Erdély, a part of Hungary before it was taken and given to Romania."

Her voice was low and musical, mesmerizing.

Savich found himself staring into the smoldering fire, the occasional sparking flame. Her words seemed to flow smoothly into his mind. Something wasn't right. He pulled his eyes away from the fire and back to her face. "Zoltan died of a curse? Is that a tale for your clients' benefit? And now mine? To give you credibility? To make yourself out to be a sorcerer's apprentice?"

10

"Sorcerer's apprentice? As vastly romantic as that sounds, I did not have to invent Zoltan. He was a living, breathing man, my mentor and lover, and he bestowed his gifts on me."

Savich knew he wasn't thinking clearly, which felt odd. He rose and walked to stand against the mantel, facing her, his arms crossed over his chest. He said very precisely, "There is no such thing as transferring psychic power. I'm surprised this claim would impress anyone, Zoltan, or should I remind you your name is Weatherspoon and you grew up in Willicott, Maryland?"

"Weatherspoon is my parents' name. What a common name it is. Naturally you investigated me the moment Rebekah told you about our visit with her grandfather. If I had the resources you do, I suppose I'd have done such a check on you. As for Willicott, it's a sad little town near Lake Massey, where I remember listening to my parents scream at each other, and where I learned to hug my secrets close. Ah, old history. I left for New York when I was eighteen, attended City College, and met Zoltan. There's really not much more to say about my past, Agent Savich.

"I changed my name six years ago, after Zoltan died. I took his name to honor him, to show the depth of my love for him. And to thank him for what he'd given me. Can we get on with it? You look rather tired. You've had a long day. Your saving Rebekah Manvers from kidnappers is all over the news, and of course that's why you're here. You believe I may have had something to do with her attempted kidnapping, since Rebekah was with me last night."

Savich decided to take a shot in the dark. "It's obvious her attempted kidnapping was precipitated by your having her here for a séance, telling her her grandfather had come, having him tell her things she didn't want to hear." He watched her closely.

Zoltan threw back her head and laughed. "A frontal attack, that's good. If I were responsible, you'd have me quaking. But alas, I'm a simple medium, my only purpose to connect the Departed with the living, nothing more, nothing less. So

Rebekah told you about what her grandfather told her. I'm surprised. She told me she wanted it to stop here, never speak of it again."

"Evidently she changed her mind after someone tried to kidnap her. It wasn't lost on her that what happened was only hours after her meeting with you. And that makes what she and her grandfather discussed a motive, doesn't it?"

Zoltan fanned her hands in front of her. "Agent Savich, I had nothing to do with anything. I was only the conduit for her grandfather. It was he who told her about the Big Take that happened so long ago."

Savich kept his face impassive. "Do you think her grandfather murdered his supposed best friend, Nate Elderby, because of the Big Take?"

"Well, it appears Rebekah told you everything. But not murder, that wasn't ever discussed." She frowned. "Although her grandfather's words about his friend were somewhat ambiguous. A falling-out among thieves, then, that's what you believe."

Savich said, "I imagine Rebekah was quite surprised, didn't want to consider her grandfather could have been involved in something like the Big Take, much less murder." He took another sip of his tea.

Zoltan shrugged. "So who would care one way or the other? Rebekah, as you know, doesn't want anything to do with the Big Take, not even to consider returning it to the original owner. She doesn't want her grandfather's legacy tarnished in any way.

"I believe it makes more sense that whoever tried to take Rebekah today did so because her husband is a very rich man, not to mention Rebekah herself must have inherited a good deal of money from her grandfather." She sighed. "I was still hoping Rebekah would agree to come back here tomorrow to speak again to her grandfather, if he was able to come through the Verge. But now? I doubt she will."

Savich said, "You're right. Rebekah won't be back. She believes, as do I, that you gave a brilliant performance as her grandfather last night, that you somehow found out about the Big Take and that's why you invited her here."

"I am not a fake, Agent Savich."

"Tell me then, Zoltan, how you got Rebekah to come to you in the first place. She wasn't clear to me on why you called her."

"It's no secret. Her grandfather came to me three times during séances with other clients. He finally gave me enough information to identify both him and Rebekah and to find her. He told me a nickname he had for her, Pumpkin. There's nothing more to it. He told her about this Big Take and that she knew where it was hidden. She didn't want to know what they'd stolen, didn't want to discuss it, as I'm sure she told you. I now realize her grandfather was right to warn her—he told her there's a wolf in the fold, as he put it. Perhaps this wolf tried to kidnap her, and that would mean the wolf is someone close to her. If only she could come back, perhaps her grandfather would tell her who the wolf is."

She sipped her own tea. "It always surprises me what the Departed have to say to the living, and the living to the Departed. And what they don't want to say."

He watched her rise slowly to her feet and thought again how graceful she was. He agreed with her for a moment that what the Departed would have to say to the living might be surprising. Then he put on the brakes, realized what she'd done. "What did you put in my tea, Zoltan? A psychotropic drug? LSD?"

She flapped her white hands at him. "Goodness no, Agent Savich. It's merely my own special blend of herbs, designed to help my clients relax, to put them in an easy state of mind."

"Don't you mean make them more receptive to whatever you say? Did you give the same blend to Rebekah Manvers last night?"

She studied him. "How very curious. No one has ever noticed anything different about my special tea, except you. There's nothing to be alarmed about, but that's not the point, is it?" She walked to the fireplace. She fiddled with an antique andiron, straightened it, and went to stand behind a love seat. "Of course, you think my special tea is some diabolical attempt to manipulate my clients into believing what I want them to believe. That is not it at all. As you can imagine, when people come to me, they're upset, often in distress. I provide the tea because it helps level them out, calms them, makes them less afraid, if you will. Speaking to the dead isn't an easy thing to face, Agent Savich. Better, I've found, to ease them into it, when they're a bit more relaxed and calm. If there is communication, it's far more comfortable for them, and, I've learned, less emotional.

"The fact is, Agent Savich, I'm a simple but lucky woman, well aware of the benefits to others my special gift provides. I could never have imagined such a thing possible before I met Zoltan. I didn't ask for this gift, nor have I ever lied about any of it. I help grief-stricken people reach their Departed and speak to them. Nothing more, nothing less." She paused, looked rapt. "Zoltan gave me the keys to his kingdom, Agent Savich."

And what did that mean exactly? Savich wanted to ask her, but for the life of him, he couldn't remember why. He nodded to Zoltan, picked up the thermos, and walked out. He closed the front door quietly behind him.

11

Denny Roper walked into the CAU carrying the second package at nearly the same time he'd brought the first one. There were more than a dozen agents behind him this time. Roper had clearly gotten the word out when the second package had arrived. Savich, knowing there was no choice, motioned them all into the conference room.

"It's the same, marked 'PERSONAL,' to you, Savich." Roper was broadcasting excitement.

Everyone crowded around as Savich slit open the box and lifted out another red box. "Only a day after the first red box arrived, as expected." Savich carefully unfolded the red paper. "Either good luck or very fine planning."

No one was surprised to see more puzzle pieces.

Once they were fitted together and placed above the pieces from yesterday, they showed more buildings, part of a commercial area, but no printed names that could identify them, and a single street sign— Main. There was also more of the ancient pier, the focal point. Was the town on the Potomac? The Chesapeake?

Agent Davis Sullivan said, "Looks like the wacko added a few more bones, nothing else. And how did he manage to find a time when no one was around to snap a photograph?"

No one had an answer for that.

Lucy said, "It has to be a photograph someone took, not a precut puzzle you'd buy. There are tons of companies that take photos you send and make them into puzzles, like Shutterfly. I looked some up. There's Puzzleyou.com and goodness, even Walgreens does it, pages of them and that's only here in the U.S."

Sherlock said, "The person who's red-boxing you could even have access to whatever equipment he'd need and make the puzzle himself."

Ruth said, "And that would make him as good as invisible. We couldn't track him."

Ollie said, "I'm wondering if there's more than one person involved, and that means—"

Shirley finished his sentence. "—the greater the chance of our catching them."

Savich looked around at the group of agents. "We have more now, but still not enough. I don't suppose anyone recognizes this place?"

To everyone's surprise, a woman's voice called out, "Yes, I do. It's my hometown, St. Lumis, Maryland, on the Delmarva Peninsula, south of Mayo in Anne Arundel County, right on the Chesapeake." At the blank looks, she added, "Just south of Annapolis. Yes, I'm sure. Growing up, I fished off that pier with my mom for striped bass and red drum." She paused, added, "But I don't remember any dead seagulls on the pier or human bones on the sidewalk."

Everyone in the conference stared at Agent Pippa Cinelli. She was newly assigned to the CID, the Criminal Investigative Division, one of the recent stars to graduate Quantico. Most everyone was aware of who she was, even if they hadn't been introduced. She was tall with long blond hair worn in a French braid, green eyes, a looker, no doubt about that. And at the moment, she was munching on a bagel, a dot of cream cheese on her upper lip. She popped the last bit of bagel into her mouth, patted her upper lip with a paper napkin, pulled out her cell, and scrolled through her photos. "Here we go, way back in my archives." She handed her cell to Savich. "St. Lumis is a destination for weekenders who know the area, mostly. There are nice beaches, good fishing, and it's rarely too hot in the summer. It's a cute town, with a few tourist shops. At least that was true seven years ago, the last time I visited." She smiled. "My family moved to Boston, so no, I don't have any relatives left in town. Now? I'll bet it's probably triple the size." She stuck out her hand. "We haven't met, Agent Savich. I'm Agent Pippa Cinelli, Financial Crimes."

Savich shook her hand, smiled really big. Did she realize she'd made his day?

Pippa was looking at the puzzle again. "Everything looks the same. Almost. The person who sent this is seriously disturbed."

Agent Davis Sullivan said, "Or crazy like a fox. Why would this wack job send Savich puzzle pieces to put together of your hometown, Cinelli? And with the bones and dead birds? Did something horrific happen there? Something that might have involved Savich personally? Is the puzzle announcing some sort of weird payback?"

Everyone thought about this. Pippa said, "I can't remember hearing about anything really bad happening, nothing violent, only what you'd expect—domestic violence, pilfering from local stores, some vagrancy, but no murders. We were neighbors with the chief of police, Barnabas Cosby." She turned to Savich. "You want me to call, see if he's still there? See if he can help us?"

Savich said slowly, "No, hold off. I think the person sending the red boxes doesn't believe anyone will recognize the location until the puzzle's complete. This might give us an edge." He smiled at Sherlock, who'd told him about Cinelli. She'd said they'd sweated together a couple of times in the gym at Quantico, practicing martial arts. She'd told him Cinelli was smart, focused, and as fit as, maybe even stronger than, Sherlock was. She was, Savich thought, just the ticket.

"Let me give your chief a call, see if I can spring you from Financial Crimes for a couple of days. You interested?"

"Yes, sir, I'm very interested. I finished up a case only two days ago, so maybe—" She was nearly dancing in place, her eyes sparkling.

Savich held up a hand. "Everyone, I'm sure we'll meet here again when the third red box arrives, probably on Monday. Agent Cinelli, come with me. Happy Halloween tomorrow night, everyone."

Sherlock gave a little wave as Pippa followed Dillon into his glass-fronted office. Savich pointed Cinelli to a seat, sat behind his desk, and called her unit chief, Jessle Tenley, a hard-nosed veteran, and proceeded to negotiate the quid pro quo for lending Cinelli to the CAU.

A deal was struck and it wouldn't cost Savich a thing, but Agent Griffin Hammersmith probably wouldn't be too happy to hear about it. Savich grinned. He would tell Griffin to suck it up and take himself to a surprise birthday party for Jessie's nearly eighteen-year-old daughter, Paige. She'd seen Griffin and begged her mother to introduce her. Well, Griffin could deal with a smitten eighteen-year-old, a whole roomful of eighteen-year-olds. He'd be the highlight of Paige's birthday party Sunday afternoon. At least Griffin liked cake.

Savich turned back, studied Cinelli a moment, then stuck out his hand and shook hers. "Agent Cinelli, you're now a temporary member of the CAU."

Pippa's cell sang out the Black Keys' "Lo/Hi." "It's Agent Tenley."

"She's calling to give you a pep talk. Go ahead and speak to her, and I'll check on the chief of police to see if he's still there. Barnabas Cosby, right?" He called the police station in St. Lumis. When he punched off his cell, Pippa had already slipped hers back into the breast pocket of her white shirt.

Savich said, "Did Jessie give you the gung ho speech?"

"She told me I was representing her and the unit and suggested I shine bright. The 'or else' was unspoken, but understood. Even when Jessie doesn't say it out loud, she's still very clear."

He grinned. "Here's the deal in St. Lumis. Chief of Police Cosby retired three years ago. The new chief is Matthew Wilde. Now, Agent Cinelli—"

"Please, call me Pippa."

"Call me either Dillon or Savich."

Pippa cocked her head to the side, sending her thick French braid swinging over her shoulder. "Dillon, if that's okay. It's what Sherlock calls you. Now, I've never heard of a local family called Wilde. He must be an import from outside, new to St. Lumis."

"I didn't ask to speak to him. His dispatcher sounded bored. Give me a minute." Savich typed Wilde's particulars into MAX. When he looked up, he was silent a moment. "Matthew Carlton Wilde, age thirty-three. He was a detective in the Philadelphia Police Department for three years, resigned three and a half years ago after one of his team members and his best friend was shot when Wilde was in Cleveland bringing a prisoner back to Philadelphia. To date the murderer has not been identified."

Pippa shuddered. "Imagine carrying that memory around with you. I bet he investigated his team member's killing, couldn't solve it, and ended up leaving. I wonder how that works, teams rather than partners? No matter. How long has he been chief of police in St. Lumis?"

Savich looked down, read. "About three years."

"Talk about making a big change, not only his responsibilities, but the atmosphere, the people, the smallness of St. Lumis compared to Philadelphia." She paused, then, "Like I told you, when I left, St. Lumis was a quiet town. Seemed like half the people there were visitors during the summer months, but they caused few problems." She shook her head. "I imagine nothing's changed. St. Lumis is about as different from Philadelphia as Paris is from Bermuda."

She was so hyped, she was very nearly vibrating. Savich could practically see her nerves firing. He said, "Pippa, I want you to go in as a civilian there for Halloween, a short holiday. You can make up your own cover story. See if you can find out why that particular town is part of this bizarre message aimed at me."

"You don't even want me to introduce myself to Chief Wilde? Give him my creds? Tell him to keep it under wraps?"

He tapped his fingers on the desktop. "Not right away. You need to get to know him, assess his value to you if you get into trouble, then maybe yes."

Pippa said, "All right, Dillon, I'll become his new best friend. Luckily, I've never done much social media, well, at least since high school. But people could look me up, see I'm an FBI agent. Shouldn't I use an alias if I want to stay unnoticed?"

Savich shook his head. "Too much risk someone could recognize you. Since you haven't advertised you were at Quantico, you should be good for a while. You should be well in place before the person sending the red boxes gets to the point of this puzzle. Email me photos of all the players, and call me with daily updates. And, Pippa, be careful. With all the work this person is doing to set the scene, he could be seriously disturbed. And dangerous."

He watched Pippa Cinelli stride out of his office, stop by Sherlock's station, and give her a light punch on the shoulder. He heard Sherlock laugh, saw them speak for a few moments. He had a gut feeling Cinelli was the right agent for this job. He thought about adding a partner but decided to let Pippa go in alone. From the gleam in her eyes, she wanted to do this, bad.

He called Jessie Tenley back to get her assessment of Pippa. Tenley said, "It's early yet, but I have a feeling Pippa's got the nose, Dillon. She's a lawyer with an accounting minor from NYU. She can read a financial document and tell you there's a sentence in paragraph four that could point to the whole scam. She reads people, too, adapts well to the different roles she has to play. From the short time she's been in my unit, I already know she's a bulldog. She gets her teeth into something and gnaws away. She knows how to handle herself. I wish she would give more thought to some situations before rushing in, but she'll learn.

"A week, Dillon, you've got her for a week. That's the deal. I'll need her back. The Calypso case is heating up, banking fraud, of course. The bankers involved are funneling money in and out of accounts in the Caymans. I hope Griffin can handle an infatuated eighteen-year-old at her birthday party who very well might puddle at his feet. Or faint. And all her eighteen-year-old friends as well." Jessie sighed. "Was I ever eighteen?"

"Don't worry, Jessie, Griffin's fast on his feet."

"Then maybe he'll have a chance. A pleasure doing a deal with you. Happy Halloween, Dillon."

12

Pippa Cinelli pulled her small black-and-white Mini Cooper into the rear gravel lot of Major Trumbo's B&B on Flounder Court. She'd forgotten how many streets in St. Lumis had fish names. It was nearly four o'clock in the afternoon, the drive from Washington had taken longer than she'd expected with weekend traffic. She had only a couple of hours before it was dark.

She lifted her go bag and a single carry-on from the skinny back seat and made her way up the flagstone walkway to a large Victorian house, once owned, she remembered, by the Calder family, and now, evidently, by the Trumbos. It looked prosperous and well-maintained, painted white with blue, green, and yellow trim. A large skeleton hung in a downstairs window, and jack-'o-lanterns lined the sidewalk. She'd snagged the last room available, the honeymoon suite on the third floor. Half the nightly rate was coming out of her own pocket, but she wanted to stay in the very center of town. She was so excited, she was nearly bursting through her skin. This wasn't about pulling crooks off golf courses, this was about a maniac with a flashy preamble, obviously proud of himself for his originality, proud of the alarm and fear his puzzle would cause. Dead birds? Bones? He was showing off, matching wits with Savich, and now with her. He had set the game in motion with no one watching, no one chancing to see. It was up to her to find out who and why.

She remembered Halloween was a big deal in St. Lumis, and sure enough, she'd seen dozens of carved pumpkins as she'd driven in, and assorted skulls and goblins adorning some houses and businesses. Most of the town would turn out for the yearly Halloween party at Leveler's Inn and Conference Center, a local happening as big as the Fourth of July. She'd checked, and the Halloween bash was still being held at Leveler's Inn. She'd come prepared for the festivities with an ornate Venetian mask, bought two years earlier when she'd visited Las Vegas for a bachelorette party, and a long crimson cloak to go with it. What a fine opportunity to start nosing around.

She was shown to her honeymoon suite by Mrs.

Trumbo, a big woman with silver-and-black skeleton earrings hanging from her earlobes and an apron with a picture of a growling red cat on it tied around her substantial middle. She smelled great, and Pippa said so. "Oatmeal cookies?"

Mrs. Trumbo beamed. "Yes, and wait until you taste one. Just look at me." Mrs. Trumbo patted her middle. "My special Halloween oatmeal cookies are shaped like ghosts and goblins and monsters. I decorate them all in orange and black—well, the ghosts are white. They'll be out of the oven in exactly six minutes. Do come down and have one while they're nice and warm and gooey. I don't suppose there's a Mr. Cinelli coming? To make proper use of this marvelous suite?"

"Sorry, I'm alone, a real shame. This will be my home away from home for a while, maybe a week. I heard about the Halloween party at Leveler's Inn. Do you go? Will it be fun?"

"Oh my, yes, it's always a drunken hoot. I hear it'll be even bigger this year. Guess what, Ms. Cinelli. I have a special circular bed for you. I'm told it's all the thing for young people. Me? I think it's strange, myself, feels like I'm sleeping on a big round cookie."

"First time I'll be sleeping on a round bed," Pippa said. "I'll let you know. Thank you, Mrs. Trumbo. I'll be down as soon as I can for the cookie. Have you been here long?"

"You know, I lived here, then left, then moved

back, and when the Calders left five years ago to retire to Maine, not Florida, I bought the house and turned it into a B&B." She paused a moment. "My husband, the late Major Trumbo, had thoughts, too, of a B&B, but then he up and died of a heart attack. When you have breakfast tomorrow in the living room, I'll show you his urn on the mantel, all gold and shiny. So now it's my B&B, all mine." She beamed at Pippa. "I had to spend a pretty penny updating the bathroom here. Cut out a utility closet to make it nice and big, and to fit the Jacuzzi tub, large enough for a party, if you ask me." She sighed. "Major Trumbo would have gotten a kick out of it, poor old geezer."

When she was alone, Pippa walked to the two wide windows at the front of the room and stared out over three blocks of St. Lumis toward the Chesapeake. The water looked cold and gray in the dying daylight. She saw most of the boats were already docked and secured for the night. She remembered the police station was on Main Street, a pedestrian name for a street in St. Lumis, and good luck for the person who'd sent the red box and the puzzle pieces. If Main Street had been named Bass Lane or Speckled Trout Avenue, a computer search would have found it quick as spit, as her grandfather loved to say.

She made a stop downstairs to get her oatmeal cookie, a ghost with gobs of white frosting. Her first bite tasted like pure warm sin. She could practically feel her blood sugar shoot up. Mrs. Trumbo gave her an orange pumpkin, carefully wrapped in a napkin, and Pippa slipped it into her jacket pocket. She walked out of Major Trumbo's B&B, her beautiful crimson velvet cloak swirling around her black-booted feet. Leveler's Inn stood three blocks west, set well back from Tautog Street, its deep front grounds beautifully planted and maintained. She remembered it had started out in what was then a poorer part of town, until it was bought by a corporation and made into a hotel that had lasted into the early new century. Then it was bought by Mr. Field Sleeman, St. Lumis's only wealthy local, who'd revamped it into the new Leveler's Inn, the town's only destination for company retreats and conferences.

It was full-on dark now, a three quarters moon low on the horizon. She'd passed only a couple of kids trick-or-treating, since it was getting late. She saw some teenagers laughing, shoving one another, talking on their cell phones, a couple of them wearing their mom's sheets around their necks. Bedroom superheroes? She wondered what this teenage pod would do if no one answered the front door. Was toilet paper draped in trees still the big thing?

She pulled on her mask as she walked into the inn, tugged her French braid out over the elastic, and strolled into the large ballroom. It was decorated to the hilt with skeletons dancing on the walls, and loop after loop of black and orange crepe paper was strung from the ceiling. The huge room was filling up fast, the noise level rising. A band played an enthusiastic rumba in the corner, and she saw three costumed couples performing quite well. There was a large rectangular table at the other end of the room with a huge punch bowl and plates of fresh veggies and dip, untouched, and a score of different kinds of pies, all nearly gone. There were several dozen circular tables, each with ten chairs, most of them filled with costumed locals. A small grinning pumpkin with a lit candle inside sat on each table. More people arrived behind her, sending the noise level even higher.

Nearly everyone wore masks, and many were decked out in elaborate costumes, like Captain Hook or Bluebeard, she didn't know which, several Musketeers laughing at their own jokes, and a Captain Kirk doing the rumba with Lieutenant Uhura in her twenty-third-century miniskirt.

And there he was, Chief of Police Matthew Wilde, standing by the large food table chatting with two couples drinking orange Halloween punch from clear plastic cups. She watched Captain Picard dump the contents of a flask into the punch, probably vodka, and wondered how many other partiers had done the same thing and would continue to. She remembered her dad used to carry a flask to this shindig every year, her mom laughing and shaking her head at him. He never said a word about the small vodka bottle in her purse.

She paused a moment and studied the police chief. In the photos she'd seen of him as a detective in Philadelphia only months before he'd quit the force, he'd looked dour and stiff-lipped, showing about as much life as a stick of wood. But tonight, he was smiling and looked relaxed, his once military-short hair now on the long side. He wasn't wearing a mask or a costume, but sharp-looking civilian black wool slacks, a white shirt that was open at the neck, black boots, and a black leather jacket, what she thought of as the Savich School of Fashion. His eyes were a mix of green and blue, heavily lashed. He looked rangy, lean like a runner. She knew he was three years older than she was, divorced, no children, and she wondered what had happened to break up the marriage. In the photos she'd seen, he'd been clean-shaven. No longer. Now he sported dark beard scruff, a look she normally didn't like, but on him, it fit. He looked a little tough, maybe a little mean, but overall, he projected calm and trustworthiness. *I know what I'm doing and I'll keep you safe.* Was he what he advertised? In her first six months as an FBI special agent, she'd met two police chiefs she'd wanted to punch out for how they'd treated her, a woman FBI agent.

Pippa looked away from him, over the fast-filling ballroom. Probably at least one hundred and fifty people were here. What with the masks and costumes, she hadn't recognized anyone, but that also meant no one would recognize her.

Time to meet Wilde. She made her way to the food table and poured only half a plastic cup of the spiked Halloween punch to go with the oatmeal cookie she gingerly slipped out from her pocket beneath her red velvet cloak. She sipped her punch, chewed her cookie, and watched him. He was only six feet away. Soon he would see her and come say hello, realize he didn't know her, and introduce himself.

Sure enough, here he came. "I'd recognize that smell anywhere—it's one of Mrs. Trumbo's famous oatmeal cookies."

He had a deep voice, and a smooth cadence, an accent more mid-Atlantic than Southern.

She broke off a piece from the pumpkin-shaped oatmeal cookie, handed it to him. "Here you go."

He smiled, popped it into his mouth, wiped his hand on his slacks, and stuck out his hand. She shook it. "I don't believe we've met. I'm Matthew Wilde, chief of police here in St. Lumis."

"I'm Pippa Cinelli." She eyed him up and down. "You could have at least duded up like a Wild West lawman and worn a yellow duster, a nice big Colt .45 strapped to your leg. Maybe some black gloves."

"A yellow duster, hmm, like in the old spaghetti

westerns with Clint Eastwood? That's quite an image—maybe next year."

Pippa pushed back her mask and eyed him. "You'd mosey when you walked, too, make the duster flare out, show off your boots. Men would fear you, and women would want to jump you. Well, at least maybe the teenage girls."

13

Wilde laughed and looked at Pippa more closely, "Now, there's a visual. It's off-season, and we haven't met. Does that mean you're here visiting relatives, or did you come for our famous drunken Halloween bash?"

"Actually, I'm here to take a break from the big bad city. A Halloween party at Leveler's is an overdue treat." She pointed to the punch bowl. "I wonder how much vodka is swimming around in that orange punch?"

"I've already seen at least half a dozen vodka dumps. The noise should increase exponentially as the evening goes on. So, what do you think of Mrs. Trumbo?"

"She's been nice, she makes marvelous oatmeal

cookies, but I wouldn't want to mess with her. She's built like a tank. I'll bet the late Major Trumbo didn't mess with her, either."

"She's a pussycat when you get her talking about her son, Ronald, a textile artist in Baltimore. But you're right, I wouldn't want to tangle with her, either."

"I made plans at the last minute and ended up in the only room available—the honeymoon suite. She was pleased to get a customer, but I could tell she was disappointed I was alone. She hoped to get a groom on the premises to liven things up."

"I've never seen the honeymoon suite. I'm picturing a big waterbed, a mirror in the ceiling, and bordello-red towels in the bathroom."

"Sorry, no water in the bed, no ceiling mirror. There are, however, red draperies, and the Jacuzzi in the bathroom could host a party."

"Is this your first visit to St. Lumis, Ms. Cinelli?"

"Actually, I lived here years ago, before my folks moved to Boston. I remember there was another police chief. What was his name?"

"Barnabas Cosby, a fine man with a firm grip. He and his wife took off for Montana. Not to hunt or raise buffalo, he told me. He's a big skier. His wife isn't so much, but luckily she likes to shoot snakes and make belts out of them."

She stared at him. "You made that up."

He put his palm over his chest. "No, I swear. Evidently there are lots of snakes in Montana, slithery ones and, of course, the all-too-common two-legged ones, I'm sure. Do you ski?"

She nodded. "Colorado. Vail, Aspen, my two favorite places. Snow's like fine powder. And you?"

"Last time I skied was in Switzerland. Good skiing, good fun, until I got plowed into by a kid, another American, who nearly sent me flying off a thousand-foot cliff. An older woman, gray hair flying all over her head, saw it all. Quick as a flash, she was right there, planted her pole and rammed me sideways, saved me from a swan dive into eternity. I asked her to marry me, but alas, she was already married, although she thought I was a cutie. At least I think that's what she said. A lot of this is supposition since her English was nearly as bad as my French." He grinned really big as he spoke. "I think her name was Yvette."

Pippa decided she liked him. "Good story. I wonder if it's true?"

He crossed his heart.

Pippa waved at the punch bowl. "The vodka-laced punch tastes too good. I've got to be careful, or I'll be out there on the dance floor trying to do the rumba, clothing optional."

A dark eyebrow went up, then a flash of a smile. "That image just neon-lit my brain. If I weren't the chief of police, I'd offer you another cup and ask you to dance with me."

Pippa took another tiny sip and made herself set down her cup. "Best not slug down any more of that very fine liquid sin. I remember St. Lumis was pretty peaceful, no real crime, just minor stuff. People locked their doors only in the summer when the tourists invaded, if at all. Maybe that was because of Chief Cosby's firm grip? I'm wondering why you came here."

Too much too fast. Well, she couldn't take it back, so she waited, acted nonchalant, and looked out over the crowded room, listening to the laughter. The band was playing a waltz now, and a good three dozen couples were whirling around the dance floor. Or trying.

"A change of pace," he said at last, his voice almost smooth and easy, but not quite. "It's a nice town." He shrugged, looked beyond her shoulder, and nodded hello. "Excuse me, Ms. Cinelli, one of St. Lumis's prominent citizens is beckoning." He paused. "Maybe he has an oatmeal cookie to share." He gave her a smile and walked away. Prominent citizen? She turned to see a man wearing a plain black mask and a black suit. As Wilde got closer, the man lifted the mask, and she stared at Mr. Field Sleeman, owner of Leveler's Inn. He'd been St. Lumis's most prominent citizen when she'd lived here, too. She wouldn't be surprised if Mr. Sleeman was one of the richest men in Maryland by now. He owned the local bank, Leveler's Inn, a half dozen tourist shops, and a dozen other businesses, and that was only in St. Lumis. She watched the two men shake hands, heard

Mr. Sleeman laugh. She remembered Sleeman's house—or mansion, as her parents called it—a huge, sprawling affair clearly announcing he was king of this mountain. Suddenly, a drunk zombie grabbed her arm. Before she could punch him, he grinned and asked her to waltz with him. Why not? He sported hanging rags and a mask right out of *The Walking Dead.* Turned out he was an insurance salesman and a good dancer. He didn't recognize her, didn't recognize her name, but after their dance, he introduced her to a dozen more people. She smiled and chatted, hoping to find out something interesting, but everyone had visited the punch too many times. Pippa wasn't all that sociable, but she gave it her all. She met as many people as she could. Some remembered her and her family. In her experience, people here loved to talk, particularly to a former local, still considered one of them, but not tonight. Everyone was having too much fun and too much spiked punch. But tomorrow they would remember her. Maybe.

She kept half an eye on Wilde. He'd spoken with Sleeman for only a couple of minutes, then after scanning the room, as if checking to see no one had stabbed anyone, he slipped away. Where was he going? Maybe to trick-or-treat? She saw Sleeman standing silently, staring after him. She'd met Mr. Sleeman several times when she was a teenager, before she went off to NYU to get her law degree to give her the best chance of being accepted by the FBI. She watched another man walk over to Sleeman and pull off his mask. The younger man looked like Sleeman. She remembered he had sons and one daughter. They spoke, then the younger man walked back to a woman, held out his hand to her, and off they went to the dance floor.

She didn't see the chief again.

She was exhausted when she walked back to Major Trumbo's B&B after eleven. She found Mrs. Trumbo standing behind the high mahogany reception desk with its orange and black streamers still looped across the wall behind her. She heard conversation coming from the sitting room to her right. Only two oatmeal cookies remained on a plate on the counter.

"Where's your bag?"

Pippa blinked. "My bag?"

"Your trick-or-treat bag, dear. I was too busy to get out this year. Last year, I dressed up as Little Red Riding Hood and collected candy for the children's hospital in Annapolis. People were so surprised. I really cleaned up. I didn't know there were that many Snickers bars in St. Lumis."

Pippa couldn't imagine Mrs. Trumbo as Little Red Riding Hood. It boggled the mind. She smiled. "I'd rather have another one of your cookies," she said, and snagged one. She said good night to Mrs. Trumbo and climbed the two flights of stairs to her honeymoon suite, wondering if Major Trumbo had been as outgoing and friendly as his spouse. Out of habit, she locked the door and slipped on the chain. She double-checked the bathroom. Not a single red towel, only white.

She showered, put on black flannel pajamas covered with red cats, and sat cross-legged on the bed, her tablet on her lap. She read more about Wilde. Three years with the Philadelphia Police Department, married three years, three medals for bravery, divorced. On the fast track until his team member and best friend was murdered and he failed to find the killer. After Wilde had resigned, he dropped out of sight for a few months until he'd become the chief here in St. Lumis.

Pippa read until her eyelids were at half-mast. She turned off her tablet and the lamp beside the big circular bed and lay back, wondering why Wilde's best friend had been murdered and why he hadn't found whoever was responsible.

When she slept, she dreamed she was in a jail cell, seated on a bench fastened to a wall, with a beautiful woman with thick dark hair like a mantle around her shoulders seated next to her. There were plates stacked high with Mrs. Trumbo's oatmeal cookies in front of them. The woman told Pippa she knew it was wrong to eat them, but she had anyway, until she could only lie there, blissfully full. Suddenly Chief Wilde appeared on the other side of the jail cell bars, his eyes on the woman, and he was shaking his head, telling her she shouldn't have eaten the cookies and look where it got her.

She told him he was pathetic because he didn't know what the cookies meant. The woman laughed at him and was fluffing her hair when Pippa awoke with a start, her heart pounding, sweat dampening her sleep shirt. What in heaven's name did that weird dream mean? Who was the woman? And why was she dreaming about Chief Wilde? What did Mrs. Trumbo's oatmeal cookies have to do with anything? Then she remembered. She'd seen that woman when she was looking into Wilde. It was his ex-wife, Serena Wilde.

She huffed. What could she expect except weird dreams after swilling that vodka-laced punch?

14

Savich and Sherlock left Sean with his grandmother and Senator Monroe, a longtime fixture in her life, to attend church, eat his grandmother's fried chicken and potato salad for lunch, and play Frisbee in the small park across from his grandmother's house. As they left, they heard Sean explaining in great detail how Marty, his future wife and next-door neighbor, had dressed as Wonder Woman and lassoed all the adults and made them tell the truth, which made them laugh and got them more candy.

"At least he didn't make himself sick," Sherlock said as she slid into the Porsche.

"Through no fault of his own," Savich said as he closed her door and walked around to ease into the driver's seat. He started the engine and smiled when his beauty roared to life. "I'll bet he and Marty stuffed themselves before coming back into the house. And then they chowed down on popcorn while they watched that Scooby-Doo movie."

She laughed, leaned her head back against the sinfully soft Porsche leather. "I think if I see that movie one more time I'll be able to say all the characters' lines. We've seen it with him, what, half a dozen times already?"

"Nah, no more than four."

Sherlock sighed. "I'd have enjoyed playing Frisbee with Sean in the park with your mom and the senator. The senator's gotten pretty good, says Sean keeps him on his toes. He's gotten lots of practice what with his seven grandchildren. Well, if he and your mom get married, he'll have a step-grandchild, too."

The thought of a stepfather didn't give Savich a jolt like it once would have. "I doubt marriage is in the cards. Mom told me last month she likes things the way they are between them. Like me, she misses Dad. On the other hand, the senator is quite a debater, and he's smitten, a big point in his favor. And he's proven he can stick. They've been seeing each other nearly three years now." Savich slowed and carefully steered around a dozen bicycles, mostly tourists weaving in and out, having too much fun to be careful. Thankfully, traffic was lighter on Sundays.

Sherlock said, "I wonder what Congressman Manvers thinks about Agent Griffin Hammersmith protecting his wife. An alpha male in the same house as another alpha, only this one is twenty-five years younger and so good-looking he stops traffic."

"Griffin won't be there all day. About now, he's leaving for his command performance at Jessie Tenley's surprise birthday party for her eighteen-year-old daughter, Paige. He looked hunted when I told him about his assignment. Of course, I also told him his sacrifice meant we got Agent Cinelli on loan. He sighed and accepted his fate."

"And you thanked him for taking one for the team?"

"Yes. I told him he was bound to get cake, and maybe that'd make his sacrifice worth it."

She laughed. "I can't wait to meet Rebekah Manvers. You said her husband won't be there? He's up to his ears in meetings, even on Sunday?" She gave him a sideways grin. "Imagine, having to work on a Sunday."

Savich steered around an SUV filled with a family, obviously tourists, the driver moving slowly enough to see the sights with his family. "We need to speak to her husband, find out what he knows, what he's gotten out of Rebekah. You'll find this interesting: Rebekah claims her husband never trashed Zoltan, never questioned her about seeing a medium. He wouldn't be human if he didn't have strong feelings one way or the other. And after her attempted kidnapping, I imagine he got in her face about telling him what happened, about what Zoltan said, what her grandfather supposedly told her."

"He might not believe her attempted kidnapping had anything to do with Zoltan and this Big Take."

"And he could be right."

"But you doubt it."

"Yes, I do. I'm about ready to bring Zoltan in for questioning, see what shakes out. Regardless, Congressman Manvers will have a lot of questions. I know I would in his position."

"Do you think she told her husband everything?"

"If I were her, I would have. We'll see what happens. But you know, I'm surprised Zoltan's played her cards this way. Even if Rebekah's kidnappers had succeeded, it would have painted a big X on her chest."

Twenty minutes later, Savich pulled into a wide driveway behind Rebekah's Beemer on Belmont Road NW in beautiful Kalorama Heights. Savich had long thought the Heights was the prettiest place in Washington. He and Sherlock occasionally walked here with Sean, and, of course, visited the ice cream shop in Kalorama Circle. The lots were big and filled with trees, denuded now on November 1. "The silver Beemer, that's Rebekah's car," Savich said. "Behind it is Griffin's new Range Rover, isn't it?"

"Yes, an identical twin with his last one, but with that lovely new car smell. I wonder if the story about his now-deceased Range Rover going over a cliff was a new one for the insurance company." She waggled her eyebrows. "Nah, I bet they've heard it all."

Sherlock got out of the Porsche and looked around. "This is quite a place." The house was two stories, with ivy climbing up the age-mellowed redbrick walls. The grounds were beautifully maintained, like the rest of the yards in the neighborhood. The house itself looked well settled, probably more than a hundred and fifty years old. Sherlock said, "I bet before the War of 1812, this site was probably a lovely wooden colonial. But after the Brits burned Washington, wood was out, only brick."

"At least in this old neighborhood."

Griffin answered the door, greeted them, and turned to Rebekah Manvers, standing behind him. Savich introduced her to Sherlock.

Griffin said, "Rebekah, like I told you, I have to go to a birthday party."

"You didn't say who's celebrating. A friend, relative?"

"Nope, I only know the person giving the party. Please, don't ask. I'll be back about three o'clock, hopefully, and I'll stay until your husband gets home. About six, you said?"

Rebekah nodded. Griffin gave Savich a salute and left, whistling.

Rebekah looked after him. "What's that all about?"

Savich merely smiled and said, "Ask him when he gets back. You'll find it amusing." He studied Rebekah's face and saw no obvious signs of stress, though he knew she still had to feel afraid. But looking at her now, it wasn't obvious. "Is your arm all right today?"

"Yes, only a little sore." She rotated her shoulder to show him. She was wearing a white camp shirt over black skinny jeans and black socks on her feet, no shoes. Her hair was pulled up in a ponytail. Rebekah looked back and forth between Savich and Sherlock, cocked her head. "You're not only partners, are you? You're together, right?"

"Yes," Sherlock said, and gave her a sunny smile. "You're very perceptive."

Rebekah smiled, shook her head. "The two of you—it's obvious to me you guys have a connection."

Sherlock decided on the spot she liked Rebekah Manvers.

They followed her into a high-ceilinged, old-style living room filled with early American antiques.

Sherlock said, "How lovely. The antiques fit the room beautifully. Everything is from about the same time period, right?"

"Yes, 1838, to be exact. Needless to say, the house has been transformed many times during its lifetime. As you can see, though, all the beautiful molding and fireplaces have been kept and dutifully restored. As to the furniture, my husband seems to think a congressman needs to surround himself with American period pieces, to give him gravitas and a solid sense of embracing history. Me? I prefer Danish modern, which my husband finds appalling. At least this stuff is fairly comfortable. Let me introduce you to Kit Jarrett, my partner, my friend, and my one and only investigator in our art consulting business."

A petite young woman stepped forward, smiling. She was loaded with curves she displayed in black leggings and a long black turtleneck sweater to her hips. Kit shook their hands and cocked her head to one side, sending her glorious straight hair swinging against her cheek. Her words nearly jumped out of her mouth. "Believe me, it's a great pleasure. Goodness, Agent Savich, if you hadn't been in Celeste Manvers's neighborhood when Rebekah needed you, she would have been taken. Do you know yet who did it? The bastards. It makes my heart stutter to even think about it." She grinned really big, showing a crooked eyetooth. "Well, you can see I don't do 'measured and mature' very well." She looked at Sherlock and drew a deep breath. "Does your husband have a habit of swooping in just in the nick of time?"

Sherlock said, "I've always found his timing to be excellent." She realized how what she'd said could be interpreted and blinked up at Dillon, who smiled at her.

Rebekah's cell buzzed. She looked down. "Excuse me a moment." She walked a couple of steps away from them. A moment later, she turned back. "That was my husband. Turns out his meeting was cut short. He'll be home in about twenty minutes."

It was perfect timing, just what Savich wanted. He said, "He plans on being home the rest of the day and evening?"

At her nod, he said, "Then you won't need our protection." Savich quickly texted Griffin, told him to go straight to the birthday party and have a great time with all the teenagers and the cake.

A text came back immediately: *Understood. Fingers crossed for chocolate, tons of frosting, little chocolate flowers on top.*

Savich said, "Twenty minutes should be fine."

Rebekah said, "Please, sit down. May I get you something to drink?"

"No, thank you," Savich said. "We need to get started. Rebekah, I want you to tell me everything about your meeting with Zoltan on Wednesday night." He looked at Kit Jarrett and cocked his head.

Kit said, "I know it all already, Agent Savich. I won't interrupt, and you can trust me not to blab, despite my being a motormouth when you walked in. Believe me, I would never do anything to harm Rebekah. She pays me very well." She lightly poked Rebekah's arm.

Rebekah studied his face, stilled. "You went to see Zoltan, didn't you?"

"Yes, Thursday night."

She sighed. "I suppose she told you everything, then? About pretending Grandfather was there and what he said about the Big Take?"

"Despite the psychotropic herbs she put in her special tea, yes, I managed to get her account of what happened."

"What? You're saying she drugged the tea?"

Savich nodded. "When I called her on it, she claimed there was nothing harmful in the tea, that she meant only to relax her clients, make them more at ease."

Rebekah stared at him. "You mean her blasted tea was meant to drug me into not questioning her version of reality?"

"I'd say that about nails it, yes. When I left her, I took the thermos with me and had the tea checked. There was a mix of poorly understood Chinese herbs in the tea but nothing illegal."

Rebekah smacked her fist against the arm of the sofa. "I never questioned it, never. I knew I was mellowing out—I was less stressed, and I really liked the taste of that tea. That bitch. But you realized what she'd done."

"I'm suspicious by nature. Rebekah, it's time for you to tell me exactly what happened that night. From your perspective. You can trust our discretion."

She sighed again. "I guess there's no point trying to keep it private any longer. I finally broke down and told Rich all about the séance. I thought I'd have to coldcock him to keep him from driving over to Zoltan's house and attacking her. I wouldn't be surprised if he passed the story along to his sons, even his best bud, Chief of Staff Arlan Burger."

"Why didn't you add me to your list?"

She blinked away tears. "I didn't think on Thursday to tell you more about it. I couldn't admit to myself the story might be true. My grandfather was a good man, at least I believe so from everything I know to be true about him. I preferred to think that story really was made up, and who knows, maybe it was, that's what I told Rich. He laughed and said if the Big Take was made up, then why would someone try to kidnap me?"

"He's right," Savich said. "Someone found out about the Big Take story and believes it's true. Rebekah, do you really know where the Big Take is hidden?"

"No, really, although I think I left Zoltan with the impression I did. Of course, I didn't recite Grandfather's poem to Zoltan, but I did hint I knew where it's hidden. She wanted me to say the poem, but I didn't. I told her it didn't matter what the poem said, I intended to let whatever it was, even if it's real, stay hidden forever."

"Someone attacked you to hear that poem, Rebekah," Savich said. "You need to let it go now. I'm not sure we can help you if you don't trust us with it."

Kit sat forward, took Rebekah's hands in hers. "Do you still remember it?"

Rebekah sat back against the sofa cushions, clasping and unclasping her hands in her lap. "I promised Grandfather I'd never say it out loud, except to him, and I haven't, not to anyone. I know it's silly keeping a child's promise, but it's hard for me to break it, even now. In many ways, my relationship with my grandfather was the most important one I had growing up, other than with my mother, of course. It was his story and his poem, and now it's mine. I couldn't stand it if I let whatever it leads to tarnish his memory."

"After what's happened to you, Rebekah," Savich said, "a grandfather who loved you would understand. He'd want you to tell us."

"Then you have to promise not to repeat it, to use it only to find out who attacked me. Can I trust you, Agent Savich, Agent Sherlock, and you, Kit, not to repeat it to anyone?"

After their nods, she closed her eyes, and recited quietly:

> *Don't let them know it's hidden inside*
> *The key to what I wish to hide*
> *It's in my head, already there*

And no one else will guess or care
Remember these words when at last I sleep
And the Big Take will be yours to keep.

She opened her eyes. "A silly little poem, one of several he wrote for me. I asked him what the words 'it's in my head' meant, and all he said was I would know someday. Of course, he never had a chance to tell me. He had the strokes and fell into the coma. I remember I thought he was only adding some charm to his story, never anything more than that—until now." She studied Savich's face and sighed. "I know you're on my side, Agent Savich. I should have told you before."

"Then you can tell me all the rest of it now."

Rebekah laid out exactly what had happened in the séance, and Savich noted that her story was very similar to Zoltan's.

Sherlock said, "Seems to me Zoltan knew about the Big Take and put on a big production to convince you her shtick was real, hoping you'd tell her where your grandfather had hidden it or work with her to find it. Only you didn't do that. You shut her down. And when that didn't work, she tried to get you kidnapped. And then that blew up in her face."

Rebekah said, "Only thanks to Agent Savich."

Savich said, "That would mean Zoltan is very organized and has some bad people on speed dial. She acted fast."

Rebekah said slowly, "Is it possible she thinks she's for real? That she really brought Grandfather to me?"

"No," Savich said.

Kit sat forward. "All right, but it's still possible someone we don't know about wanted to kidnap Rebekah for ransom, that it has no connection to this Zoltan. It's not a secret Rich is—excuse me—rich. And Rebekah is, too, for that matter, a legacy from her grandfather. Even if Rich didn't adore Rebekah as much as he does, he'd still pay the ransom. He'd have to."

"Yes, he'd have to, wouldn't he?" Rebekah looked down at her hands pleating the brown afghan folded next to her on the early American sofa.

Savich didn't want to ask her, but he knew he had to. It was a part of this mad mix. "Rebekah, have you ever thought your grandfather might have been involved in the death of his friend Nate Elderby?"

"What?" Rebekah sat back, her eyes wide on Savich's face. "My grandfather? No, no. He wasn't, he couldn't have been. He wasn't that kind of man." She calmed and drew a deep breath. "I wish I had some of Zoltan's tea about now. Listen, Agent Savich, I was a little kid when Nate Elderby drowned in 1995, but I remember Grandfather was very upset, pacing around his study, tears in his eyes, cursing Nate. Thinking back, he really was distraught.

"You're checking into his death since he may have been Grandfather's accomplice in this Big Take. With one thief murdered, the other thief gets everything? No, even as young as I was I remember his grief vividly. There was something snarky about Nate that Grandfather said in the séance. But that's stupid. It was Zoltan who made that snark up, not Grandfather."

Kit said, "If Rebekah's grandfather did murder his best friend, for gain or for some other reason, what does it matter now? I mean, there's no one left to prosecute. It happened years ago. Who would care now?"

Savich said, "I've learned that violence in the past has a way of forcing itself into the present." He suddenly thought of the puzzle pieces, of St. Lumis. Could Cinelli be in danger?

Rebekah said, "Nate Elderby's wife would care, wouldn't she?"

Everyone in the living room turned when they heard the front door open. Savich's cell beeped with an incoming message. He stared down at a photo sent by Agent Pippa Cinelli.

15

Savich sent her a quick text and slid his cell back into his jacket pocket. He slowly rose when Congressman Rich Manvers came into the room. Rebekah quickly walked over to him and took his hand. Manvers studied her face a moment, then kissed her lightly on the cheek. Manvers said over Rebekah's shoulder, "Good to see you, Agent Savich. Let me say again I owe you a great deal for saving my wife. Have you made any progress in finding the men who attacked her? Do you know yet if there was any connection to this charlatan, Zoltan?"

"That's what we're looking into and why we're talking with Rebekah now, Congressman," Savich said.

"Rebekah already told me a lot of what happened, the faked séance, that Zoltan was after some kind of information? I wanted to go to Zoltan's house and shake her by the neck until she coughed up the truth." He hugged his wife to his side. "But Rebekah was quite right. Involving myself probably wouldn't have ended well. We will need to trust you to get to the bottom of this." He grinned. "You might have saved me from an assault charge." He glanced at Sherlock, did a double take. "You're Agent Sherlock—the heroine of JFK." He pumped her hand. "A great pleasure to have you in my living room."

"Thank you. It all happened months and months ago."

Manvers smiled. "And bringing down that terrorist at the Lincoln Monument? I'm a politician, Agent Sherlock. That makes it my job never to forget anything that important to our country. I don't believe acts of heroism like yours should ever be forgotten."

Sherlock found herself smiling back at him. So he knew how to be self-deprecating and charming, not to mention he was freely stroking her ego. Still, she wondered why Rebekah had married a man old enough to be her father. She was young and smart, and her art authentication business was taking off. Maybe she'd been badly burned by a younger man? Sherlock planned to find out. "Sir, what did you think about Zoltan's revelation?

Of the Big Take? After you'd calmed down, of course."

He sat down in a big armchair that fit him nicely, facing them. "I knew Rebekah's grandfather, John Clarkson, actually I interned with him in the nineties. What he—Zoltan—was saying sounds preposterous, I mean, the Big Take? The John Clarkson I knew would never do anything illegal.

"I think the woman's a criminal, and she may be responsible for all that's happened. I think you should arrest her, Agent Savich, or at least haul her into the Hoover Building for questioning." He sat forward, clasped his hands between his knees. "Rebekah is frightened, and so am I. If you hadn't been in Celeste's neighborhood at just that time, what would have happened to her? I know you're concerned as well, enough to assign an agent to guard my wife."

Savich said, "I'd already decided to bring Zoltan in for an interview. Sir, who have you told about the Big Take?"

"Only Arlan Burger, to help me think it all through. He'll keep it to himself."

Savich said, "So you didn't tell Beck or Tucker?"

Manvers shook his head.

Sherlock said, "I understand Beck still lives here with you?"

Manvers visibly tightened, then relaxed. Sherlock wondered if he had to protect his younger son often. Manvers said, his voice matter-of-fact with a touch of humor, "Yes, for the short term. I hear he has a girlfriend, so my fingers are crossed."

Savich said easily, "Tell me, sir, has anything unusual happened in your congressional office the past month? Anything to concern you? Unsolicited emails or threatening letters, perhaps?"

Manvers fanned his hands. "Unusual? No, nothing unusual. Every politician gets their share of nut-cake threats. There are always unhappy people out there who want to blame somebody in government. Staff hands them over to Justice if they're at all concerned. Why? Are you thinking this isn't about Rebekah's grandfather? That it's something else entirely?"

"We're trying to cover all the bases," Savich said. "After what happened to Mrs. Manvers, we will double down and examine any questionable emails or letters you've received in the past month or so."

"You mean you think they might have gone after Rebekah when they were really after me?" He shook his head. "That would mean this whole thing is some sort of convoluted conspiracy against us. But for what hoped-for outcome?" Manvers pulled his wife closer. "Where is the FBI agent who's supposed to be guarding her from these people?"

Savich said, "Agent Hammersmith will continue to be here with Mrs. Manvers whenever you are unable to be."

Back came a charming grin. "Kit tells me I should demand another agent."

"Goodness, why?" Rebekah asked her husband. "Griffin is very nice and you know he's—what's the matter? What are all these grins about?"

Kit laughed. "Rebekah, I told Rich that Agent Hammersmith's a danger to womankind, and he'd best be careful." She gave Rebekah another poke on the arm. "Earth to Rebekah."

Rebekah shook her head. "Sorry, I'm on the slow side today. Actually, I was thinking about Beck, wondering what he'll say about Agent Hammersmith."

Manvers said easily, "Beck hasn't been around in the past couple of days, and though I can say with certainty Beck will hate his guts the minute he lays eyes on him, he isn't stupid. No way would Beck take on an FBI agent. But maybe Agent Hammersmith being here will motivate Beck to move out sooner."

Sherlock laughed. "Or perhaps, you, Congressman Manvers, could give Beck thirty days' notice."

Manvers nodded slowly, a smile on his mouth. He saw, too, the humor had put color in Rebekah's cheeks, at least for a little while.

16

Mrs. Trumbo's dining room held half a dozen tables, each one covered with a red-and-white checked tablecloth topped with a single chrysanthemum in a skinny red vase between the salt and pepper. Everyone was talking about the party at Leveler's Inn, comparing notes and hangovers. A woman said, "It was my flask of Grey Goose that rocketed the punch over the top."

An elderly gentleman at the next table said, "So that's why I wanted to fly south at three a.m."

Mrs. Trumbo raised her voice over the groans and said to Pippa, "Full house and not enough tables, so sit here, dear." She pulled out a chair for her next to a coffee table. It was fine with Pippa. She wanted to be by herself to think, to refine the plans she'd made on her drive from Washington yesterday.

Mrs. Trumbo appeared at her elbow. "Coffee? It's strong enough to put extra pep in your step."

The coffee, even with Pippa's liberal dose of milk and two Splendas, was more than strong enough. As she sipped the high-octane coffee and waited for her breakfast, Pippa made her plans for this Sunday morning. She knew not all stores would be open this time of year, but she'd visit the open ones and cozy up to the owners, friendly as could be, and see what she could learn. Maybe she'd tell them she'd once lived here, get them to tell her if anything hinky happened here lately. She'd been told by a judge she'd interned for that she really knew how to listen and draw people out. Time to put what Judge Vena said to the test. It would be easier with people who recognized her. She'd play the family card, see if she could open them up. Of course, Chief Wilde would probably be her most valuable source, but she wouldn't bring him in yet, didn't know him well enough to know how he'd react or what he'd do. She wanted to be very sure about him first. This was her show until she nailed something down or needed his help.

Pippa looked up at a loud harrumph. Oh dear, she hadn't heard Mrs. Trumbo, too deep in her plans. Her mouth watered when she saw a plate piled high with scrambled eggs, crispy bacon, and wheat toast. She took the cutlery and spread a white napkin on her lap. "That looks wonderful, Mrs. Trumbo. Thank you."

"Major Trumbo always liked my scrambled eggs. It's the pinch of dill, you know. You've got nice long legs, time to fill 'em up. Be a good girl and clean your plate."

Pippa crunched on a piece of bacon and looked around at the mix of guests—several older couples, two families with a total of five kids, the kids too busy eating to make much noise yet, and a young man and woman who looked barely old enough to vote. The young woman was yawning, probably wishing she were still in bed with a damp cloth on her forehead and four aspirin down her gullet. Pippa heard her say to an older couple next to them during a brief lull, "This is our third year coming back to visit Barry's parents and go to Leveler's Inn with them, and every single year I swear I won't go swimming in that awesome punch. But the devil whispered in my ear again and won. Again."

Her husband had a bad case of bed head. He stopped shoveling down his scrambled eggs and said, "Before I got wasted on that Halloween punch, the local police chief warned me he never touched the stuff, said he never knew when he'd have to deal with ghosts stringing toilet paper all over town. I wanted to ask him who cared, it was Halloween, but then a guy dressed as Frankenstein handed me another glass of punch. Shelly, what was his name? Not Frankenstein, the police chief?"

An older woman called out, "Wilde, Matthew Wilde. He's a nice boy. He spent three years in the Philadelphia Police Department before he took over from Chief Cosby. I wonder why he left?"

"Got to be a woman," said a gentleman with a huge mustache decorated with some whole wheat toast crumbs. "Always is."

"Or a man."

"Nope, not Wilde. The chief shoots straight arrows."

"No, I meant it works both ways," his wife said, exasperated. "If the chief were a woman, it would have been a man."

On it went. Everyone seemed content to stay in the dining room, talking and sharing stories. And Pippa listened. You never knew what nugget might drop into your lap.

Pippa ate two pieces of toast slathered with strawberry jam and finished up her scrambled eggs.

Mrs. Trumbo appeared in the doorway. Arms crossed, she waited until everyone was quiet and announced, "Services begin in twenty minutes at St. Mark's on Columbo Square, on the back side of General Columbo's statue. And no, for those of you who don't know, our Columbo isn't named after the old Peter Falk character. Our Columbo was a buddy of Theodore Roosevelt's, rode up San Juan Hill with him way back when, before even I was born. Father Theo can assist you to repent your Halloween sins, and then you can have a nice walkabout, digest your wonderful breakfast, and clean the rest of the vodka out of your heads. Many of our shops are closed on Sundays in the off-season, but most will be open today with so many people in town this weekend. You might want to visit Harry's Pawn Shop on Big Bass Street. His specialty is old handguns, strings of tatty pearls—the kind your mother-in-law used to wear—and old guitars, including one Harry claims belonged to Elvis. Then there's Maude's Creepy Puzzles. Maude Filly's got snake puzzles and all sorts of monster puzzles your kids and grandkids will like. It's on South Looney Street. If you take North Looney, you'll go straight to Sleeman's Used Cars, one of the son's dealerships, though daddy did give it to him. They're open every day except Christmas.

"Since it's November, don't be surprised if it gets chillier as the day goes on, even with the sun, so be sure to layer. Go on. Out. Dinner's at five thirty. Roast beef with all the trimmings. Don't be late." She stood back by the dining room door, arms still crossed, and waited until everyone cleared out.

Pippa's heart was pounding. A puzzle store? She smiled at her hostess. "Thank you, Mrs. Trumbo, for the delicious breakfast. Maude's Creepy Puzzles, you said?"

Mrs. Trumbo nodded. "Yes, on South Looney Street. Maude Filly owns it. That's her maiden name, and it so happens she was Major Trumbo's first wife, lived with him here in town when he was a big pooh-bah in the army. She's been a good friend of mine since Major Trumbo passed to the hereafter, where he belonged, not before, it would have been too weird. She'd already changed back to her maiden name so there was no confusion. I always mention her store to my guests. Maude designs and makes most of her own puzzles, got a gift for it. I once asked her why the fascination with monster puzzles. You know what she told me? She said, 'Lill, you can always pull apart puzzle pieces and the monster is gone, not like those monsters who come in your nightmares. People like that.'

"If you can figure that out, tell me. During the summer, when tourists are thick on the ground, she makes a fortune. Everyone with a kid wants a monster or a snake puzzle, says she can hardly keep up. It tides her over during the winter. Would you look at the time? Back to my kitchen. Have a good day, Ms. Cinelli." She paused and gave Pippa a big grin, showing beautiful white teeth, possibly her own. "You're a pretty girl. Not many young available men around St. Lumis, particularly now in November. That's a pity. You'll have to come back in the summer. All you'd have to do is walk around and look available."

Pippa accepted this advice with a smile, but she wasn't paying attention. *Creepy puzzles.* No, couldn't be that easy, that obvious. She was already wearing a white shirt under a dark blue V-neck sweater, jeans, sneakers, and a leather jacket over her arm, ready to rock 'n' roll. Her first stop would be Maude's

Creepy Puzzles, on South Looney Street, only a two-block walk from Major Trumbo's B&B.

Five minutes later, she was already there, facing a deep, narrow storefront set between Sharpest Tools and Buzzy's Burgers. *Maude's Creepy Puzzles* was written in bold Gothic script above the door. One large front window showcased puzzles from ancient horror movies, like *Creature from the Black Lagoon*, the original *Godzilla*, and Jack Nicholson in *The Shining*, grinning manically, his eyes quite mad, a thick green snake wrapped around his waist, mouth open wide, fangs dripping venom. The snake looked nearly as terrifying as Nicholson. And there was a kraken, a giant bulbous beast rising above a ship, crushing it and eating the sailors, the kraken's long, fat teeth dripping blood. Talk about giving kids nightmares.

Even the *Closed* sign was in fancy Gothic script. The door opened as Pippa studied a puzzle of a serpent winding its way up what looked like the Tree of Life. The Garden of Eden? If that serpent spoke to her, Pippa knew she'd have run away, not hung around and munched on an apple.

An older woman wearing an orange turban that rose a good five inches above her head and a flowing black caftan with yellow stars looked over at Pippa and gave her a big smile. She was about seventy, comfortably large, her eyes slightly almond shaped and nearly as dark as Dillon Savich's. So this was the first Mrs. Trumbo.

"What a blessed Sunday morning. It's good to see someone out of bed, looking alert, after those wicked revelries at Leveler's Inn last night." She touched her fingers to her orange turban. "Yes, yes, I'm still celebrating Halloween. Come in and look around. I think there's a couple of Snickers bars in the basket on the counter if you still have a sweet tooth left. Just let me hang the Open sign. There."

I've found the mother lode.

17

Pippa was so excited, for a moment she couldn't think of a thing to say. She beamed at Mrs. Filly and out tumbled, "I can't wait to talk about your puzzles, Mrs. Filly. They've always fascinated me. Mrs. Trumbo said you designed and made most of the puzzles in your store. I am so pleased to meet you."

Mrs. Filly patted her arm and drew her into the shop. Unfortunately, a moment later Pippa heard a jangling bell, and two families poured in, the children shouting and pointing. "Yes, dear, we can talk all about puzzles, but as you can see it will have to wait a bit."

Pippa watched Maude Filly speak to the parents, answer their questions, and point the kids to some puzzles Pippa supposed were appropriate for their ages. She walked through the store herself as she waited, astounded at the variety of puzzles, most with a twist of some kind, and as advertised, very creepy. Then, on a corner shelf—she couldn't believe it. Her heart skipped a beat; her brain went on full alert. She stared at a puzzle of St. Lumis from the water looking toward town. It was the same long pier, the same narrow waterfront sidewalk, and the bottoms of the buildings—identical. She was looking at the bottom two-thirds of the puzzle sent to Dillon—well, without the bones and dead birds. She stepped closer. Near the top of the puzzle, leaning out from an upper window was an older man, shown from the waist up, wearing a purple Grateful Dead T-shirt that didn't cover his paunch. He was bald, with saggy jowls and a snarl on his mouth, and his eyes promised mayhem, mean and dark as night. A long, thin yellow snake wound around his neck like a multi-stranded choker necklace, touching his cheek, almost a kiss. It was creepy and ridiculous.

She looked more closely and realized she recognized the building. It was the Alworth Hotel, a once-thriving waterside hotel that had closed when she still lived in town. The big ALWORTH HOTEL sign was long gone now.

Would the old man with the snake be in the next section of the puzzle sent to Dillon? She took a photo of the puzzle, sent it to him, and texted about finding it in Maude's Creepy Puzzles. She saw she'd used three exclamation points. She hoped he'd be as excited as she was.

She studied the puzzle, obviously professionally made. In comparison, the St. Lumis puzzle pieces sent to Agent Savich definitely looked amateurish, more homemade. Someone must have copied this puzzle, added the dead gulls on the pier and the scattered human bones on the sidewalk digitally, and sent it to Agent Savich. Which meant it had to be someone who lived in St. Lumis or at least had visited, maybe often, someone Maude Filly might remember.

Pippa jumped when Maude Filly's voice said near her ear, "I see you're fascinated by that puzzle." She pointed a long blood-red fingernail to the top of it. "In the window there, trying to look malevolent, that's Major Trumbo, my ex. Lillian, his second wife, that's the Mrs. Trumbo who owns the B&B, she told me it's the best picture she's ever seen of him and that snake kissing him had to be one of his relatives. Ah, Lill, she loves to tell visitors how the B&B was Major Trumbo's dream, how he wanted more than anything to have his own place right here in St. Lumis." Maude leaned close. "What a whopper—don't believe a word of it. It was always Lill's dream, not his. It didn't take long before she hated the old codger, but not as much as I did. I kicked him out when he cheated on me with her." She glanced at the puzzle, lightly touched her fingers to the man's face, then snorted. "To this day, Lill claims she didn't know the major still had a wife until after he'd asked her to marry him, admitted it might take a little time since he had to get a divorce. When we've both croaked, I'll ask her again in the afterlife, that is if we both end up in the same place. The major didn't look like this when he was married to me or when he first married Lill. He could look mean, if he wanted to, but it was a sexy sort of 'I'm dangerous and don't fool with me' mean. But the last couple years of his life? He was that man in the window, well, with a bit of whimsy on my part. At least by then he was her problem, not mine." She shuddered.

Pippa said, "You put that nasty snake around his neck, like he's a monster. And why do you have him leaning out the window?"

Mrs. Filly shrugged. "I decided to make it my last memory of him. I actually saw him up there and took a photo. I decided to immortalize him. Believe me, the snake fits him. But, to be honest here, he didn't really have a paunch, I added it because he was such a two-timing bastard. And the Grateful Dead T-shirt? Like I said, a bit of whimsy on my part."

"And this was when it was still that old hotel, the Alworth?"

"Yes, you can see the sign. The hotel wasn't ever renovated and no one wanted to stay there. Old Mrs. Alworth sold it, and Mr. Sleeman—he's our local wealthy robber baron—he turned it into some St. Lumis memorabilia shops. How did you know about the hotel?"

Pippa gave her a big smile. "I grew up in St. Lumis. My family left seven years ago. I decided to come back and visit my old stomping grounds." She looked back at the puzzle. "When did Major Trumbo die?"

Mrs. Filly stroked her jaw, hummed. "I think it was five years ago, the same year Lill bought the Calders' place and turned it into a B&B. She said it was very sudden, he simply fell over and croaked while they were on vacation. She said she couldn't cremate him in life, so she did it when he died. I believe his urn sits on her fireplace mantel. All her guests see it at every meal."

Pippa smiled. "It was one of the first things I noticed."

Mrs. Filly snapped to and called out, "Sir, that puzzle's wooden, indestructible, very good for small children, perhaps not quite as scary as the one he's clutching to his chest, which I don't recommend for any child under thirty." She laughed at her own joke, patted Pippa's arm, and walked over to ring up a sale, a large puzzle of Harrison Ford as Indiana Jones in a room filled with snakes, one crawling up his leg, another wrapped around his waist. His mouth was open in a scream. Pippa shuddered. No, thank you. She saw a father and one of his sons arguing. The boy wanted a Frankenstein puzzle that showed purple goo coming out of the monster's enormous mouth. She hoped the father won that round. It was then she saw a sign posted against the back wall of the shop:

LEARN HOW TO MAKE YOUR OWN PUZZLES

If she'd been in a bathtub, she'd have jumped out and shouted, "Eureka!" Pippa snapped a photo with her cell when she was sure Maude Filly was otherwise occupied, walked to a corner of the shop, and shot off another text with the photo to Savich.

She waited, studied Mrs. Filly as she rang up another sale and interacted with her customers. When there was a break again, Pippa walked back up to her. "I see your sign about making your own puzzles. Do you give classes?"

"No, not exactly classes. If someone asks for advice I help them with the design they want or recommend several different designs to them. Help them set it up."

"I'll bet people love to turn photos into puzzles, right? Like with Shutterfly? You send them your photo and they make a puzzle out of it?"

Mrs. Filly nodded. "Many people want to give their puzzles a personal touch."

"You're so talented. I bet people from all over have heard of you and come in."

"Aren't you sweet. Yes, I have a lot of visitors."

Pippa pointed to Major Trumbo leaning out

the window. "That one is fascinating. Did anyone want to make a puzzle like it?"

"Hmm, I don't think so. That's not to say that someone couldn't simply take a photo of it if they wanted to. I'd never know."

"Have you sold many of Major Trumbo's puzzles?"

"Not all that many. Mostly only to folks who knew him and get a good laugh. The few others who've bought the puzzle only see a nasty old dude with a snake kissing him. Gives lots of people the willies." Mrs. Filly cocked her head at Pippa in question. "Why all the interest in that particular puzzle? You never knew Major Trumbo, did you?"

"No, I didn't know him. The puzzle's unusual, makes me wonder about the nasty old dude."

Mrs. Filly didn't smile, but she nodded. "People prefer the monsters and the gore, and maybe the Jack Nicholson. Now, the Jack one makes my skin crawl."

More customers poured into the store, and Mrs. Filly turned to greet them. Pippa had so many more questions, about her records, about how her puzzles were made, but she didn't want to make Mrs. Filly suspicious. The way the woman had looked at her when she'd asked how many Major Trumbo puzzles she'd sold—maybe she already was. It was time to move on. She'd swing back around later.

Pippa left Maude's Creepy Puzzles, snapped another photo of the storefront, and sent it to Dillon.

Then she headed to Columbo Square, another two blocks inland.

The air was fresh with a slight breeze, and the sun was bright overhead, a perfect fall day for the tourists strolling around town. After a block, Pippa pulled off her leather jacket as she walked toward the square. She felt euphoric, amazed at how quickly the puzzle mystery seemed to be coming together. But she realized, even with her meager experience, that something seemed off. The puzzle had almost been served up on a platter for her where she couldn't miss it. Was someone trying to lure the FBI to St. Lumis? She'd asked only a few questions before Mrs. Filly had looked at her oddly. Why? Had she given herself away by showing all that interest? When she went back, she'd have to be more careful.

It was time to talk to more of the locals. Pippa turned right off Columbo Square, with its giant bronze statue of General Columbo in the center astride his rearing horse, its hooves flying high. The square looked wilted from the hot summer, and the grass was brown. She started to sit on one of the benches, thinking perhaps someone she recognized would come by, but she decided to keep walking toward her former family home and see how it was faring. Maybe the owners would come out and talk. She walked two blocks down Pilchard Street and turned onto Blue Lagoon Lane. Her former home was on the left, three houses down. She stopped and stared. She couldn't believe her once-tidy clapboard house and immaculate yard with flowers blooming everywhere, thanks to her mother, was now painted a virulent pink, a car on blocks in the driveway. The yard looked like it hadn't been tended or a flower planted since her parents left. She wanted to scream, or cry. She remembered her parents saying they'd sold the house for a great price to a lovely couple from Norway. Apparently the folks from Norway had decided to go back to Oslo and sold it to some yahoos. She wanted to burst through the pink door and yell at whoever lived there. *Calm yourself. It's only a house. It has nothing to do with you now.* Still, she snapped photos with her phone. Should she send them to her parents? No way. She deleted them instead. As she stood staring at the house, the front door opened, and a young man stepped out, yawning, wearing only a pair of tatty jeans, looking buff and scruffy. He made a sprint to the driveway to pick up the *St. Lumis Herald* and stopped in his tracks when he saw her.

18

_____

"**H**ey, who are you? Why are you standing there?"

Pippa shook herself. What the house looked like didn't matter. The derelict yard that would make her mother weep, it didn't matter, either, not for seven years. She called out, all bonhomie, "I stopped to admire the lovely pink paint."

The man guffawed and gave her a white-toothed smile. "Yeah, right, funny girl. It's a bloody nightmare, but that's Ma for you, loves her pink. The pinker the better. I'm only visiting. I couldn't live here. It'd make me nuts, send me screaming into the night. My name's Hunt. You want to come in for a cup of coffee? Ma's at church. Hey, once you're inside, there's no more pink, I promise."

Too bad Hunt didn't live here. The chances of his being of any help were close to nil. She gave him a big smile. "Not today, but thank you."

He waved and turned back to the house, whistling.

Pippa walked another block inland, past an older square brick apartment building, circa 1970, surrounded by denuded maple trees and small older houses with smaller front yards built nearly to the worn sidewalk. There was a new sign for a hair salon in one window. Otherwise everything seemed the same. There were children playing football in a side yard, young girls going wildly high on swings hanging from low oak branches. She heard parents' voices from inside the houses and the sound of TV cartoons, but mainly football games blasting out. She supposed as long as Sunday football was king, things would remain the same.

She kept walking through the neighborhoods, getting a feel again for the town she'd once known down to her callused bare feet. She saw a new café on her right, June's Eats, and thank goodness, it was open. She walked into an art deco movie set, beautifully done, with booths and tables, a long counter with stools, the open kitchen in the back. A pretty young woman stood behind the cash register, giving change to a customer. Pippa recognized her immediately. June Florio, her dad a banker in Annapolis, her mom a schoolteacher in Mayo. And now she owned a café? Amazing what paths people took. Look at Pippa, from lawyer to FBI agent. The place was popular, already filling up for lunch. There was a waiter tending to the dozen customers.

June looked up and smiled. "Can I help you?" The friendly smile changed to a dawning look of recognition. "Wait, I know you. Pippa—yes, that's right, Pippa Cinelli. Goodness, I forgot how pretty you were. Welcome home."

Pippa gave June Florio a big smile. "Thank you. What a beautiful café, and I love the black-and-white art deco squares on the floor. Were you at the party last night at Leveler's?"

"You wouldn't know it now, but last night I was Marie Antoinette. My husband, Doug, came as one of my lovers and draped himself all over me the entire night. As you can see, he's not around. The idiot is home in bed, groaning. I was tempted to pour cold water over his head. Between moans, he said everyone would be hungover today after last night at Leveler's Inn, and we should just stay closed. Happens every year. Look around, he was dead wrong." She waved her hand toward the dozen or so people seated around the café. "Over there's a big tub of cold bottled water, great for a hangover, in case you drank too much of that vodka pretending to be punch?"

Pippa smiled. "I didn't have another drop after I saw yet another Einstein with electrified hair pour in a full flask of vodka. I'm out for a walk on this beautiful November day. Visiting all my old haunts."

"Where do you live?"

"Down the road in Washington. This is a mini-vacation for me. It's good to see you, June. So far, I've got to say, nothing much has changed."

"No, nothing ever changes here. Well, except I'm married to the guy holding his head at home. I'm June Sweazy now. Do you remember Doug Sweazy? He was our running back in high school, had a smooth tongue, a great body?"

"I do indeed. He also had a great sense of humor, I remember. I had a crush on him."

"Yeah, I did, too. I remember your dad. He was always so nice."

"Thank you, I'll pass it along." Pippa looked down at her watch. Where had the time gone? She heard a man call out June's name. "I'm keeping you away from your customers. Maybe I could have a tuna salad sandwich, and we can talk when you're free?"

In short order, Pippa was eating her sandwich while June dealt with customers, smiling and friendly. In free moments, she asked June to tell her about what had happened in the seven years since she'd visited.

Not much, apparently. Pippa mentioned the puzzle store.

June shuddered, then grinned. "That place gives me the creeps. It's fitting, I guess, since 'creepy' is in the name of Maude's store. I've only been in there a couple of times. Now, if you ask me, Maude is on the strange side. She's too obsessed with snakes and monsters. Wouldn't that warp your brain?"

Pippa nodded. "She told me she helps people who want to make their own puzzles. I guess you've never done that?"

"Goodness, no, and I don't know of anyone who has. She has a boyfriend, an older gentleman from around Annapolis. Every two weeks she closes her puzzle shop, and the two of them leave St. Lumis for a couple of days. It's like clockwork. She always puts a sign in the window: *Going on a short honeymoon.* Where, I asked her once, and she only smiled and shook her head."

That was interesting. Perhaps she could bring it up casually when she went back to the puzzle shop later in the afternoon. "I visited her puzzle store this morning. You're right, 'creepy' is the perfect word for it."

"I think Maude Filly's a hoot, always wearing hippy tie-dye and Birkenstocks, except for Halloween when she turns into Madam Rasputin and wears a turban and flowing robes. But hey, she's nice and does great business with tourists, especially with their kids. The more gore the better for the kids."

"Does she talk much about Major Trumbo?"

June shook her head.

"She told me about him when I saw a puzzle

with him hanging out of a window of the old Alworth Hotel. I got the impression there's not much love lost there."

"Since she and the second Mrs. Trumbo appear to be good friends, I guess not." June was off to fill coffee cups.

When she was free again, Pippa asked her about Chief Matthew Wilde. "He took Chief Cosby's place, right?"

June said as she wiped down the counter, "Now, there's a pleasing hunk of man, been here maybe three years now." She leaned closer. "Field Sleeman's youngest daughter, Freddie, is after him now. I think he even went out with her a couple of times, then sheared off. Freddie is her nickname, which her parents hate. She's maybe twenty-four now, went to school to be an interior designer. And no, I haven't seen any of her work."

Pippa's eyebrow went up. "A bit young for him, isn't she?"

June shrugged. "Only nine years between them, or thereabouts. In any case, who cares? A hunk's a hunk."

Pippa laughed. "True enough. So Chief Wilde decided he wasn't interested?"

June nodded as she measured coffee into the pot. "Alas for Freddie, she's not giving up. Would you like a slice of apple pie? Mrs. Hodkins makes them for us, renders our customers mute with pleasure, and gives her extra income."

"What I'd really like is another one of Mrs. Trumbo's oatmeal cookies," Pippa said.

"Aren't they delicious? Now, there's a friendly woman, gruff and smiling, all at once. Tells you what to do, then gives you a cookie. She's always talking about how important family is, but then she never speaks of her own family. I don't know how many are left."

"Her husband, Major Trumbo, he died before she bought the Calder Victorian and made it a B&B, right?"

June laughed. "Do you know, I'm not sure. She, Major Trumbo, and her son, Ronald Pomfrey, moved here half a dozen years ago. Mrs. Filly already lived here." June shrugged. "The two former wives are the best of friends. Go figure. They still like to talk about the infamous Major Trumbo." A customer called out, and June patted Pippa's arm and was off.

Why was Major Trumbo infamous? But June was gone. Pippa called after her, "The sandwich was delicious. Thank you, June. I hope to see you again before I leave."

June sent her a little wave. "Do come back, Pippa."

It was nearly one o'clock when Pippa stepped onto the sidewalk and breathed in the fresh, clean St. Lumis air. It was chilly now, but tourists were still thick on the ground, eating ice cream, laughing, enjoying themselves. She smiled at everyone she passed and walked toward Whale Head Court and the Sleeman mansion. The house was still mostly colonial, with two stories, painted white with dark green trim. It was set back from the lane on a slight rise, with lots of maples and oaks and pines surrounding the beautifully maintained grounds. It was the only house on Whale Head Court with a big circular driveway. A BMW and a Lexus SUV, both silver, shined bright beneath the afternoon sun. The house was even bigger than she remembered. They'd built an addition that looked like a conservatory, with lots of windows and a lovely green domed roof.

A child's voice said, "I don't know you. Why are you staring at my grandma's house?"

19

Pippa turned to see a little girl in jeans, sneakers, and a Baltimore Ravens sweatshirt, too large for her. She was holding a basketball she'd been bouncing up and down on the driveway.

Where was the hoop? "Hi, I'm Pippa. What's your name?"

"I'm Anjolina Sleeman, Jo for short. That's what everyone calls me, but my mama hates it. She always says I'm Anjolina, with an *O*. I think she was stoned when she picked that name and Daddy let her. She didn't even spell it right." She paused. "Maybe Daddy was stoned, too. When I grow up, I'm going to ask them why they weren't stoned when they named my brother. His name is normal—Christopher."

Pippa was charmed. This kid could rule the world someday. She said, "So your grandparents live here? It's a lovely house."

Anjolina dribbled a couple of times, nodded. "Yes, Grandpa and Grandma live here. I told you, it's their house. My pain-in-the-butt brother and I visit on Sundays so my folks can drive to Washington to eat at their favorite restaurant in Foggy Bottom." The little girl thought a moment, frowning. "Do you know why it's called Foggy Bottom?"

"I guess I knew once, but I forgot, sorry."

The little girl shook her head. "That name makes it sound like they were stoned, too."

Pippa laughed, couldn't help it. "So what's your dad's name?"

"Mama calls him 'jerk' a lot, but his real name is Mason. Mama said it was his great-granddaddy's name and that's why he got stuck with it."

The little girl leaned over and started bouncing the basketball from right to left, left to right, imitating Steph Curry. She was smooth and looked up, never at the ball. "My stupid brother got sick because he ate too many candy bars last night. I told him Captain America wouldn't stuff food down like a baboon, but he wouldn't listen. Well, he puked it all up. My parents still went to Foggy Bottom. Grandma is letting him lie on the couch and watch TV. She brought him saltine crackers and ginger ale. Do you know, he doesn't even like basketball? Can you believe that?"

"No, I can't," Pippa said. "And here you are, doing Steph proud. You take it easy, Jo." Pippa was turning to leave when the front door opened and a large older woman appeared. Solid-looking, that was Pippa's first impression, and she wasn't dressed like the lady of the manor, either. No, she was wearing jeans and a red turtleneck and she was wiping her hands on her apron. Was this Mrs. Sleeman?

"Jo, don't bother the lady."

Pippa took a chance and called out, "Mrs. Sleeman?"

"Yes, I'm Joyce Sleeman. Who are you?"

"Pippa Cinelli. I grew up in St. Lumis. I'm back for a short visit. I remembered your beautiful home."

Pippa could see the woman relax from twenty feet away. Whatever else she might be, Pippa was a local and thus harmless. "Come in, why don't you, and have a cup of oolong tea. My precious little brain-dead grandson isn't moaning so loudly from his bellyache. Field just got home—Mr. Sleeman, my husband. I remember you now. Your mama had such a green thumb. She could make any place in St. Lumis look as green as Ireland. And her flowers, I miss all the gorgeous colors. I remember neighbors would bring her dead plants and I swear she'd have them dancing the hula within a week. Your mama had amazing juju. I trust she still does?"

"She does indeed."

"Do come in, Ms. Cinelli." She said to Jo, "It's

not too cold, Jo, so you can stay outside and practice your dribble."

Pippa gave Jo a little wave and followed Mrs.
Sleeman into the grand house. She hadn't remembered how spectacular it was inside, all golden pol-
ished wood and rich Persian carpets, a chandelier
overhead sparkly as diamonds.

A man's voice came from behind her. "And who
is this? Wait, I saw you last night at the Halloween
party at Leveler's Inn. Sorry, didn't get your name."

Mrs. Sleeman said, "Field, this is Pippa Cinelli.
She grew up here in St. Lumis. You remember her
parents, don't you?"

"Of course. How are they?"

"They're great, thank you, sir. They moved to
Boston seven years ago. I saw you, too, last night at
Leveler's Inn."

"A great party, as usual."

Mrs. Sleeman said, "I couldn't make it this year,
I was part of the kid patrol." She turned to her
husband. "You weren't tipsy when you came home,
Field. How come?"

Mr. Sleeman said, "Business last night. Had to
keep my wits about me."

His wife rolled her eyes. Joyce Sleeman looked
like his housekeeper standing next to him. Today,
he was dressed in a dark gray pinstriped suit with a
pale gray shirt and dark blue tie. He had a headful of
iron-gray hair, beautifully styled. Fact was, unlike his
wife, he looked rich. Had he been at church sitting

through the homily, or buying more real estate? And what was his business last night? Pippa's dad had always been cautious of Mr. Sleeman but only shook his head when Pippa asked him why that was.

"You don't look any the worse for wear, Ms. Cinelli. Did you enjoy the party?"

"Yes, along with a couple hundred other people. I saw you speaking with Chief Wilde."

He shrugged. "There's always something coming up that requires my attention. Let's go into the living room."

Mrs. Sleeman said, "Yes, I'll bring some tea."

Pippa spent an hour with Field and Joyce Sleeman while their grandson napped on a gorgeous blue brocade sofa. "You don't have to keep your voice down, Ms. Cinelli. Christopher sleeps like the no-longer-walking dead. Would you like sugar in your tea?"

"No, thank you." Pippa wasn't much of a tea drinker, but she dutifully tapped her cup to theirs in a welcome-home toast.

Pippa complimented them on the new conservatory they said they'd built five years ago, and they asked her what she did for a living. She said she was a lawyer. Conversation stayed social, and Pippa couldn't see a way to segue smoothly into anything helpful, like gruesome puzzles. At least they were friendly, the grandson was a great sleeper, and the tea, without sugar, wasn't bad.

Everything changed when Freddie Sleeman came into the living room, wearing, of all things, ski clothes. So this was Freddie, twenty-four, who'd studied interior design, and was on the hunt for Chief Wilde. "I'm off!"

She saw Pippa and stopped cold. "What are you collecting for? Or are you a religious cult member selling newly discovered books of the Bible?"

"Yes, that's it," Pippa said, smiling. "It's a short chapter, said to be hidden in northern Africa, and it's all about giving women the vote before the change of the millennium."

This brought a laugh from both Mr. and Mrs. Sleeman, but not from Freddie. Mrs. Sleeman said quickly, "Pippa grew up in St. Lumis. She's back for a short visit."

Freddie said, "You're so much older than I am, it's no wonder I don't remember you."

A nice sharp jab. Why the animosity?

Before Pippa could answer, Freddie shot her a look. "I heard Wilde was laughing with a new woman at the party last night. I also heard she was making a fool of herself, flirting with him like mad. It was you, wasn't it?"

Pippa cocked her head. "Not me. I think it was Cleopatra. Why weren't you there to save him?"

Mrs. Sleeman gave her daughter a warning look, then shrugged. "Who cares? Forget about Chief Wilde, Freddie. He's too old for you in any case."

Freddie shot Pippa another look and glanced at her watch. "I have to go. I'm meeting Kenny and Gretchen in Peterbrough."

"Where's the snow?" Mr. Sleeman asked his daughter.

"It's a party," Freddie said, nothing more. She left and gave the front door a good closing snap. Mr. Sleeman rose, shook Pippa's hand, and excused himself. Pippa couldn't very well ask him to stay and talk about, say, making puzzles. She looked at Joyce Sleeman and saw a guileless face with rich humor in her dark eyes. She glanced down at her own watch. Time to get back to the puzzle shop and speak to Mrs. Filly before it closed.

Before she could leave, Mason Sleeman and his wife arrived to pick up their kids. After introductions, Mason walked to the sofa and ever so lightly touched his kid's arm. The boy rose straight up and gave him a lazy smile. "I'm all well now, Dad. Can we go out to dinner? Maybe pizza?"

"You're a heathen," his grandmother said.

Pippa arrived at Maude's shop twenty minutes later to see a *Closed* sign in the front window. She'd closed early. What rotten luck. Well, it was Sunday. It would be all right. Pippa would see her tomorrow, early, before many customers came in. She could ask for her help in making a puzzle, see how it was done. Maybe she'd even show Maude the photos of the puzzle someone had sent to Dillon, see what kind of reaction she got. She'd have time to make out a list of questions for her.

When she reached the B&B, the lights were fully on, making the lovely old Victorian glow in the late-afternoon sunlight. She walked in to see everyone already gathered in the living room, waiting for the promised roast beef dinner with all the trimmings. Soft music she didn't recognize was playing on an old-fashioned turntable. She didn't bother to change, just joined in with the others and accepted a German beer, Major Trumbo's favorite, Mrs. Trumbo told the group.

Later, still full from the amazing dinner, Pippa sat in the middle of her honeymoon bed on the third floor and emailed Dillon a summary and photos of the Leveler's Inn Halloween shindig and the people she'd met today, primarily Mrs. Filly and her girlhood friend June.

Savich called her. "Sounds like tourist Cinelli is doing fine and making headway. I checked out Sleeman. He's a big deal in commercial real estate, as you told me, Pippa, with a reputation for not always being on the up-and-up. Nothing to tie him to the FBI or to me specifically, or to the puzzle yet, but I'll have MAX do a deeper check on him. Let me know everything you find out from Mrs. Filly about her puzzles tomorrow. MAX will do a search on Mrs. Filly's relatives and her background and give us more information about Major Trumbo."

"Dillon, you really believe we'll get the third red box tomorrow?"

"Yes. I'm betting we'll see Major Trumbo hanging out of the hotel window." Savich paused a moment. "Be careful, Pippa. We have no idea yet what we're dealing with, but this isn't some bizarre joke."

She spent the next half hour reading about the people she'd met that day. She was surprised when she discovered Mrs. Joyce Sleeman spent a good deal of her time in Annapolis at a halfway house for mentally disturbed patients newly out of psychiatric prison. She actually owned and operated Felber House, Felber being Mrs. Sleeman's maiden name. Interesting. Pippa read all about the halfway house, but she couldn't find a specific reason why Mrs. Joyce Sleeman had opened it. Maybe a disturbed uncle in the family whose life hadn't ended well? Someone closer?

When she finally fell asleep in the big circular bed, she dreamed everyone in St. Lumis had found out who she was. She was walking down Great Heron Street, and people were shouting she shouldn't be there, she had lied to them, shame on her. And Mrs. Sleeman was telling her in a gentle voice to come stay at Felber House because that's where she belonged.

20

Her late breakfast of scrambled eggs was a bit on the runny side for Pippa's taste, a surprise after the perfect scrambled eggs on Sunday. She left the B&B before Maude's puzzle shop was set to open at noon, per a sign in the window. She was anxious and wanted to explore more of St. Lumis, but still be first at the door to speak to Maude Filly. She had to see Maude again since this would be her last day in St. Lumis before the third red box was due to arrive at the CAU. The puzzle would be complete, and St. Lumis would be quickly identified. The sender would know that, of course, and know to expect the FBI here soon. She would lose any advantage she had of no one knowing who she was.

She strolled west this morning, away from the tourists still left in town, greeting the few locals she saw with smiles and hellos. She ended up on the less gentrified edge of town, where she remembered a small industrial district. She saw three buildings pressed together. They looked like long-abandoned ancient mercantile supply stores.

There was an antique sign hanging at half-mast over the doorway of the nearest building: Howzell's Marble Tables. The front door was gone, so she walked in. She saw broken windows, rusted, partly dismantled machinery, mildewed boxes, and rat carcasses strewn on the floor. She remembered the once-thriving manufacturer had closed its doors long before her family had moved. Why had the building been left in ruin? She did a quick walk-through, winding around the broken old machines scattered across the large space like giant iron ghosts from a former time.

She'd been about to skip looking at the other two buildings when she checked her iWatch and saw she still had time before the puzzle shop opened. She walked out to the second building, which looked ready to collapse in on itself, maybe even more derelict than the first, its wood-planked door barely held up by rusted old nails. She stepped inside and nearly choked on the musty, stale air. There was no sign left to announce what the business had been, but much of the space was divided by rows of ancient metal shelves, a good eight feet high. She saw three cobwebbed jars lined up on one shelf. She wasn't about to look inside them. A store of some kind, groceries and assorted dry goods probably. She took a cursory look around for anything that shouldn't be there. What had she expected to find here anyway? She sneezed. Time to head into town. She'd gone out far enough. There was no reason to visit the third building.

She'd turned back toward the battered door when she heard a groan and stopped dead in her tracks. She stood perfectly still, cocked her head. Another moan, this one not as loud, but it sounded like someone in pain. She thought the moans were coming from behind one of the long metal shelves at the far end of the building. She waited but heard nothing. She started walking toward the sound, adjusting her eyes to the deepening gloom, and made her way down a narrow aisle with the huge empty shelves boxing her in. She paused, called out, "Anyone there?"

Another moan. She suddenly felt spooked. Something wasn't right. She pulled her Glock from her belt clip, racked the slide, and walked forward, careful not to step on the scattered debris—cans, shards of paper, cracked and shattered bottles. She paused, listened, but heard nothing more.

"Where are you?"

She heard a gasping whisper, "I'm here. Back here. Help me." A man? A woman? She couldn't tell. She rounded the last cobwebbed shelf, stopped, and looked into a dim corner, empty, as far as she could tell.

"Talk to me, I can't see you."

She didn't hear him coming. His blow was fast and hard to the back of her head. She was down.

21

When Savich opened the door to the interview room at precisely 9:00 a.m., the stage would be set. Ollie and Ruth had appeared at Zoltan's door and threatened to arrest her if she didn't accompany them to the Hoover Building right away. Savich knew Ollie's hard voice would work on Zoltan to good effect, and Ruth had doubtless given Zoltan her patented dead-eye stare. The two of them stood against the wall, arms crossed, flat-eyed, mouths seamed, looking ready to break out the brass knuckles.

Savich met Zoltan's eyes when he entered, saw they were filled with anger and a flash of fear. Her fingers were beating a furious tattoo on the table-top. She jumped to her feet, slapped her palms on the table. "Why did you have these FBI agents come to my house and order me to go with them? Why did you bring me here? I have done nothing wrong, yet those two rottweilers"—she pointed to Ruth and Ollie, who didn't blink, and if anything looked even more threatening—"treated me like a criminal. Did you honestly think these two thugs were necessary? Did you think I would try to run? You could have simply called, asked to speak to me again. Of course I would have seen you."

"Thank you for coming, Zoltan," Savich said in his calm FBI voice. He paused a moment as he walked over to sit across from her at the interview table. He waved his hand. "Do sit down."

Slowly, she sat back down, her eyes not leaving his face. She was wearing little makeup, and her dark hair was clipped at the back of her neck. She'd covered her dark green wool dress with a formal black blazer that gave her the look of a consummate businesswoman. He said nothing more as he watched her get hold of herself, watched her expression segue from outrage to calm seriousness, with a dash of bewilderment, an innocent woman unfairly attacked. It was well done. He appreciated her obvious talent.

She said, her voice as cold as an ice floe, "What do you want from me, Agent Savich? I have told you everything I know. Should I call my lawyer? Have her roast you for harassing me?"

Savich said, "You are not under arrest, Zoltan, as

I'm sure my agents told you. However, a lawyer is your right, naturally." He sat forward, bulleted out, "You've lied to me from the beginning. That's very unwise of you, given it's a federal crime. Are you ready to tell me the truth now?"

He saw fear spark in her eyes again. Excellent. She leaned forward, her hands clasped in front of her, and her voice throbbed with sincerity. "I have told you the truth, and it remains the truth, Agent Savich. I am a medium, nothing more, nothing less. I only contacted Rebekah because her grandfather begged me to."

Savich said quietly, "I am worried for you, Zoltan. I'm very glad you're still alive. You have to realize what you know is a threat to those in this scheme with you. You failed in your assigned role and now you're of no further use to them. You're a liability. You may wish to believe you're protecting yourself and your career by continuing your lies, but unless you're completely honest with me now, and tell me who's responsible for the attack on Rebekah Manvers, I doubt you'll be alive for much longer."

Zoltan rose straight out of her chair again. "Wha—what did you say?"

He fanned his hands. "Listen, you're not stupid, Zoltan. Your assignment was to get Rebekah Manvers to tell you where her grandfather hid the money. Yes, I'm assuming it was money he stole all those years ago. Your partners were sure Rebekah knew, and they wanted you to get her to tell you—that is, tell her grandfather—with no one the wiser, not even Rebekah."

"That's not true!"

Savich continued without pause, "You were to find out where the Big Take was hidden. But she told you flat-out she wanted nothing to do with the money. You failed, though you tried to get her to come back again, tried to convince her that her grandfather was really there, desperate to see her again. You're excellent at reading people, Zoltan, and you believed her when she told you she didn't want anything more to do with you. And that's what you had to tell your partners."

"No, no, that's not why I wanted Rebekah back. There were other reasons—"

Savich continued over her, "When you told them they were out of luck, your partners set the kidnapping in motion. I've got to say, it was all done in an amazingly short time. So it was always the fallback plan, wasn't it? Or did you even know that would happen if you failed?"

She stared at him, mute, shaking her head back and forth.

"Face it, Zoltan. You failed to deliver. And look what happened."

She remained silent. Savich rose, splayed his palms on the table, leaned in close, and kept pushing. "Now that everything has gone sideways, there's no way they can get to Rebekah. She's guarded twenty-four/seven." He straightened. "But you're not guarded, Zoltan. You're all on your own. They can get to you. It's time to save yourself, time to talk to me. Tell me how this all came together. Tell me who's really in charge. Tell me who brought you into this scheme."

Savich sat down, crossed his arms, and stared at her. He saw her pulse pounding hard in her throat, but she didn't move, didn't deny what he'd said. He watched her smooth her expression again, until she looked almost bored. He was impressed. The woman was formidable. Of course, she'd already known what he'd told her. Was she planning on getting out of Washington as soon as she could?

He added, "It's no secret Rebekah's grandmother has attended séances for years. She's a believer in communicating with the dead. Is that why they picked you to talk to Rebekah? They thought you could convince her? My big question is how you and your partners found out the Big Take was real. Congressman Clarkson was in a coma for sixteen years until he died last month. To the best of my knowledge, he never woke up. So how did you know?" He waited a beat, then, "You know I will find out and then it will be over for you. If you're still alive, you'll be in prison for a very long time.

"You have to face it, Zoltan, you're of no more use to anyone. You're a walking liability. I am not exaggerating, and you must know it. I fear for you."

Remarkably, she laughed, fanned her hands at

him. He watched a sneer twist her mouth. "Agent Savich, what a remarkable tale you've spun. I don't have any partners. I don't have an agenda. Yes, I know Rebekah's grandmother believes in speaking with the Departed. Rebekah herself told me that. I don't care about this wretched Big Take, whatever it is, if it even exists. I will say it again. I am a medium. Rebekah's grandfather came to me three times, anxious to speak to her. I succeeded in connecting them. There is nothing more to it than that. You have tried to frighten me, and you still refuse to believe I have done nothing wrong. I have no one to fear. You've dragged me in here for nothing. I want to leave."

Savich said, "When your partners tried to take Rebekah, they had no reason to think they would fail. Only luck put me there. But their failure to nab Rebekah has landed you squarely in their crosshairs. For your own survival, I strongly recommend you tell me who your partners are, now, before it's too late."

Zoltan started tapping her fingers on the tabletop again, tap, tap, tap. She looked both amused and disdainful. She gave him another splendid sneer. "You're concerned for my survival, Agent Savich? I'm touched. For the last time, I am a medium—I have no partners, I have nothing to do with Rebekah's attempted kidnapping." She snapped her fingers in his face. "Nothing. I did want another opportunity to work with Rebekah and her grandfather, try to iron out their issues, but Rebekah didn't want to continue. A pity, but it happens."

"Issues? What issues did Rebekah have with her grandfather?"

"I believe her grandfather wanted to justify his actions to her. He wanted to convince her he'd done it for her. He wanted her respect."

"That's a tall order, isn't it? Respect a man of substance, a member of Congress, who put it all aside to commit a crime? How were you going to convince her to respect him? Selling what he did to her would be quite a challenge. You must have given that some thought."

"Disbelieve my abilities—many do—but I tell you, I've found the Departed want those still alive, those they loved, to understand why they did what they did. Good or bad, it seems to be very important to them." She shrugged. "But I doubt he will come back to me again." She gave him a cold smile, then yet another sneer at full bloom.

She rose slowly, her hands fisted on the table, and looked Savich in the eye. "I wish to leave now, Agent Savich. May I?"

Savich studied her. He found her self-control amazing. She didn't fidget, didn't say anything more. She simply stood patiently and waited. He really couldn't guess what she was thinking.

"Do you know Mrs. Gemma Clarkson, John Clarkson's widow?"

"No, I do not. I only know what Rebekah and

her grandfather said about her, nothing more. May I leave now?"

"Did you know Rebekah and her grandmother weren't on good terms? That they've never been close?"

"No, there is no way I could possibly know that unless Rebekah told me, and she didn't."

"How old are you, Zoltan?"

She cocked her head at him. "What sort of question is that? You want to find that out, Google me."

"Whatever your age, Zoltan, you are too young to die." He said nothing more and nodded to Ollie, who opened the interview room door. He and Ruth fell into step on each side of her. Savich stood in the open doorway and watched them walk with her to the elevator, stolid and silent.

Savich walked back to his office, sat down, thought a moment, and pulled out his cell phone.

22

A pleasant older woman answered Savich's call to the CEO of Clarkson United Industries on the first ring. "Mrs. Clarkson's office. How may I help you?"

"I'm Special Agent Dillon Savich, FBI, calling from Washington, D.C." He paused a second to let this sink in. He knew it had when he heard the woman suck in her breath.

"The FBI? I don't understand, sir, Agent. Mrs. Clarkson has never had any dealings with the FBI."

"No, I imagine not. Please tell Mrs. Clarkson it concerns her granddaughter, Rebekah Manvers." If nothing else, that should be enough to get Mrs. Clarkson on the line.

"Oh my, yes, certainly, Agent Savich. A moment, sir."

Almost immediately Savich heard the clipped no-nonsense voice of the top dog. "The FBI? Agent Savich? This is Gemma Clarkson. I suppose this has something to do with Rebekah and her attempted kidnapping?"

It wasn't concern he heard, it was a sheen of impatience, and wasn't that curious? Rebekah had told him she and her grandmother weren't close, but this?

"Mrs. Clarkson, as I told your assistant, I'm Agent Dillon Savich, FBI. Rebekah said you were the best person to speak to about her grandfather and that's mainly why I'm calling. I believe the two are connected."

There was a moment of silence, then again, that hint of impatience. "Why on earth would Rebekah send you to me? She and her grandfather were like two peas in a pod. Surely she knows everything you would need to know. But that begs the question, Agent Savich. Why do you want to know about my husband? He's dead now, at last, buried a month ago. Actually, he was dead for all intents and purposes when he fell into a coma sixteen years ago. Putting him in a casket was only a formality."

"Mrs. Clarkson, Rebekah was attacked last Thursday in Washington. If you didn't see Congressman Manvers briefly speak about it on TV, please don't be alarmed. She was uninjured, but we have reason to believe her attack involved your late husband, Congressman Clarkson."

"What? How in the world? I don't understand any of this. I mean, of course I knew about the supposed attempted kidnapping. I saw her husband on TV say the FBI believed kidnapping her for ransom was at the root of it and the FBI was dealing with the situation. Well, her husband *is* rich, and so is she, what with the trust her grandfather set up for her a long time ago. I would have thought Rebekah would have the maturity to call me herself, but she didn't. Are you certain Congressman Manvers didn't stage this attempted kidnapping? For the publicity? He's up for re-election, and an attack on his young wife would certainly garner him sympathy. I don't understand how you could believe the attempt to kidnap her has anything to do with her grandfather. He's dead and buried."

"That's why I'm calling you, Mrs. Clarkson. To provide me with information Rebekah is unable to. We know she held a special place in her grandfather's life, but still, she was very young when he fell into a coma and so wasn't able to answer a number of concerns."

Silence. It felt calculated to Savich. He pictured her tapping her fingernails on her desktop, ready to what? Lie to him? Give him the heave and hang up? She said at last, her voice calm and matter-of-fact,

"So it appears all the money her grandfather left her came to the attention of the wrong people. I hope you find the criminals responsible."

"I'm certain we will. Now, what we believe, Mrs. Clarkson, as I already said, is that her attempted kidnapping is very probably connected to her grandfather and had nothing to do with a ransom demand. As I understand it, after Congressman Clarkson suffered the strokes that left him in a coma, he was placed in a private sanitarium. Is that right?"

"Yes. That is public knowledge, Agent Savich. What does this have to do with Rebekah's attempted kidnapping?"

"I'm not at liberty to give you any details, ma'am. I'm asking you to verify. What is the name of the facility?"

"No details? You're worse than a politician. Ah, very well. For sixteen years, my husband was in the Mayfield Sanitarium. It's one of Virginia's finest long-term-care facilities. He had round-the-clock nursing there for each and every long year. The nurses and doctors who tended him were kind and attentive. I hired private nurses for him as well. As you probably already know, the series of strokes brought on the coma, and he never woke up. And then he died, only last month. Is there anything else?"

"Did Rebekah visit her grandfather often?"

Mrs. Clarkson gave a short, brittle laugh. "Oh

certainly, she was there at his bedside as often as possible. She worshiped him in life, as he worshiped her. I can't imagine how his years in a coma could have anything to do with this—situation."

"Let me ask you about another important person in Congressman Clarkson's life: his longtime friend Nate Elderby. I understand Mr. Elderby drowned in the nineties. What can you tell me about him?"

"I do not see what Nate Elderby has to do with anything, alive or dead, Agent Savich."

He plowed right over her again. "I imagine you remember his death, ma'am, since it must have affected your husband profoundly, and you as well, I imagine."

If she considered arguing with him, she thought better of it. She said, her voice even more clipped, "Nate died in 1995, Agent Savich. It's hard for me to even call his face to mind now, it's been so long. Yes, he and Johnny were childhood friends, and they remained close until Nate drowned. My husband never spoke of it to me, but I know he mourned his friend deeply."

John hadn't talked about Nate's death to his own wife? Savich said, "I know your husband had to deal with rumors insinuating he was responsible for his friend's death, rumors it wasn't an accident, that they'd had a falling-out and he murdered Nate. What happened between them to give rise to such rumors?"

She gave a full-bodied, let-it-all-loose kind of

laugh. "Of course he didn't kill Nate. There was no falling-out—I would have known about it if there had been. I blame his political enemies at the time. As you well know, once a rumor starts, it's impossible to stop it. Anything that juicy breeds like mold in the dark. And the press at the time, they were pushing, always pushing, to find something shocking, something to boost their sales. And people, no matter who they are, even supposed friends, are always interested, always seem to take pleasure in the misfortunes of others. The more gruesome, the better. The Germans even have a word for it—schadenfreude. The truth, of course, was very uninteresting. Nate was drunk. He fell overboard and drowned. It was an accident."

"Here's the thing, Mrs. Clarkson. Even though Nate Elderby's blood alcohol level wasn't high enough to be debilitating, according to the autopsy report, the local police ruled he fell overboard and drowned. How do you think such a thing could happen?"

"The fact is, Agent Savich, I believe Nate was an alcoholic. Maybe he hadn't drunk himself stupid that particular day, but he really loved his bourbon. He was always careful—he didn't want to jeopardize his criminal law practice. Still, he always drank a single shot before court, said it smoothed him out and fired up his brain. Then, of course, he always had a breath mint or two as a chaser. But he remained a firecracker in the courtroom, that's what Johnny always said, until his untimely death. Yes, I believe he was drunk enough to be careless, and he did fall overboard. Believe me, Agent Savich, my husband was not responsible for his death. There wasn't any earthly reason."

Savich said, "So Nate was a successful lawyer?"

"Yes, he was, but he had the ethics of a man for hire. That is to say, he didn't have many ethics. I do know Nate defended some bad people, got many of them off. I remember the police did look into one of his criminal clients in particular, a Mr. Showalter, but they couldn't find any necessary proof.

"Johnny left town after Nate died, went into seclusion for several weeks. I have no idea where he went. I never asked, and he never told me. Again, he didn't discuss anything about Nate's death with me.

"Agent Savich, like most people, Johnny wasn't all good or all bad, and he worked tirelessly for his constituents during his years in Congress, as well as the years before when he was mayor of Clairemont. He was no murderer."

Savich said, "You and Nate Elderby were friends as well, I'm sure, for many years until his death, despite his questionable ethics, correct?"

"We all spent time together, of course, mostly with Nate and his first wife, Lorna. Yes, we were all close, even after Nate divorced Lorna and married a woman young enough to be his daughter. Miranda, a ridiculously dramatic name. I do not remember her maiden name."

Savich heard it clearly, cold dislike when she'd said Miranda's name. "Would Mr. Elderby's second wife know any more particulars about her husband's death, ma'am? And his relationship to your husband at that time?"

She huffed out a breath. "Miranda, know something important about anything? She was about as smart as a head of lettuce, a silly, vain young woman of questionable moral character. She wasn't his equal, in either intellect or interests. She married Nate for his money, no doubt in my mind. If he hadn't died, he would have divorced her within months. You know the type, flaunted herself in front of him, treated him like the king of the world, and Nate, being a man, fell for it." She seemed to realize her voice had gotten louder, faster, so she paused, collected herself, and said in a calm voice, "Now, I still fail to see the importance of any possible disagreement between my husband and his friend for your purposes, Agent Savich. And what are your purposes, may I ask?"

"You're being very helpful, and I appreciate it. We were talking about Mr. Elderby's wife?"

She must have realized how her diatribe against Nate's young wife had sounded, but she couldn't take the words back. "They were married only six months before he died. After his funeral, she cashed out, sold the house, his cars, his boat, and left. I heard she moved to Maryland, married a dentist." She gave a world-weary laugh. "It goes to show her sort always lands on her feet, always flourishes."

Time to push. Savich asked, "Why all the venom toward the young wife?"

"Venom? The fact is, Miranda was a disaster. She ruined Nate's life. If she hadn't trotted out such a good alibi, I bet the police would have arrested her for Nate's murder. Who knows?"

Jealousy, rock-hard jealousy, and it still burned. Savich asked, "Nate had no children?"

A contemptuous laugh. "No, although Lorna wanted a child." She added, as if she couldn't help herself, "As for Miranda, if Nate hadn't died, I doubt she would have ever agreed to a pregnancy. She wouldn't have wanted to ruin her figure."

She was silent for several moments, then said in an emotionless voice, "It's been too long even to remember clearly what one felt, what one believed. If someone murdered Nate, it wasn't Johnny. I have no idea who it would have been." She gave a short laugh. "I remember thinking if Johnny and Nate were gay, it would have been perfect for both of them. They were that close. You must excuse me now, Agent Savich. I'm needed in a meeting." And without another word, she punched off.

Savich leaned back in his chair, closed his eyes, and thought. Was she telling the truth? Or did she not remember the events that clearly anymore? He'd bet his last dollar she remembered every detail of her own fourth birthday party. She was a fascinating woman, a woman still carrying a trail of bitterness after so many years. At her husband? He'd give that a yes. And Miranda. It was obvious to him she disliked Rebekah as well. Why? Was it again a case of simple jealousy because her husband loved his granddaughter so much? Maybe more than his wife? There had to be more. There was always more. He'd have to speak to Rebekah.

Savich looked up to see Denny Roper at his office door, grinning and holding another large brown paper–wrapped box. "Here you go, Agent Savich— just as you predicted."

Savich led Denny and the agents who'd followed him to the CAU into the conference room. They gathered around the conference table, every eye on Savich as he cut off the wrapping paper, pulled out the third red box, and poured out the puzzle pieces. A couple of minutes later the new puzzle section was complete. Savich fitted the three sections together, and they stared down at an older big-bellied man wearing a purple Grateful Dead T-shirt and hanging out a window. Above him was a sign that read AL-WORTH HOTEL. Flames were pouring out of the window, surrounding him, enveloping him. He was screaming.

23

A man's low voice brought her back to an aching head. Pippa listened but couldn't make out his words, yet she knew instinctively to play dead. She slitted her eyes. Her vision was blurred at first, but she could see a man in a black hoodie standing near her, listening to someone talking from the cell phone in his hand. She could tell he was slightly built, his blue jeans loose, and his voice sounded on the young side, maybe thirties.

Turn around. Turn around so I can see you. But he didn't. He paced away from her. He was wearing black high-top sneakers. Had she seen him during her walkabout yesterday? The jeans, the black hoodie. She didn't think so. If she'd been alert, would she have noticed him, noticed something was off? She didn't know. She held very still, eyes still slitted, and listened.

Then he raised his voice. "Yes, yes, I know." She saw him shove his cell phone into his pants pocket. Before he turned back to her, he pulled up a hand-kerchief from around his neck and tied it over the lower part of his face.

Kill the fear and think cold, that's what Hibbard, an instructor at Quantico, had preached. She heard Black Hoodie crunch over some broken glass, coming closer, until he stood over her. She imagined him studying her face. *Don't move. Play dead.* Finally, she heard him step away and she slitted her eyes again. The only light came from weak sunlight through a high broken window. She gathered herself mentally and waited for him to come close again, but before she could act, he leaned down and whispered against her ear, "I saw you blink. So you're playing possum?" He struck her with the butt of his gun behind her left temple. Pippa saw a flash of light, then nothing.

24

Veronica Lake pressed herself against the prison wall, out of the stiff, cold wind, trying to keep warm. It didn't help. She was alone and cold, always cold. She looked out over the yard with its dozen or so prisoners, some sitting on benches and gossiping, trash-talking, some shooting basketballs at the ragged metal net. She hated and feared these women, at least the coarse, violent ones who preyed on the rest. The few who were nice tried to keep to themselves and out of sight of the leaders, like she did. She saw three of the bullies approaching Leah, pitiful little Leah, who was awaiting trial for credit card fraud. She was small, no more than twenty-two, and rabbit-scared all the time. She sat huddled on a bench, knowing they were slowly moving in on her from all sides, trying to look nonchalant and not succeeding.

Early on, Veronica might have gone to help her, but not now. She knew she wouldn't stand a chance. She had to protect herself. Her left arm still ached like a rotten tooth where one of Angela's thugs had kicked her. She turned away when she heard Leah cry out. Where were the freaking guards?

Leah was crying now, deep gulping sobs, begging them not to hurt her. Angela wasn't there, but the rest of them were mocking her, calling her vicious, ugly names, taunting her about what they would do to her. Veronica looked away again, she didn't want to see it. She heard a punch, heard a guard shout—about time—and turned to see three guards running toward Leah, who still cowered on the bench, her arms covering her head. One of the prisoners cracked her knuckles in Leah's face and motioned to her friends, who melted away. Another prisoner picked up a basketball from the ground and began bouncing it and whistling, as if she didn't have a care in the world. Veronica knew Leah wouldn't tell the guards anything. She would be fine for now, until the next time.

Veronica automatically looked down to check her watch, but of course they'd taken even that away from her. She looked at the clock above the door to the yard. Ten minutes until she'd be escorted to the dining room. She began pacing, slapping her arms to keep warm, and, as always, wondered what would happen now that she'd given Marsia up to the prosecutor for a reduced sentence.

Beautiful Marsia. Her lover, so smart, so talented, the one she'd believed would be with her forever. But she'd had to face it. Agent Savich was right—Marsia had manipulated her from the get-go. She'd drawn her in, lied to her, all the while professing her love, and Veronica hadn't seen it. More likely, she hadn't wanted to see it. She'd jumped like a fish to bait. All she'd seen was this brilliant, wonderful person who'd complimented her, told her how much she loved and needed her, would always need her. Blah blah blah. She'd been a fool, a blind fool. It sounded so trite. She hated being a cliché.

Marsia had no conscience. She lied fluently when she needed help getting what she wanted, no matter the cost to anyone else. Veronica had even killed for her, no hesitation.

Veronica accepted now that Marsia was a psychopath. It had never made sense to her, Marsia's endless desire—no, obsession, a sick obsession—for wealth and her absolute disregard for anyone else. Veronica was thankful they were kept apart here, awaiting trial. The last time she had seen Marsia, she'd looked at Veronica sadly and shaken her head, nothing more.

Veronica realized she was hitting her fist

against her palm. *Stop it. It's done. You're going to testify against Marsia, and she's going to stay in jail forever.*

Yes, she would testify. It was the right thing to do. It was what she deserved. The prosecutor, a middle-aged matron who badly needed a makeover, had guaranteed Veronica a maximum sentence of ten years. Ten years? She'd be forty-six when she got out, with no friends and very little money, since most every dollar she had was already in her hotshot lawyer's pocket. He liked to pretend he was the one who'd talked the prosecutor into the lighter sentence in return for her testimony, acting like he'd scored a huge win for her. Who cared? She'd testify, then do time in a minimum-security prison, without inmates like Angela there—at least that's what her lawyer had assured her. And hey, he'd said, I got you only ten years! The prick.

The warden had warned her her life could be in danger, despite all his precautions. What precautions? The prison grapevine was high octane, he'd said, every tidbit, big or small, always got out in no time. Within hours everyone knew she'd turned on her partner and would be the star witness for the prosecution against Marsia Gay. She'd gotten nasty looks, but no one had confronted her, so far. The guards were supposed to keep a close eye on her, the warden had said, and maybe they had for a few days. Veronica tried to make sure she was rarely alone or without a guard nearby to escort her wherever she needed to go. Even when the door of her cell clanged shut behind her, she was still afraid, more so with each passing day. She had only one goal: to survive the night. She was being transferred tomorrow.

She looked again at the clock. Only two more minutes and she could go back inside. She looked blindly around, lowered her face into her hands, not to cry—there were no more tears, only the endless ache in her heart at what had happened, at what she'd done and couldn't ever undo. Even when she got out of prison in ten years, she had no one left to care if she lived or died. How would she possibly live?

When her time was up, a guard escorted her to the prison dining room and left her at the door. He nodded across the room at another guard, who took one last look around the cafeteria and nodded.

Veronica stood a moment, frozen in the doorway, prisoners walking around her. She kept her head down, no eye contact with any of the other prisoners. She knew many of them condemned her for testifying against Marsia, the ultimate betrayal.

She smelled spaghetti sauce. She hoped some stingy meatballs were in the sauce but doubted it. She met the other guard's eyes. He nodded to her and motioned her in. She squared her shoulders and walked into the cafeteria, chin high.

Ignore all of them. What they think of you doesn't matter. You'll be gone from here tomorrow. Eat your dinner. Go to bed. That's all you've got to do.

25

WASHINGTON, D.C.
MONTROSE PARK
R STREET NW
MONDAY AFTERNOON

Griffin tossed the neon green Frisbee toward Sean, who ran, jumped, and managed to snag it. The Frisbee was Sean's birthday present from Marty Perry, and it glowed bright at night. Sean whooped, did a fast fist pump, and threw it to his mom.

Sherlock caught it and threw it on to Dillon, who plucked it out of the air, grinned at everyone, and waved toward the blanket they'd spread on the nearly dead grass in Montrose Park. Even so, it was a beautiful spot, wide open, perfect for whatever a kid would want to do.

Everyone was warm enough still, but Savich knew it wouldn't last, and that's why he'd had the idea to bring Sean to the park with them while they still had some sun. Savich knew all of them were tired and needed a bit of time to decompress.

Savich flipped the Frisbee to land on top of their ancient red-and-white-striped wool blanket, a witness to many a picnic. Everyone took a drink and a cookie. Between bites, Sean told them all about a video on YouTube about the best ways to throw a Frisbee. He took them through every single step. He told them the boy who made the video, Ellery, lived in Australia and could throw a Frisbee so far his friends spent days looking for it. "Even farther than you, Papa. I emailed him. I hope he'll email me back, maybe give me some private pointers."

Sean's attention veered from the Frisbee when he saw a half dozen teenage boys throwing a football around twenty yards away, having a great time hooting and hollering. Sean walked closer to watch them, all the adult eyes on him. Savich said, "You've seen all the photos Pippa's sent. She planned to go back this morning and question Mrs. Filly, but I haven't heard from her. I reminded her last night to check in with me, told her again to be careful." He looked down at his Mickey Mouse watch. "She hasn't called, and all my calls have gone to voice mail."

"Dillon, call her again while Griffin and I pack everything up. It's getting too cold to stay out much longer anyway."

As Savich stepped away and pulled out his cell, he heard Griffin say to Sherlock, "You wanted to know about Jessie's birthday party for her daughter. Picture a dozen eighteen-year-old girls, all laughing and talking and slurping down ice cream smoothies when Jessie brought me into the living room and yelled out, 'Surprise, girls!' All eyes turned to us. There was instant silence, not a single slurp, and then they rushed me. It was like a tsunami. I gotta say, though, the chocolate cake was delicious, pecans whipped into the chocolate frosting. Almost made it worth it."

When Savich walked back, Sherlock was laughing so hard she was holding her stomach. Sean looked over, realized he'd missed out on something, and ran back to go down on his knees beside her. "Mama, what? What's the joke? What did Uncle Griffin say?"

Griffin said, "Sean, I was telling your mama about a birthday party, and the chocolate cake, nearly as great as the one your mama served at your birthday party back in September. Here, let me show you some photos." Sean was treated to photo after photo of girls he didn't know, girls way too old to hold his interest. He paused at one photo. "Mama, I think Marty will look like her when she grows up."

Sherlock looked at a young girl with an impish face, capped by spikes of black hair, tiny diamond studs in her ears. She didn't look as mature as the other girls, more like a bud nearly ready to bloom. She didn't look a thing like Marty Perry except for the wicked intelligence shining from her dark green eyes. You knew looking at her she was fun. Sherlock said, "Griffin, send me her photo, and we'll show it to Marty, see what she thinks."

Savich took a quick look at the girls' photos and smiled at the one Sean had talked about. She looked clever and smart. He lightly poked Sherlock's arm. "Would you mind packing up? I need to speak to Griffin. Sean, there's one cookie left with your name on it."

Savich and Griffin walked a bit away while Sean munched his cookie and helped his mother fold the blanket and close down the drink cooler.

Savich said without preamble, "I still can't reach Pippa Cinelli, only voice mail, no answer to my texts. I think something's wrong."

Griffin said, "I can leave right now, Savich. Wait, Congressman Manvers said he had to go out for a meeting this evening, which means Rebekah would be alone. I know her assistant, Kit Jarrett, would stay with her, but is that enough?"

Savich shook his head. "You go watch over Rebekah. I'll go to St. Lumis."

Savich pulled Sherlock aside. "I've got to go see what's going on, make sure Pippa is all right. Rush hour traffic shouldn't be too bad on a Monday night. I'll call you, keep you updated."

Sherlock was as worried as Dillon, but she didn't want to pile on. "Do you want to call Police Chief Wilde? He's right there."

"Not really. That last puzzle section with Major Trumbo hanging out the Alworth Hotel window, surrounded by flames? Until we find out what it all means, I want to keep this as private as possible."

26

When Pippa came to, she could barely breathe, then realized there was cloth stuffed into her mouth. She managed to spit it out and swallowed, trying to get saliva back in her mouth. She breathed in moldy, stale air—she was still in that derelict building. He'd tied her up, bound her wrists behind her back and her ankles and knees with rope, the knots strong and stout. How much time did she have before he came back? The man in the black hoodie? Who had he called? What had that person told him to do with her? If not kill her, then what? None of it made sense to her. She'd been in St. Lumis for less than two days. How could anyone know she was an FBI agent or even why she was here? Who would even wonder? Well, obviously someone did know, and it didn't matter how. So why attack her? Surely whoever they were, they had to know killing her would only bring the full weight of the FBI down on their heads. What did they hope to gain? Did they think she'd found out who they were? But how? Maude Filly? Suddenly she was afraid Maude Filly had closed early yesterday because someone had forced her to. No time to think about that. Right now she had to get out of the building before Black Hoodie came back. She looked down at her wrist. Of course her iWatch wasn't there. Smart. Savich could have used it to locate her.

Pippa started to sit up, felt a wave of dizziness and eased back down. She lay perfectly still. She wasn't going anywhere until she got herself together. She remembered how she'd come to after the first time he'd struck her, but only for a minute. Her head still pounded.

She had to move more slowly, not take any chances. She lay there until she knew she shouldn't wait any longer. She had to move, free herself, and ignore her pounding head. She was concussed, how badly she didn't know, but now, at least, she wasn't nauseated. Her vision was clear, and, best of all, she could move. And that meant she had a chance. Who cared about an aching head?

She had to get her wrists free. She tugged and worked the ropes, but there was no give. She had to find something sharp enough to cut through them. She looked out a high broken window. No more sunshine. How late was it? There was still enough light for her to see the rubbish and debris lying around her. She didn't see anything sharp enough to cut through the ropes, except some small shards of glass scattered on the floor. Then she saw an ancient rusted hook half buried under a tattered pile of filthy clothes in a corner, several feet away. She inched slowly toward it, little by little, quietly, because she had no idea if Black Hoodie was nearby. Her hands brushed against the hook. It was at the end of a long wooden pole, decades old, probably used to hook the latches on the high windows to open them in the morning and close them for the night. The hook tip felt sharp enough to do the job. She backed onto the hook until she felt the blade against her wrists. Carefully, she played her fingers over it, adjusting her hands until the ropes were directly beneath the tip, and started slowly rubbing the rope across it. Eventually her hands cramped, and she had to ease off.

She started again but realized she was cutting her hands as well as the rope. She didn't know how long she kept at it, but the room became almost completely dark as she worked the knots. When at last the rope gave, she pulled her hands apart and brought them in front of her. She couldn't prevent a hiss of pain. Her hands were bloody and numb and hurt. She patted them on her T-shirt, raised them to the back of her head, and felt dried blood through her matted hair where he'd struck her. She didn't seem to be bleeding now, and that was good. When she pressed against the wound slightly, she felt a jolt of pain. She stopped and breathed until the pain faded. It was time to forget about her head and her hands. She had to move fast now. She went to work untying the ropes around her ankles and knees.

Her hands were throbbing fiercely by the time she was free. She braced herself against a rusting shelf and slowly stood. She took a small step, felt a stab of vertigo, and stumbled. She caught hold of an old mildewed crate and breathed in deeply until the vertigo eased off. She stamped her feet to get the feeling back. She had nothing to wrap around her hands, certainly not the moldy rags scattered on the floor, so she'd have to be very careful.

Her cell phone, her Glock, and her wallet were gone. So was the small Glock 380 she kept in her ankle holster. She checked her jacket pocket. He'd taken her creds, too. He knew exactly who she was now, but of course he'd known she was FBI before he'd struck her down. She started to shake. She was so afraid, it threatened to sweep away any logical thought. This was her first time face-to-face with real danger, and she was alone, with no one here to back her up.

Stop it! Kill the fear and think cold. She saw Agent Hibbard's face again, in the classroom at Quantico. He'd had them repeat his mantra to themselves in his deep Southern drawl. "You're in trouble. You're alone. You don't have your weapon. What's the first thing you do?" He had everyone in the classroom say it aloud. But saying it was easier than doing it. Pippa took deep breaths to slow her breathing, ignored her throbbing head, and quietly stamped her feet again. She could handle herself in a hand-to-hand fight, she knew it, but her hands were a mess. She could try to take Black Hoodie down if he came back for her. But he had a gun, and she didn't. She felt another wave of dizziness. What symptom would hit her next? Would she black out again? She had to get out of this ancient rotting building, find Chief Wilde, and give him a treat to make his Monday night. She knew Wilde lived on Upper Marlin Road, only a short distance from downtown St. Lumis. She'd call Dillon from the chief's house. He had to be worried. Was he already on his way?

She made her way carefully through the rows of shelves, got to the ramshackle door, closed now on its rusted hinges, and drew it inward quietly. She looked outside. The derelict old buildings stood like desolate monoliths framed by the darkening sky. She didn't see or hear anyone.

She set out, keeping to the side streets, close to buildings. It was nearly full-on dark now. She heard voices from inside houses, heard a TV and a father yelling at a kid to get himself to bed. Already? When did it get completely dark in early November? Six o'clock?

She didn't see anyone as she made her way through downtown, except for a couple of teenagers on a corner, trying, she imagined, to find something to do. It had to be late enough for the stores to have closed. As she neared the Chesapeake, the wind picked up. It felt like November now, and she was wearing only her jacket. But the cold kept her head clear and took her mind off the pain. The police station was on the way to the chief's house, so Pippa headed there, hoping Wilde hadn't left yet. There was a light on in the large front window of the station. She saw an older man, wearing a parka indoors. Was the heat in the station out? He looked to be working on a crossword puzzle. No one else seemed to be inside. She didn't even consider going in. She turned away and walked to the corner of West Main and Faire Street, toward Wilde's house. Then she heard a man's low voice not twenty feet from her talking on a cell. Was it Black Hoodie's voice? Was he looking for her? It didn't matter.

Pippa ran.

27

Pippa hugged the shadows as she passed a half dozen houses and finally reached Upper Marlin Road. The houses were set a good distance apart from one another, thick stands of trees dividing them. She had a stitch in her side, but she kept running under the shadows of naked-branched trees. She was breathing hard when she saw a small white cottage. There was a light on in the front window and a nondescript compact car in the driveway. He had to be at home. She hoped he was alone, but if he wasn't, well, she'd think of something. She held her side as she walked up the flagstone path to the small front porch.

She didn't have her FBI creds or her Glock,

couldn't prove who she was. She knew he'd take her in, but how he'd react when she told him what had happened was another question. She looked around again, didn't see any sign of Black Hoodie or anyone else.

Pippa took a deep breath and knocked. She heard a loud bark and scrabbling paws on hardwood racing to the door. Then Chief Wilde's voice, "Calm yourself, Gunther."

Pippa drew a deep breath. What to say? *Hello, Chief. Happy Monday evening. Have I got a bit of a story for you. And, oh yes, I think they're looking for me.*

Wilde opened the door and did a double take. "You're Pippa, right? Cinelli? What's happened to you? There's blood on your face. Well, blood a lot of places."

She managed a smile. "I know I look like I've been mugged, but I'm basically okay. There is a problem, though. The man who did this—he's wearing a black hoodie—is probably looking for me. Could I come in, and can we lock all the doors and windows? And maybe I can borrow your cell phone? Black Hoodie took mine."

He grabbed her hand and pulled her inside, slammed the door. "What? My cell phone?"

"Yes, Black Hoodie took mine. He also took both my Glocks and my creds. I escaped and must have just missed him coming back to the building where he tied me up. Like I said, he's probably out there, looking for me."

He started to say something, then shook his head. "No, Gunther, stay down." Pippa was hit with another wave of dizziness and grabbed the closest thing—his arm.

"Whoa, you need a doctor."

"No, no, give me a second. I'll be fine. I'm a bit concussed is all." The dizziness passed, and Pippa straightened. She saw she'd gotten blood on his sleeve. "Please lock the front door, Chief. He must be out there, maybe close, watching the house. I'm sorry I got blood on you."

"Don't worry about the blood. Stay put." He drew his Beretta and went outside, closing the door behind him. Pippa stood there, tense, afraid Black Hoodie would shoot him. Minutes rolled by. Finally, he was back. He locked the front door, slid the dead bolt home. "No one's around that I could see. We're all secure. Come with me to the kitchen, and I'll see if I can fix you up while you tell me what happened to you."

"I really do hate to lay this on you, Chief, but I was ordered to come to see you if I got myself into trouble. And I did."

He came to a standstill. "Ordered? Who are you?"

"I'm Special Agent Pippa Cinelli, FBI. Ah, I really need to borrow your cell phone right now. My boss has got to be worried I didn't check in. He isn't going to like this at all. Could you please shut off the living room light? Just in case he's snuck up on the house?"

She was a fricking FBI agent? Why would the FBI send an agent to St. Lumis? What was going on? Why hadn't she identified herself Saturday night at the Halloween party? Par for the course, the federal yahoos hadn't bothered to alert him, to give him any warning at all. He'd find out why soon enough, but first things first.

A moment later, they stood in the dark and he was speaking to the single deputy she'd seen in the police station. "Yes, I want you to patrol around my house, make a circuit of the neighborhood, call me immediately if you see anyone, specifically a man in a black hoodie." He punched off, said, "All right, let's go to the kitchen."

Wilde took her arm, led her down a short, dark hallway, and flipped a light switch. He walked her into a roomy, old-fashioned kitchen with dark cabinets and scarred granite surfaces that were, to her surprise, covered with gleaming modern appliances. Blue wallpaper with huge hydrangea blooms covered the walls. The room was cozy, welcoming, and warm. He sat her down at an old oak table topped with a mason jar filled with dai-sies, a small basket of napkins, and old-fashioned glass salt and pepper shakers. Why was she paying attention to any of that? To distract from her fear? She rose and walked to the back door, locked it. She pulled the curtains over the three kitchen windows. "Chief Wilde, would you please turn on the hall light and turn this one off? He could still see us through the windows."

Wilde said nothing, did as she asked. When he came back, she was again seated at his table. He said, "Could you identify this man looking for you? This Black Hoodie?"

"Unfortunately, no, only his profile, really, but I got the impression he was on the younger rather than middle-aged side."

"All right. Stay seated. You're safe here."

Pippa started to pick up the salt shaker, realized her hand was bloody, and pulled it back. "My hands—I didn't realize I'd cut them so badly." She looked up at him, blinked. "You see, my hands were tied behind me, so I had to cut myself loose on a sharp hook."

He said, "I should take you to our urgent care facility."

"No, please, I'd rather not leave here. I don't think the cuts are bad enough to need stitches. But the blade was filthy, and I need to clean them. Do you have a first-aid kit?"

He stared at her hands a moment, slowly nodded. "All right. I'll get it and some hot water." He looked down. "What's this? Your head—"

"He struck my head twice with his gun.

There's only a bump and a bit of blood. Nothing, really."

"Yeah, right. I'll get the blood out of your hair, see what we've got. And in the meantime you can talk to me, Ms.—Special Agent Cinelli."

"First, I have to call my boss."

28

Chief Wilde handed Pippa his cell. She picked up a paper napkin, wrapped it around her bloody hand, and dialed.

"Chief Wilde?"

"No, Dillon, it's me, Pippa. I had to borrow Chief Wilde's cell."

"You're all right, Pippa?"

"Yes, a bit on the ragged side, but okay. I'm at Chief Wilde's cottage. It looks like I've stirred up the hornet's nest, though I have no idea how anyone could have found out who I am or why I'm here so fast."

"Tell me what happened. Put it on speaker so the chief can hear everything, too."

As she spoke, Chief Wilde listened and Gunther

moved closer, snuggled his head on her leg, and looked up at her with unwavering eyes, his waving tail metronome steady on the wooden floor. "I checked the police station and saw the dispatcher working a crossword puzzle, bundled up to his ears. Since you weren't there," she added, looking up at Wilde, "I came here." She gave no hint of the grinding fear she'd felt, of running until she thought she'd vomit, her side on fire.

Savich heard Wilde say, "Davie always feels cold, even in July, drives everyone nuts."

Savich said, "You're still with me, and that's what's important. I didn't expect you'd be attacked. I'm on my way to you. Chief, be honest and tell me how bad her injuries are."

Pippa started to reassure him, but Wilde shot her a look. "Her hands are bloody from cutting herself loose from some ropes, and her head's bloody from being struck. I've just started examining her and cleaning her up. She doesn't want to hear about any doctors. Yes, I already looked around outside and didn't see anyone, and I've got Davie cruising the neighborhood. You should come directly to my house, 107 Upper Marlin Road."

Pippa said, "I'm all right, Dillon, I promise. No dizziness, no nausea, only a headache. After the chief bandages me up, I imagine he'll want to know what the FBI is doing here in St. Lumis. Do you want me to tell him? From the beginning?"

A pause, then, "Yes, there's no way to keep him

out of it now. If Chief Wilde believes you should visit the hospital, then you're going, and that's an order. All right, Pippa?"

"Yes, but really, I'm okay. And I'm sorry, Dillon, I messed up—"

"Be quiet, Pippa. You were right to involve the chief. He had a good close rate as a homicide detective at the PPD, so he's competent."

"Thank you for the vote of confidence," Wilde said, "but it seems you know a hell of a lot more about me than I know about your agent here."

"You're welcome. I hope you'll back it up," Savich said. "Go ahead, Pippa, tell him everything. I'll be there as soon as I can."

Pippa punched off Wilde's phone and handed it back to him. "Agent Savich drives a Porsche. Now he has a good reason to speed all the way from Washington to St. Lumis. I bet he'll use his flashers."

"A cop drives a Porsche? That's something I haven't heard before."

"It's red."

He didn't laugh. He filled a stainless-steel bowl with hot water and opened a fresh bar of soap. She could tell he was pissed even though he was gentle when he lifted her hands into the water and washed both hands and wrists.

"You've got a dozen small nicks from the very likely rusted blade. And your wrists are bruised from the ropes. Hang in there, I know this hurts. I hope you've had your tetanus shot."

She nodded, but otherwise she didn't move, didn't make a sound. She saw the water turning red with her blood. She drew a deep breath and looked up at Wilde. "I'd have thought you'd drive a truck, say a Silverado or an F-150."

"I traded in my truck when I came to St. Lumis. Now I drive that old compact outside. Easier to park, draws less attention. I'm going to call a doctor I know, see if he thinks you need some antibiotics. No, be quiet." When he finished cleaning both hands, he wrapped white gauze bandages around her palms and wrists, but left her fingers free. "Now, talk, Agent Cinelli, while I clean those bloody bumps on your head."

Pippa moved her fingers, stiff but workable. "Thank you. I don't need a doctor poking around. Really, I'm fine, only banged up a bit. Listen now, it all started when a red box addressed personally to Agent Dillon Savich arrived at the Hoover Building on Thursday, filled with puzzle pieces." She repeated how she'd recognized St. Lumis when the second red box had arrived on Friday and that was why Agent Savich had assigned her to come here. "Agent Savich wanted me to find out what was going on. I planned on cozying up to people who knew me back when, striking up conversations and asking questions, finding out if anything unusual has been happening here in St. Lumis. I haven't met many people who remember me yet, but I've only been here two days. Here's the thing, though: someone already knows I'm an FBI agent and came after me. That's what's surprising. I don't know how anyone found out I'm FBI so quickly."

Wilde said, "Not much of a stretch with the Internet and social media. Someone could have looked you up, saw you're FBI."

"When I was accepted to the FBI, I was told to keep who I was and what I did under the radar. I laid down the law with my friends and relatives. As far as I know, no one has posted anything about my being an agent. I certainly haven't. I'm also a lawyer, and that's what anyone would find if they looked. Sure, they could have looked deeper, but why would they?"

He said nothing and began pulling her hair away from where the gun had struck her. She felt warm water run over the bumps, felt him pressing against them lightly with a wet towel. Her breath caught, and her eyes watered. He said, "Sorry, I'll be more careful. Keep talking, it'll be a distraction."

Pippa gritted her teeth and told him about what she'd found in Maude's Creepy Puzzles. "If the third installment of puzzle pieces arrived today, I'll bet Major Trumbo is hanging out that window, looking just as nasty and mean, but changed somehow. I still have no idea how all this fits together. But obviously there's someone playing with the FBI, with Savich in particular, and this someone is very serious. Look how they found out about me"—she snapped her fingers—"that fast." She sighed. "We'd hoped to have a leg up when I identified St. Lumis early." She looked up at him. "It didn't work out that way." She flinched.

"Sorry. Hang in there. I'm going to daub some antibiotic ointment on your scalp. There's only a little blood left in your hair. If Dr. Salovitz thinks it's all right, you can soap it out. Keep talking, Cinelli."

She told him about the old abandoned grocery store with its rows of rusted shelves, and how she was attacked by Black Hoodie when she went to investigate.

"You said you only saw some of his profile, that he was youngish, slender, wearing loose jeans and a black hoodie."

She paused, frowned. "Yes, that's right, and I saw him talking on a cell phone. Too bad I couldn't hear what he said."

Wilde said, "He doesn't sound like a local, but I can't be one hundred percent sure. Whoever he is, he's got to know I'm armed. And my deputy can be here in under a minute for backup. So I don't think he'll be hanging around."

He inspected his handiwork and nodded. "I've gotta say, I haven't been this surprised since I left Philadelphia. Do you or Agent Savich have any guesses as to what this is all about?"

Pippa flexed her fingers again. She said slowly,

"No, except that someone seems to have a hate on for Agent Savich."

He smiled. "I'm just now realizing how much I've missed real police work. Okay, now we wait for Agent Savich."

29

Rebekah Manvers sat on the white wall-to-wall carpeting in her bedroom, a large, well-appointed room furnished with nineteenth-century English antiques and an enormous sleigh bed. She pulled the last envelope from the rubber-banded pile of letters in her girlhood keepsake box, a gift from her grandfather for his letters to her.

She wasn't finding anything useful. The letters were loving, but mostly chitchat about his work in Congress and whatever new bills he was hoping to pass to help his district. She eyed the last envelope, a birthday card, which birthday she couldn't remember. She did remember the crisp one-hundred-dollar bill she'd found tucked inside, a fortune for a little kid, and felt her long-ago excitement. She remembered her mother telling her it was going into her college fund. She'd sulked, but she never could budge her mother when she was set on something. She pulled out the card—a dog jumping off the end of a pier, about to splash into the water, a Frisbee in its mouth.

She read:

> *Happy Birthday, my beautiful girl.*
>
> *Here you are, already quite the reader. On your birthday I find myself wondering where life will take you. Things happen in life, things you don't expect, things you are forced to face and deal with. Even though you were small, I know you felt very sad for me when my best friend, Nate Elderby, died. It still hurts me. We had so many years together. As it turned out, in the end he wasn't the lucky one. I was. Ah, but that's not important; you're what's important to me now, and always.*
>
> *My sweetheart, there will come a time when you outgrow my stories, but don't forget I made them up only for you. Remember them and the promises we made to each other. You must always keep your promises. And now, a final*

bit of advice: When you grow up, stay in
charge of your life. It's yours alone, no
one else's.

> *My love forever, Rebekah,*
> *Your Grandfather*

She looked up to see Griffin holding out his hand for the birthday card. She handed it to him. "You're only the second person in the world who's read that card or any of his letters. Grandfather made me promise I wouldn't share them. I didn't even let my mother read them. That birthday card—he writes about his stories, about his friend Nate and my promises. I think he was reminding me about the poem he had me memorize, the poem he made me promise not to tell anyone. Yesterday, I told Agent Savich and Agent Sherlock, and of course Kit, the poem. I suppose Agent Savich told it to you?"

"Yes, he did. He also told me to keep it close." Griffin opened the birthday card, looked it over. "The poem seems a major clue, but you have no idea what it means?"

"No, it's quite mysterious. At least he was clear in the poem about hiding something."

"And his telling you to keep the rhyme secret. I wonder what he meant about the key being in his head?"

Rebekah shrugged. "So do I. Actually, I don't know if I even want to figure it out. I don't want any stolen money, especially if it was Grandfather's, and I'll have no part in ruining my grand-father's legacy."

He raised his head, looked at her straight on. "I wonder what Nate Elderby did? Rebekah, do you have any idea?"

She said, keeping her voice emotionless, "I was a little kid when he drowned. Of course I don't know. I know Agent Savich wonders if Grandfather might even have killed Elderby, but I can't believe that. I won't believe that. Do you?"

Griffin tapped the card against his palm. "I'm sorry, Rebekah, but if I had to guess, I'd say he might have. Can you speak to your grandmother about this?"

"If I even brought it up gently, innocently, my grandmother would fry my liver. I can't remember a time she ever liked me. Even when I was little, I knew she hated to be around me, but it didn't bother me because I had Grandfather and my mother. Once, my mother told me to ignore her. When I was older, I wondered if she was jealous of the bond between Grandfather and me." Rebekah shrugged. "That sounds petty, but it's all I've got. Even at Grandfather's funeral last month she was distant. It was obvious she didn't want anything to do with me. When she had to speak to me, she never looked directly at me. The staff at the May-field Sanitarium told me she very rarely visited. Why not? I don't know."

"What are you two doing up here?"

Congressman Richard Manvers stood in the bedroom doorway, staring at them—no, he was staring at Griffin, his hands fisted at his sides.

Griffin and Rebekah were sitting on the floor facing each other, a pile of letters between them, Griffin still holding the last one.

Rebekah jumped to her feet. "Rich, you're early. If you'd called, Agent Hammersmith could have gone home."

"What are you doing?"

Griffin got slowly to his feet. He knew instantly, of course, Manvers was pissed because Griffin was alone with his wife in their bedroom. It hadn't even occurred to him when Rebekah waved him in that it was inappropriate. It wasn't the first time he'd faced a pissed-off husband or boyfriend. It seemed there was always suspicion whenever he was within three feet of a woman. *Get it through your brain, Hammersmith. Never go into a woman's bedroom, no matter the reason. Well, unless it's at gunpoint.*

He said easily as he got to his feet, "Good evening, Congressman. Mrs. Manvers and I were reading letters written to her by her grandfather. They're very interesting. In this last one he mentions his best friend, Nate, and how he, Nate, wasn't the lucky one." Griffin held out the card to Manvers. Griffin said nothing more. Rebekah said nothing, either, but her face was flushed.

Manvers quickly read the card, looked down at the pile of letters on the white carpet, and slowly, he eased. He stepped forward and took his wife's hand, brought her close against him, and kissed her cheek. Then he smiled at her and read the birthday card again. "I don't understand. What is this all about?"

Griffin said, confiding now, man-to-man, "I think it's time to add your own thoughts to this mystery, sir. Rebekah, tell your husband about Nate Elderby."

Manvers cocked an eyebrow. "Nate Elderby?"

"I was very little when Nate died, and honestly I don't remember him, even though he must have been around a lot. Rich, do you remember what happened?"

"The police ruled Elderby was drinking, fell overboard, and drowned. Why the interest now?"

Rebekah said, "I'm not sure. It's sort of like a blank canvas I'm trying to fill in. Rich, after those two men tried to kidnap me, I wanted to do something, to help somehow. That's why I'm showing Agent Hammersmith my grandfather's letters. I hoped we might find something." She shrugged. "But probably not."

Griffin said, "Do you know of any trouble between the two men back in the nineties? Any idea what her grandfather meant by Nate not being lucky?"

Manvers said, "No, I don't remember his ever talking about Nate with me, but it's possible I've forgotten. It was a long time ago." He looked down at his wife and lightly kissed her cheek. "Believe me, sweetheart, after you told me about your séance with Zoltan, I've given your grandfather a lot of thought. I honestly don't know if this Big Take was real, but maybe when your grandfather wrote that Nate wasn't lucky, he was referring to this Big Take. Maybe they were partners but then Elderby drowned, leaving your grandfather with the prize, whatever it was. Would that make sense?"

Rebekah shook her head. She pulled away from her husband and began to pace the bedroom. She paused a moment to straighten an impressionist painting of a field of lavender, a painting she'd selected herself. She looked from Griffin to her husband. "I remember clearly that Grandfather was devastated when Nate died. Even as young as I was, I remember him crying. Could the two of them have stolen a huge amount of money? "

Manvers said, "I trust not, but all we can do now, Rebekah, is to keep you safe until the authorities find out who attacked you."

Rebekah thought of the poem and her promise to her grandfather. She only nodded.

When Griffin left a few minutes later, Manvers was holding Rebekah, stroking her hair. Griffin heard him say, "I'm so sorry about all this, Rebekah. I know Thursday was terrifying for you. But I'll keep you safe, I promise."

Griffin started to call Savich but decided his

boss and Cinelli had enough on their plates at the moment. He was surprised when he realized he was driving toward the Savich house in Georgetown, but he didn't stop. Something was nagging at him. He dialed Sherlock. On the third ring, she said, "Griffin? What time is it? Oh goodness, it's not all that late. I was wiped out and went to bed early, out like a light. What's up?"

He felt foolish and guilty for waking her. Nothing was wrong. "Sorry I woke you, but with Savich gone, I guess I wanted to check in with you, make sure everything was all right. I'm close by if there's anything you need."

She laughed. "I'm fine without Dillon for a night. Hey, maybe even two nights." She paused, and he could picture her smiling into her cell phone. "I'm okay, Griffin. Thank you for checking."

In that instant, he heard a sound blast, a loud whoosh, like a giant grill lighting. He knew that sound. "Sherlock, there's a fire starting at your house. Get out now! I'm calling 911. I'll be there as fast as I can. Go!"

30

Savich, Pippa, and Chief Wilde sat in the cozy living room dominated by an oversize ancient sofa, both ratty and charming. Pippa laughed and pointed. "Your mom? Grandmother?"

"Actually, my great-uncle Marlbury's third wife, Irene. Yeah, I know it's chintz, that's the word she used." He shrugged. "I haven't gotten around to buying much of anything new." He stared at the sofa, realizing he'd been in St. Lumis three years and hadn't even tried to make this rented cottage his home. What he'd been doing was marking time. And for what?

He walked to the fireplace and set a match to the wadded-up newspapers he'd stuffed between logs. He rose, wiped his hands on his jeans. "The fire should get going soon. Odd how quick it's turned into November."

He looked at the two FBI agents drinking coffee in his living room and marveled at what life could dish up with no warning at all. He'd told Cinelli the truth. The red box, the puzzle pieces of St. Lumis, the attack on her—he hadn't realized how much he missed feeling the excitement, the beating pulse of real police work. He hadn't felt anything like that since he'd left Philadelphia. He looked over at Agent Cinelli, at the drying clumps of hair still sticky with her blood. Her thick French braid was in bad shape, long blond hanks hanging around her face. Every few minutes she shoved the hair behind her ears only to have it slither back. At least she didn't need stitches. He'd pulled the skin together with butterfly strips. He looked at her hands, covered with ointment and wrapped in soft gauze. Did she feel the same sort of excitement he did after all she'd been through? There was an intense focus in her eyes as she reported to Agent Savich what she'd already told him.

He said, "I recognize you, Agent Savich. I've seen you on TV—the Kirsten Bolger case? Most detectives in the squad room were jealous you'd gotten her and not one of us."

Savich smiled. "It was a team effort, always is. She'd kidnapped one of my agents, Cooper McKnight, and he was the one who ended it in Florida. In a tobacco field."

"I wish I'd been in on that, too. Sherlock told me how scary it was." Pippa yawned. "Sorry, guess my exciting day is catching up with me."

"No wonder. You sure you don't want to get checked out, Pippa?"

She waggled her fingers at Savich. "No, please, Dillon. The chief fixed me up. I'm sorry I screwed up and got myself bashed in the head and made you come out here. All right, don't blast me. I can see you don't want any more apologies from me, so no more mea culpas. Sherlock told me you wouldn't dress me down if something went wrong, you believed your agents bashed themselves enough. You don't like to pile on."

Sherlock had told her that? He said, "You did what I would have done, Pippa. You did well to get away. I don't imagine your deputy has reported seeing anyone out there, Chief Wilde?"

"I checked a few minutes ago. Davie hasn't seen anyone. I think this Black Hoodie will keep his distance tonight."

"Now that I'm here, I want to stay awhile," Savich said, "go back to that old grocery store in the morning with you, Pippa, have you show me exactly what happened, then talk to Maude Filly, look at her puzzles. The third red box arrived today, and the last part of the puzzle was altered. The hotel window Major Trumbo is leaning out of is on fire."

Pippa stared at him, said slowly, "That old hotel never burned. Maude may be our best chance to find out what the fire means. As I told you, when I went back to speak to her again, the shop was closed early. I don't know why, but tomorrow we can sit her down."

Savich looked at Wilde. "I hope you'll join us, Chief. This is your town. You'll catch anything unusual more easily, maybe point us toward someone who could be involved."

A compliment from a Fed. Wilde was surprised, given the few times he'd dealt with the Philadelphia FBI. He hadn't warmed to them. At all. But both Cinelli and Savich seemed different. "As I told Agent Cinelli, I can't place Black Hoodie as anyone in town. And if he's not a local, someone might have spotted him."

Pippa said, "Chief, do you have an artist available? I can't give many specifics since I saw only a part of his profile. When he leaned over me, he didn't take any chances and pulled a handkerchief over his nose. But I can try."

Wilde said, "Yes, my artist lives in Annapolis. She's an amateur, usually does flowers, but I saw a charcoal sketch of her son. She's good."

"If you would set her up with me tomorrow first thing, I can work with her, give your officers a general idea of the man to look for. I doubt we'll be lucky enough for Dillon—Agent Savich—to get enough for facial recognition."

"From a drawing? How is that possible?"

Pippa said, "Dillon and a colleague at Scotland

Yard have developed software that can work not only with photographs but with drawings." She sighed. "But again, I strongly doubt anything will come of what little I saw of his face."

How'd she know about that? Savich said, "Still a work in progress, Chief, but it helped on an important case a year or so back. Pippa, I want to go back to Major Trumbo's B&B with you. I don't want you alone tonight. I don't know how secure the B&B is, so if it's all right with you, I'll stay in your room."

Pippa laughed. "Wait till I tell Sherlock I shared my honeymoon suite with her husband. Did you bring a go bag?"

Savich shook his head.

"We'll ask Mrs. Trumbo if she has an extra toothbrush." She turned to Wilde. "Do you happen to have an extra gun? Mine's a Glock nine-millimeter, but a Beretta's no problem, either. I grew up with one."

"I've got an old Walther P99, semiautomatic, my grandfather's."

"That'll do."

Savich's cell rang. He held up a hand. "Sherlock? What's going on?"

A second later Savich yelled over his shoulder as he ran to the front door, "Chief, keep Pippa safe here with you."

He ran out.

31

*G*asoline? Did she smell burning gasoline? Didn't matter. She had to move. Sherlock pulled on jeans, jerked a heavy Redskins sweatshirt over her head, shoved her feet into her sneakers and her Glock in her pants, slipped her cell phone into her jacket pocket, and raced down toward Sean's bedroom.

The smoke alarm went off, loud enough to wake the neighborhood. With the warning Griffin had given her, she had a bit more time. Soon after Sean was born, she and Dillon had planned out what to do in case of a fire and practiced every step. But this was different; this was real. It was all up to her. Sean ran out of his bedroom to her, Astro on his heels. "Mama, what's wrong? What's that smell? Is it fire? Are we on fire?"

So much for Sean not understanding. No time to be calm and reassuring. "Yes. Sean, don't move!" She ran into his bedroom, grabbed the blankets off his bed, and ran back to where he stood, exactly where she'd left him. She wrapped him up, lifted him in her arms, and headed down the hall to the stairs, Astro barking madly at her heels.

"Mama, I can run by myself."

"Let me carry you tonight, sweetheart. Arms around my neck, real tight." Sherlock double-stepped down the front stairs and luckily didn't stumble.

Thick smoke was gushing out of the kitchen, filling the living room, moving fast. Soon the smoke would engulf the house in a choking gray fog. She felt the heat from the flames behind them and pulled the blankets over Sean's head. She unlocked the front door and ran full tilt out of the house, Astro right beside her, the security alarm blasting an ear-splitting accompaniment to the smoke alarms. She turned and stood panting in the front yard, rocking Sean, Astro hugging her leg, whimpering. She jerked out her cell, punched Dillon's number. "Dillon, our house is on fire. We're all right. Hurry!" She heard someone shout her name. She saw Luke Mason, a firefighter, jump off his porch five houses down and race toward her, shrugging into a jacket as he ran. She quickly slipped her cell back into her pocket. He grabbed her arms, did a quick once-over, and pulled back the blankets. "You're good, Sean, and so's Astro. You'll be okay. Your mama was fast. Savich isn't here?"

"No, unfortunately."

"Didn't matter, you did great. My guys are on the way, another couple of minutes. Hear the sirens? Stay put, Sherlock. I want to check this out."

She shouted after him as he ran toward the back of the house, "Someone set the fire!"

"Sherlock!" It was Thomas Perry from next door. Then she remembered. "Thomas, take Sean!"

Before he could stop her, he had an armful of little boy. Sherlock ran back into the house, her sweatshirt pulled up over her mouth and nose. She didn't think, didn't pause, just raced up the stairs into Dillon's study. She grabbed MAX and raced back down, wheezing from the smoke, thicker with every passing moment. She felt heat pumping out of the kitchen like a blast furnace. She heard the flames crackling, making terrifying sputtering noises, pictured her kitchen, and swallowed convulsively. *It's only a kitchen. Get a grip.*

Sherlock couldn't believe it when she saw Griffin carefully lifting Dillon's grandmother's painting down from above the fireplace. He gave her a manic grin. "Got it. Let's get out of Dodge!"

They ran out of the burning house to the sidewalk just as the ear-splitting sirens stopped. Two fire trucks pulled up, one on the street, one on the sidewalk. Firefighters jumped out of the trucks with dizzying speed. In a couple of minutes, they had hoses trained on the back of the house, now lit up like a torch. Thick, arcing streams of water shot into the heart of the fire, turning the flames into smoke that gushed upward like a mushroom cloud. It was like a Bosch painting of hell. A firefighter waved them across the street onto Mr. McPherson's yard. She saw neighbors pouring out of their houses, those close by grabbing hoses and watering down their roofs. Other neighbors from farther away gathered around Sherlock and Griffin. Mr. McPherson came out of his house to stand beside Sherlock, Gladys at his side, her tail wagging. He was wearing what Sherlock called his Nanook-of-the-North padded coat. He was old and frail, but that didn't matter. He was there for them, one of his veined hands lightly rubbing Sean's back, Sean once again in Sherlock's arms. She heard one neighbor wonder aloud how the insurance company would try to weasel out of paying for damages this time and nearly laughed.

Sherlock felt immense gratitude at that moment to Griffin for giving her those few extra precious moments. She was light-headed, realized Sean was choking her, his arms tight around her neck. She tickled him, gave him a smacking loud kiss. Sean laughed, music to her ears, but soon he was sucking his fingers, something he hadn't done in at least three years. She felt his tears against her neck, listened to his little-kid hiccups. She rocked him and softly sang Bob Marley's "Three Little Birds" to him.

When Sean hiccupped a final time, Sherlock turned to Griffin, saw he was grinning. "Good song."

She nodded. It was still hard to comprehend, even looking at the flames, that someone had set fire to their house. Someone had wanted to burn it down with them inside. She felt a ball of bile rising in her throat, and swallowed. She took Griffin's hand and squeezed. "Thank you, Griffin, for calling, you gave me enough time—" She gulped, and her voice fell off a cliff.

He said nothing, only stared at the flames and the gushing smoke. She looked at the painting plastered against his leg, covered with his own coat. "Thank you for saving Dillon's painting. He would have been heartbroken if even one of his grandmother's paintings had burned, but you know he'll call us both idiots for running back into a burning house." She sighed. "I guess we are idiots. But can you imagine MAX burning up?"

Griffin shook his head and moved closer. Together they watched the water winning the battle, but clouds of smoke still spurted upward. She kept rocking Sean, now only whispering the words from "Three Little Birds" against his cheek. He was calmer, no longer sucking his fingers.

Luke Mason's teenage daughter had picked up Astro and was cuddling him close by. Mr. McPherson stood straight and tall, one hand on Gladys's head and the other still lightly stroking Sean's back.

It was the weirdest thing. Sherlock felt oddly disconnected from the burning house in front of her. The rancid smoke, the flames didn't touch her because it didn't seem real, but like a fire she'd seen on the news. How could it be her house? How could it be happening? She coughed, and it snapped her back. Her house, Dillon's house—their home— was burning. And it wasn't an accident. She began shaking. Someone had wanted to kill them.

She heard the neighbors talking, getting organized. Mrs. Rodgers, a neighbor three houses down, handed her and Griffin a glass of water each, and a small cup for Sean. "For your cough, dears." Sherlock hadn't realized her throat was raw. It hurt to swallow, but the water felt heavenly. Sean swiped his hand over his eyes and drank.

Soon there were thermoses of coffee and hot chocolate for everyone, piles of blankets, and hugs, lots of hugs. Everyone crowded in. No one left.

She nearly dropped Sean when he suddenly reared back in her arms.

32

Sean had seen Marty, not only his best friend but, he'd told them many times, his future wife. Sean sniffled and whispered fiercely against Sherlock's cheek, "Mama, Marty's here. I can't cry in front of her. She'll think I'm a sissy and she won't marry me. She's going to be really mad when she finds out I don't have my basketball anymore. Don't tell her, Mama, promise."

About his crying or his basketball? She heard Griffin stifle a laugh. She wanted to laugh, too, but knew this was serious business for a five-year-old. "I promise, on both counts. Look, Sean, she's bringing you some of your clothes." Some of Sean's clothes hung in Marty's closet from their sleepovers, just as Marty's jeans and T-shirts were in Sean's closet.

Sherlock watched Sean run to his five-year-old soul mate. She waved and shouted a thank-you to Marty's parents, the Perrys. Astro struggled out of Lauren Mason's arms and dashed after Sean.

Sherlock pulled out her cell and dialed their longtime insurance agent's number. Sure it was late, but she was up and so she figured Ethan Brothers should be, too. When she punched off, she said to Griffin, "Ethan, our insurance agent, will be here in thirty minutes."

Griffin said, "Is he afraid Savich will arrest him if he doesn't drive right over and give you a check?"

"I hadn't thought that far. Maybe he will. That'd be good. Dillon's called me three times, so I know he's driving like a maniac. It shouldn't be long now." She looked down at her watch.

Griffin said, "I've spoken to him as well. And no, I didn't mention arson. He's scared enough as it is. Knowing him, he'll have a police car on his bumper."

Luke Mason, his face blackened, ran around the side of the house toward them, still wearing his civvies. He smelled like nasty smoke, but he was smiling. "Sherlock, it looks like we've got the fire under control, and your neighbors' houses are safe. First, let me say the kitchen's gone, but the guys assure me the fire didn't gut the rest of the house." He started to pat her shoulder, realized he was filthy, and drew back his hand. "All I know is the fire started at the back of the house. Hang in there,

Sherlock. I'll be back when I have more to tell you."
Lauren handed her and Griffin each a cup of coffee,
strong and sweet, from her mother, Lauren told
them, to ward off shock.

A red Porsche roared around the corner.

Griffin smiled when he saw a Metro car pull
in behind the Porsche. He checked his watch and
grinned. "Thirty-seven minutes from St. Lumis.
That's pretty impressive, maybe a record."

Savich jumped out of the Porsche and turned off
his flasher, yelled, "Sherlock!"

Sherlock held tight to the blankets wrapped
around her and ran to meet him. She saw his face
was hollowed and grim in the light from the neighboring houses. She'd been willing him to hurry, to
run every red light in Maryland and in the District.
She felt everything inside her break apart. She
shucked off the blankets and threw her arms around
him, squeezed him as tightly as Sean had squeezed
her. "I'm all right, really, I'm okay. So is Sean, and
Astro. Sean's not crying because he doesn't want
Marty to make fun of him, but he's upset because
he lost his basketball. I remembered MAX and ran
back to get him. Griffin brought out your grandmother's painting. I called Ethan Brothers, and he's
on his way." She realized she was spurting it all out
a mile a minute, stopped, panting, and hugged him
tight again. "I'm so glad you're here. Thirty-seven
minutes. I bet dispatch knew about the fire and told
them to let you through."

Of course he fastened on to the most critical thing she'd said. He spoke calmly, but he was so scared he wanted to shake her. "You went back into a burning house for a fricking computer?"

She smiled up at him. "No, not just any fricking computer. I went back for MAX. He's your creation, Dillon. I didn't even think about it. I pulled my Redskins sweatshirt over my nose, and I was in and out fast. Dillon, I hardly even breathed."

He wanted to yell at her for what could have happened, but he didn't. He drew a deep breath and hugged her close again. He wouldn't let her go, even though she'd assured him she was all right when he'd called her several times on his mad drive to Washington. He called out, "Griffin, thank you for saving my grandmother's painting." At the moment, he didn't even wonder why Griffin was there.

"Papa!"

He turned to see Thomas Perry holding Marty's hand on one side, Sean's on the other. Alice Perry was rocking their small baby boy, keeping away from the smoke a breeze was blowing toward them. Thomas gave Sean a hug. "Your daddy's here. Go." Sean shouted and ran full tilt toward him. Sean was fully dressed, and how could that be? Astro was barking his head off, and now Gladys joined in. The black Labrador Boris from down the street filled out a trio. Savich felt his throat close as he scooped Sean up in his arms and hugged him close. All the while

Sean was talking nonstop. "Mama carried me, Papa, and she was fast. She wrapped me up like a hot dog so I wouldn't get smoke up my nose, and Astro was barking and jumping. And Mama leaped down the stairs, and we ran outside." Sean stopped, studied his father's face, and patted his cheek. "It will be okay, Papa." Had Sean seen the empty fear? "Marty said I could sleep with her new little brother tonight if I wanted to. She said he'd wake me up every ten minutes because he was hungry. Mama, you're crying. What's wrong?"

She gulped but managed to smile. "Happy tears, Sean. We're all safe and together." She hadn't thought of where they'd sleep tonight, or for that matter, for the foreseeable future. Not in their own house, that was for sure. It didn't matter. They were together; they were safe.

Savich continued to hold Sherlock and Sean against him until Luke Mason trotted over to them. It took Savich a moment to recognize him, as his face was black, his clothes filthy. Why wasn't he in his fire gear? Luke raised his voice. "Folks, all your houses are safe. The firefighters got here fast enough." He turned to Savich and Sherlock. "As I told Sherlock, the kitchen's destroyed, but nothing else structural is burned, only smoke and water damage that couldn't be avoided. Savich, I'm glad you're here." He beamed at the three of them. "Your family's all right, and that's the most important thing. It's good Sherlock got out so fast, didn't try to fight it. A house is only a house, after all—well, in this case, a kitchen is only a kitchen. Tell you what, let's get a little away from your neighbors."

Luke walked them toward one of the ladder trucks. "Good, no one else can hear us here. I'm sure you're wondering, so let me spit it out. The fire inspector will make the final decision, but I can tell you now this was no accident. Sherlock was right. We found a can of gasoline behind the kitchen, and one of the guys found one of the kitchen windows smashed. Someone started this fire. And whoever it was also left the gasoline can there on purpose. They wanted you to know."

"Not an accident," Savich said slowly. He felt a cold rage, nearly shook with it. Sherlock and Sean could have died. Whoever had set the fire had brought a war to his home. He would make sure he finished it. He looked at Sherlock's face. Of course, she'd already known. He looked at Griffin. He nodded.

33

Sean pushed against his father's arms and shouted, "Grandma!"

Savich set him down, and his son ran to his grandmother, Senator Robert Monroe smiling really big at her side.

Minna Savich scooped Sean up and squeezed him so tight he yipped. She looked into her son's eyes and saw huge relief, mirroring her own. She looked him over, then Sherlock, and closed her eyes a moment, squeezing Sean again. "I never prayed so hard in my life."

Senator Robert Monroe looked toward the smoke still pluming upward, then back at Savich and Sherlock, and slowly nodded. He patted Sean's small shoulder. Sean looked up. "I'm glad you brought Grandma over, Uncle Bob."

Savich started to say something, but Minna said over Sean's head, "You have Bob to thank for our getting here so fast. One of his friends at Metro called him on his ham radio to alert him about a 911 call to your home, Dillon. He picked me up, and here we are."

Savich felt surprise at the brief stab of resentment he felt at seeing his mom with Senator Monroe, though they'd been together for several years now. He remembered he'd once disliked the senator on principle—he wasn't Savich's dad—but he'd proved he could stick and he loved Sean. Savich shook the senator's hand. "Thank you for helping, sir, and for bringing my mom."

Sean was leaning back in Minna's arms, talking a mile a minute, about how Mama ran back into the burning house and Uncle Griffin, too, to get his great-grandma's painting, you know, the really big one over the fireplace. His basketball was still stuck in his closet—if it got real hot would it melt? Would it still bounce? Minna listened with half an ear, though Sean would never realize it, her eyes on Sherlock. Her face was streaked with smoke, but her breathing seemed fairly normal, thank heaven.

Senator Monroe scooped up a barking Astro and held him up for Sean to hug.

Sherlock said, "So Sean's told you most of it already, except that someone dumped gasoline in through a smashed kitchen window and outside the kitchen door. The firefighters say they contained it in the kitchen and saved the rest of the house. And we got out all safe and sound, didn't we, Sean?" She hugged him, couldn't help it. It had been too close, too close.

"You're saying someone set fire to your house? It was arson?" Minna's voice climbed two octaves as the enormity of it hit her.

"Yes. Our firefighter neighbor told me we'll have an arson inspector and the police department working together on it."

Minna put her arm around Sherlock, Sean between them, hugged them both close. "You and Dillon will catch the people who did this."

"You can bet on it," Sherlock said. "We're working two current cases. You know there's a connection to one of them."

Senator Monroe said, "At least you won't have any problems with the insurance company. I'm a senator, and you're FBI. Do you think they'd want to mess with either of us?"

For the first time that night, both Savich and Sherlock grinned.

Minna said, "Bob's house in Hannibal, Missouri, burned down a couple of years ago—ancient wiring that finally gave up the ghost. Bob knows exactly how to deal with them." She saw Ethan Brothers, the family insurance agent, speaking with a firefighter, and gave him a big shark smile. Minna added, "You'll come to my house tonight. We'll see to clothes and whatever you need tomorrow." She drew Sherlock and now Savich into her arms, sandwiching Sean again. "When Bob called me about the fire, I was so scared." Her voice caught, and she began to cry.

It was Savich who held her close and whispered in her ear he loved her while Sean patted her face. "Grandma, please don't cry. Are you sad because you weren't here and Mama had to carry me down the stairs?"

Minna sniffed, swallowed. "Maybe after she carried you down, she'd have come back for me."

"Mama's real strong. She could do it."

"Here now, Minna," Senator Monroe said, "tears are for sad occasions. Most of the house will be good as new once it's repaired. And everyone is all right. As for the man who set that fire, his days are numbered."

Savich found himself looking at the people he loved, finally accepting that they were safe and unharmed. He felt so thankful it smothered his rage, at least in this moment. It wasn't important right now. He had things to do.

He called Ben Raven, who told him their people and the arson investigator would set up a forensic team. He accepted a check from Ethan Brothers to cover short-term living expenses. He made the rounds of their neighbors, thanked them for their care, and where did anyone get doughnuts this time of night? He listened to their outrage at someone setting fire to his house, and underneath it he heard their fear that something far worse could have happened, maybe to them. He knew there was no way to reassure them, except to find the person who'd done this. He walked with Captain Ells, the fire chief, and Luke Mason to the back of the house and looked into his burned kitchen. The appliances were scarred and black, but still in one piece. His once-proud coffee machine, what was left of it, was melted into the counter. The cabinets, table, and chairs had burned to cinders. All the dishes, pots, and pans were scattered, breaking where they'd dropped, or melted. The beautiful oak floor was still intact, and amazingly, he saw a single black mug lying on its side in the sink, unharmed. It was his gift from Sean last Christmas. My Dad was written on it.

Savich looked up at the ribbons of black smoke still drifting slowly upward out of what was once their kitchen. For the first time, he realized how noxious the smell was and knew it couldn't be good for Sean, or any of them.

When he, Luke Mason, and Captain Ells rejoined his family, Savich shook the firefighters' hands and thanked them for saving his house. Ells said, "You'll get this figured out, Agent Savich. Right now, though, it's time to take care of your family." Griffin gave him a doughnut. Ells laughed and ate it. "Sorry, guys, here come the media. Looks like you're newsworthy, Agent Savich."

The media was all they needed. Savich hadn't even thought of them and was surprised they'd come. How did they know so fast? One of the firefighters or dispatchers, no doubt. Three reporters and their cameramen piled out of their cars and vans, all of them homing in on him, questions flying from six feet away.

34

It was well after midnight. Senator Monroe had left, Savich's mother had gone to bed, and Sherlock was upstairs in Sean's bedroom, holding him close as he cuddled an exhausted Astro. Savich wished he were with them, but not just yet. He and Griffin were speaking quietly downstairs in his mother's living room.

Griffin nodded toward a photo set on the mantel. "That's your dad, isn't it?"

"Yes." Savich looked at the large photo in its place of honor. His larger-than-life dad, FBI agent Buck Savich, had been a big-time cowboy in an office full of cowboys in the FBI New York Field Office. In the photo, he was laughing, his arms around Minna and his children. Savich remembered when the photo was taken by one of his dad's FBI friends. He'd been about twelve. Savich wondered what Senator Monroe thought about Buck Savich being so prominently displayed. He was brought back, his throat closing, when he thought again, *Sherlock and Sean could have been killed, burned to death, and I wasn't there.*

However much time Griffin had bought them when he'd awakened Sherlock had helped save their lives. "Griffin, I owe you more than I can ever repay. Thank you."

Griffin looked down at his smoke-streaked hands. "I'll tell you, Savich, what I heard, I knew that sound meant fire. It nearly scared me to death. I was afraid I wasn't close enough to your house to help Sherlock."

"Where were you then, Griffin?"

"I found myself driving toward your neighborhood, no idea why really, and I called Sherlock, just to check on her. I heard a loud whoosh, sounded like a big-ass grill being fired up, and like I said, I knew. After I called Sherlock, I called 911. She left the line open, and I heard the smoke alarm go off, then after a moment, your security alarm. When I got there, I remembered your grandmother's painting and ran in to get it and there came Sherlock down the stairs carrying MAX." He paused. "It was close, Savich, too close. Do you have any idea who's responsible?"

"No, not yet. But it's got to be about the St. Lumis case. That's a lock, after that third part of the puzzle they sent me showed a man burning in a fire the same day someone tried to burn down my house with Sherlock and Sean in it. The question is why."

Griffin nodded. "Tell me what you want me to do."

"Keep protecting Rebekah Manvers."

Griffin suddenly grinned. "Do you know your mom kissed me and patted my cheek, told me I was an angel, even with a smoky face?"

Savich said simply, "You are an angel. And Mom doesn't know the half of it."

Griffin, embarrassed, said, "Ah, but still with an *eau de smoke* smell. Maybe after I shower I'll smell sweet enough for your mom to hug me again."

Savich said, "Our firefighter neighbor told Sherlock it would take at least three rounds of soap and water for people not to cross the street to get away from her and Sean. Of course, Sean doesn't want another bath. He can't wait for the other kids at school to smell him."

Griffin said, "I want a Sean." He shrugged, looked down at his sooty hands. "Sorry, I don't know where that came from."

Savich thought of Anna, Griffin's former fiancée, who'd broken up with him that past spring and left for Seattle. He said, "Having your very own kid is a life changer. Everything shifts, sharpens. Don't worry, Griffin, you'll have your son or daughter, and when you do, you'll be good at it."

"That's what Delsey, my little sister, says about herself. She and Rob Rasmussen are serious." He looked shocked. "Already talking about kids." He paused, took a sip of his tea, and set the cup down next to a *Sports Illustrated* magazine with the whole Warriors team on the cover, set there for Sean, of course. He said, "The fire captain said the house should be cool enough by tomorrow morning for a more thorough investigation. There'll be a number of experts there, arson specialists. Would you like me there, too? About nine o'clock?"

"Sure. Both Sherlock and I will try to be there, too. There are so many balls in the air right now." Savich knew he was crashing, could hardly make sense anymore. "Sorry, Griffin, for the life of me I can't think straight."

Griffin rose. "I'd give you a hug, but I smell too bad. Go to bed, and kiss Sherlock and Sean. We both need some sleep."

Savich walked Griffin to the door. "I want to stay involved, Savich," he said. "So you think it's connected to the burning man in the puzzle?"

"Got to be. The man in St. Lumis who knocked Pippa out and tied her up did it to pull me away from Washington. The puzzle itself was meant to draw me out there, and when I sent Pippa instead, they had her disappear so I'd go out there after her."

"So someone could set your house on fire and kill Sherlock and Sean."

Savich nodded. "I'm thinking it could even be the same man who knocked Pippa out and tied her up. Tomorrow she and Chief Wilde will be working with a local artist to see if they can come up with any sort of decent sketch."

Savich's expression never changed, but his voice was cold as an ice floe. "I don't think he's the one behind the red-box puzzle. He's a hired tool. What are they after? To hurt me? By killing my family?" Savich paused, then said quietly, "When I find the person behind this, I'm going to destroy him."

When Griffin's car disappeared around the corner, Savich set the alarm and turned off the lights. He paused. Did the arsonist know about his mother's house? If they stayed here for more than a couple of days, it would be easy to find them. They would have to be very careful.

Soon, he was spooning Sherlock, who was spooning Sean, Astro tucked close. But, despite his exhaustion, he had trouble falling sleep, with Sherlock and Sean in the crosshairs.

When he finally slept, he dreamed he saw the shadow of a woman staring at his house. Even though he couldn't see her face, he knew she was smiling. He called to her, but she didn't turn to him, only laughed and pointed. He saw a match burst into flame and watched her hold it up. He yelled at her to stop. But she threw the match, and the house exploded.

He jerked away when Sherlock shoved him. "Wake up, Dillon. You're having a bad dream, and no wonder. Keep close, all right?"

He fell back asleep, breathing in the smoky smell of Sherlock's hair.

35

Savich looked at his burned-out kitchen and smelled the acrid odor of charred paint and wood coming off the walls and appliances. He actually wished he could still feel some of the heat he'd felt last night, since it was a cold morning, hovering in the low forties, but there wasn't a trace. He, Sherlock, and Gabriella, Sean's nanny, had already gone through the rest of the house, accompanied by Flash Randy, the fire department arson investigator. The water damage wasn't as bad as it might have been, according to Flash, though it looked bad enough to Savich and Sherlock. He'd seen her staring at the soaked furniture and sodden rugs in the living room and taken her hand, squeezed it. He'd looked at the empty spot over the fireplace where Griffin had taken down his grandmother's painting. Griffin's act was a debt he'd be hard-pressed to pay back.

Upstairs, there was a light veil of soot on the walls where the smoke had hovered near the ceiling. "The walls will need a thorough cleaning and some paint," Flash said. "Pack what you need, but be careful. Stay away from any damage you see. You never know. I'll be right here."

They collected clothes, badly in need of washing, and gathered bathroom essentials. The smell was the worst in Sean's room, directly above the kitchen. They packed his clothes in his Captain Corbin roll-on and gathered his favorite games and, of course, his beloved basketball and Steph Curry sneakers. When Savich walked into his office, the foul mixture of burned wood, smoke, and water nearly overwhelmed him. At least MAX was safe, thanks to Sherlock.

They met with the fire forensic team, huddled in a small group, not that there was much of a mystery—someone had smashed a kitchen window, tossed gasoline into the kitchen and onto the walls, and left the can outside the kitchen door, announcing what he'd done.

Savich's cell sang out "Zombie" by the Cranberries. "Excuse me." He turned away from a Metro fire investigator. "Savich here."

"Agent Savich, it's Candy. You've got to come.

Zoltan's gone. She might be dead. There's blood, I don't know, I don't know—"

Savich blinked, dialed in. Candy was Zoltan's assistant. "Candy, take a deep breath. That's right. Now, go slow and tell me exactly what happened."

He heard her take some deep breaths, heard her panic slowly lessen, and waited. Finally, she gulped and said, her voice a bit less shaky, "I got here maybe ten minutes ago. I sang out hello, like I always do, but Zoltan didn't answer. That's not unusual, a late client, a late night. She could still be in bed or she went out early to the store, or whatever, so I went to my office and started to work. Then it hit me. She had a client coming this morning—a strange time, I know—but she should be getting ready, making her special tea. I thought maybe she was sick and went looking for her. When I went in the living room, I found blood on the floor, a lot of it, black and horrible. She's dead. I think she's dead, and someone hauled her away—"

He heard hysteria bubbling back and interrupted her. "Breathe, Candy. Settle yourself." He settled himself, too. Savich knew that to a layperson, a lot of blood could mean anything from a cut finger to an artery fountaining. He said, "Candy, was the house alarm on or off when you arrived?"

Silence, then, "Oh goodness, I didn't think anything of it, only that Zoltan must have already gotten up, you know, for a cup of tea, maybe an early muffin—she loves blueberry—and she'd turned it off for me. But she usually doesn't go back to bed. The alarm's off, Agent Savich. Off." She hiccupped. "Is she dead?"

"Candy—what's your last name?"

"Spindler, I'm Candace Spindler. What's happened, Agent Savich?"

"Candy, stay near the front door. I'll be right there." He turned to Sherlock, who simply nodded at him.

"She was really upset. I heard her clearly." Sherlock turned to Gabriella. "Gabriella, please take all this stuff over to Dillon's mom's. Sean's in school, so you'll have enough time to unpack everything." She gave Gabriella a hug, told her to be careful, and thanked her again.

Gabriella said, "I still can't believe it. Imagine, someone wanting to hurt you and Sean." Her voice cracked, and Sherlock pulled her close. "We weren't hurt, and everything here is fixable. It will be all right." She stepped back and took Gabriella's pretty face between her palms. "Everything would be so much harder without you, so thank you. There's not enough room for all our stuff in your sexy little Mazda, so take my Volvo. I won't need it today. We'll pick up your car later."

They watched the firemen help Gabriella load the suitcases into Sherlock's Volvo. She said, "Dillon, there's nothing more we can do here. We can come back later to get more stuff if we need it. Our insurance agent has assured us he's taking care of everything. Let's just go. I want to meet Candy."

When Savich pulled the Porsche into Zoltan's driveway, Sherlock was staring out of the windshield, looking at nothing he could see.

"Sweetheart?"

"Oh, we're here? Sorry, Dillon. I was thinking about last night. It all happened so fast I didn't have time to be scared, but I'm scared now. Believe me, I'm really working on being mad instead. But then I think maybe it'd be better if you and I were insurance brokers or veterinarians. It'd have to be a safer life."

What could he say? "Well, you'd make a great vet, but since we're FBI agents, you and I, we need to suck it up and find the maniac who did this."

She whooshed out a breath, nodded. "Yeah, okay, but he's not a maniac, Dillon. Whoever did this isn't crazy; he's evil. You know it has something to do with the red-box puzzle. You know it. I know it."

Before Savich could answer, they heard a shout and saw Candy Spindler standing in the open front doorway, waving wildly at them.

"Time to let the red boxes go for the moment. Let's see what this blood is all about. Then we'll give Ben Raven a call at Metro."

Sherlock climbed out and said over the roof

of the Porsche, "You warned her, Dillon, but she didn't listen. You know, I don't think Zoltan's dead. I can't think of a reason why the attacker would haul her body away. Maybe someone did try to kill her, to snip off a loose end, and she managed to run. Either way, it proves she was in on this up to her ears." She paused. "I hope she managed to run."

They walked toward Candy Spindler, who was wringing her hands like Lady Macbeth. She was in her late twenties, small and lithe as a gazelle, with short, wavy black hair. She was wearing pink sweats and pink sneakers.

Candy grabbed Savich and leaned up, her voice a mix of anger and fear. "I told her, Agent Savich. I told her trying to fool Mrs. Manvers wouldn't work. Zoltan knew Mrs. Manvers wasn't a believer, but still she went along with it."

"Went along with what, exactly, Candy?" he asked, rubbing his hands up and down her arms.

"She didn't tell me, if only she had. All I know is she got a call from someone—she wouldn't tell me who—and she set up a séance with Mrs. Manvers right away. She was excited about seeing her, really upbeat. She said we'd make enough money to maybe go to France, to Cannes, lie on the beach, hold a séance once in a while, order up French spirits. She was so pleased with herself, but now look." She put her face in her hands and sobbed. "I told her. I told her."

Sherlock said, "Candy, show us to the living room, to the bloodstain."

Candy let them into the house, but she stopped at the living room doorway. "It's blood. I don't want to see it again. I can't. It's hers, I know it. Agent Savich, she was usually so careful, researched all her clients down to when they had their last cavity filled."

The blood was on the edge of the Oriental carpet, next to one of the sofas. It looked hours old, smudged and streaked at one edge where someone had struggled to stand or was pulled up. They found two slugs. Nothing else seemed disturbed or damaged. Savich called Ben Raven at Metro and the FBI forensic team, then he asked, "Candy, do you know where Zoltan's cell phone is?"

"Her purse is gone, and her cell isn't charging, I checked. They took her car, too. But maybe it makes more sense Zoltan took her own cell phone and her car? Not some stranger who didn't know where she kept her car keys? Well, they were always in her purse, but still. Zoltan isn't dead, please, she can't be."

Sherlock walked back to Candy and lightly touched her hand to the woman's arm. "Candy, we'll do DNA testing and know soon enough if that's Zoltan's blood. Tell us, do you think Zoltan was the real deal? Not with Mrs. Manvers, but with her other clients? Do you believe she really could contact the dead?"

Candy blinked up at her. "Good heavens, no, Agent Sherlock. She even told me once if she died, the last thing she'd want would be to have to deal with any idiots she left behind." She paused a moment. "But you know, she thought she was helping some of her clients deal with their grief and their loneliness, and some of them certainly left happier. But sometimes she took advantage, charging clients too much, and too often. She had no qualms about that, especially those clients who wanted to find something the dead person left behind, like money or jewelry." Candy paused, huffed out a breath. "She was very upset when someone attacked Mrs. Manvers. I know she made some calls about it on her cell, but I don't know who she called. Then you made her go to the Hoover Building to talk to you, Agent Savich. She was even more upset when she came home. She tried to hide it, but I know her very well. She even canceled some clients. She's never done that before."

Sherlock said, "How long have you worked for her?"

"Zoltan and I have been together since I graduated with a degree in human studies with nothing but debt to show for it. I was waitressing in the Village in New York when she found me. She always paid me well—I mean, she *pays* me well. I refuse to believe she's dead. I've always admired her for how well she put on a show. She laughed when I called it performance art."

Savich asked her to wait outside for the FBI forensic team while he and Sherlock went upstairs to search Zoltan's office. There were drawers of meticulous files on her clients going back more than a decade, their personal histories, their likes, their dislikes, their relationships with both the living and the dead, but there was nothing they could find on Rebekah Manvers.

36

Pippa hugged herself against the cold as she hurried into Major Trumbo's B&B, Chief Wilde behind her. Mrs. Trumbo was coming out of the dining room with only a small stack of plates in her arms. Most of her Halloween crowd had left St. Lumis.

"Ms. Cinelli! I was worried when you didn't come down for breakfast. I was going to go up and check on you—" She broke off and stared at Chief Wilde, an eyebrow rising nearly to her hairline. She said slowly, smiling, "But I see if I'd knocked on your door, I wouldn't have gotten an answer." She looked at each of them. "Chief, what are you doing here with Ms. Cinelli this early on a chilly Tuesday morning, as if you're just now bringing her back? You only met on Saturday night, isn't that right?"

Mrs. Trumbo was teasing them about sleeping together? Talk about fast work. Well, maybe his bed would have been more comfortable than the rock with a thin mattress in his small guest bedroom. "Good morning, Mrs. Trumbo. It's very kind of you to be concerned about me. You're right. I didn't sleep in my beautiful honeymoon suite last night. You see, yesterday someone hit me on the head and tied me up in that old abandoned grocery store on the edge of town. I escaped to the chief's house."

Mrs. Trumbo blinked, laughed, and wagged her finger at Pippa. "You're making that up, Ms. Cinelli. Not that it's any of my business who you want to play with. Why, I remember my first husband, he—well, that's not important. No need to spit out a wild story. Someone hit you and tied you up? That wouldn't be funny, young lady, though I suppose it makes a fine tale."

"To be totally accurate, he hit me on the head twice, ma'am."

Mrs. Trumbo shifted the plates in her arms. "I know young people hook up faster nowadays—that's what you call it, isn't it? Like fish? No reason to be ashamed about it, but I am surprised at you, Chief Wilde. Don't you have rules about not fraternizing with the community whenever you're tempted? A reputation to uphold? Aren't you supposed to be our moral beacon, as our mayor claims to be?"

Wilde stared at her. "I don't recall being a moral beacon listed in my job description, Mrs. Trumbo, and no, our fine mayor didn't mention it, either."

Pippa realized the conversation was rapidly deteriorating and raised her hand.

"Mrs. Trumbo, Chief Wilde and I did not hook up, and believe me, that tale I told you is true, though I wish it weren't because I still have a headache. And look at my wrists, all bandaged up." Mrs. Trumbo simply looked at her, a thick salt-and-pepper eyebrow raised. What was she thinking? Bondage? Surely not. If only Pippa had her creds, she'd have a better chance of convincing her. But she didn't, so she shut up. Let Wilde handle Mrs. Trumbo.

He said easily, "We sure would like a cup of coffee, Mrs. Trumbo. I don't suppose—"

Trumbo stared between them, amused, and nodded. "Very well. You two go into the dining room. Ignore the two tables we used for breakfast. I'll clean them up soon enough. Ms. Cinelli, I have your breakfast warming since I was expecting you any minute. Chief, I'll have to see about you. I know I have a couple of scones left. I hear you're a strawberry preserves man?"

He nodded. "Yes, ma'am, that'd be very kind of you."

"My scones were Major Trumbo's favorite."

Mrs. Trumbo gave Pippa a last look and a wink and walked back toward the kitchen.

Once they were seated in the dining room, Pippa sat back in her chair and sighed. "I know she was teasing us, but I still feel like I have a scarlet letter on my forehead. She didn't believe me, not for a second."

"I wouldn't have believed you, either. It sounds like a tale a seriously embarrassed person would dream up. I liked your effort at a frontal assault, though, Cinelli, right out there with the truth."

Pippa shrugged. "Yeah, yeah, but it didn't work out well, did it?" She began drumming her fingernails on the table. "When it's a question of who's sleeping with whom, why is it always the woman who's the instigator, not the man?"

"Excuse me? I was the one she accused of moral turpitude."

"When everyone in St. Lumis hears about our wild night, it'll be me who jumped poor Chief Wilde. You wait and see. How I wish I had my gun and my creds. I feel half-dressed."

Wilde grinned. "Know what you mean."

Pippa sighed. "Dillon called me about the fire, said he drove back to Georgetown in record time last night. Thank heaven Sherlock got Sean out in time and the fire stayed in the kitchen. Can you imagine someone breaking one of your windows and throwing in gasoline?"

"I've been giving the situation a lot of thought

and I have to agree. The arson at Savich's house last night has to connect to someone here in St. Lumis."

Pippa sat forward. "Otherwise the red boxes and the puzzle showing Major Trumbo hanging out of a burning window right here in town make no sense. If no one here is involved, why did they pick St. Lumis, and why attack me here?"

Wilde said, "Maybe St. Lumis is part of some larger scheme they're betting none of us can solve. The only clue we really have is the puzzle, and that means we start with Maude Filly."

He paused, fiddled with a salt shaker.

"What?"

"I was remembering when I was a cop in Philadelphia. I investigated murders, faced off with violent drug dealers, you name it, but I never came across something this—well, convoluted. It's like some madman with a hate on for Savich has come up with a weird kind of revenge, daring us to catch him."

Pippa unfolded a napkin and spread it in her lap. "It makes me think of a fat spider weaving a web. No, I do not want to think about spiders. Everyone agrees it could be some kind of payback, revenge, whatever you want to call it by someone Agent Savich arrested or harmed, or maybe someone close to them." She shook her head. "Okay, after I've had a shower and changed, we'll go see Mrs. Filly. Don't forget, I've got to meet with your sketch artist."

"It's all set up. Lisa Trout's her name. She's excited."

"The more I try to remember him . . ." She shrugged. "We'll see what pops out."

They heard Mrs. Trumbo's heavy tread even before she appeared in the dining room doorway, two big platters held expertly on her arms. "Chief Wilde, I figured I should always be generous to our local police, no matter what you've been up to, so I brought you some scrambled eggs and bacon. Might keep you from stealing some of Ms. Cinelli's." She carefully set down the plates, straightened the silverware, finally nodded to herself. She paused, looked at each of them again. "Tell me, is this love at first sight? Or do you young people not believe in that anymore?"

"I don't know," Pippa said. "Love at first sight has never landed at my door."

Mrs. Trumbo smiled at Chief Wilde, but when he only smiled back, she walked out of the room and returned with a tray of coffee and cups. As she poured out their coffee, Pippa said, "Why do you think Mrs. Filly has a puzzle with Major Trumbo hanging out of a window in the old Alworth Hotel?"

For a moment, Mrs. Trumbo froze, then she shook her head. "Why would you think I'd have the faintest idea why Maude Filly framed the major in a window? I will say she can be a vicious old bat about the major when the mood strikes her, not that I blame her." She paused, eased the cream closer to Pippa. "I know you like your coffee black, Chief. Do you know, when Major Trumbo asked me to marry him, he was so nervous, the poor man. It took me a while to realize Maude had been smart to divorce him. He became a real pain in the butt, nasty old bugger, until he had the good taste to croak." She nodded toward the mantel. "Ms. Cinelli knows his ashes are in that lovely urn. Six pounds is all that's left of him, and believe me, it's more than enough. Ms. Cinelli, would you like some cream? Sugar? I have real, raw, and fake."

Pippa said, "Black is perfect, thank you. Mrs. Filly told me you'd been seeing Major Trumbo while they were still married. She said you claimed you didn't know, and you were clever enough to use all your assets."

"Well, now, that's the truth, isn't it? Poor Maude never had much in the way of assets. I've always wondered what's with all the snake and monster puzzles." She gave one final look at their plates, nodded to herself, and left them alone.

Wilde forked up a bite of scrambled eggs. "You made that up, didn't you? Mrs. Filly didn't say that about Mrs. Trumbo's assets." He gave a little shudder. "Her assets don't bear thinking about."

Pippa chewed on a piece of bacon and smiled. "So sue me. I wanted to see what she had to say about Mrs. Filly."

He raised his coffee and saluted her. "We can talk

to her more seriously after we've spoken to Mrs. Filly."

She crunched on another piece of bacon. "Thank you, Wilde. Wilde—that doesn't feel right. Does anyone call you by your first name? It's Matthew, right?"

"Actually, no one calls me Matthew. Even my mom started calling me Wilde when I turned thirteen. There was nothing I wouldn't try, including joyriding my uncle Tommy's prized BMW nearly off a cliff, and brawling with my friends after a football game, coming home with a banged-up face. It's been Wilde since that first bloody nose."

She laughed, then sobered quickly. He saw it.

Wilde added some pepper to his eggs, offered it to her. "Back to business, then. I'm thinking it's you and me who need to find out who set the fire at Savich's house, if it's someone from town."

Pippa turned down the pepper. "Makes sense it is."

"I want to visit that old grocery store, too, see what we can find."

Pippa saw he was looking at her bandaged wrists. "Don't even think about it, Wilde. No doctor."

"Let me see them."

She rolled her eyes, stuck out her hands. The gauze bandages were in place. "All right, no doctor." He picked up a slice of crispy bacon, pointed it at her. "I like to see tough on the hoof, but take three aspirin, okay?"

Mrs. Trumbo wasn't at the reception desk when they left the dining room to go upstairs to Pippa's honeymoon suite. "Black Hoodie took my key along with everything else." She stepped behind the desk and took the master key from its hook on the key rack. "Do you think he could have come here?"

"Let's go see."

She unlocked the door and Wilde simply pushed her away and went in first, his gun drawn.

"All clear," he called out a moment later only to see she was right on his heels.

Pippa looked around the room. "I don't think anything's been touched. Well, Wilde, what do you think of my room? Does it meet your expectations?"

He stopped and stared at the circular bed and the bordello-red draperies. "This is amazing."

"Ah, there's my tablet, right where I left it. Why don't you have a seat, and I'll take a shower and change." She picked up her tablet and punched in her password. "Take a look at my notes, under 'Red Box.' I'll be fast."

He sat down on a plush red-as-sin circular chair by the window and opened the file while Pippa carried some clothes into the bathroom. "If you have questions, jot them down in the notes section."

When she came out of the bathroom eleven minutes later, he looked up and saw an FBI agent—black pants, white blouse, a kick-ass black leather jacket, and low-heeled black boots, her hair pulled back in a ponytail. "You have my Walther?"

She pulled back her jacket to show him.

"You clean up well, Cinelli. Your notes are thorough, but they show how little we know. It's time to go check out Mrs. Filly's assets."

37

HOME OF ZOLTAN
TUESDAY MORNING

Savich started his Porsche, listened to his baby roar to life, and smiled. He always did. He loved the sound of those cylinders. His cell sang out Jimi Hendrix's "All Along the Watchtower." He frowned. "It's Sonja Grayson, the lead prosecutor in Marsia Gay's trial." Ever since Grayson had told him Veronica Lake had agreed to make a deal with the prosecution and testify against Marsia Gay, he had been waiting for this call. He knew exactly what had happened. "Ms. Grayson?" He said nothing, only listened. Finally, he punched off.

Sherlock laid her hand on his. "Veronica's dead, isn't she?"

"Amazingly, she survived surgery, but the surgeon says her odds aren't good. She's in the ICU at Washington Memorial. Grayson is frothing at the mouth at the prison personnel. What's worse for her is she specifically asked to be assigned the case, and now it's blown up in her face. She told me news of their deal with Veronica got out faster than they thought it would." He sighed. "They were moving Veronica to Regional today, a day too late."

"It sounds like a monumental screwup on all sides."

Savich said, "Now there are consequences. I'd like to drop you off at Washington Memorial to deal with all the folk there, media, Metro, politicians looking for a sound bite. It'll be a madhouse. Grayson said she tried to call me last night, but she'd heard someone set fire to our house." He grinned at Sherlock. "Grayson made it sound like I was a slacker."

"Not a problem. I'll get a whip and a chair if I need to, keep control of the zoo. You, a slacker? Find out how this happened, see how Marsia Gay managed it."

Savich dropped Sherlock off at Washington Memorial Hospital with a quick kiss for good luck and drove directly to the D.C. Jail on D Street, fighting the ever-insane morning traffic. Grayson had asked to meet him there so they could question Marsia together, but Savich had asked her to wait. He wanted to speak to Marsia himself first.

The D.C. Jail, as the facility was called, was a huge campus housing both men and women, its large, plain buildings standing stolid behind well-maintained grounds. There were always lots of parking spaces. Savich looked around as he climbed out of his Porsche. He walked to the main entrance and was met there by Warden Putney, a tall, thin man with a bit of a stoop. He looked like he'd already been beaten about the head and shoulders since Veronica Lake's attempted murder happened on his watch.

Savich wondered if Warden Putney would try to find excuses for what had happened, and sure enough, he started talking fast as he shook Savich's hand. "I hate it when you think you've done everything right, when the guards do what they're supposed to be doing, and still something like this happens. Veronica Lake was under watch by rotating guards. She had no contact whatsoever with Marsia Gay in the months they've been incarcerated here. After Lake made her deal to testify, we amped up her protection until she could be transferred to Regional. She was to be transferred today." He drew a pained breath. "A frigging day too late. I'll take you to the security room. It's down the hallway."

They were met by Wallace Freed, head of security for the women's wing. He was comfortably in his fifties, bald with a bit of a beer belly, thick brows, and sharp eyes behind black-framed glasses that kept sliding down his nose. Freed showed them into a small security office where six large screens displayed live feeds from both inside and outside the prison. Freed sat down and typed on a keyboard, and soon they were watching a recorded video from the cafeteria. The warden said, "There are currently three hundred–plus inmates to feed, so meals are served in shifts. This is the early shift, for about eighty prisoners."

Freed pointed. "Here's Veronica Lake, head down, walking toward the serving line. See, there is no roughhousing, not a whiff of impending violence. Everything appears calm. Now watch." Again, Freed pointed. "Look, eight prisoners are walking toward Lake, each from a different part of the cafeteria. It all looks accidental, their movements are fluid, easy. They're even talking to each other, nothing loud, nothing threatening."

Freed said, "Watch now, see Lake's face? She knows something is wrong." The prisoners are weaving around her, smooth and easy, until finally they begin to melt away and there's only Veronica Lake left, lying on her back on the floor with a knife wound in her chest.

Savich leaned in close. "Did you find the shiv?"

"No. They got rid of it somehow, out of sight of the cameras," Freed said.

Putney picked it up. "No way to know who stabbed her, either."

Savich said, "Did you get anything from the prisoners who were in on this murder dance?"

"We've identified them from the video, isolated all eight. Prosecutor Grayson and two Metro detectives have interviewed each woman. None of them knows a thing. They claim they didn't even see Veronica. They must have rehearsed what to say afterward when questioned. I've got to say, for a murder in plain sight, it was well planned and perfectly executed."

Savich said, "I wouldn't expect an amateur job from Marsia Gay. Of course, she's behind it. You're seeing her fine brain at work. Somehow, she got herself a small army she could trust to take Veronica out. I'd say to start, she picked one specific prisoner who has enough juice to keep the others in line, even now. I imagine each of them was offered a good deal to talk?"

Putney nodded. "Even early release for three of the nonviolent prisoners. No go. No one will say a word. Wallace, wind it back. There, stop. See that big woman with the tattoo of the rattlesnake on her biceps? Long dark hair in a braid? Looks like she eats nails for breakfast?"

At Savich's nod, he said, "That's Zanetti, Angela Zanetti, awaiting trial for murdering her boyfriend and his lover, for want of a better word, when she caught them in her bed. She's one of the gang leaders, rules with an iron fist. Believe me when I say no one refuses a demand from Zanetti. She enjoys violence, incites it. Funny thing is, three of the eight weren't under her thumb, at least that's what I thought. The one prisoner with enough juice to pull in the others? Zanetti's got the juice. She gets my vote."

Savich nodded. "All right. Let's say Gay enlisted Angela Zanetti, made Zanetti her front man—woman. Then if any of the eight confess, it would be Angela they'd have to answer to, not Gay. She'd have stayed well out of it. Ask the guards in their unit if Angela and Marsia spend much time together."

Putney said, "Sure." His eyebrow went up. "You make Gay sound like a Mata Hari."

"Gay would leave Mata Hari in the dust, but it's a lot more complicated than that. I don't see Gay in the video. She kept away, another smart move. She must have hated missing the show."

Putney said, "Gay was in the common area speaking to a guard, all chummy, nowhere near the cafeteria. Let me put the video on the monitor."

Savich pointed at the young man. "Who's the guard?"

"That's Crowder, Junior Crowder, a nice kid, conscientious, been here two years. I spoke to him myself. He said Gay is always friendly to all the guards, said she told him she was a famous sculptor until she was framed and sent here. He said he couldn't tell if she was pleased or upset when someone shouted Veronica Lake had been stabbed.

Then he had to run off to control the prisoners in the cafeteria. There's always a risk of a rampage after violence like that. Violence begets violence here."

Savich asked Freed to back the tape up to look again at Marsia. She was striking, not beautiful in the accepted sense, but there was something compelling about her face that made you look twice. Her dark hair was longer, pulled back in a ponytail. All her attention appeared focused on the guard she was speaking to, though Savich knew she was aware of exactly what was happening in the cafeteria. He said, "She not only directed the show, she gave a performance of her own."

Putney said, "However Gay managed it, we've got a wall of silence. I'm betting not one of those prisoners will ever give Zanetti up. Like I said, they're too afraid of her. Grayson was throwing out threats like water, but the prisoners looked right through her.

"It's amazing Lake is still alive. I didn't think she'd make it to the hospital. There was so much blood. It was the purest luck our physician happened to be here, and he got to the cafeteria fast, applied pressure until the ambulance arrived. She had to be brought back twice, I was told."

Putney met Savich's eyes. "I wish I could say Lake will make it, but I don't think so, not after seeing her. The prosecutor is very upset, with me, with the guards, probably at the staff serving the spaghetti."

Savich followed Putney to a small meeting room away from the new visitor's area with its comfortable chairs and unscratched glass partitions. He wanted a private face-to-face with Marsia Gay. He had no doubt Angela Zanetti had helped Marsia set up Veronica's grand finale. And he also had no doubt Marsia had seduced her as she had Veronica. Had she offered her another sort of payment, other than sex and her undying love?

He sat on the far side of a scarred laminate table. When Marsia Gay was brought into the interview room, a guard behind her, she wasn't wearing a prisoner's three-piece suit, only ties on her wrists. Her orange jumpsuit actually fit her fairly well, and orange was a good color for her. She looked as she had in the video—maybe a bit paler in person, but composed, her face serene as a Madonna's. She saw him seated at the table and smiled, showing lovely white teeth. Her eyes sparkled. She knew he'd come, and she'd looked forward to it.

She walked to the table, her smile well in place. "My, my, what a lovely break in my routine on this cold November morning. I suppose you're here to ask me about poor Veronica's murder."

38

"**S**it down, Marsia."

She sat gracefully in the seat opposite him, gave him a big smile. "May I call you Dillon, since we appear to be on a first-name basis?"

"No."

A large female guard with pretty dark eyes and a tight mouth stood behind her, arms crossed. She looked like she could bust heads if she needed to, but when she glanced at Marsia, her face relaxed into a near smile, like she was looking at a friend. Her reaction to Marsia reminded Savich that Gay was a psychopath with the ability to draw people to her, a kind of charisma that camouflaged what she really was.

Marsia sat back and crossed her arms, still smiling. "So it takes a death to bring you in for a visit. I must say you're looking fit, Agent Savich, and quite handsome. I always thought you put the Rasmussen males to shame. Do you think I'll be allowed to attend Veronica's funeral?"

"If you were allowed to go to her funeral, you would have to go dressed in orange. A pity it makes you look rather sallow, since it's the color you'll be wearing until you're too old to care."

He saw a blaze of rage, then it was gone. Marsia laughed, wagged her finger at him. "Not a bad color on me, actually. We'll see how long I'll be wearing it, Agent Savich."

She sat forward suddenly, enough to make her guard twitch, but not enough to caution her. "I know you believe I was behind Veronica's murder in the cafeteria, but I didn't know anything about it until a guard told me. I was in the common area, speaking to that very sweet guard. Junior is what he's called. I don't know his last name."

"What were you talking about?"

"There's only one thing you talk about in Washington if it's not politics. Football and the status of the Redskins."

Savich let her words settle a moment, then leaned back, crossed his arms over his chest. "What I'd rather talk about is how you orchestrated Veronica's murder like a ballet, planned the whole production. It was artistic, even, wasn't it? Had your fingerprints all over it, crazy and unique.

Come on, don't be shy, Marsia. Wouldn't you enjoy taking credit?"

"And you'd enjoy sticking me with her murder, wouldn't you, Agent Savich? Sorry, but as I said, I had nothing to do with what happened to poor Veronica. I was actually very fond of her until she turned on me, implicated me in her own attempts to murder Venus Rasmussen. I understood. Veronica was desperate, didn't know what to say, and not being very bright, she picked anyone she could to throw to the wolves."

"Don't be modest, Marsia. It really doesn't fit you at all. You weren't Veronica's accomplice; you ran the whole Rasmussen plot just like you ran the murder show in the cafeteria—by having someone else do it."

She waved her hands at him. Savich saw her fingernails were manicured, buffed. Did she get a guard to give her a file?

Marsia said, "Let me tell you something you probably don't know, and yes, I said the same thing to Warden Putney. You can ask anyone you like, actually. Veronica didn't make any friends here. She didn't realize how much she needed friends. She acted like she was better than the others, and no one likes to be treated like that, with no respect. I heard she complained about some of the prisoners, got them into trouble. And what did that crappy attitude get her? A shiv in her chest. Yes, a little over the top, but she should have known you never want to make enemies in prison."

She cocked her head to one side, her eyes not leaving his face. Again, she smiled. "How remiss of me. I forgot to ask. How are your lovely wife and your little boy? Sean's his name, right?"

Savich wanted to leap over the table and strangle her, but instead, he said without pause, keeping his voice calm, "Which one of your private gang shoved the shiv in Veronica's chest? Did you or Zanetti select the prisoner who did the job?"

Another brief flash of rage in her eyes, then she shook her head at him, like a disappointed schoolteacher. "A gang? I do not have a gang. Sure, some of the prisoners tend to stick together, and there are some natural leaders. I steer clear of them, and when I can't, I am always courteous and attentive. I'll only have to be here until I'm acquitted at my trial in a few months, after all. If I go to trial, that is."

"How long did it take you to decide Angela Zanetti was the one to not only keep you safe but solve your biggest problem? And so you seduced her, just as you seduced Veronica."

"I seduced her? You're not being very clever today. Actually, Angela—Angie—is very nice, if you show her respect. All Angie and I do is talk, play some basketball, watch TV, since there's little else to do in this place. Angie really likes *Wheel of Fortune*. We watch the show together sometimes."

"So does Angela believe in your undying love, just as Veronica did? Aren't you afraid of how she'll react when she's charged with murder and finds out you've only used her, just as you did Veronica?"

Savich saw her stiffen all over, then it fell away, and she eased and gave a little laugh. "That's a fascinating tale you're creating."

"I'm curious, however did you manage to sleep with Angela? You don't share a cell."

She cocked her head at him, tap, tap, tapped her fingers on the table.

Savich said, "All eight women who surrounded Veronica will be tried for conspiracy unless they come forward. They were all part of it. Their wall of silence will collapse sooner or later. Do you think Angela will be willing to go down alone for Veronica's murder? Or, like Veronica, will she turn on you?"

Marsia said in a low, flat voice, "How dramatic of you. It's really straightforward. Prisoners hate snitches almost as much as they hate betrayal. It's how many of them got here. Veronica's deal to lie about me made her a target. That had nothing to do with me. Ask the guards. There was lots of talk." She shrugged. "Prisoners are unforgiving, I've found. Don't you agree?"

Savich sat back in his chair. "You're dreaming if you think Veronica's death will get you off at trial."

"There you go again, wishful thinking. My lawyer tells me my case might not even get to trial now that Veronica's dead. The prosecutor has only circumstantial evidence, hearsay, and your own speculation to tie me to anything. Otherwise I'm nowhere in the picture. I know it was you who convinced the prosecutor I was the mastermind behind Veronica, that I manipulated her, even slept with her to buy her loyalty. I admit you're an excellent salesman. Talk about manipulation, you're the expert."

He talked right over her. "You acted fast when you found out Veronica was being moved today. But you've been planning her death, probably ever since you heard she and the prosecutor were talking. Actually, I'll bet you've been thinking about how to kill Veronica ever since you were both arrested. Congratulations. The whole production was impressive." He sat back and clapped, slowly, once, twice, three times. "The reason you'll fail, Marsia? You believe you're smarter than everyone else, but you're not. You had to manipulate only Veronica the first time, and look what happened. You didn't learn from that mistake. This time you involved eight people. Very stupid."

She jerked up, yelled, "I am not stupid! We'll see who's stupid before this is over!" She stopped when the guard started toward her, looking worried, and eased back down in her seat. She drew a deep breath. "I saw on the news this morning there was a fire at your house in Georgetown last night. I hope Agent Sherlock and your little boy are all right. Such a pity you weren't there."

It all slid into place. "And that fire at my house

happened on the same day you had Veronica stabbed. Hard to miss that, Marsia. It took you long enough to bring it up, but you couldn't help yourself." He leaned forward. "Are you finally taking credit for something you've done?"

An arched dark eyebrow went up. "Come, Agent Savich, you're being dramatic again. One never knows when a fire can start. Faulty wiring, leaving the oven on, who knows? You can never be sure. Anyone can die at any time, can't they? Even in a cafeteria surrounded by a hundred people."

He half rose and leaned toward her, his voice hard. "That was your biggest mistake, Marsia. You tried to kill my family, and you failed. I'm going to find the man you hired, and that crime will keep you in prison for the rest of your life, this time in maximum security."

She leaped to the bait. "You're going to what? Find a nonexistent man I supposedly hired? You, a no-talent cop? Look at your boorish little excuse for art—whittling! I'll be back in my studio soon, sculpting the female form as only a true artist can envision it. What you do is laughable, pitiful." She paused, got control, and gave him a full-bodied sneer. "Actually, it's too bad I'm not content to whittle like you do, lots of wood here, you know?"

"You'd have to chew the wood, Marsia, no knives for prisoners. I doubt a shiv would do the job."

Fury and hatred pumped off her in waves. Savich sat back, gave her his own sneer. "Your sculptures

are grotesque, random pieces of metal unrecogniz-
able as anything meaningful or inspiring. You said
you admired my grandmother's paintings. Sarah
Elliott's art is in museums. And what you call your
art, Marsia? Nothing you've ever done will gain
you that kind of recognition. You're the one who's
pitiful. You'll be in an institution for the rest of your
natural life, with nothing to do but seduce other
prisoners in return for less and less, until you're too
old, and they turn on you."

She was panting, hitting her tied fists against the
tabletop. "You bastard! You'll never prove a thing.
Fact is, *Dillon*, Veronica Lake was a loser in life, but
in death, she'll be my salvation. And you? We'll have
to see, won't we?"

Savich looked at the woman who wanted not
only him to die, but also Sherlock and Sean. But
now he knew. She'd taunted him with it.

His voice was dismissive. "You'll find prison slowly
leaches the life out of you, Marsia, hollows you out
until you have no real substance. Life becomes a matter of enduring, nothing more. You really think you
can get away with murdering Veronica? Get away with
setting my house on fire, endangering Sherlock and
my son? Are you that stupid?"

She screamed at him, "Just try to screw with me!
You're the one who'll regret it! I always win!"

Savich said to the guard, who seemed frozen in
place, "I'm done with her. Take her back to her cell."

39

Mrs. Filly was no longer a gypsy. She was all businesswoman: black slacks, a slouchy black linen jacket over a white sweater, a string of pearls around her neck. She was explaining to a couple of parents why she didn't carry Winnie the Pooh puzzles while trying to keep an eye on their four children roaming around the store, yelling and pointing, praying they wouldn't try to pull any of the puzzles apart.

Chief Wilde's cell buzzed with a text from Dillon. He read it and looked up at Pippa. "Dillon says he couldn't reach you so he texted me. He's sure Marsia Gay is behind the fire at his house, says it makes sense Black Hoodie could have struck you down to lure him away from his house, then driven to D.C. and set the fire while he was away. He wants us to find out how Black Hoodie's connected to Marsia Gay here in St. Lumis. Marsia Gay? Who's she?"

Pippa said, "All I remember is she was arrested for attempted murder some months ago. I'll read up on her on my tablet when we get back to Mrs. Trumbo's. It was Dillon who arrested her. She'd be in the D.C. Jail awaiting trial."

Wilde said, "But why lure him away? Wouldn't she want him in the house? See him in the flames like Major Trumbo? Wasn't that the point?"

"I don't know, but whoever set the fire knew Sherlock and their little boy were there."

"It's about revenge, then, and she went after family first. It would have been possible for Gay to communicate through a visitor, her lawyer, or maybe through another prisoner. I had one prisoner in Philadelphia who asked his priest to mail a letter for him. Did Savich tell you how he connected the fire specifically to Gay?"

Pippa said, "He'll tell us when we see him again. Did the priest mail the letter?"

"You bet. The priest felt sorry for him, believed he was falsely accused, which he wasn't. And yes, he's in jail now for fifteen to life. The prisoner, not the priest."

She reached into her pocket but came up empty. "I keep forgetting Black Hoodie took my cell. Call up the photo of the red-box puzzle Dil-

lon sent to you. Let's compare it to the original."
She pointed toward Mrs. Filly's Major Trumbo
puzzle on a shelf next to them. Wilde stared from
it to Dillon's puzzle. He said, "Aside from Major
Trumbo getting burned alive and the dead birds
on the pier and human bones on the sidewalk, the
main difference is it looks homemade."

"Good morning, Ms. Cinelli, Chief Wilde. A bit
on the nippy side this morning, isn't it?"

Pippa looked up and smiled. "Good morning,
Mrs. Filly. Let me introduce myself properly. I'm
Special Agent Pippa Cinelli, FBI. I can't show you
my credentials—they were stolen yesterday—so
Chief Wilde has to vouch for me."

Maude gaped at her. "What? You're an FBI
agent? But—I don't understand, Ms. Cinelli." She
looked at Wilde, who nodded. "But you're here
visiting, aren't you?"

Pippa said, "I was here in St. Lumis undercover,
Mrs. Filly. I couldn't tell anyone."

"But you're not undercover today? Why? What is
going on? Why are you here to see me?"

"The people I'm here to investigate already know
I'm here. Let me explain." Pippa told her about
being struck on the head in the abandoned grocery
store and left there, unconscious and tied up, and
how she'd escaped. "I ran to Chief Wilde's house
last night. My boss, Agent Dillon Savich, drove here
from Washington."

Maude blinked at her, slowly nodded. "That's

horrible, but I don't understand. Are you all right? Were you hurt?"

"My head aches a bit, and my wrists are still raw, but nothing debilitating."

Mrs. Filly was shaking her head. "I've never heard of such a thing, not in St. Lumis. What about your boss, Agent Cinelli? Is he still here?"

"No, Agent Savich had to go back to Washington."

"Why on earth are you talking to me? What is this all about?"

Pippa pointed to Major Trumbo's puzzle. "It all started with this puzzle, Mrs. Filly."

"That silly puzzle of Major Trumbo? I remember you were very interested in that puzzle when you were here on Sunday morning, asked me all sorts of questions, but what does it have to do with the FBI? Why you were hit on the head?"

"The man who struck me also took my cell phone, so Chief Wilde will have to show you." Wilde held his cell phone out to Mrs. Filly. She pulled a pair of glasses out of her jacket pocket and leaned close.

"Oh dear, is that a copy of my puzzle? But wait—" She gulped. "Major Trumbo is burning. And all those birds and bones are scattered on the pier and sidewalk." She took off her glasses and looked from Pippa to Chief Wilde. "What is this all about?"

Pippa told her about the three red boxes and how

the third had arrived only yesterday, the same day Pippa was attacked. "Agent Savich drove here when I called to tell him what happened. While he was at Chief Wilde's house, his own house was set on fire in Washington with his wife and son inside, asleep. Yes, they're all right, but Agent Savich drove back immediately. Mrs. Filly, we need to know the names of everyone who bought this puzzle."

Mrs. Filly fiddled with her pearls. "Well, I've sold maybe half a dozen, mostly to locals who knew Major Trumbo and got a kick out of seeing a puzzle of the town with the major in it. I remember I sold one to Joyce Sleeman for her husband's birthday. Mr. Sleeman and Major Trumbo had what you'd call a complicated relationship. She thought he'd get a kick out of seeing the major all paunchy and sneering, wearing a Grateful Dead T-shirt."

Pippa said, "Anyone else local you can remember?"

"There was Harber Fossen, an old drinking buddy of the major's. I remember joking with him about the T-shirt. And there was Jamie Frost, who lived next door to us when we were married, but he's a nerd, always fixing computers, harmless. Those are the only locals I remember off the top of my head."

Pippa said, "Do you have records you could check?"

"I have some credit card records, going back, but

I doubt I could remember who bought what. A lot of people in town have bought my puzzles over the years."

Wilde said, "Have you ever had a customer copy the puzzle, maybe someone you gave instructions to?"

She shook her head. "Never. Most everyone wants to copy Indiana Jones in the pit with all the snakes, or the kraken."

"Have you ever seen anyone take a picture of this puzzle?"

"No, never did, but that doesn't mean someone didn't. Of course, when I finished it, Lill snapped countess shots with her iPad, while laughing her head off."

Pippa said, "Could you tell us how someone would make a puzzle like that, Mrs. Filly?"

"All you would need is a drawing or a photo to copy and enlarge, an X-Acto knife, acid-free glue, and cardboard. You find whatever puzzle template you like online, outline the puzzle pieces on the back of the cardboard, and cut. Here I apply acrylic to finish them off, you know, make them look professional, but a seal isn't necessary if you're using a photograph. Of course, whoever made that puzzle on your phone altered the picture digitally first, easy enough with Photoshop. Agent, Chief, what strikes me is he didn't even bother to make it look good. See here, the shapes of the pieces match the original, but some of the edges are ragged, some bent. I doubt he used an X-Acto knife, probably a pair of scissors."

Pippa said, "The puzzle wasn't the point, it was the subject."

Wilde said, "I never met Major Trumbo, Mrs. Filly, but it seems to me you took some artistic license. The big belly? The yellow snake kissing his cheek? He doesn't look like he has much of a mouth."

"Oh, Major Trumbo had a mouth all right, but he could seam it into a thin line when he wanted to put you down. He could still sneer, blight you, with that thin line. I guess you could say the puzzle was my payback to that philanderer."

"Philanderer?"

Mrs. Filly's eyes showed some heat, not much, but enough for Pippa to see it. So there was a little anger left. "He was always going on out-of-town trips, never told me why, said it was none of my business. I knew he was cheating on me—lipstick on his clothes, bits of paper left on the dresser with phone numbers, names, you get the gist. I think he did it on purpose. He was proud of his cheating. One day he told me he wanted a divorce. I asked him her name. He smiled from ear to ear, told me her name was Lillian Pomfrey. She had a son by a previous marriage, and she managed a hotel in Baltimore, where he'd met her. He said she understood him, she'd do anything for him, things I wouldn't. Can you believe he actually used that tired old cliché? I told him good luck with her and let me know what she'd be doing for him six months from now. He didn't hit me, but I knew he wanted to. I filed for divorce myself. Of course, I should have done it long before. My only demand was he pay off the mortgage on my puzzle store, which he did. After fifteen years of dealing with the major, believe me, I was glad to have another poor woman take him on. I celebrated with a bottle of champagne."

She beamed at them and laughed.

40

Mrs. Filly hiccupped and shook her head. "Forgive me. Now, I will admit I was surprised a couple of years later when Major Trumbo and Lill moved back to St. Lumis to retire here."

Wilde said, "I know the major died five years ago, right? How did he die?"

"All I know is he and Lill went to visit her son at his vacation cabin somewhere in the Poconos. Her son is a textile artist, creates beautiful pictures with thread on his loom. When Lill came back to St. Lumis two weeks later, she was carrying the major in an urn, said he'd fallen over with a heart attack, died instantly."

Pippa said, "And over the years you and Mrs. Trumbo have become friends?"

"That's right. It didn't take long. We had coffee and talked about marriage to the major, about how he could be mean and nasty as all get-out. There wasn't much left for us to do but laugh about him and thank the powers that be we didn't have to deal with him ever again. Now I think about it, having him in common is what made us friends. I made the puzzle to remind us we were free of the old lecher." She smiled.

Pippa said, "When did you make the puzzle, Mrs. Filly?"

"Ah, I made it shortly after he ended up in that urn on Lill's mantel, not in the basement, where he belonged. She did it as a joke, I think, although she said it was a fitting place for him. She told me one of the visitors at the B&B asked her about the urn and she told a fine tale about how Major Trumbo was a big game hunter in Africa and he was gored by a rhinoceros." She gave them a big smile, only to have it fall off her face. "Oh dear, she's spotted you, Chief."

Pippa looked up when the shop door opened and Freddie Sleeman burst in like she'd been shot from a cannon. She did not look happy.

Pippa had more questions for Mrs. Filly, and now this. Freddie Sleeman was all she needed. She forced a smile. "Hello, Ms. Sleeman. How are you this chilly morning?"

Freddie ignored her. "Wilde! What a surprise to see you here of all places."

"Good morning, Freddie," Wilde said.

Freddie turned to Pippa, sent her chin up. "What are you doing here? And with Chief Wilde? I thought you'd have left town by now."

"Nope, still here and we're puzzle shopping."

"Puzzle shopping? That's ridiculous."

"Good morning, Freddie," Mrs. Filly said. "How is your mother?"

"Mother? She's like she always is, spends more time with the downtrodden than she does with her own family." She turned back to Pippa. "Of course you know my name, everyone knows my name, but I don't remember yours."

Mrs. Filly tried, she really did. Pippa appreciated her effort. "And your dear brother? How are he and his sweet family?"

"Sweet? How very nice for us. So, what's your name? And why are you here?"

"I'm Special Agent Pippa Cinelli, FBI."

Freddie stared hard at her. "You, FBI? An agent? Are you joking?"

Wilde said, "No, she's not, Freddie. Actually, Agent Cinelli grew up here in St. Lumis. Are you also here to look at puzzles? We were studying Major Trumbo's puzzle."

Freddie spared half a glance at Major Trumbo's puzzle, shook her head. "That ridiculous old man was disgusting. I hate it that my dad has his puzzle in his study at home."

Wilde said, "If you didn't come to buy a puzzle, then why did you come in, Freddie?"

Freddie grabbed up a puzzle of Saint Patrick surrounded by snakes. "Anjolina has a birthday next week. This will do."

"Anjolina's too young for this puzzle, Freddie. It would give her nightmares. And isn't her birthday in March?"

"Anjolina's age is irrelevant. No puzzle in this store would frighten her. No, her birthday is next week. Gift wrap it, Mrs. Filly."

Mrs. Filly took the puzzle. "Agent Cinelli, let me check how many Major Trumbo puzzles are left. I've remembered a couple more people, and I'll make up a short list." She turned on her heel and was through the door at the back of the shop fast, as if escaping.

Wilde said, "Freddie, have you seen any men around St. Lumis you didn't recognize?"

"What is this all about?" She pointed a sharp fingernail at Pippa. "If you are an FBI agent, then why are you all over Chief Wilde? It's unprofessional. And no, I haven't seen any strange men. What does that have to do with Major Trumbo's puzzle?"

This young woman, either a born pain in the butt or spoiled to death since the cradle, was the last thing Pippa needed. Pippa didn't think she'd ever been considered a threat before. If not for everything being at a critical point, she might be amused. But not now.

Pippa said, "Of course you have lots of questions, Ms. Sleeman, but I don't have time to answer them right now. Tell you what, would you entertain Chief Wilde while I speak to Mrs. Filly?" Pippa turned on her heel and walked toward the back of the shop.

Freddie yelled after her, "You won't get Wilde, do you hear me? He'll get tired of you really fast, and you're not even pretty. That French braid of yours looks ratty, probably because you slept with him last night at his cottage, didn't you? I know the truth, so don't lie."

That brought Pippa up short. She slowly turned back.

Wilde raised a dark brow. "And how do you know Agent Cinelli was at my cottage last night, Freddie?"

"Davie told me."

Davie Hauck, his night deputy, was normally a clam, but Wilde had heard Davie really liked Freddie Sleeman. He probably tried to impress her by telling her how he'd cruised the chief's neighborhood, keeping watch for a suspicious character who was after a woman. He said, "Actually, we did spend the night at my house, then went back to Major Trumbo's B&B for a good breakfast this morning."

"My father will make sure you're gone soon enough." And Freddie gave Wilde nothing short of a steaming look, turned on her heel, and left the shop, slamming the door.

Mrs. Filly came out of her office, holding the wrapped Saint Patrick puzzle in one hand and a piece of paper in the other. She said blankly, "Sorry, I have to admit I waited until I heard her leave. Freddie can be such a trial. You should marry her, Chief, put her out of her—and our—misery. But wait, you're a good boy, you'd suffer too much. Here's the list, very short, as you can see. I wonder if I should keep the puzzle wrapped?"

"You should make it a surprise puzzle, charge a dollar more for it," Pippa said. "Just one more question, Mrs. Filly, and we'll leave you alone. Have you noticed any strangers around town who've stayed on after the Halloween bash at Leveler's Inn?"

"Of course, but not many, mostly older people and a couple of families, like the one you saw when you came in." She rolled her eyes.

"How about men who came into your shop? Any strangers you noticed, wondered about?"

Mrs. Filly thought a moment, then shook her head. "I'm sorry, Agent Cinelli, but no. You're thinking about the man who hit you, aren't you?"

When Pippa and Chief Wilde left the shop, the weather had turned even colder. Pippa pulled her leather jacket close and carefully pulled on leather gloves over her bandaged hands. She said, "Well, we did learn some interesting history." She poked his arm. "And Ms. Sleeman certainly enlivened the morning."

"She always does." Wilde looked down at his watch. "The sketch artist should be arriving at the station. Let's go see what you can remember. Oh yeah, your French braid looked ratty last night, not today."

41

Sherlock looked up from her tablet when Savich turned off at the Sinack exit. "Apparently Sinack's known for its early American antiques and its six white church spires." She put down her tablet and turned to face him. "Enough about Sinack. Dillon, what I'm really worried about is my Steinway. I called Ian—you remember Mr. Phipps—and he's coming today to check out how bad the water damage is." She sighed. "There's so much we have to do. We haven't even finished sorting through all our clothes, Dillon. We'll have to rebuild the kitchen, and once that construction is done, we'll need all new appliances." She groaned. "Every time I think about what needs to be done, something new pops up, and the list gets longer. Bless your mom for dealing with the cleanup crew today, but I don't want her doing too much."

Savich reached over and took her hand. "I've got a surprise for you, Sherlock. It's a secret weapon. Senator Monroe called this morning when you were in the shower. He gave me the name of a woman here in Washington, Janet Mickelson. She's a logistics expert. She specializes in the aftermath of home fires, from determining what needs to be replaced to dealing with contractors for any necessary rebuilding, the kitchen in our case. I didn't know such a person existed. Robert said he didn't, either, until his home caught fire three years ago, said the logistics expert earned every dime he paid her. And yes, Mickelson will get our approval at every step. She'll do as much or as little as we want." He gave her a big smile. "Best thing? She works directly with insurance companies and makes sure they don't try to slither out of their responsibilities. She gets their approval as she goes along."

Sherlock shook her head at him, smiled. "I wish you'd stuck your head in the shower and told me about this fire fairy godmother while you washed my hair. Janet Mickelson sounds amazing. Dillon, I think I'll make Senator Monroe an apple pie—when I have my kitchen back and my new appliances. Knowing we'll have our own personal rottweiler really changes the landscape." She gave him a huge smile. "All right, now we can talk about Miranda Stirling. I thought you'd have asked Griffin to interview her."

He was silent a moment as he smoothly passed a Chevy Silverado. "Rebekah needs protection, and that means Griffin has to stick close. Also, Griffin and Rebekah are going to see her grandmother in Clairemont."

"Yes, yes, all true, but you know what I think? You're hooked. What with Zoltan disappearing, and all the drama from so many years ago. You want to stay right in the middle of it, don't you?"

He shot her a smile. "Miranda Stirling was right in the middle of everything back in 1995. She and Rebekah's grandmother are the two people closest to whatever happened to Nate Elderby. I'm hoping she'll tell us what she thought actually happened at the time, and what she thinks now after so many years have passed."

They drove through Sinack's charming colonial downtown, turned on East Jacobs Street. Savich carefully steered around an ancient pale-blue-and-white Cadillac, a gray head barely visible above the steering wheel.

Three blocks later, they turned onto Elm Street, into an older settled neighborhood with big houses and bigger yards, shaded by maples and oaks. Savich found himself thinking the neighborhood would be a great place to bring kids on Halloween. He pulled in behind a white Lexus. "Mrs. Stirling seemed excited we were coming to see her. I didn't tell her what it was about, and she didn't ask."

"I wonder why she didn't ask. I mean, the FBI

calls you, wants to come over, and you don't ask what it's all about? Maybe she already guessed."

They were met at the freshly painted dark blue front door by a tall, very fit woman wearing a big fuchsia shirt, black leggings, and black ballet slippers on long narrow feet. They'd called up photos of her and knew she was forty-eight, good-looking, and stylish. But Miranda Stirling in person was more, lots more. Her high, sharp cheekbones and her sloe-eyed dark looks were striking. Sherlock imagined she'd still be beautiful at ninety. She wore her dark brown hair in a bob around her face, not a single gray hair showing. But it was her nearly black eyes that were the draw—mysterious and compelling. Sherlock imagined she'd been a knockout as a young woman, probably got whatever she went after.

"Mrs. Stirling?"

She nodded. "Agent Savich?" At his nod, she looked at Sherlock, blinked, then smiled really big. "Of course I know who you are, Agent Sherlock. It's an honor to meet you. Do come in."

They showed Mrs. Stirling their creds and followed her into a large entry hall, its wide-oak-plank floor scattered with early American carpets, all dark colors and patterns that should have made the space dim, but didn't. It looked rich. The living room, like the entrance hall, was right out of the colonial period, with a dark-beamed ceiling, cream-painted walls covered with an assortment of stylized co-

lonial paintings, and inset dark mahogany bookshelves. A brick fireplace sat between two long,
narrow windows, facing an arrangement of sofas
and comfortable chairs. An old, dark-patterned carpet covered most of the living room floor. There was
even an antique broom leaning against the fireplace.

Sherlock said, "I feel like I've stepped back in
time."

Mrs. Stirling smiled, very pleased. "I found a
print of the colonial living room I wanted, and
my husband, Frank, helped me bring it to life.
I had the interest and the contacts, and in addition to taking great care of people's teeth—he's a
dentist—he has quite the eye. As for stepping back
in time, it's all quite lovely until it's too hot or too
cold, like today, and then I'm grateful for the cen-
tral heating. Do sit down." She pointed to a brown
rolled-arm sofa.

Mrs. Stirling sat opposite them in a high-backed
chair, her incredible eyes intent on their faces. She
said without hesitation, "I was very surprised and
pleased to hear from you. I have to say, it's about
time. Are you here about Nate's murder or about
the money? Or both?"

Savich didn't get surprised easily, but Miranda
had managed it. He'd planned to steer her slowly
back in time, help her recall memories and details.
He smiled at her. "Yes, you're right. I imagine you'd
think it is about time. Your thoughts about Mr.
Elderby and what happened to him are exactly

what we'd like to know. And, of course, anything you know about stolen money."

She paused a moment. "When I heard about John's death last month, I wondered if what happened back in 1995 would resurface. I'm very pleased to see it has. And no, I didn't go to the funeral. I didn't want to have to see Gemma, John's widow, again. To be blunt, I know she would have hated seeing me."

Miranda drew a deep breath, cocked her head to one side. "Where to start?" She sat forward and looked back and forth between them. "I was only twenty-three when I married Nate, who was some twenty-five years my senior. I know how that sounds, but when you're twenty-three, you don't think about him being on Social Security by the time you're forty. All you see is a man in his prime, well-known, smart, successful, and the biggie? He loved me." She rolled her eyes. "Ah, one's optimism at twenty-three. As you know, Nate was a big-time criminal lawyer, really talented in the courtroom. I knew firsthand about some of his clients since I'd seen him in court a dozen times. That's how we met. I'd been assigned to spend a year on the court and the crime beat with a senior reporter at the *Richmond Tribune*, so I was well aware he defended some scary people. As I said, he was a big name locally, a beautiful man, really. We were married three months later.

"We'd been married maybe six months when

he told me in bed one night we were leaving the country in two days. He said money wouldn't be a problem, we'd live anywhere I liked. I said Bali, thinking he was joking, but of course, he wasn't. When I realized he was perfectly serious, I asked if one of his criminal clients had threatened him, and he said yes. I knew he was concerned about one particularly vicious client's criminal father, a man named Showalter. Nate lost the son's murder case. The son had stabbed his wife, and the evidence was overwhelming. I had no trouble believing someone like Showalter, the father, could kill him as well as me in retribution. I asked Nate if it was Showalter, but he only wanted to talk about how perfect the timing was for us, how we'd have a lifelong honeymoon. He grinned really big, kissed me, and made me promise I'd only wear bikinis on the beach in Bali."

She paused, splayed her hands in front of her. "Agents, I was in love with my husband, still had stars in my eyes. Leave the country? It sounded like pure romantic adventure to me. I still had my mom, but we could certainly keep in close touch. So I readily agreed to leave the country with him. I remember before I fell asleep, Nate told me I was to pack only the clothes I needed, to leave the rest. It was then he dropped the money bomb. He said he was getting a lot of money due to him the next day. I asked him what money, where was it coming from, but he wouldn't tell me anything else. I knew he was very well-to-do, no money problems, but the way he talked about that money, his excitement mixed with fear, it seemed like a very big deal to him. I wondered if he had stolen some of that money, but I couldn't ask him, I simply couldn't. He was my husband, and the fact was, I wouldn't believe he was a crook. But Nate never got that money, and he drowned the next day while fishing by himself, they said, something he rarely did. John Clarkson was usually with Nate. I never found out why they weren't together that day, but I do remember John was home and not in Washington the day Nate drowned."

42

Savich said, "Nate and John Clarkson had been friends since they were boys, isn't that right, Mrs. Stirling?"

Miranda looked toward the fireplace when a big spurt of flame shot up from the stacked logs. She sighed. "Actually, once we were married, I soon came to realize I didn't know the half of it. It didn't take long for me to feel like I was married to both men. They were inseparable when John was home from Washington. He and Gemma were always with us, always. I was the last part of a foursome, the very young newcomer. I started to wonder whether Nate married me for the sex and because I looked good on his arm. But he kept saying he loved me, easy enough words to say.

"As for John Clarkson, I liked him, and he liked me. He seemed larger than life like Nate, sexy like Nate, and powerful in Congress, serving on important committees, a really big deal." She shook her head. "The problem was Gemma. She couldn't stand me. I thought it was because she'd been close to Lorna, Nate's first wife, but when I mentioned it to Nate, he said Gemma hadn't particularly liked Lorna, either, that Lorna never paid her any mind and neither should I. The three of them had such a long, rich history together that it never occurred to him Gemma's not liking me might change that.

"I suppose Gemma thought I was a gold digger. She was old enough to be my mother, just as both John and Nate could have been my father. When my own mother met Gemma, she pulled me aside and told me it had to be difficult for her, having someone her daughter's age marrying her husband's best friend. She told me to be patient but to hold my own. Then my mother, bless her, never said another word.

"Of course, Gemma and Nate were also very close, had been for years, and she was very protective of him. Sure, in front of Nate and John, she'd be civil, but no matter what I tried, complimenting her, asking her advice, nothing worked. She always kept me in my place, always treated me like a little sexpot with fluffy hair."

Savich said, "When we arrived, you said you

thought Nate was murdered. Could you tell us why you believe that?"

"Let me say right away I heard all the rumors about John killing his best friend. After all, didn't they always fish together? I don't know who started those rumors, but wondered if it was the woman running against John for his congressional seat. Let me be very clear about this, though: John didn't murder Nate. That's ridiculous. They were closer than brothers; they shared most everything.

"Of course, I was the first person the police focused on. It would have been so easy, so convenient for them if I was guilty—the young wife bored with her older husband, wanting his money. But alas for them, I was out of town that day, saying goodbye to my mom. As you know, the police ruled Nate was drunk and fell overboard. He did have alcohol in his blood, and the M.E. decided it was enough to debilitate him, so they ruled accidental drowning. It's true Nate liked to drink, but he held his liquor well. It never made sense to me he'd be falling-down drunk in the middle of the day by himself. Let me add, the local police owed John a lot of favors—he helped their new police station get funded. They wanted to protect him from those silly rumors in his upcoming election, and I believe that's the main reason they were so fast to rule accidental death by drowning. I told them Nate said he'd been threatened, probably by a criminal named Showalter, that we'd been planning to leave because of the threat. They looked at Nate's client list, especially those he failed to get off at trial, but it didn't lead anywhere."

Miranda paused, shook her head. "Six months with Nate and then I was a widow, my husband probably murdered, and everything was—just over. It seems like a different life now, and I'm certainly not that young woman anymore."

Savich said, "Mrs. Stirling, you didn't know how Nate died, didn't understand what he'd told you the night before he drowned. You must have spoken to John about it, about the money Nate was expecting to get."

"Yes. John said he didn't know anything about it, couldn't imagine what Nate was talking about. Then he fell apart again and held me close and cried. We cried together. I didn't ask him again about the money. I wouldn't have had any right to it anyway."

Savich sat forward. "But it makes sense to you he was meeting someone about the money the next day and that's who killed him?"

"Ah, yes, if there was a partner, it had to be John, or at least he'd have known about it. Could the stolen money have come from the government somehow, have something to do with John being on those committees in Congress? I don't know. I had to let it go, so I did."

Savich said, "Mrs. Stirling, did you know Rebekah, John and Gemma's granddaughter?"

"I remember her very well. I saw on the news Rebekah was attacked, last Thursday, wasn't it? But Congressman Manvers said she was fine and the police were investigating. I hope she is. I don't suppose you'd tell me if Rebekah is somehow involved in all this?"

"We believe she is, Mrs. Stirling. But what her husband said is true. She's fine. What do you remember of her?"

"I remember she was with John whenever he could manage it. Her mother, Caitlin, never seemed to mind. In fact, I only met Caitlin a couple of times. But Rebekah, yes, such a pretty little girl, eager, bright, and she had a kind heart, unusual, I think, for a child that young. John was always talking about how smart she was, how she loved the children's stories he made up about him and Nate and their adventures. I remember thinking more than once that John loved her more than he loved Gemma, more than he loved his own daughter, Caitlin. I remember there was no love lost between Gemma and her daughter, either. I don't know why, but I thought it odd, since I've always been so close to my own mother.

"Rebekah looked quite a bit like Caitlin and a lot like John. And now Rebekah's all grown up. Imagine, she even married a congressman like her grandfather. I was surprised she married a man so many years her senior, just as I did. I wondered if she felt so comfortable with him because of her grandfather.

I saw a wedding photo of her in the *Post*. She looked striking."

Sherlock said, "Is that a photo of your husband, Mrs. Stirling?" She nodded toward a framed photo.

"Yes, that's Frank. I met my prince at a New Year's Eve party in 2010. Glad to say he keeps my teeth in perfect condition." She gave them a big grin, showing straight white teeth. "He's my junior by ten years," she added, and grinned even bigger.

43

Pippa and Chief Wilde ate hamburgers at the Wave, a popular tourist greasy spoon opposite the ancient pier in the red-box puzzle. Thankfully, there weren't any dead birds or human bones scattered about, no Major Trumbo hanging out of a window of the Alworth Hotel.

Pippa stared sadly at the final two bites of her cheeseburger. "Juicy and perfect. Alas, no more room. Ah, there's one fry left." She popped it into her mouth, chewed slowly, eyes closed. Wilde started laughing at her. She patted her mouth, wagged her finger at him. "You're jealous because I nabbed it before you."

He ate the final bite of his own hamburger and sat back. "Too bad you and Mrs. Trout had no luck with that sketch of Black Hoodie, but she did say up front she's better at drawing a cactus than a person."

"Mrs. Trout is really good. She tried, and I was hopeful. But you're right, what we came up with isn't anything useful. It was dark and I guess I was still woozy from the knock on the head. About all I could tell her was he had a slight build and was younger rather than older. And I only had an impression of his profile inside that hoodie. Good luck with that."

"You done scraping up fries? Good. I want us to go to that old abandoned grocery store where Black Hoodie attacked you." He waggled a dark eyebrow. "If this was Philadelphia, we'd have had a team in there by now."

They stepped outside into a cold afternoon under a sullen sky that promised rain. There weren't any tourists in sight, only locals hunkered down in coats, stoically going about their business. They walked the same route Pippa had taken. Twenty minutes later, they stood in front of the derelict grocery store. In the dull gray light, the building looked even more desolate than it had the day before.

Wilde said over his shoulder as he pushed open the creaking door, "When I first arrived in St. Lumis, I spent a week exploring every inch of the town, even checked out this old store. When I happened to mention this particular eyesore to Mr.

Sleeman, he told me he'd tried to buy the building from Hubert Duncan, a retired dentist whose grandfather had run the store way back when, but no go. Evidently the two men hadn't gotten along for many years. Sleeman didn't tell me what his plans were if he had gotten ahold of it. Maybe he'd have built a skating rink, cold enough for it today."

They stood in light dimmer than it had been on Monday, and breathed in cold, fetid air. Wilde looked around. "Hasn't changed a bit since I was in here three years ago." He pointed to Pippa's footprints, clear in the dust. "Okay, Cinelli, lead me through what happened."

"I was standing here when I heard a low, muffled voice that sounded like a man in pain. 'I'm here. Back here. Help me.' Because I'm an idiot, I didn't think, didn't even pause. I jumped on my steed and went off to find him."

He tapped her on the shoulder. "I don't want to hear that idiot crap. You're a cop, of course you acted. Did he have an accent you could make out?"

She shook her head. "I didn't hear anything distinctive, so mid-Atlantic, I'd say." She gave him a crooked grin. "As in right here. Easy to say, I know, since we're here and not in Texas." She stared around the dilapidated space, breathed in the mold. "Over there is where he struck me down."

Wilde pulled out his cell, punched on the light, went down on his haunches, and studied the area. "That was where he was hiding," she said, "behind one of the storage racks." Wilde saw Pippa's footprints clearly, and others, larger prints more smeared.

"When I got my brain back together, I heard him talking on his cell, and that's when I got a glimpse of him. He hit me again. See this clear path through all the dust? That's me. When I woke up the second time, I inched my way across the floor on my butt, since my hands were tied behind my back and my ankles were wrapped tight."

Wilde rose, followed her progress through the dust, and saw the long hook attached to a wooden pole with her blood on the sharp tip. He said, "Show me your hands."

Pippa arched a brow, then carefully eased off her gloves to show her hands, still partly covered with gauze bandages. He cupped one at a time in his palm but saw no sign of blood. He looked down at her. She was wearing no makeup and a red ski cap over her long French braid. He raised his hand, but then lowered it and shook his head. "I gotta say, Cinelli, scooting across the floor on your butt, your hands tied behind your back, sawing away on that hook, that took grit. You did good, really good. I'd still like to have the doctor check out your hands."

"My hands are fine. They don't hurt, not after the three aspirin I took this morning. Let's see if we can follow Black Hoodie's footprints."

"He stayed on the outside perimeter," Wilde said, pointing, "then he moved inward behind the racks, stopped where he could hide and wait for you to come in."

Pippa touched her fingertips to the back of her head. "Do you know, I nearly didn't come in here. He couldn't have known, either. But he took the chance, and it paid off for him. I suppose he would have tried to take me down someplace else if he'd had to."

Wilde said, "Probably. With all the dirt and dust, it isn't hard to see where he was hiding. Here, hold my cell and aim the light down here." Wilde set his boot next to one of the prints behind a storage rack. "I wear a twelve. This print is no more than a size nine. Goes with your description of him being slight. He went down on his haunches when he heard you. I'll bet he leaned forward, probably steadied himself with a hand on this rack. Let's see what we can see." He pulled a small black plastic carry case out of his pocket. "This, Agent Cinelli, is my own personal portable latent fingerprint kit, given to me by my dad when I made detective. I always carried it in Philadelphia." He opened it to show a stack of two-by-three black cards, a jar of latent powder, a roll of lifting tape, and a fiberglass fingerprint brush.

Pippa said, "A fingerprint kit? Wow, I'm impressed you thought to bring it with you today." She stepped back, out of his way.

"Keep the light right here." Wilde dipped the brush into the latent powder. "No doubt a gazillion people have handled these storage racks over the decades, but it's worth a shot." She watched him carefully dust on the powder.

She craned her neck to look over his shoulder. "Well, that's not a surprise—nothing but smudges."

"Have faith, Cinelli." Then Wilde whistled. "Look at that, a clear thumbprint, higher than I'd have thought, which means he stretched up to get a better view of you." He lightly pressed down a thick strip of tape and lifted off the print. "I'm using white powder, so black cards, as you already know. Here we go. Digits crossed, Cinelli."

She watched him carefully press the tape onto the card. And there it was, a distinct thumbprint.

"Amazing. But why only a thumbprint? I would have thought he'd use his whole hand to steady himself."

"I think he did. He asked you to come help him, then he had to push off fast to hit you, and that smeared his other fingerprints."

"This may be all we need," Pippa said, and felt a punch of optimism.

"If we're lucky and his thumbprint's in the system."

Pippa rose, rubbed her hands over her arms, and winced. She watched him repack his kit and slip it into his pocket. She looked back at where she'd been standing when Black Hoodie hit her. She stared at the bloody hook still lying in the corner, saw herself moving her wrists back and forth on it, gritting her teeth against the pain, her blood smearing the tip. "It's humiliating how easily he brought me down. He must have dogged my every step yesterday, from the time I left Major Trumbo's B&B. And I never saw him, never felt someone was watching me."

"You weren't expecting anyone to be tracking you. You'd only been here a day and a half. Even the few people who recognized you couldn't know you were FBI, here undercover. Hey, I'm a cop, and I had no idea who you were."

"Yeah, make me feel better. Fact is, he dealt with me easily. It's humiliating, really humiliating."

"It's a good thing he didn't want to kill you, only put you out of commission. That makes me wonder what he was going to do with you if you hadn't gotten yourself free. Would he have let you go? Maybe left you here until someone found you?" He slowly rose, dusted his hands on his jeans. "Either way, it seems there was a lot of luck on their side, or Black Hoodie and whoever he was getting his instructions from knew Savich well enough to know if he believed you were in trouble, he would rush right over to St. Lumis."

"It makes sense they'd know Agent Savich was my boss. But I wonder what they would have done if he hadn't come."

"Probably something more obvious, more violent. Like I said, they got lucky, got exactly the result they wanted. But now that we have Black

Hoodie's thumbprint, their luck might be about to change. We have to find out how they knew you were FBI so quickly."

"Only one place to start. We need to talk to Mrs. Trumbo."

44

Rebekah pushed the up button in the elevator lobby. As they waited, she said to Griffin, "When Grandfather was elected to Congress back in the early eighties, he had to divest control of his holdings. He signed Clarkson United over to a blind trust, but arranged it so my grandmother could continue to run things. Grandfather was never much interested in the business, it was more pro forma for him, though the business thrived under him. He had a knack for it. He was charismatic, and people loved working for him. But politics was his true love. When he was elected mayor of Clairemont, he'd already handed the company over to my grandmother. This was three years before he was elected to Congress." She laughed, shook her head. "Politics and me, both of us his true loves." She paused a moment, smiled. "It helped that the incumbent was caught in a love triangle."

"Do you find it a little unusual how much he loved you, now that you're an adult?"

She nodded. "Unusual, sure, but I was lucky. I was well loved and I knew it." She paused a moment, then said, "You think he loved me too much? Why? Don't you think I was lovable enough?"

"I'm sure you were. What did your mother have to say about it?"

"I think she saw him as stepping in to fill a gap, since I didn't have a father. Do you know, because of him, I never missed having a father, I had Grandfather."

"What happened to your father?"

The elevator pinged, the doors opened. There was no one inside. Rebekah punched the button for the eighth and top floor. "I was told he abandoned Mom—well, I started calling her Caitlin when I was a teenager, her choice—and me right after I was born. I don't know why. That's all she told me. It didn't matter that much to me, though. Again, I had Grandfather."

"And how did your grandmother react to her husband adoring you?"

"She was never a part of my life, only a presence in the background, nothing more. To be honest, I doubt that will ever change. When I grew up I realized she'd ignored me whenever she could. I remember when she'd look at me, there was nothing there, no expression at all. Looking back, I think she simply didn't like me, or maybe she resented me because Grandfather loved me more than he loved her and he made it obvious. But I think she'll be civil to me today, it's the way she is, the ruler in control, the queen bee. How do you like that for a screwed-up family dynamic?"

"Sorry, that doesn't even make my top ten."

The elevator pinged again, and they stepped out into a reception area filled with plush, comfortable Americana—love seats and chairs in nubby browns and golds within easy reach of a big glass-topped coffee table stacked with magazines and coasters for coffee. The walls were lined with a procession of photos, from a black and-white of the original Clarkson textile mill built in the 1920s to the new office building built in the early eighties. She said to Griffin, "I've given you fair warning, Agent Hammersmith. Even though I said my grandmother would be civil, I really have no idea how she's going to react to me, much less you, an FBI agent."

An older woman, short, plump, and wearing a black suit and sensible black pumps, came out of an office down the hall, saw them, and smiled. "Goodness, it's you, Rebekah. Look how you're all grown up, and so pretty. Although you were such a cute little girl, it was easy to see you'd only become more so. I hear you're becoming an art fraud expert.

And you, sir? You're not Rebekah's husband, you're far too young."

Rebekah was laughing. "Mrs. Frazier, it's amazing you got all that out in a single breath. On one of my visits here, I remember you gave me gummy bears and a Beatrix Potter coloring book."

Mrs. Frazier gave her a pat on the shoulder, then hugged her. "What a memory you have. I'd forgotten those silly gummy bears. They were your grandfather's favorites, you know. I always kept them in case he dropped by to visit with employees. He was so very popular. And look at you now, Rebekah, married to an important congressman, just like your grandfather. I see your handsome husband on the TV now and then. I remember when he was an intern with your grandfather back in the day. I wish I could have come to your wedding, but I was visiting my sister. It's so good to see you, but who is this young man with you? He's too good-looking to be on the loose, so if you like I can keep him here with me, all to myself." She gave a big belly laugh.

Griffin said, "Thank you for the compliment, Mrs. Frazier. I'm Special Agent Griffin Hammersmith, FBI."

Mrs. Frazier glanced at his creds, then back to his face. "Goodness, Rebekah, you haven't done anything wrong, have you?"

"No, no, Agent Hammersmith is with me for another reason. Oh, hello, Grandmother." Gemma Clarkson stood in the doorway of her office, not saying a word, simply observing them, unsmiling.

Mrs. Frazier turned around. "Oh, Mrs. Clarkson, isn't Rebekah lovely? She's grown up very well. This handsome young man is an FBI agent. Can you imagine?"

Gemma turned to Mrs. Frazier, nodded. "Olivia, I'm expecting Mr. Neilly from accounting in twenty minutes. I'm sure we'll be done by then. Let me know when he arrives." She looked at Griffin. "I don't believe your presence is needed, Agent. Please remain here." She stepped aside to let Rebekah walk into her office.

Griffin said, "Sorry, Mrs. Clarkson, but I have questions, too."

Rebekah smiled at Olivia Frazier, shook her hand. "It's so good to see you again."

She turned with Griffin to follow her grandmother into a large rectangular office with a row of wide windows behind her grandmother's desk. It was all in shades of gray, from the walls to the sofas and chairs to a thick carpet, the color broken only by a dozen or so Dutch paintings on the walls. She wondered what the office had looked like when her grandfather had run Clarkson United. Rebekah's mother had told her the day he'd won his first election, he'd been the happiest she'd ever seen him, nearly danced out of the building. He was glad to leave everything in Gemma's capable hands.

Griffin said to Gemma, "Ever since someone

tried to kidnap Rebekah last Thursday in Washington, I've been assigned as her bodyguard." He pulled out his creds again and handed them to her. Gemma waved them away.

Gemma said, "Yes, yes, I know all about it. I saw your husband's TV appearance. As I told an Agent Savich, who called me on Monday, it occurred to me it might have been a stunt set up by your husband, Rebekah, since he is up for re-election. Publicity is always useful, particularly if it involves a perceived danger to a loved one. He did say you were all right. Why don't you tell me what happened?"

Griffin said, "It was no stunt. The kidnapping attempt was quite real. You would have known that if you'd called Rebekah."

"Or if Rebekah would have called me," Gemma said.

Rebekah said simply, "I didn't think you'd be interested, Grandmother."

Gemma touched the diamond studs at her ears. "Of course I would have been interested. Now, what does this have to do with why you're here today, with an FBI bodyguard?"

Rebekah sat forward. "I'm in trouble, Grandmother. I'm hoping you can help."

A dark eyebrow went up. "Help you? How can I possibly help you, Rebekah?" Left unsaid but clear to Rebekah's ear was the smear of contempt in her grandmother's voice. Rebekah hadn't seen Gemma since her grandfather's funeral, and before that, at her wedding six months earlier. Her grandmother had arrived at Rebekah's wedding with her car and driver and left shortly after the ceremony. Gemma had looked amazing in a stylish Armani suit, so dark a purple it was nearly black, and a white silk blouse. One of her bridesmaids had told her Rich was very attentive to Gemma before the service, brought other politicians and businessmen over to meet her. Well, she was a big deal, rich and influential. She'd sat next to her daughter at the service, because it was expected of her.

Gemma was wearing Armani again today, black this time with a white blouse and black pumps on her small feet. Her short black hair didn't show a single strand of gray, and she looked fifteen years younger than her nearly seventy-seven years. Rebekah remembered her mother saying at Grandfather's funeral as she'd looked over at Gemma, her voice stone cold but oddly accepting, "I see the phoenix has shaken off the last of her ashes and risen."

Gemma walked to her desk and sat down. She steepled her fingertips as she said, "Sit down, Rebekah, Agent Hammersmith, and tell me what I can do for you."

Rebekah said, "As Agent Hammersmith told you, my attempted kidnapping was real. Rich didn't stage anything. I was actually saved by another FBI agent."

An eyebrow went up again. "You always were amazingly lucky," she said, and smiled.

Rebekah thought of Agent Savich's call, sat forward in the pale gray leather chair, and said without preamble, "Did you know Miranda Elderby, now Miranda Stirling, is convinced Nate was murdered? I'd like to know what you think."

45

Gemma lightly tapped her fingertips on an exquisite gray leather desk pad as she shook her head. "It amazes me Miranda is still tossing out that old chestnut. Nate, murdered? What an absurd thing to say, but of course, Miranda was never very bright, always flirting, even with my husband. I never understood how she got that nonsense about murder in her head." She paused. "It did bring her attention, though, and a lot of sympathy for the twenty-three-year-old widow."

Griffin said in his smooth FBI voice, "I imagine it upset you, Mrs. Clarkson, when Miranda flirted with your husband."

"I'll admit it, several times I wanted to gut her." Gemma stopped cold, stared at Griffin. "That was well done, Agent Hammersmith. But it's the truth, and I'm not ashamed to say it. I imagine I felt like most any woman would if another woman went after her husband."

Griffin continued, "Did you say anything to your husband about it?"

Gemma eased; they clearly saw it. "Of course I did. Johnny laughed, said Miranda was a cute kid and maybe that's how Nate would come to see her as well. In other words, he saw right through her and trusted Nate would do the same when he got over his midlife crisis."

Rebekah said, "But Nate never saw through her, did he, Grandmother? He loved her."

Gemma shrugged. "So he died before he grew bored with her, but he would have, I'm sure of that. But all of it is nothing more than ancient history, isn't it? Why are we even speaking of it?"

Griffin smiled at her. "You're right, Mrs. Clarkson. We certainly have other, far more important things to discuss. For example, I know you've attended séances most of your adult life. Have you ever worked with a medium named Zoltan?"

"Zoltan? I've heard the name, of course. She has an excellent reputation, but no, I haven't had the opportunity to work with her."

It was a lie, he saw it, but she'd said it so smoothly. Had he imagined it? "Did you know she asked Rebekah to meet her to speak with her grandfather?"

Gemma grew utterly still, her face expression-less. She looked from Griffin to Rebekah and said slowly, "What is all this about? I thought you wanted to talk about Nate and his death, his acci-dental death."

"We believe Zoltan and Rebekah's attempted kidnapping are connected, Mrs. Clarkson, that they both had to do with a great deal of money your hus-band intended Rebekah to have, money he called his Big Take."

"Big Take? That sounds like one of his silly stories. John's estate was thoroughly accounted after he died, including Rebekah's share. He had no hidden fortune. And if he did, why would he want to give it all to Rebekah? And why would Zoltan call her?"

Griffin wasn't about to let her bog him down. Maybe she knew all of it already, but it didn't matter. He said easily, "A good question, ma'am, and we'll get to it. First, though, to be clear—you believe Nate's death was an accident?"

She shrugged. "It all happened years ago, and, thankfully, those memories are blurred now. But I do know this. Nate wasn't murdered. He was drunk, he was alone, and he fell, hit his head, and drowned. I remember Miranda was so pleased to be in the spotlight, and she played the bereaved widow to the hilt, the drama queen. She gloried in it until every-one realized there was no evidence of murder and finally dismissed her absurd accusations. Blessedly, she shut up and left Clairemont, her pockets full of Nate's life insurance money."

"What did Grandfather think?"

Gemma sat perfectly still. She cocked her head at Rebekah and stopped tapping her fingernails. "May I remind you your grandfather recently died? Those wounds never healed. Why do you want me to revisit such a painful time?"

"Please, Grandmother, it's important."

"Very well. Certainly your grandfather believed Nate was drunk, believed his death was an accident. He was buried in guilt because he thought he should have been with Nate."

"What do you mean about those wounds never healing, Grandmother?" At her grandmother's silence, Rebekah's voice hardened, and words came out that had festered for years. "You can't be talking about Grandfather and what happened to him. His wounds didn't touch you. The sanitarium staff told me you rarely visited him yourself, though you sent in a series of private nurses. I know *I* never saw you there, and I visited him regularly all through those long sixteen years."

Gemma laughed. "You really don't understand anything about it, Rebekah. Yes, I was told his precious little darling was always there, crouched by his bedside, stroking his limp hands—" She broke off abruptly, shook her head. "I was very busy, Rebekah, and frankly, I do not understand why you bring it up. It's none of your business what I did or didn't do over the years. You know, one of the nurses asked me if you were hoping for a bigger inheritance, absurd since John was in a coma. Believe me, I assured the nurse you didn't need it, not with the trust your grandfather had set up for you all those years ago."

"Do you know, I've wondered if you ever loved my grandfather, your husband. Why else would he heap his love on me, his granddaughter? He didn't have a wife who cared."

Gemma rose straight up out of her chair, banged her fists on the desk. "He felt sorry for you, you idiot! A poor fatherless child. What was he to do? Ignore you? Pretend you didn't exist? No, he heaped love and attention on you."

"Did you expect him to ignore me like you did, Grandmother? Why didn't you feel sorry for me, too, a poor fatherless child of your blood? You knew my biological father, didn't you? You know why he left my mother and me."

Gemma straightened tall. "You want honesty? Your mother, my only child, was such a disappointment. She was rebellious, slept around. Which of her stream of boyfriends fathered you? I don't know, nor do I care. I have no idea if I met your actual biological father.

"But she always worshiped her father, always did exactly what he wanted her to do. Just as you did. I imagine she complained to him about me trying to control her, just as I had to take control over the business your grandfather never wanted in the first place and was delighted to drop in my lap. He felt no responsibility for anything except politics and how he would rise to the top. And you, of course. You and politics."

"You said your daughter—Caitlin—disappointed you. What did I do to disappoint you, Grandmother? I wasn't old enough to sleep around, and I never rebelled, not with Grandfather there to guide and love me. After the strokes, when he fell into a coma, I was focused on him." She searched her grandmother's cold face, and the words poured out. "Why do you hate me? Why have you always hated me?"

The words sat stark in the cold silence.

"Hate you?" Gemma gave a contemptuous laugh. She waved her hand at Rebekah's face. "I don't hate you. Hating you would mean I spend time thinking about you, which I don't. You are not and never were important. You were always simply there, to be endured."

Griffin saw the devastation on Rebekah's face, watched her absorb the blow. Then he saw anger and realized this moment had been coming for a very long time. He held perfectly silent and waited to see what Rebekah would do. She said slowly, "When I was a child, I always looked at you like some powerful being who occasionally came into the room when I was there. You rarely spoke to me or even acknowledged me in any way. It was as if I didn't exist. I've never understood your dislike of me. Why? Were you punishing Grandfather for stepping up and being a father to me? Were you jealous he gave me affection?"

Gemma sat down again, turned her chair, and said to the bank of large windows, "No, I have never liked you, Rebekah, but I was not jealous of you. My reasons are my own. Did you come here to accuse me of ignoring your grandfather during those endless sixteen years he lay there, a husk with a faint heartbeat, nothing more? If so, you may leave. Nothing between your grandfather and me was ever any of your business." She rose. "I've told you Nate's death was an accident. Is there anything else?"

Rebekah said, "You've told me nothing."

Griffin said, "Mrs. Clarkson, do you still visit mediums? Have you tried to reach your husband, for example?"

Gemma slowly sat down again. "No, I have nothing to say to him. If you must know, our marriage became more of a business partnership as the years passed. In fact, even if he hadn't been in a coma, I doubt he would have cared if I visited him or not."

Griffin decided to tell her all of it, about Zoltan claiming Rebekah's grandfather had come to her, about her séance where John Clarkson supposedly appeared and spoke of Nate Elderby and their Big Take. Gemma didn't interrupt, merely sat there, listening. When he finished, she said, "That is a remarkable story." She turned to Rebekah. "So you actually spoke to your grandfather?"

Rebekah shook her head. "If I'd been inclined to believe in the dead returning to talk to loved ones, I'd have believed her. She's an excellent researcher and entertainer."

Griffin said, "Did you know Zoltan has gone missing? There was blood in her living room. It appears someone after this money thought Zoltan not only failed in her assignment, but she'd also become a risk."

Gemma said, "You obviously believe Nate and my husband planned and stole this money together. You probably also believe my husband murdered Nate because of this stolen money, to which I say, it is impossible. Now, Nate gloried in not-guilty verdicts, even for criminals at trial, but his biggest flaw? He was a liar. He had no loyalty, not to me, not to your grandfather. Tell me, Rebekah, what does your husband think of this extraordinary story you've concocted?"

Rebekah said, "Rich is upset. He loves me and doesn't want to see me hurt."

Griffin said, "Mrs. Clarkson, you said your husband never mentioned any of this to you?"

"Of course not." Gemma's phone buzzed. She picked up, said, "Yes, send Mr. Neilly in." She rose. "I expect I won't see you again, Rebekah."

"And you don't want to, do you, Grandmother?"

"Any more than you want to see me."

Rebekah rose slowly to face her grandmother across her big mahogany desk. "Do you really think Nate's death was an accident?"

"Of course it was an accident. Your precious grandfather was many things, but he wasn't a murderer." She looked over at the trio of old Dutch countryside paintings against the light gray wall. "Your grandfather loved Nate. Perhaps as much as he loved you. As for any stolen money—what you're calling this Big Take—I suppose your grandfather could have stolen it. He had what I call flexible ethics." Her face stiffened. "Unlike Nate, who, as I said, had no ethics at all. Now, you've put on quite a show for Agent Hammersmith. Are we finally done here?"

Rebekah nodded. "Thank you for seeing us." She and Griffin walked to the door, her heels sinking into the gray carpeting.

Rebekah turned back to face her grandmother. "Do you know what I told Zoltan? If there is such a thing as the Big Take, I intend to let the money rot for eternity. As you said, I don't need it, and the last thing I'd ever do is harm Grandfather's legacy."

They didn't speak until they were in Griffin's black Range Rover. He turned to her. "How do you feel?"

She fiddled with her seat belt, her hands trembling. Then she turned to him and smiled. "I still don't know why she dislikes me so much, but I finally said what I needed to. Sorry we couldn't get much out of her."

Griffin started the Range Rover. "I'm not so sure about that," he said. "Your seat belt still isn't fastened."

46

Savich punched off his cell when he saw Sherlock coming toward his office. He rose automatically at the look on her face.

"What's up? You're grinning like a fool. Is it something to do with the house?"

Sherlock laughed. "I'm grinning like a fool for two reasons. I spoke with Mrs. Mickelson—our logistics expert—about the home front. Dillon, she's already looked at the fire damage with contractors and scheduled the cleanup in the kitchen and the repairs that won't need permits on Friday. She wants to discuss the new flooring for the kitchen and what brand appliances we want. She even said we might be all finished by Christmas. Unbelievable, right? And my piano tuner says my Steinway will play like new once he's done. So yay!

"Now, the second thing I'm grinning about is really unbelievable news."

He grinned at her. "Lay it on me."

"You remember when I spoke to Philly in forensics, told her it was super critical to run the DNA from the blood from Zoltan's living room as quickly as possible? I nearly begged her on my knees, even said I'd offer you up as a bonus. Well, Philly rang me up, said she called in some favors and got the DNA results. You won't believe this, Dillon: some of the blood belongs to Zoltan, and some of it belongs to a Gary Duvall, a thug out on parole for the past seven months."

He whistled. "So someone sent a thug out to get rid of Zoltan, a loose end, but it didn't work out well for him. Both of them wounded, but no reports of gunshot wounds at the local ERs or urgent care clinics. Well, we can put out a BOLO for Mr. Duvall. How about an apple pie for Philly?"

"No, a Christmas fruitcake, with lots of bourbon. Philly would love that. I already called in a BOLO on Duvall. Here's his booking sheet. The guy's thirty-four, Dillon, looks like a preacher, with the long Elmer Gantry black hair." She added, "You know, Zoltan didn't break any laws we know of. I hope she's still alive."

"I do, too."

He watched Sherlock speaking on her cell as she

walked back to her workstation, her step light. Was she thinking about a new double-door refrigerator or Duvall? Probably both; she was a born multitasker.

Savich made his own call to Sonja Grayson, Marsia Gay's federal prosecutor. When he punched off his cell, he closed his eyes and said a silent prayer. Veronica Lake was alive, but her surgeon still wasn't optimistic. The knife had nicked her heart, one millimeter closer and she'd have died on the cafeteria floor. Both Grayson and Savich hoped he was being overly cautious. Sonja was desperate for Veronica to survive because she was afraid Marsia would go free without Veronica's testimony at trial. "Would I even be able to make a case beyond a reasonable doubt without Veronica's testimony?" she asked him. "Even with you and Sherlock testifying, I don't think so, Dillon."

Of course, she blamed herself for not getting Veronica out of the D.C. Jail in time. Once the bureaucracy got involved and everyone up the ladder wanted to chime in with opinions, it was enough to delay the transfer, and that was all Marsia needed. There was more than enough blame to spread around up the chain of command, but Sonja would take the fall.

Savich said a prayer for Veronica. She'd been the perfect patsy for Marsia, a single woman in her mid-thirties, hungry for love, easily manipulated, and willing to do whatever her goddess asked of her. He hoped she'd make it.

He pictured Marsia in his mind, but she was quickly replaced by Major Trumbo enveloped in flames—and the sight of his home on fire. His hands fisted, and rage bubbled up. It was Sherlock and Sean Marsia had been after. In that moment, he knew he would move heaven and earth to make her pay.

He heard loud voices and looked up to see Ruth and Sherlock barreling toward his office, excitement pouring off them.

Sherlock yelled out, "We found him!"

47

Mrs. Trumbo eyed her up and down. "So, it's you again. I suppose I shouldn't call you Ms. Cinelli any longer, Agent Cinelli, excuse me, Special Agent Cinelli. Yes, Maude Filly called me, told me who you were and all the questions you had for her. I'd like to know why I had to hear this from Maude."

"Yes, Mrs. Trumbo, I'm Special Agent Pippa Cinelli."

Mrs. Trumbo studied them, then turned to Wilde. "I suppose you were in on this deception as well, Chief Wilde? You knew she was coming here under false pretenses, spying on everyone?"

Wilde shook his head. "No, ma'am. Agent Cinelli was sent to St. Lumis undercover. I only found out when she came to me for help after she was attacked yesterday in that abandoned grocery store out on the edge of town."

"We'd like to talk to you about everything that's happened, Mrs. Trumbo."

Mrs. Trumbo clearly wasn't ready to make peace. She huffed, tried to smile, then jerked her head toward the living room. "All right, for all the good it will do you. I don't know a blessed thing about who sent you that stupid puzzle of Major Trumbo you told Maude about, nor do I like my place or my guests being spied on, well, not that you've been spying on any of my guests, but still."

Mrs. Trumbo sat herself in a large wing chair opposite them. "Now, Agent Cinelli, Chief Wilde, say what you have to say." She looked down at her watch. "I have a pot roast in the oven for dinner, and it needs watching."

Wilde said, "Mrs. Filly told us you disliked Major Trumbo as much as she did. She told us he was a cheater, and that's how he met you."

"That's right. I met him when he came to Baltimore on business and stayed at the Wilson, the hotel I managed. He was very smooth. Until after we married." She snorted.

Pippa pointed to the urn on the mantel. "Then why did you put his urn in a place of honor?"

Mrs. Trumbo shrugged. "It was the most expensive urn the funeral home had, perfect for the mantel, a lovely reminder the old coot's dead. Do you know, I picture him in that urn sailing down the River Styx, on his way to hell. It's enough to make me smile.

"Now, you said you wanted to talk, so talk. I have a pot roast in the oven, as I told you. By the way, will you be staying here tonight, *Agent* Cinelli, or will you be going back to Chief Wilde's lovely little cottage?"

Pippa said, "Since you serve such wonderful breakfasts, Mrs. Trumbo, I'll be staying in my honeymoon suite. You mentioned you spoke with Mrs. Filly about our visit to her this morning."

"Of course, Maude called me right away. She thought nothing this exciting had happened in St. Lumis in years." Mrs. Trumbo sat back in her chair, crossed her arms over her ample bosom, and waited.

"Mrs. Trumbo, no one here in St. Lumis knew I was an FBI agent, not even Chief Wilde. As he said, I was here undercover. Yet within a day and a half, someone found out who I was and attacked me. Did you happen to see anyone go into my room while I was out at the Halloween party at Leveler's Inn?"

Mrs. Trumbo gave her the stink eye. "So the two of you think I'm a dim bulb? Why not say it right out? You have the gall to wonder if I snooped around in your honeymoon suite, found out who you really were, and then told everyone the FBI had invaded St. Lumis?"

Wilde said, "So did you, Mrs. Trumbo?"

"Well, of course I went into her room Saturday night. I go into everyone's room to straighten up, make sure there are clean towels, fluff pillows, and the like. Saturday night was no exception. Did I search your things? Of course not. Neither would my daily woman, who does all the deep cleaning. I do not search my guests' rooms. And if I did, I certainly wouldn't brag about it."

Pippa said, "Mrs. Trumbo, I left my tablet on the table by the sofa. I was in a hurry so I suppose I could have left it on, which I try never to do, and that's on me if I did. Did you look in my tablet, Mrs. Trumbo? Happen to notice what I was reading?"

"No, I did not."

Pippa hardened her voice. "Then tell me this, Mrs. Trumbo. Do you know of anyone other than yourself or your daily woman who could have gone up to my room?"

Mrs. Trumbo drew a deep breath. "All right, I remember Grizzlie Cole was here to check on the heating in the guest rooms. You know old Grizzlie, Chief. He was here for only a half hour, made a few adjustments, and charged me thirty bucks. Thirty bucks! It's a crime."

Wilde said, "So besides Grizzlie, only guests went up those stairs?"

"That's right."

"Did anyone come in and ask about Ms. Cinelli?"

"No, no one."

Pippa said, "Mrs. Filly mentioned you have a son, a textile artist who works on a loom. He lives in Baltimore."

"That's right. He's very talented. Baltimore is his home. But he visits me on occasion." She studied Pippa a moment. "Tell me, Agent Cinelli. Did you bring your gun into my house? Would I have seen your gun if I'd gone searching?"

Her sarcasm made Pippa smile. "No, ma'am. I had my gun with me until the man struck me down and took it, along with my cell phone and my wallet."

"I don't suppose you saw the person who struck you?"

Pippa started to say no, but instead, "His face? I tried to do a sketch with Mrs. Trout, but I didn't see him well enough. I might recognize his voice, though. It's pretty clear he's involved with whoever sent the FBI the bizarre Major Trumbo puzzle."

"Maude told me someone sent that silly puzzle in three parts, in red boxes of all things. Of course, I have an original puzzle here somewhere, but I can't imagine why anyone would want to do such a thing."

Pippa said, "Mrs. Trumbo, do you remember meeting a young woman named Marsia Gay, perhaps at the Wilson hotel in Baltimore when you were manager there? Since I don't have my cell phone, Chief Wilde can call up her photo on his."

Wilde had no trouble finding a photo of a Marsia Gay and handed his cell to Mrs. Trumbo. Mrs. Trumbo looked at the photo, studied it a moment, then shook her head.

48

Savich was on his feet in an instant. *"What? Who did you find, Sherlock?"*

Ruth said, "Dillon, we found Gary Duvall, the guy whose blood was at Zoltan's house. Not twenty minutes after Sherlock put out the BOLO, we got a call from Porterville, Virginia, about forty minutes northeast of Richmond. A Porterville police officer named Theodore Janko saw the BOLO, realized he'd seen Duvall bent over, walking up the outside stairs to the second floor and into a side door of a Dr. Milton Hodges's office on High Street. He called it in to his chief, Walt Collette, who called us."

Sherlock picked it up. "Turns out Officer Janko is young, six months on the job, and, well, now we've got complications."

Savich sighed. "I can see it all. Janko knew Duvall was wounded, so he figured he could take Duvall down himself. Right?"

Ruth said, "That's it exactly. So our boy wonder roared right in, didn't wait for backup. And now we have a hostage situation. Duvall is holding Dr. Hodges, a nurse, and Officer Janko in the office and is threatening to kill them. Says he isn't going back to Red Onion prison and he's ready to put slugs in the heads of all three of them. That's all the Porterville dispatcher knew."

Savich grabbed his leather jacket off the coat rack. "Ruth, we've only got the Porsche, so follow in your car unless you want Sherlock on your lap. Sherlock, you call Chief Collette, let him know we'll be there as soon as we can. And I'll concentrate on getting us to Porterville in one piece and in record time."

Thirty-four minutes later, Savich pulled his Porsche behind a Crown Vic on High Street, on the edge of a heavily wooded area three blocks off the small Porterville downtown, Ruth's silver Audi behind him. The area was cordoned off by four cop cars, an ambulance, and a gaggle of police officers and EMTs, all focused on the medical building. And someone who looked to be the hostage negotiator had a cell phone in her hand.

Ruth said, "All these trees, even with next to no leaves, are so thick it's hard to see clearly. Hard for Duvall, too. We should be able to get close."

A tall man in uniform, fit and straight as a flag-pole, broke away from a group of cops and strode quickly toward them. He was in his late forties with thick graying brown hair, no doubt Chief Walt Collette himself. Savich would bet he was ex-military. Collette snapped to a stop, looked at them with a dispassionate eye before he quickly introduced himself. He only glanced at their creds. "The cock-up is our own fault. We can't try a direct assault, can't take the chance he'll kill all three hostages."

"Tell us what happened, Chief," Savich said.

Collette said, "A nurse who got out, Glennie Franks—she's standing over there by her mother—told us Duvall came dragging in through the side door, bent over, holding his side and moaning. She said he screamed at her to get a doctor and to keep the other patients away or he'd shoot them all. He pulled a gun, she said, waved it around, and Glennie saw thick gauze wrapped around his middle, black with dried blood. It was obvious he'd tried to take care of the wound himself but was afraid he might die unless he got himself to a doctor. Dr. Hodges was already treating Duvall when Teddy, Officer Janko, came rushing into the office reception area, waving his weapon, asking questions, and ordering everyone in the office to leave. That's all she could tell me." He paused a moment, his jaw working. "I can see the young idiot rushing in and getting himself in trouble. His mom will skin him, after I get through with him. There's been one shot, about twenty minutes ago, only one, with a lot of loud cursing and a scream. It was probably Jenny Connors, the nurse, who screamed. I'm praying Duvall hasn't already hurt her. He's hardly talked with our hostage negotiator, Eliza, keeps hanging up, but he sounds violent, screams at her he's not going back to Red Onion prison. He sounds like he's near the edge, could go off at any time.

"Come with me, and I'll show you what we've got." They trotted through the woods to the side of the medical building. Collette continued in his clipped sergeant major's voice as they walked to the edge of the oak trees, "As you can see, the building is older, built in the eighties, two floors. The medical suite on the second floor has both a front and a side door. You see the upper floor overhangs the patients' parking and more than half of the ground floor. Thankfully, there are only a few cars since it's late in the day and our people finished clearing the building. There's an elevator and stairs that go up to the second floor. We might get as far as the office door using the stairs before Duvall would know about it, but that would be dangerous. He's probably barricaded in one of the exam rooms, which means we couldn't get to him before he shot the three hostages. We called the SWAT team from Richmond, but they're still a ways out. I don't know how useful they'll be, too many trees in the way, no clear shot even if Duvall pressed himself against a window and called out."

Sherlock asked, "Where is the fire escape?"

Collette pointed upward. "On the far side, actually connects to Dr. Hodges's office, only one or two rooms away from where we think Duvall has the three hostages. He could have moved them, we don't know. The fire escape works, but it's old, probably creaks, and we're worried Duvall would hear us given where we believe he is. We decided it's a no-go."

Sherlock said, "You said he screamed he wouldn't go back to Red Onion. On our ride here, I called Warden Hendricks myself, spoke to him about Duvall. Hendricks said Duvall thought of himself as a badass, but he isn't that big, plus he's good-looking and was always fighting off the bigger guys. He'd go into rages, and everyone knew he'd kill without hesitation. The warden said he was arrested with an ancient Colt and a stiletto. And he was unpredictable. Hendricks has no doubt he'd murder the hostages."

Chief Collette said, "None of that surprises me." He looked through the thick trees toward the medical building. "We know we can't let Duvall go free, no matter what happens. Any ideas?"

49

Savich said, "Chief, you know Duvall had to be in pain from his gunshot wound by the time he got in there, his only hope that Dr. Hodges could fix him up and he'd get out of there fast. The first thing he'd have asked for is some pain meds, morphine from the doctor's medical cabinet, once the doctor started treating his wound. It would have been enough to make him woozy, and that gives us a chance. Chief, do you have plans to the building?"

Collette nodded. "Marvin brought them over. They're in my patrol car. I'll show you."

Collette took the rolled-up plans from a young man with oversize glasses falling down his nose, thin as a Popsicle stick, his uniform perfectly pressed. Collette said, "This is Marvin, my right hand, young enough to keep my brain on track. He's the one who thought to bring the plans." Collette spread them out on top of his Crown Vic. Sherlock pointed at a small electrical room. Savich nodded, but he wasn't looking at that. He stepped back and stared at the medical building. Sherlock opened her mouth to ask him what he was thinking when Chief Collette laid three photographs on top of the plans.

"Here are the hostages. This is Teddy, the young idiot who wanted to play cowboy. This is Dr. Milton Hodges, an older man who's not so spry anymore, near retirement, but still a good doctor. And this is his new nurse, Jenny Connors. She's twenty-six, married two months, husband's an EMT."

Savich said, "Make sure to circulate those photos to the SWAT team when they arrive."

"Will do. You put out the BOLO, so Duvall is part of an FBI case? What can you tell me?"

Sherlock said, "Duvall was hired to murder a witness, a loose end, if you will, and got himself shot instead. We don't know how badly he was wounded, only that there was a lot of blood."

Savich said, "We need to speak to Eliza, your negotiator."

Chief Collette introduced the three of them to Sergeant Eliza Crumb. They saw she topped out at no more than five feet tall on a good day. The

Kevlar vest she was wearing over her black turtle-neck made her look like a tough sort of dumpling. She was remarkably pretty, with big liquid gray eyes, and when she spoke, she sounded six feet tall. She said right away to all of them, "I keep trying to engage him, but he either screams at me or curses up a blue streak and hangs up. He claims he didn't shoot anyone, says it was a warning. I heard a woman's scream, and it had to be Jenny Connors. He sounds drugged up to his eyeballs but he still knows what he's doing. Guys, I'm scared he's going to lose it if anything sets him off."

Savich said, "Do you think you could call him again? I'd like to hear his voice."

Eliza set her cell to speaker, punched in the number, and drew a deep breath, slowly letting it out. She nodded to Savich and said, "Mr. Duvall, we were all concerned when we heard Jenny scream and you fired off that shot. Are you sure Jenny's all right? Are Dr. Hodges and Officer Janko all right?"

"Shut up about her. Ain't none of your business what I do with these yahoos."

Eliza talked over him. "Why did you fire your weapon, Gary?"

Hot silence, then, "I wanted to see if the sucker still worked. It belonged to my granddad, and he always said his old Colt wouldn't fail me." He laughed, a manic laugh. "He was right."

"Are you ready to talk to me again, let us resolve this situation so no one gets hurt?"

"You sound like one of those idiot shrinks at Red Onion, the brainless dicks. You want me to pour out my guts to you, keep me busy so you can get cops in here before I kill these cockroaches. Ain't going to happen. I'm running this show." He muttered to himself, then said, his voice calmer, "I've made up my mind. I want out of this place, it stinks like antiseptic. I want fifty thousand dollars and a helicopter here in thirty minutes or you'll have three dead folk, none of them worth anything to me, but maybe something to you. Move it, bitch, or you'll hear three gunshots, not one. Hey, sweet Jenny, they want to know you're all right. Do you want to say hi to hubby?"

They heard a young woman's fierce voice clearly over Eliza's cell. "You're crazy up in your head, you know that? My *hubby* will twist your skinny neck off and stuff your brains down your pants. That wall is thin, only a painted wallboard partition, what with us dividing up the one exam room into two, so he'll hear you if you try anything with me."

They heard him hiss out curses, fast and loud as a machine gun, but nothing else. No gunshots.

Savich grinned like a bandit. *Thank you, Jenny*.

"That's my girl," Eliza whispered to Collette. "Guts and grit." She said calmly into the cell in her negotiator voice, "Gary, we can get the money, but you know it takes time to get a helicopter here, has to fly in from Andrews Air Force Base."

"Don't you lie to me."

"No, Gary, I'm not lying, I need at least an hour to get the helicopter here."

They heard him arguing with himself, then, "Forty minutes and that's it. I'll shoot these bozos or maybe stab young Jenny in her belly with one of the doctor's scalpels here? Stick it in deep, then rip it out, you know? Let her watch her blood pour out through her fingers.

"I'm thinking I might take the boy cop with me, make sure none of his buddies lose it." Duvall's voice had gone from mocking and flat to colder than death.

Eliza said, her voice firm as a hanging judge, "No, you will not take Officer Janko with you. That's nonnegotiable. Look, Gary, I'll call the authorities, see what we can do to speed them up. But let me make myself perfectly clear. If you kill any of the hostages, you won't be leaving; you'll be killed. You know that, don't you?"

He hung up on her.

Eliza said, "He sounds high as a kite, but you can hear he's getting desperate, and under it all, coldness and meanness. When he finds out there won't be any helicopter, we're going to have three dead hostages, three dead friends."

Savich knew they'd reached critical mass. He said, "Eliza, when you dial up Duvall again, assure him the helicopter's on its way. Remind him we'll blow his head off if he kills any of the hostages."

"But what—" Collette said.

Savich only shook his head. "Trust me. Eliza, do it." She got a nod from Collette.

"I'm going to need a long rope."

Marvin nodded and brought him one from the trunk of the Crown Vic.

Savich said, "Chief, please keep everyone here in place and see no one follows me, all right? Under no circumstances will you send the SWAT team or any of your people in after me. If Duvall makes himself visible, it's important the SWAT team and your people don't shoot him, unless there's absolutely no choice. We need him to tell us who hired him to commit murder, and believe me, that's not the end of it." He smiled at Sherlock, whispered, "Here's what I want you to do when I text you."

They watched Dillon head toward the building, the coiled rope over his shoulder.

Collette said, "He saw something on the plans." He shook his head. "Well, crap, a Fed hot dog. Take me, Lord, I've seen it all. Why the rope?"

Sherlock had an insane desire to laugh. Ruth said in a clear, certain voice, "Stick with this, Chief. Our boss is tougher than the old boots from your army days in the back of your closet. Don't know what the rope is for." But Ruth knew that rope was headed for the fire escape.

Between prayers, Sherlock decided she'd punch him out at the gym when this was over.

50

Gary Duvall's brain was humming, sparking, working at top speed. Morphine was new to him, and he loved it. No more pain, amazing. He felt good, maybe too good. He'd seen the wound in his side up close and personal when he'd tried to take care of it himself, seen all the blood, felt pain he'd never imagined. He slowly turned from his post at the front window to face his three hostages, all sitting on the floor lined up next to one another, their backs against the wall. He said, his voice mean, "Shut up, old man. I've already said I won't kill any of you if your hick police do what I tell them to do exactly when I tell them to do it. And there won't be any CT scans or surgery. You're going to load me up with some more of your morphine, and I'm getting out of here. So stop your begging."

Dr. Hodges said, "I'm not begging, you ungrateful whelp. I'm telling you what you're doing is stupid. Without tests, I can't know if the bullet nicked your bowels. Antibiotics and a few stitches won't help you if it did. And you listen to me, I'm not an old man. I'm late middle age. Stop waving that scalpel around. Officer Janko can't hurt you; you tied him up."

Duvall eyed Hodges. Late middle age? The old dude probably couldn't see himself clearly when he looked in the mirror. He had wispy gray hairs sticking up in all directions, and his jowls sagged. Only his eyes were sharp, still some fire in that ancient brain. He looked at the blood smears on Hodges's white coat, his blood. The doctor had stitched up his side quick enough and told him the bullet had gone through and out his back, got some muscles and some fat on its way through, and he was damned lucky. But the bowel deal? He'd take his chances.

Duvall said, "You want to know what I really want, old man? Your bottles of morphine and some needles in a bag so I can shoot up myself later when you won't be around."

Dr. Hodges said, "Look, we all heard you're going to get your helicopter. Will you keep your word to the negotiator? You'll leave us all here, unharmed?"

"Well, sure," Duvall said, and gave him a big

grin, showing nice white teeth. "I'm the model of rectitude. That's the right word, isn't it? Don't think I ever said it before." He laughed, said "rectitude" three more times as if savoring the feel of the word in his mouth. "The prison chaplain said it a lot."

He heard a growl and waved the Colt toward Janko, who looked both scared and angry. Duvall eyed him. Talk about young. Janko didn't look old enough to be in the Boy Scouts, much less a puppy cop. He'd set Janko's Beretta on the exam table within easy reach. Compared to his compact Colt .25, it was clumsy and big. Still, he'd take the extra magazine the puppy cop carried. Let Janko growl. Duvall had already shown him how easily he could take him down, even wounded. He looked at the nurse, young, pretty Jenny, and wondered if he shouldn't take her with him instead of the puppy cop. Yeah, she could take care of him in lots of ways. She was sitting perfectly still next to Janko, her hands resting on her knees. He hadn't tied her up, no reason to. She was a girl, no threat to him, but she had a big mouth on her. He could correct that fast enough. As for Hodges, the old man would probably fall over with a heart attack if he tried to jump him, and he was tied up anyway.

Duvall said, "What you better hope is the cops show me some rectitude, otherwise there'll be an eye for an eye, right?" When no one answered him, he started whistling "Whole Lotta Love," his favorite Zeppelin tune, marveling again at the absence of pain. It was like that weird psychic bitch hadn't shot him. Suddenly, he was there again and he saw her stagger, blood blooming on her arm. He wanted to shoot her again, a death shot. But she shot him, and he saw himself stumble to the floor, saw her staring at him, her gun still pointed at him. The pain in his side nearly froze him, but he pulled himself up and ran. Duvall blinked, shook his head. He didn't want to think about that long, skinny living room, that place where he nearly died. He knew now he should have shot her again, at least tried, but he'd felt like he was dying himself. He wondered what had happened to her.

He shouldn't have waited a day. He could tell right away the wound was bad. And now he was trapped in this bum-crap town. He wondered if one of the sick old geezers in the waiting room had heard him in the back and given him away. Whatever. Soon he'd hear helicopter rotors, and he'd be on his way, with cash and morphine in his pockets. No way he would ever go back to that prison, where the prisoners eyed him like he was a Snickers bar.

He looked down at his watch. Nothing to do but wait. Duvall smiled. Why not mock out the old codger some more? He knew he was smarter, so it'd be fun. Maybe he should be thinking about where he should go, making plans, but his brain was hopping around too much, all sorts of weird thoughts. The morphine. So what if he'd given himself too much? It would wear off, and he could give himself more if the pain came back. Who cared? He loved feeling like he could fly. He smiled again.

Savich knew If he made any noise, Duvall would hear him. He studied the ancient fire escape with its open steel gratings and drop-down ladder on the upper floor. No doubt in his mind, the old contraption would gladly creak out his presence if he unhinged the ladder and pulled it down. He uncoiled the rope and made a loop out of it. He swung the coil to give it momentum and sent the loop upward toward a strut anchoring the platform to the building. He missed, and the metal groaned from the impact. He went silent. No sound from above. He managed to loop the rope around the strut on the third try. He tied off the rope, yanked on it, and it held. He took off his boots, said a prayer, and slowly pulled himself up the rope, hand over hand, his stockinged feet holding the rope steady, careful not to swing enough to touch any part of the fire escape. He reached the landing, paused, and listened. Nothing. He pulled himself quietly onto the platform. Now the window. It was closed, as expected. He took out his pocketknife, pushed it under the bottom edge of the window frame, and torqued the blade steadily and gently until he got enough purchase to slide the window smoothly up.

He climbed into the doctor's office, looked around, and walked on cat's feet out into the hall. He heard voices. They were in Exam Room 1, the door shut and no doubt locked. He eased farther down the corridor and spotted the exam room Jenny had told them was separated off only by a wallboard partition. He stepped inside as quietly as he could. It was dim, the shades drawn. There were contractor tools stacked neatly in one corner, an exam table and two chairs next to them. To the right was the Sheetrock wall. Savich pressed his ear to the Sheetrock and listened, heard Duvall say, "Hey, old man, are you getting it on with this sweet young nurse? No way you could keep up with her. What you need is an old bag as ancient as you are and the both of you could go to a retirement home in Florida."

Jenny Connors spurted out a mocking laugh, and Savich felt a stab of fear. He heard Duvall take a step, probably toward Jenny, then stop. "Shut up! Why are you laughing?"

Savich breathed easier when Jenny stopped and hiccupped. The Sheetrock was so thin, he even heard her swallow. She said, her voice steady, "It's what you said. It really was funny. Dr. Hodges said he hired me because he was too old now to appreciate my youth and vigor, so I'd be safe. You swear you're not going to kill us?"

Before he could answer, Janko said, "Who shot you?"

Duvall said, "A weird bitch. I wasn't expecting her to be in the living room, but there she was."

Dr. Hodges started laughing. Duvall yelled, "Stop laughing at me, old man, unless you want a bullet in your feeble brain right now."

Dr. Hodges said, "Listen, you young fool, I've got two ex-wives spending all my money, and with a malpractice insurance company charging me more than the national debt and cutting back what they pay me every year, I haven't got that much to look forward to. Why do you think I'm still here? I have to be here, to keep a roof over our three heads, three different roofs, three different heads. I'm the one living in a ratty apartment, not those two harpies."

Savich heard Duvall laugh. He was distracted, perfect. He texted Sherlock, typed only *Now*. In the next second, earsplitting music erupted from bullhorn, a Sousa march, so loud it shook the building. He heard Duvall curse and run to the window.

Savich stepped back and ran full tilt at the wallboard, hit it at full speed. It buckled and splintered, and he burst through. "Duvall, drop the gun! Now!"

For a wild, confused instant, Gary Duvall didn't know what was happening. He whirled around, saw a big man pointing a gun at him, and raised his Colt, but he wasn't fast enough. He heard a shot and felt a sledgehammer slam into his shoulder. He screamed, felt his precious grandpappy's Colt slip from his fingers as he sank to the floor. He lay there only a second, still aware enough to know he couldn't let it end like this, couldn't go back to Red Onion. He made a grab for his Colt.

A boot heel smashed down on his wrist, and he screamed again as he felt the bones crack.

It wasn't Savich's boot; it was Teddy Janko's. His hands were still tied, but he'd managed to stumble to Duvall and kick down. Then Janko kicked Duvall's Colt across the room, managing to keep his balance. He stood over Duvall, panting.

"Good going, Officer Janko," Savich said.

Jenny Connors leaped up, her intentions as clear as water to Savich. She raised her foot, then slowly lowered it, blinked, and stepped back. "Sorry, I nearly lost it. I'd still like to put his lights out."

Dr. Hodges said, a good deal of satisfaction in his voice, "Better not to smash him more, Jenny. I don't want you killing the idiot." He grinned big at Savich. "Whoever you are, that was one amazing rescue."

"I'm Special Agent Dillon Savich, FBI. I must say it's a relief to see all of you in one piece."

Jenny turned to Savich. "Thank heavens you understood what I was saying about the Sheetrock. I wouldn't care if you were the coffee maker repairman. Thank you. Now, Dr. Hodges, let's get you and Officer Janko untied. I can put this bozo's lights out later."

Savich called Sherlock. "All clear. The hostages

are fine. Get an ambulance here fast for Duvall. I had to shoot him in the shoulder to bring him down, and Officer Janko broke his wrist."

They heard shouts and cheering from outside. Savich turned to Jenny Connors. "Yes, I understood what you meant. Along with the building plans, your information made all the difference." He paused, then said, "Dr. Hodges, I think Jenny deserves a raise. Officer Janko, I'll tell Chief Collette what you did here, maybe it'll mitigate the butt-kicking he's planning."

Teddy Janko took a deep breath. "Thanks, I'll probably need any good words you can say. But you know, I can tell him if I hadn't seen Duvall, if I hadn't come in, things might have turned out differently." He gave Savich a huge smile and looked hopeful.

"Good luck with that," Savich said.

51

ST. LUMIS
POLICE STATION
TUESDAY NIGHT

When Pippa stepped into the warmth of the St. Lumis police station, she saw Deputy Davie Hauck bundled in a heavy coat, handmade fingerless mittens on his hands, hunched over, talking on his cell. Davie looked up, punched off his cell, and waved. "Hello, Chief, Agent ma'am. I got a call from Mrs. Gilly about a varmint, probably a possum, raising a ruckus in her she-shed. She locked it in." Davie lumbered to his feet. "I guess I gotta go see what's what." He walked toward the door, still hunched over in his coat.

Wilde said, humor in his voice, "Looking at Davie, you'd think the station was the North Pole." He pointed to another older man, his brown uniform starched cardboard stiff, expertly twirling a pencil between his fingers. "~~white~~ hair on

Agent Cinelli, FBI. Cle~~~~

proud of his full ~~~~

Clem ~~~~

with~~ead.~~ That's right. My mom calls it allit-
eration. I'm Clement Collin Clark, ma'am—
C cubed." He grinned, showing very white buck
teeth. "So, Chief, it's all over town this lovely lady
is your new girlfriend. Davie said she was a looker,
and she was in some kind of trouble. But I don't see
why she can't take care of herself, seeing she's a fed-
erale." Clem paused and eyed Pippa. "You sure don't
look like an FBI agent."

Pippa arched a brow at him. "I don't? Oh my,
that's not good. I guess I'll have to try harder. Any
suggestions, Clem?"

"Don't mean anything by it, Agent Cinelli. You
can't help it if you're pretty. I'm happy to help if I
can, otherwise I'd have to be dealing with the little
ghostbusters who threw tennis balls at the Har-
mons' house Halloween night when they weren't
home to give out candy. Broke a window and the
neighbors reported it. Chief, please give me something I can do for you instead."

"As a matter of fact, Clem, we do need your help.
I'd like you to take a walk around town, talk to
people, see if you hear about anyone new in town.
Agent Cinelli and I will be in my office."

Wilde's office was long and narrow with windows across the back looking out at a scraggly tree and two bushes Pippa didn't recognize, a parking lot off to the left. A nice oak credenza sat behind an ancient military-looking desk, probably from World War II. There were wire baskets, a pile of papers, and a brand-new computer on top of the desk, nothing else. Two chairs sat in front of the desk. Wilde motioned her to a chair, sat down, and booted up his Mac.

While he waited, Wilde said, "By the way, I know Grizzlie. If he was guilty of dropping a gum wrapper on the sidewalk, he'd come to me and confess. Grizzlie didn't look at your tablet."

"I can see Mrs. Trumbo snooping," Pippa said. "Not a big deal, simple curiosity about her guests, maybe telling herself she was protecting the others. But then who did she tell? Did she consider an FBI agent staying at her B&B only an interesting bit of gossip? Or did she have another reason for searching my room? Do you think someone paid her to keep an eye out for a stranger who could be FBI?" Pippa shook her head. "But who would pay her?"

"All good questions."

Pippa looked down at her tablet. "Before we start dumpster-diving, let me tell you what I already know. Major Trumbo was career army, retired, honorably discharged. He and Mrs. Filly were married for fifteen years, no children. After he divorced Mrs. Filly, he married Mrs. Trumbo, also divorced. The major did consulting work on government contracts with the army. He died of a heart attack, was cremated, and sits, as you saw, in a beautiful gold urn on the mantel in Mrs. Trumbo's living room.

"Mrs. Trumbo's son by her first husband—Ronald Pomfrey's his name—is a textile artist. He moved back to Baltimore after staying here in St. Lumis with his mom and the major for a couple of years. That's all we've got."

There was a knock on Wilde's door. A dazzling young woman with long, dark brown hair in a French braid thicker than Pippa's danced in, no other way to put it. She looked insanely happy. "I wanted to meet the FBI agent, Chief." She stuck out her hand to Pippa, who obligingly shook it. "I'm Deputy Lorraine Carr, but everybody calls me Mouse."

Pippa nodded and smiled. "I'm Agent Cinelli."

"It's a total pleasure. Chief, is there anything special you want me to do?"

"Do what you do best, Mouse, but keep your eyes open. Let me know if you see anything unusual."

"You got it."

After Mouse danced out, Pippa asked, "And just what does Mouse do best?"

"Parking meter patrol. No one ever gets pissed when Mouse gives them a parking ticket. It's like she waves fairy dust on them and they smile even though she's taken twenty bucks out of their pockets. So do you want to call Savich?"

"No, he and MAX have enough on their plates. Actually, I'm pretty good at this myself. How about you?"

He smiled, and they settled in to work.

After a bit, Pippa raised her face. "Wilde?"

He looked up. "Yeah?"

"I think I might have something. Here's Major Trumbo's obituary in the *St. Lumis Herald*." She read: "'Major Corinthian Ellis Trumbo died unexpectedly of a heart attack while vacationing in the Poconos with his family.' It lists his age, sixty-two, and briefly mentions his military service and that he had no surviving children. No mention of Mrs. Filly. I guess Mrs. Trumbo wrote the obit." She typed a moment, then looked up. "And here's another obituary in a veterans' magazine. A bit more here. Yes, it says Major Trumbo was vacationing at his stepson's cabin with his wife, stepson, and one of Ronald's female friends, in the Poconos, near Cold Bluff. Sounds like a girlfriend to me. Just a second." Pippa called up the Poconos on her tablet map. "Here we go. Cold Bluff is a tiny hamlet, maybe half an hour from Bushkill, which is very small, too. The obit goes on to say the heart attack was sudden, with no medical warnings. He was cremated, and a memorial service was held at his home in St. Lumis, Maryland."

Wilde held up his hand and punched in a number on his cell. "Davie? Do you remember a memorial service for Major Trumbo here in St. Lumis? Really? Okay, I see. No, no problem." He looked up. "Davie says there was no memorial service held here for Major Trumbo. I wonder where the major was cremated."

"Hang on. Okay, no funeral homes in Bushkill; it's too small. Here we go, the closest funeral home is in Stroudsburg. Give me your cell, Wilde." He listened to her talk a clerk at the funeral home into checking her records. When she hung up, she shook her head. "He wasn't cremated in Stroudsburg. Of course, there are other funeral homes in the wider area, but you know what's smacking me in the face?"

He clasped his large hands in front of him on the desktop and raised an eyebrow.

"If Mrs. Trumbo and her son and his unidentified girlfriend didn't take the major to the local hospital, there wouldn't be a physician's report, no death certificate, no autopsy, even though it was an unattended death. There were evidently no questions because no one knew to ask any. He was cremated. Mrs. Trumbo came back to St. Lumis and bought the B&B and put an obituary in the *St. Lumis Herald*. Ronald went back to Baltimore. And that leaves the question: Did Major Trumbo really fall over dead with a heart attack? Or did something else happen, something Mrs. Trumbo doesn't want anyone to know? And what happened to Ronald's girlfriend? Hang on a second." Pippa found Mrs.

Trumbo's Facebook page without difficulty and scrolled through her public photo gallery. "Wilde? Here's a photo of Ronald Pomfrey and his mother. Given the date, the major was already dead."

Wilde looked down at the photo on Pippa's tablet of a slight young man with a big smile, carrying several books.

Pippa said, "He's handsome as sin even with his hair beginning to recede. I don't see any of Mrs. Trumbo in him, so I guess his dad was a looker. Here's another photo of him with his art." Ronald Pomfrey was standing next to a loom covered with a kaleidoscope of colored yarns forming a vivid picture of a dozen different fruits all tumbled together, so real you felt you could pluck out a plum or a pear and munch. His long, narrow hand rested possessively on the loom. "He studied at the Maryland Institute College of Art, a private art and design college in Baltimore."

Wilde waited, then cocked his head to one side. "And?"

Pippa grinned. "Drumroll . . . I've studied Savich's file on Marsia Gay. She also studied at the MICA, for one year. She's an artist, modern sculpture in metals."

He sat forward, eyes gleaming. "Tell me, how old is Ronald Pomfrey?"

She typed. "He's thirty-six. Young enough to be Black Hoodie."

"Sure is. And Marsia is in her late twenties. That

puts them both at MICA, but, Cinelli, there are years between them."

"Well, Ronald didn't go to MICA until he was thirty. He was an assistant manager in a hotel in Baltimore his mother managed before she married Major Trumbo. So we have Marsia Gay and Ronald Pomfrey at the same place, same time. That doesn't prove they knew each other, but it's way more than a start."

Wilde said, "You're thinking Marsia Gay was the girlfriend at the cabin in the Poconos when Major Trumbo died?"

"If she was the girlfriend, then Mrs. Trumbo lied about knowing her."

Wilde smiled. "Okay, we're getting somewhere, Cinelli. I can think of a bunch of phone calls to make, but they'll have to wait until the morning. Maybe it's time to call it a night." He rose and stretched. "You want a taco?"

52

After a dinner of meatloaf, mashed potatoes, green beans, and an excellent vegetable frittata for Savich, everyone adjourned to the living room. With Savich's mother and Senator Monroe cheering him on, Sean played a video racing game with his dad that Sherlock had rescued from the house. She stood in the doorway of the living room, her cell against her ear, listening to their logistics expert, Janet Mickelson, who never seemed to run out of new wrinkles in the home repairs, from replacing the old wiring in the kitchen to another week's delay in shipping the living room draperies she and Dillon had picked out. Sherlock knew she should be taking notes, but she only listened as Janet addressed one problem after another.

"Sherlock, I saved the good news for last, guaranteed to bring a smile. My contractor can start work in the morning, and he promised when he's done with the painting, there'll be absolutely no more smoke smell in the house. All of Sean's new bedroom furniture will be ready for delivery as soon as the painting's done, exactly what he wanted. So, we're all on the same page. I'm still hopeful we'll be done a week before Christmas." She paused. "Well, unless they delay the inspections, which, alas, is known to happen more often than I'd like."

The week before Christmas seemed like a perfect new mantra. When Sherlock punched off, she stood a moment in the arched doorway and looked at her mother-in-law, her shoulder touching Robert Monroe's as she laughed at Sean's super-serious efforts to beat his father, or rather Magic John. It struck her what a blessing it was to have this time with Dillon's mom, and to really get to know the senator, who'd been a rock, tossing in the occasional nugget on what to do about this or that problem concerning the house. Sherlock had no doubt Sean was having the time of his life being the only kid in a house with four adults. Not to mention Gabriella, who was helping Minna, picking up Sean from school and shepherding him to all his activities. When they finally moved back home, Sherlock imagined it would take a month to convince Sean he wasn't the king of the universe. She watched her son clap his hands and chair-dance next to his father. Dillon was distracted, the great part of his brain still focused on what he'd have to do next to keep Rebekah Manvers, and of course his own family, safe.

When Savich took Sean to bed, he listened with half an ear while his over-the-moon-excited son crowed about beating him. To calm Sean down, Savich sang him a new country-western song that had been floating around in his head the past week about a long-distance truck driver named Ed and a pretty young thing outside Yuma, Arizona. Ed woke up from sleeping with the angels in the middle of the desert, his wallet, his water bottle, and his truck long gone. Sean was out before Ed woke up.

When Sherlock joined him in the larger of Minna's two guest bedrooms, she found him sitting on one side of the queen-size bed, which was, admittedly, a bit small for the two of them, wearing only his black boxers, his hands clasped between his knees, muttering to himself.

She rubbed his shoulder until she had his attention. "Tonight was good for everyone, Dillon. You needed the distraction to let your brain simmer a bit."

She leaned down and kissed him. "Time to sleep. Talk about a long day, not to mention the small dollop of excitement. Nothing like a hostage rescue to put an end to it. But it's over now. Duvall is alive, and MAX is working. You have to close your mind down, stop your angsting, all right? You needn't worry about Rebekah. Her husband's with her when Griffin isn't. She'll be fine, and we're all safe for now. Get your very fine self into bed." Sherlock kissed him again and watched him climb into bed and pull the covers to his chest. She looked down at him, gave him what she hoped was a sexy grin. "I'll be right with you, gorgeous. I'm thinking Mama needs to make you forget your name."

She sashayed to the dresser with a mirror hanging above it and started brushing her hair. She heard him humming, a new country-western song. She frowned. "Do you know what I can't get my brain around, Dillon? How did anyone find out Rebekah knew about the Big Take? Her grandfather made her promise never to tell a soul, and she didn't. Until last week Rebekah believed the Big Take was only one of his made-up adventures."

After Sherlock made him forget his name, Savich fell boneless into a deep sleep.

He was lying on his back on a narrow white bed. Blackness surrounded him, cocooned him, but it wasn't frightening; it was comforting, like resting in his mother's arms, listening to her heartbeat as she whispered how much she loved him, how she knew he'd be a great man one day. He knew time was passing, but it wasn't important. The blackness never lightened, always stayed exactly the same, but that was all right. He was one with it, a part of it.

He heard many voices around him, but they didn't touch him. Only hers did. Rebekah held his hand, and he heard her beloved voice, telling him how much she loved him and missed him. She told him about her studies, how after she earned a master's degree, she was going to hunt for forged paintings and keep the art world honest. And it might make her rich. He wanted to tell her she already was rich. Hadn't he left her several million in a trust? But none of that mattered. Rebekah was here, and she was his.

As she held his hand, she repeated to him dozens of adventure stories he'd told her when she was young, wild hair-raising tales he'd invented about his and Nate's exploits. Nate. Where was Nate? He knew Nate was gone, gone for a very long time, but he didn't know where he was. With Miranda? Was that her name? So pretty she was. With his mother? How much time had passed? He didn't know, didn't care. His mind settled into a timeless drift.

He heard Rebekah's voice telling him about the Big Take again, her favorite story, she'd say. He wished he could tell her the Big Take wasn't only a story, it was real. The poem he'd written and made her memorize, the poem he'd made her promise never to tell another person, wafted through his head, but he couldn't seem to remember the words. He wished he could tell her he loved her, but he couldn't. He floated, content, then he heard another voice, close to his face, a voice that said matter-of-factly, "I do wonder if you can hear me, Congressman Clarkson. Can I call you John? Of course I can. You won't mind, will you, not about anything. Your granddaughter is charming. How she loves to repeat all those stories to you, but it's time for her to go now." He felt a warm hand on his forehead, felt the warm hand take his pulse. "But you'll be fine, just fine. I'll be staying here with you, John."

He fell asleep then, rocking in his mother's warm, strong arms, living in a lullaby.

Savich slowly opened his eyes. He stared into the gray predawn light coming through the window, didn't know for an instant where he was, then felt Sherlock's soft breath against his neck. She'd set the dream in motion, told him to let it all simmer. He lightly touched his fingertips to her curls, and she pushed closer. He smiled, kissed her, and whispered into the warm air, "Thank you for that, John Clarkson."

53

Mrs. Frazier looked up to see Rebekah, Agent Hammersmith, and a tall, tough-looking man she'd never seen before step off the elevator.

"Rebekah, you're back so soon? I saw you yesterday—" Mrs. Frazier's voice fell off a cliff. She stared at three stone faces. She knew something was very wrong, and it involved Mrs. Clarkson. And the company? Mrs. Clarkson hadn't been her usual self these past weeks. She'd gone from euphoric, which was rare at the best of times, to pacing her office, quiet and brooding, to sharp and curt. Olivia had heard her speaking with the Clarksons' senior accountant, heard raised voices. She'd nerved herself up and asked Mrs. Clarkson if there were any problems and could she help? Mrs. Clarkson had given her a long look and said only, "Yes, Olivia, but they're my problems. You're not to worry." And she'd walked back into her office, chin up.

And now the FBI was here again with Rebekah. What had Mrs. Clarkson done?

She slowly rose and automatically straightened her suit jacket. She looked briefly at the closed door, then turned back. "Rebekah, what is going on? Who is he?"

"Mrs. Frazier, this is Special Agent Savich, FBI, and you remember Agent Hammersmith. We're here to see my grandmother."

Mrs. Frazier nodded and held out her hand to the big man she'd never seen before. Savich stepped forward, shook her hand, and gave her his credentials. He had a hard hand, and were those scars on his finger pads? She studied his ID, handed it back to him. He smiled at her, and it changed his face utterly, made her wonder if her divorced daughter might take him out for a drink. He said, "Mrs. Frazier, a pleasure. Rebekah has told us how kind you've been to her over the years."

She didn't know what to say to that, only smiled and nodded. She saw Agent Hammersmith was still looking hard as a hanging judge. And Rebekah? She looked resolute, ready for battle. They were here to deliver bad news. She knew trouble when she saw it, and trouble was standing in front of her. She said slowly, "So you're here to see your grandmother? All of you, together?"

"Yes. Please see we aren't disturbed, Mrs. Frazier. I—I'm very sorry about this."

Olivia could only nod. She watched Rebekah open Mrs. Clarkson's door, watched her chin go up as she marched in, followed by the two agents. The door closed. Olivia sat back down and did what she did best, according to her daughter— she pulled the knitting out of her bottom drawer and worried.

Gemma Clarkson slowly rose as Agent Hammersmith and Rebekah walked into her office, a stranger flanking them. She made no move to come out from behind her desk. She said, "You must be Agent Savich? I spoke to you by phone on Monday. I pictured you in my mind, you know, I always do when I have only a voice to give me clues." She paused, studied his face, and said slowly, "I imagined you'd be a big man."

He stepped forward to hand her his creds. "I'm Agent Savich."

She waved them away. "Why are you three here so early on this chilly Wednesday morning?" She paused, pointed to chairs. There were only two set in front of her desk. She waited until Agent Hammersmith fetched another chair, carried it over, and sat down. All three looked at her a moment, unspeaking. Savich leaned forward in his chair. "Mrs. Clarkson, we've been looking into your company finances. Since Clarkson United Industries is privately held, it took time and effort to put together some of the pieces, but we now know your company has suffered financial setbacks recently, severe ones. But your own situation is rather desperate because you expanded by borrowing, which didn't work out at all for you. You have a large bank loan due in several weeks, and you'll be hard-pressed to pay it."

Gemma gave him a rictus of a smile. He had no clue as to what she was thinking. "You have been busy, Agent Savich. Let me just say that this company has been in business longer than you've been alive, and our books are really none of your business."

"Perhaps not, Mrs. Clarkson, except it might explain the puzzle of why you're suddenly so interested in getting your hands on a great deal of money. It's a puzzle that started more than twenty-five years ago, before Nate's murder in 1995."

"There is no puzzle," Gemma said. "Nate wasn't murdered; his death was ruled an accident. He was drunk and fell overboard. Now, I want to know why you three are here. I have a budget meeting shortly, so say what you have to say and leave." She shot a look of ill-disguised dislike at Rebekah, a look from Rebekah's oldest memories. She felt her familiar child's guilt that it must be her fault. She remembered the endless questions she'd wanted to ask but was too afraid to, and then she'd simply closed her grandmother out of her mind and her life.

Gemma said, never looking away from Rebekah's face, her voice hard and flat, "Particularly you, Rebekah. Look at you, a little Joan of Arc, leading your troops into battle. What did you come to complain about this time? I know it's not about where your next meal's coming from or how you will pay the rent. Did someone try to kidnap you again? Were you saved by another strong man?"

Savich saw Rebekah was used to the barely veiled venom. Then he saw her draw herself up taller in her chair. She said easily, "No, ma'am. No more attempted kidnappings and believe me, I know how lucky I am. I have a man who loves me and a grandfather who loved me, too."

Good, Rebekah was standing up to this intimidating woman, but they were getting off track. Savich said, "We're here to talk about a number of things, Mrs. Clarkson, and we can begin with Zoltan. You said you'd never met her, but we ran a facial recognition program and found a photograph of the two of you together at a benefit for the Spiritualist Society in Baltimore earlier this year."

For only a brief instant, Gemma's face went blank, then she shook her head and said smoothly, "Well, yes, now that you mention it, I do recall meeting her. We run in some of the same circles, contribute to some of the same causes. But that doesn't mean I hired her to do anything nefarious. From what you told me, she tried to help Rebekah communicate with her grandfather, and even if she misrepresented what was happening, it wasn't illegal, was it? Some believe; some don't."

"Ah, but you knew what Rebekah's grandfather would say, what he didn't know, what he would ask for."

"That is nonsense. How would I know such a thing?"

"From the private nurse who attended Congressman Clarkson in the last months of his life at the sanitarium."

A patrician eyebrow went up. "I hired many nurses to attend him. What's your point?"

Savich said, "Mrs. Clarkson, we know there had to be a trigger point, a recent one, when you realized Rebekah knew about the Big Take. She never believed it was real, at least not until after her meeting with Zoltan. I doubt your husband ever told you about the Big Take, but you found out about it regardless. From Nate Elderby.

"The trigger point was Heather Aubrey, the private nurse you hired three months before your husband died. She told you what Rebekah knew. Heather Aubrey, like all the other private nurses you hired over the years, presented herself at your office once a week to give you reports about the status of your husband, who his visitors were, what the doctors were saying. No doubt you usually heard all the same answers from the nurses throughout the years Congressman Clarkson lay in a coma at the Mayfield Sanitarium.

"But what a surprise when Mrs. Aubrey told you one incredibly valuable piece of information. That's when everything began to fall into place."

Gemma said, "I have no idea what you're talking about. Nurse Aubrey was nice enough, appeared genuinely upset when Johnny finally died. She never told me anything I didn't already know. He was unresponsive, and Rebekah was there visiting three, four times a week, hanging all over him. There was nothing more, Agent Savich. And when he finally drew his last breath, it was a formality."

Savich continued, "We spoke to Mrs. Aubrey, and she repeated to us what she told you. I imagine you tried not to show your excitement, but she saw it, nevertheless, and wondered."

Griffin turned on his cell phone recorder. "I'm sure you'll recognize Mrs. Aubrey's voice."

54

They listened to an older woman's voice speaking in a soft Virginia drawl:

My visits with Mrs. Clarkson were always short, and I understood because I knew they had to be very tedious for her after so many years with her husband in a coma. There was never much to say, only that Rebekah visited her grandfather often, always spoke with me, asked me questions. Such a kind girl, I always thought, a lovely girl. I was told by the Mayfield nursing staff that Rebekah had been coming there for years whenever she could. She'd talk to Mr. Clarkson as she stroked his hand, tell him what she was up to, and then she'd repeat one of the wild adventure stories he'd told her when she was a child.

It was the strangest thing, Agents, but when I happened to mention that story you asked me about, the Big Take story, on my last visit to Mrs. Clarkson before he died, she got very intense, and her eyes fastened on my face. She wanted to know everything her granddaughter said, so I told her what I remembered. It was her favorite of all his stories, and she'd recited a poem he'd written for her about it, about where he'd hidden the Big Take. As I said, it seemed to me Mrs. Clarkson was going to jump out of her skin. She wanted me to tell her the poem, but I couldn't remember it, of course, only something about it all being in his head. Mrs. Clarkson became very angry with me, and I didn't understand why. She told me to record everything Rebekah said to Mr. Clarkson when she visited again.

Griffin turned off the recording.

Gemma said nothing.

Rebekah said, "Mrs. Aubrey told us I didn't mention the Big Take on my next four visits, and then Grandfather died and she went on to another job. I imagine you thought the money was lost to you after Grandfather had his strokes. I know he never told you where it was, otherwise why would he swear me to secrecy? And now you thought he'd told me where the Big Take was, hidden in that poem, even if I thought it was only a story." Rebekah searched her grandmother's face. "You couldn't ask me about it outright. We've hardly been on speaking terms, and you knew I wouldn't tell you the poem. So you hired Zoltan to try to convince me Grandfather wanted to speak with me, to trick me into telling her what I know. You've always believed people can speak to the dead through mediums. You thought Zoltan could convince me. But she didn't."

Savich said, "You knew Nate Elderby and your husband had a great deal of cash or bonds hidden away that they'd stolen in the early nineties. They shared everything, no doubt being in something criminal as well. Money like that would draw a great deal of attention, particularly to a congressman, so they knew they had to wait. They stashed it.

"How much was it, Mrs. Clarkson? Fifty million? A hundred million? I wondered why your husband didn't tell you, but it's obvious he didn't want you to have it. The question is why.

"I found credit card records from Mr. Nathaniel Elderby registering as a guest at the Paulson Hotel in Richmond, a private boutique hotel in business since

1989. They continue to cater to the very wealthy who demand privacy. We tracked down the retired former manager of the Paulson. He recognized both you and Nate from photos taken of you in the nineties. And everything became clear. You and Nate were lovers, and you were at that hotel more than once. I believe Nate told you about the Big Take—probably pillow talk—until he caught himself. Then he met and fell in love with Miranda. He broke it off with you and married her. She was twenty-three years old, a knockout, and she worshiped him."

Gemma exploded with ancient pent-up rage. "That bastard told me he wouldn't break up John's marriage! He told me I was old, can you believe that? He said Miranda—that child—was perfect for him." Her voice cut off like a spigot. She seamed her lips, stared through him.

Savich continued without pause, without acknowledging what she'd said, "And then Nate decided he had to take his share of the money and leave the country with his new wife. I imagine he did plan to meet with John that day on Dawg Creek where they fished, perhaps to pick up the money. But he never got the chance.

"You met him there yourself. You'd have made threats, I'm sure, and then you lost it, hit him on the head and threw him overboard, and no one ever knew, not even Miranda. Did John find out about the affair? Suspect you'd killed his best friend? Is that why he decided you'd never see a penny of that money?"

Gemma slowly rose, flattened her hands on the desktop, and gave each of them a disgusted look. "I've been patient with you, but I will not listen to this absurd tale you've spun any longer. You've accused me of murdering Nate, with no proof whatsoever. Memories of a hotel manager from a picture taken twenty-five years ago? Is that your proof? My lawyers would have a field day with that."

Rebekah said slowly, "Do you know I was ready to believe Grandfather could have killed his best friend? I bitterly regret ever considering it, even for an instant." She paused a moment, then the words burst out of her. "What I still don't understand is why you hated me as far back as I can remember. I am your granddaughter. I am of your flesh. Why, Grandmother?"

Gemma's voice was vicious, filled with bitterness. "You stupid girl! You think your father was a young man who abandoned you and your mother, and she never even identified him to you? Didn't you ever consider that odd? You never saw him, never heard his name? You're an idiot. There never was a young man."

And then, finally, it all slid into place. Rebekah said slowly, "I never even wondered why Grandfather spent so much time with me. I thought all grandfathers were like him. I knew he loved me, knew he'd give his life for me, yes, but I never once thought he wasn't my grandfather. But he wasn't; he was my father. What happened? Your husband had his own affair, got his lover pregnant, and he asked his daughter, a footloose twenty-two-year-old, to pretend to be my mother, to raise me? It's amazing she agreed. I wonder what he gave her to claim his baby as her own. No wonder she asked me to call her Caitlin and not Mother." Rebekah started laughing, gasping for breath. "She's my older sister. It's all so clear now. You're right, I am an idiot." She hiccupped. "And there you were, considered by one and all, myself included, my grandmother. That must have burned you to the ground."

Gemma's hands were fists. "I had to look at you, Johnny's little princess, the pride of his benighted life. Do you know Caitlin told me she did love you like her daughter? She hadn't wanted to, but she began to the moment she held you in her arms. And my husband saw to it I'd never tell anyone the truth, certainly not you, or he'd ruin me." Gemma straightened, up went her chin. "In the end, who cares? None of it matters now. Johnny, your precious father, is dead and gone. It was I who took very good care of him all those long years when he was nothing more than a rotting vegetable. As for the rest of it, I did not kill Nate. That's absurd." She leaned forward, her eyes hard on their faces. "Now, I want all of you to leave. Go make your accusations to the next person on your list. If you bother me again, I will call my lawyers and let them deal with you."

Rebekah said in a pleasant voice, "Sit down, you vicious harridan. I have more to say to you."

Gemma stiffened and stared at Rebekah, her mouth agape. "What could you possibly have to say to me, you worthless brat?" But she sat down.

Rebekah smiled. "When I refused to tell Zoltan anything, did you hire those two men to kidnap me? Did you tell them to beat me until I told them the poem? Were you going to kill me after I told it to them?"

Gemma shook her head. "Don't be any more of a fool than you already are. I know nothing of your attempted kidnapping. I know nothing of any of this. As for you, Rebekah, I hope I never have to see your face again." She leaned forward, stared hard at Rebekah. "Do you know, you look more like your real mother? I wonder if you'll ever find the slut."

Rebekah actually smiled. "You want to know what scares me? You're still officially my grand-mother, and I'm still officially related to you."

No one moved. Rebekah said, "Do you know the poem Grandfather—Father—had me memorize? I have no idea what it means, none at all. Even if you'd succeeded, even if those thugs you hired had tortured me, there was nothing I could have told them."

"You're lying."

"No, I'm not. So you see, this elaborate scheme of yours was for absolutely nothing at all."

Savich said, "Mrs. Clarkson, feel free to call your lawyers. You're going to need them. We have Gary Duvall in custody, the thug you hired to shoot Zoltan. He isn't talking now, but he has very little to lose and might save himself a return to a supermax prison if he does talk. I suspect we'll be able to tie him to you in some way. What are the odds you'd be connected to two people who shot each other if you're not involved?"

Gemma threw back her head and laughed. "Oh my, do take any evidence you find to a federal attorney, and he can laugh along with me. I don't know any Gary Duvall."

As they rode down in the elevator, Griffin sighed. "I really thought she'd incriminate herself, but we got nothing solid. The old bat is right, we need more."

Savich said as they stepped out of the elevator into the lobby, "You should go home, Rebekah. Call your husband, get him home, spend some downtime with him. You two have a lot to talk about. I have to admit, your grandmother surprised me with how unconcerned she seemed about Gary Duvall. Something isn't right." He threw his Porsche fob in the air, caught it, and started whistling as he walked with them to the parking lot.

As Rebekah and Griffin watched him drive out in his beautiful red Porsche, she said, "Do you know what's grand, Griffin? That hateful old woman isn't really my grandmother. At last everything makes sense." She paused by Griffin's Range Rover. "And I don't have to feel guilty about wanting to see her in jail."

55

Pippa pumped her fist. "Halfway through the alumni list at MICA, and I finally found Jason Osbourne, now a commercial artist, who graduated with Ronald and knew both him and Marsia Gay. He remembered both of them made a good-size splash, lots of talent." She sat back in her chair and grinned like a sinner. "And he said they were an item, a couple, in the year they were there together."

"Nailed it. Good, Cinelli." Wilde sat back in his chair, rubbed his eyes. "After all those phone calls to the faculty at MICA without any luck, I thought that particular well might be dry. So let's make the assumption the girlfriend at the cabin where Major Trumbo died was Marsia Gay. Then Mrs. Trumbo lied about not knowing her and she must have had a strong reason.

"Let me ask you—do you think Ronald was the man who knocked you out, tied you up, and took your cell? And then drove to Washington and set fire to Savich and Sherlock's house?"

Pippa sat back in her chair, closed her eyes. She was tired, hyped, her brain still going a mile a minute. She cocked an eye at him and said through a yawn, "Makes sense."

Wilde pulled out his cell and punched in a number. "Call me a dolt. Ronald hasn't been in Baltimore, but here in St. Lumis." He said into his cell, "Davie, do you know Ronald Pomfrey, Mrs. Trumbo's son?"

Davie sounded out of breath. "Well, Chief, sure I know him, a nice enough guy, I guess, all into his art, does pictures on looms, real pretty. Then maybe something happened, I don't know what, but he left St. Lumis. You weren't here yet, so more than three years ago."

"Have you seen him recently? Here, in St. Lumis?"

A moment of silence, then, "Now you mention it, I did catch sight of him Saturday in the middle of a knot of Halloween tourists. He was all bundled up, but I could tell it was him, even with his sunglasses on. He seemed to be in a hurry, so I didn't speak to him."

Wilde felt his heart pound. *Gotcha.* "Thanks, Davie. You get the possum yesterday?"

"Sure did. I took him out to the marshland and let him go. He wasn't happy, but I figured he'd have a better chance of finding a girlfriend there than in Mrs. Gilly's she-shed."

When Wilde laid his cell on top of his desk, Pippa was grinning. "So that places Ronald Pomfrey right here in town on Saturday. Let's back up. Ronald and Marsia hooked up at MICA, and they were close enough that she went with him and his family to his cabin in the Poconos. After the major's death, she appears to have gone her own way. Why? Because of what happened at that cabin?"

Wilde was weaving a pen through his fingers, a longtime habit. "But how does that explain why Ronald would be willing to attack you and try to burn down an FBI agent's house for her? Is it all about money? Dillon told me she has around seventy thousand dollars in her bank account, but you know her lawyer will eat up all that. So she wouldn't have enough money to tempt Ronald into torching Savich's house. Why would he turn into an arsonist for her?" He paused a moment, then, "Savich is certain Marsia Gay is behind the fire?"

"Yes, he's positive. She as good as admitted it to him."

Wilde said, "Then it all has to go back to the four of them at Ronald's cabin. We found that community hospital about forty-five minutes away. An ambulance could have gotten to Major Trumbo and taken him to the ER or pronounced him dead at the cabin, which would have meant a doctor signed off on it. And that would have meant records, Cinelli. Why aren't there records?"

Pippa shrugged. "Maybe when they realized he was dead, they decided not to bother, took his body elsewhere."

"Maybe, but I'm hearing a drum banging, Cinelli. What if Major Trumbo didn't die of a heart attack? Remember, both Mrs. Filly and Mrs. Trumbo said he was nasty, maybe an abuser."

Pippa straightened in her chair. "So you're saying Mrs. Trumbo helped him to the hereafter? We're talking murder then, Wilde. And Marsia Gay was there to see it."

56

At ten o'clock, Pippa and Wilde huddled close in the alley across the street from Major Trumbo's B&B. Pippa whispered, "I've been texting with Dillon. He says Warden Putney at the D.C. Jail has refused Marsia any visitors or outgoing mail. Of course, he can't prevent her from speaking to her lawyer, but the guards are keeping a close watch now. So far no attempt to pass a communication. I doubt the lawyer's the conduit; he'd be putting his license and his own freedom at risk."

Wilde said, "Then she had to be using another prisoner, which could come back to bite her."

"Dillon also says Veronica Lake is still alive, but there's not much hope she'll make it. Veronica is the only direct witness against Marsia Gay, and if she dies, they might have to cut Marsia loose, or fail to convict her. That would be a nightmare for Dillon, after Sherlock and Sean nearly died in the fire. So we have to nail this down, Wilde. We have to."

"Did Savich run the thumbprint we collected at the abandoned grocery store?"

"Yes, he did, but the thumbprint isn't in the database. However, that won't keep us from matching it to Ronald Pomfrey, if it's his. But we have to find him first. Since a couple of agents at the Baltimore Field Office said he hasn't shown up at his apartment, and he was here on Saturday, according to Davie, Savich agrees our staking out Mrs. Trumbo is our best shot at getting our hands on him."

Wilde stretched. "Either he'll come tonight or she'll go to him, wherever he is. And that, Cinelli, is why we're out here in the cold. And if I'm wrong, we'll be back here tomorrow night."

Pippa leaned closer. "Trouble is, if neither mother nor son moves tonight, we'll freeze to death. My feet are cold and I'm even wearing those hiking socks you lent me. My toes aren't toasty at all, so I guess you cheaped out, Wilde."

"Hey, watch your language. Those socks are Walmart's best."

The minutes ticked by slow as syrup in the snow.

Wilde said matter-of-factly, "My gut says he's staying here. He knows St. Lumis. Even with you here, he's safe enough since you didn't see him clearly when he attacked you, even if he happened to bump into you, you wouldn't recognize him. He doesn't know we suspect him of anything yet.

"And remember, Marsia Gay has been contacting him. Look, Pippa, even if he doesn't come tonight, he will come eventually. He and his mother have to meet, talk over how to deal with what's happening, how to deal with Marsia."

They saw a figure wrapped up in a dark full-length winter coat and high boots, a watch cap pulled down tight to cover most of his face. He looked furtively around the B&B and walked in through the kitchen door.

Pippa whispered, "Hello, Ronald."

They walked quietly across the deserted street, eased up to the kitchen window, and watched Mrs. Trumbo hand him a cup of coffee. Ronald Pomfrey had pulled off his watch cap, and he looked like his photos, but there was something different. He looked exhausted and scared. He sat hunched over, cradling the coffee in his hands, and sipped.

"We need to get closer. Maybe we can hear what they're saying." They eased in as close as they could get and heard Ronald speaking. "It's him, Wilde," she whispered against his ear, "I recognize his voice."

They pressed closer, heard Ronald Pomfrey say, "I got another text from her today, Mom. She's more pissed than ever. She's losing it."

Mrs. Trumbo's hand tightened on her son's

shoulder. "What does the evil witch want you to do now?"

Ronald raised exhausted eyes to her face, gave an ugly laugh. "What does it matter, Mom? I'm screwed, no way around it. And whether Marsia throws us under the bus or not, when they find out what I've done, it will be all over. I'm only sorry I've pulled you down with me." He set his coffee cup on the kitchen table, lowered his face to his hands. Was he crying? Then he suddenly raised his head. "We should have faced up to what happened, never paid her a cent, ever." His words clogged in his throat. "A couple hundred bucks a month was never going to be enough for her anyway."

Mrs. Trumbo was rubbing his shoulders with her big hands. "What's done is done, Ron. Always, in the back of my mind, I knew she'd turn up again. She's vicious, relentless, but agonizing about it won't help. Show me that text message. I need to know what she wants you to do."

Ronald pushed his phone at her like it was a snake that had bitten him. "Here, I don't want to read it again. She's not going to stop, Mom, not until Agent Savich and his family are dead, or all of this blows up on us."

Ronald swiped his gloved fingers over his tear-shined eyes. "This is all my fault. She wouldn't have been there if not for me. I thought she loved me, believed in me. And she was so beautiful, you thought so, too. I shouldn't have let any of this happen. I'm sorry, Mom, so very sorry."

Mrs. Trumbo leaned down and hugged him to her chest as she read the text message. Then she kissed the top of his head and lightly stroked her fingers over his face. "This isn't your fault, Ron. You couldn't have known how twisted she was." She sucked in her breath. "What she wants this time can't, won't, happen. We have to deal with this some other way."

Ronald looked up at his mother and said in a voice deadened with disgust, "She wants me to go after the Savich kid, leave him in an isolated place. She knows he'd die, Mom. It's winter, and it's cold. He would die, and it would be because of me. She wants Savich to go searching for him. She wants him to find his son dead."

The words hung between them. Mrs. Trumbo said very precisely, "You won't do that." She gave the phone back to her son, straightened over him, and threw back her shoulders. She looked like a Valkyrie.

"I've thought about this, Mom, and what I need to do is run, disappear. If I don't do anything else for her, they might not be able to put all of it together. You might still be safe."

"If you run, we'd lose each other. I'd be alone. But you're right, Ron. This has to stop. Somehow. Your leaving might be the only way to keep you safe. But you're not going to be driving anywhere tonight. It's too cold, and I'm hoping we can think of some other way to deal with this. I made up a bed in the basement. Go downstairs and get some sleep. I'll wake you before anyone else is up."

They watched Ronald slowly rise, hug his mother close, whisper something, and walk, shoulders hunched, from the kitchen.

Mrs. Trumbo pulled off her apron, took her son's coffee cup to the sink, methodically rinsed it out, and set it in the drainer. She looked around the kitchen and turned off the light.

Pippa and Wilde looked at each other. "I don't know what I expected to hear," Wilde said, "but it certainly wasn't all that. Time to go say hello."

57

Pippa said quietly from the front doorway, "Mrs. Trumbo, you don't want to go upstairs. That's right, turn around."

Pippa walked to the bottom step and looked up at Mrs. Trumbo. She stared down at them, no expression on her face, but like her son, she looked exhausted. Her voice was flat, indifferent. "Oh, it's you, Agent Cinelli, Chief Wilde. I'm tired and I don't wish to speak to either of you tonight. Perhaps tomorrow. Please go. Good night."

"I can't, ma'am. I'm staying here in the honeymoon suite. Listen to me, you need to speak to us, Mrs. Trumbo. We'll go in the living room. Chief Wilde will bring Ronald up."

Mrs. Trumbo closed her eyes a moment, then

said, "How did you know he was here? No, never mind that. It's not important." She straightened her shoulders again. The Valkyrie was back. "Let me say right away: I was behind everything. Leave my son out of this."

Pippa said again, "Let's go into the living room."

They heard Wilde's voice, a muffled shout from the basement, the sounds of a scuffle, of furniture falling. Pippa started to go down, but no, Wilde didn't need her. In a moment, he and Ronald came up the stairs, Wilde's hand flat against Pomfrey's back.

Pippa and Wilde sat across from mother and son. "I will tell you again, Ronald had nothing to do with anything. It was me, only me, not Ronald."

Pippa studied them for a moment. "Mr. Pomfrey, did you hit me on the head, tie me up, and steal my phone and gun, my ID?"

He swallowed, nodded.

Pippa said, "Thank you for not lying. Just so you know, you left your thumbprint on one of the shelves at the abandoned grocery store. Now, we know you were in your final year at MICA when you met Marsia Gay."

He shot a look toward his mother, started to shake his head.

Wilde said quietly, "We heard your conversation with your mother. It's time for the truth."

"All right, Ron, tell them," Mrs. Trumbo said.

Ronald looked beaten down. He slowly nodded.

"Marsia and I met at MICA. How do you know about Marsia?"

"Chief Wilde and I have done a bit of research," Pippa said. "Now I want both of you to tell us what happened at that cabin in the Poconos the night Major Trumbo died."

Ronald's eyes blazed. He clenched his hands. "It was my fault, not my mom's."

"What was your fault, exactly?"

He licked his dry lips, looked down at his clasped hands. "Mom?"

"Go ahead, Ron," Mrs. Trumbo said, and took his hand in hers. "We've lived with this nightmare for too long, and you can't run away anymore. It needs to be over."

Ronald raised his head and studied his mother's face. He finally nodded. "Mom and Major Trumbo—he demanded everyone call him Major— sometimes visited my cabin in the Poconos, near a little town, Cold Bluff. Marsia and I had stayed at the cabin a number of times. She was with me on that visit as well. Saturday evening, Marsia and I drove into Cold Bluff to get some groceries for Mom to make her stew. We came back earlier than expected. I heard Major Trumbo yelling curses at my mother, calling her filthy names. He sounded like a snake, hissing out his insults. I heard my mother scream. I saw Major Trumbo through the window, hitting her with his fists. Mom was fighting him, but she was losing. She got one good shot—her knee in his groin—but it didn't slow him. The front door was locked. I didn't have the key, so I broke a window and crawled in. He was bigger than me, lots bigger, and stronger, even though he was old. He started yelling at me, I was a pansy with my silly little girl looms. I was a disgrace. A beautiful woman like Marsia deserved better than a little candy cane like me, he said, maybe he should be the one to have her. I jumped him, but he threw me off and hit me, kept hitting me. Mom tried to get him off me, but he knocked her away. He left me dazed on the floor and went after Mom again. I ran to the kitchen, grabbed a knife, and came flying back in. I stabbed him in the back while he was straddling her, his big hands around her neck, choking her."

58

"Where was Marsia during the fight?"

Ronald was looking down at his hands, rubbing them against each other. "She was standing in the middle of the room, in shock, I thought at the time. She hadn't tried to help me, to help my mother. She hadn't said a word, but again, I blamed it on shock. All of us were in shock. I remember standing over him, rubbing my neck and wondering why there wasn't all that much blood. I'd thought there'd be fountains of blood when you killed someone. And he was dead. Good and dead.

"Everything stopped, like we were in a bubble, no world outside, all the horror inside, right in front of us. We all stood there staring down at Major Trumbo. I remember I hurt everywhere and wondered if he'd ruptured one of my kidneys. I looked at Mom. She was rubbing her throat where he'd choked her." He slumped forward, hugging himself, as if he'd simply run out of words.

Pippa leaned toward him. "What happened next, Ronald?"

He raised his face, pale, drawn. "It was Marsia's idea to bury him and throw in the knife. She said me and Mom would go to prison otherwise, with that stab wound in his back, so we all agreed. It was awful, digging that hole until it was big enough, deep enough, to dump him in, then shoveling the dirt over him. His eyes were open. I still see his face, see him staring up at me as the dirt covered him. But I was glad." He heaved out a breath. "The next day, I drove into Bushkill to a funeral home and bought an urn. Mom filled it with six pounds of ashes from the fireplace."

Mrs. Trumbo took her son's hand. "Ron was trying to stop the major from killing me. My boy's no murderer."

Wilde said, "Why didn't you simply go to the local authorities and tell them what happened? He was a wifebeater, nearly killed both of you. It was self-defense. Even after you buried the body. With all the shock, fear, the confusion, there would have been three of you telling the same story."

"You don't understand," Ronald said. "The next morning we couldn't believe what we'd done, but still, there was no way to change it. We talked about going to the police in Bushkill, telling them the truth. But Marsia didn't let that happen. She looked from me to Mom, and she smiled her beautiful smile and said, calm as a judge, 'I'm involved now, and no way are you going to the police. If you two martyrs turn yourselves in, I'll tell the cops you murdered your stepfather in cold blood, with no provocation except his yelling at your precious mother. Good, I can see you're starting to actually believe me.'

"She told us we were going to let the old bastard stay buried and go about our business."

Mrs. Trumbo said, "I'll never forget that smile. I'd always thought her charming, clever. I would never have guessed she was capable of that."

Ronald said, "She told us she was leaving, taking my car, but before she drove off, she said, 'Don't forget, I know where the body's buried.' She laughed, pulled out her cell phone. 'Did you wonder why I didn't help you dig his grave? I had to step back so I could record everything.' She waved the cell phone at us. 'Ronnie,' she said, 'you're a fine artist and not a bad lover, but we're over.' And she gave me that beautiful smile again. 'I'll be sending you the video, Ronnie, and you and your mom will be paying me a little something from here on out. Otherwise I'll turn you both in. I'm not kidding, you know.'"

Mrs. Trumbo said, "I'll never forget what she said to me and the contempt in her voice. 'Mrs. Trumbo, you weren't very smart, were you, to marry that sorry excuse for a man? Sorry you're not done paying for it.'" Mrs. Trumbo sighed. "It made it worse because she was right."

Ronald said, "And she drove off. She left my car in Baltimore, at my apartment. She never asked for more than we could afford, only a couple hundred a month. I saw her occasionally, saw her exhibits, followed her career. Mom and I have lived knowing she could contact us or turn us in at any time. When she was accused of trying to kill that rich old lady in Washington, we didn't know what it meant for us, until last month when she sent us instructions, reminded us of what would happen if we didn't do exactly what she said. She had me change that puzzle of Major Trumbo and send it in three separate red boxes to Agent Savich. She did it to scare the crap out of us, to torture us, to reinforce to us that she held all the cards. She wanted Agent Savich to trace the puzzle here to St. Lumis. She thought he wouldn't be able to resist, that he'd come here and check it out himself. But she was wrong. You came, Agent Cinelli. She insisted we had to get him out of Washington, get him here, somehow, so his family would be left alone at home."

Mrs. Trumbo said, "Ronald couldn't bring himself to burn the house down, so he set fire only to the kitchen, to give them time to get out. Marsia was furious because he hadn't followed her instructions. She's never going to stop trying to hurt this Agent Savich."

Ronald raised dead eyes to Pippa's face. "What's going to happen to us, Agent Cinelli?"

Pippa leaned forward. It was tough to keep her voice calm. "I can almost understand why you did what you did at the cabin, with both of you in shock, in pain from his attacking you. But tell me this: If Marsia hadn't been there, what would you have done?"

Mother and son stared at her. Mrs. Trumbo said finally, "Do you know, it's hard to be sure now. I'd like to think we would have gone to the police, but I really don't know."

Ronald said, "We were so scared, I mean, there he was, lying dead, and I'd stabbed him in the back. And I remember I kept thinking he was a monster, and I hadn't even known what he was doing to my mother." He raised his chin, and his voice grew stronger, more certain. "I'd have thought about throwing him in the woods and letting the animals have him."

Mrs. Trumbo clasped his hand hard. "I can only hope, looking back, we would have come to our senses and gone to the police. I hope we would have."

Pippa looked from one to the other. "You'll have to show us where you buried the major, and there will be consequences. But when everything is explained to the district attorney, I think you'll be cleared of killing him. Of course, there'll be other charges, Ronald, some of them serious, but you'll get a lighter sentence than you might expect. Do you know why?"

They stared back at her, the beginnings of hope in their eyes. "You're going to help us put Marsia Gay away." Pippa held out her hand. "Give me your cell phone, Ronald. I believe those texts you have will be a big nail in Marsia's coffin. Do you still have that video?"

59

Rebekah, Beck, and Rich Manvers sat at the dining room table, a fresh bouquet of red roses in the middle and the warm glow of the art deco chandelier overhead.

"Well, you've certainly become famous, Rebekah, or maybe I should say infamous," Beck said as he chewed on the excellent prime rib provided by the Manvers's cook, Mrs. Bybee. "My new girlfriend won't shut up about your adventure last Thursday. She wants all the gory details, straight from the horse's mouth, well, the mare's mouth. I told her maybe my dad wanted you out of the way and picked a dramatic way to do it." He grinned at Rebekah and his father, forked down another healthy bite of prime rib. "Or maybe you and Dad put it all on together to garner sympathy votes for his next election."

"Not funny, Beck," Rich said.

Rebekah, her mind miles away, looked at Beck, cocked her head, and said, "Would you like some salad? It's Mrs. Bybee's special Caesar."

Beck arched a dark brow at her, exactly like his father, and laughed. "Sorry, just trying to lighten things up, get us in the Thanksgiving spirit, but you're off on another planet. You want to talk about my new girlfriend? Her name's Paula Land, and she's younger than you are, Rebekah, all of twenty-two, fresh out of Princeton. Don't worry, Dad, she wouldn't be a millstone around your neck if I married her; her family has more money than God. Oil wells and refineries."

Rebekah wouldn't have cared if Paula were ninety-six. "That's nice, Beck."

Beck gave up trying to get a rise out of Rebekah, turned to his father. "Seriously, Dad, about last Thursday. The FBI and Metro cops still have their thumbs in their mouths? Still no leads?"

Rich said, "Nothing definite, no. The two men who attacked Rebekah didn't leave a trail, at least not one easily discovered."

Beck patted his mouth with his napkin and sat back in his chair. "At least that FBI agent, Savich, stopped them, so he was good for something. And that other agent, Hammersmith, who's been guarding her, Kit called him a rare hunk, a girl's fantasy. So what do you think of him, Dad? Think you could be in trouble?"

Rich took a bite of his Caesar salad and shook his head at his son. "Don't you ever get tired of trying to stir the pot? Fact is, I'm very relieved Agent Hammersmith is here to keep her safe. And don't you have to get to your date, Beck? To Paula? You don't want to be late."

Beck grinned at him again. "I promised her I'd find out as much as I could, but I see you're not going to tell me much of anything, so I'll have to make something up."

Rich sighed and took a sip of his cabernet.

"Rebekah, do you want to give me some juicy details? For Paula?"

Rebekah brought her attention to her stepson's face. "Not in this lifetime, Beck, sorry."

"You guys aren't any fun," Beck said, took a last bite of prime rib, tossed his napkin on the table, and stood. He looked at his father as he walked around the table to where Rebekah sat. He leaned down and kissed her hard and fast on the mouth. "Bye, Stepmom. Dad." He left the dining room, whistling.

Rebekah called out after him, "You need to work on your technique, Beck, if you're hoping for a second date."

They heard a laugh, then the front door closed.

"Good parting shot, sweetheart. Sorry about Beck. He's been a pain in the ass ever since he lost his mother. The shrinks couldn't cure him of it. Did I tell you he let on that he's condo hunting? Keep your fingers crossed." He toyed with his mashed potatoes. "Sorry I wasn't home for you when you got back from seeing your grandmother. I wanted to call you, find out what happened, but I didn't have a chance. I trust Agent Hammersmith stayed with you?"

"He left not ten minutes before you arrived. Turns out he had a date, too, so I insisted. I think it might have been Kit, but I didn't ask. And yes, Beck was here, and I locked the front door."

"We're finally alone. Tell me what happened."

"I know you were busy. I tried to call you, too, but your gatekeeper told me you were in an important meeting with the speaker and couldn't be disturbed unless someone died. Then I couldn't very well talk about it while Beck was here." She drew a deep breath. "Here it is. Rich, my grandfather wasn't my grandfather, he was my father. That means Gemma isn't my grandmother, and hallelujah to that."

He stared at her over the rim of his wineglass. "What? Who told you that? And you believe it? I don't understand, Rebekah. You found all this out today?"

"Believe it or not, Gemma told me. And she was happy to tell me."

He set down his wineglass. "She told you in front of the two FBI agents?"

Rebekah gave him a blazing smile. "I think she told me because I stopped being a wimp. I didn't fold my tent when she ordered all of us to leave her office. I faced her down, Rich, and that's when she said it. She took pleasure in telling me. Probably believed I'd fall apart. Imagine, Caitlin isn't my mother; she's my half sister. Of course, Gemma knew all along. Only the three of them knew and never said a word to anyone." She paused a moment, then sighed. "I only wish Grandfather had been the one to tell me." Saying the words aloud sent a torrent of jangled memories through her. It was as if she'd been living someone else's life in those memories, and now she had her own life, but she wasn't sure what that life was. She felt like a phantom, hovering over herself, a different self now she hardly knew.

Rich's voice snapped her back. "You're all right with this? Really?"

"Oh yes. Well, there is a lot to think about. Rich, he was my father, not my grandfather, and he never told me."

Rich said, "Here I thought I knew your grandfather—your father. He probably would have told you, but he didn't have the chance to, sweetheart. The strokes, the coma."

"He had enough years to tell me before the series of strokes."

She'd spoken sharply, anger beneath her words.

He gentled his voice. "You were too young to

understand. He would have told you when you'd gotten older, you know that."

He was right, of course. She had to try to get it together, get over her anger at her father's charade. Rebekah tried for a smile and was vaguely surprised when a real one appeared. "You're right, I shouldn't be angry at him. He did his best by me. But what's wonderful about all this is none of that vicious old witch's blood flows in my veins. I'm free of her now, no more wondering why she always seemed to hate me, no more feeling guilty because I wondered what I'd done wrong.

"But, Rich, how do I reconcile having a father who wouldn't claim me as his own child?" She shook her head. "I'm getting angry at him again. I'm sorry."

"You don't need to be sorry, Rebekah. This is a tremendous shock to you. It is to me, too. Did Gemma tell you who your real mother is?"

"No, I still don't know. Don't get me wrong, I had a wonderful mother. Caitlin loved me always. I never doubted it. What she did, when she was still so young, it was a sacrifice for me. I can't imagine what it must have been like for her to suddenly be her sister's mother, to raise me all those years as her child without ever telling me. I thought about calling her in Spain right away, but I wanted to get my head together before I spoke with her. It's late there now, but I'll call her in the morning." Rebekah sighed. "We have a great deal to talk about, honestly now, for the first time as who we really are—sisters."

"I think it would be best if we kept this between us, not even tell my sons, particularly not my sons. Can you imagine what would happen if the media got hold of it? Beck might post it on Twitter, and even if Tucker kept his mouth shut, Celeste would trumpet it to the world."

"I hadn't thought that far ahead. You're right, of course."

"You haven't eaten much," Rich said, eyeing her plate. "And no wonder. Tell you what, if you're through, let's take our coffee in the living room. We can talk it all out."

She rose as Rich walked to her. He looked down at her a moment, then pulled her close and kissed her hair. "We'll figure our way through all this, don't worry. I want to know everything that happened today with Gemma. I only hope the new girlfriend doesn't boot Beck out early."

The living room draperies were closed against the night, the room warm and cozy. Rich built up the fire and walked back to sit beside her on the sofa. He kissed her, lightly ran his fingers down her smooth cheek. "I thought about you all afternoon, wishing I could call you." He studied her face. "Tell me what else Gemma had to say. Did she admit to anything?"

Rebekah couldn't settle. She stood, walked to the fireplace, stared down at the flames a moment, turned back, and told Rich everything. "And Agent

Savich called me, told me Duvall really doesn't want to go down for this, wants to tell him who hired him, but he doesn't know. It was all done over the phone and in cash. Man, woman? He didn't know, only that it was a scratchy, low voice. He wanted Savich to cut him a break for his honesty. So as it stands now, there isn't enough proof Gemma was involved, and she, of course, knows it."

Rich rose, took her hands, lightly stroked her fingers. "You know, Rebekah, I feel I've been of very little help to you so far. I've been busy, I know, but it's more than that. You've been shutting me out. I want to be a bigger part of helping you find your way through all this."

She felt a wave of guilt. "I never meant to shut you out, Rich. Everything's happened so fast. Zoltan, the attempted kidnapping, the showdown with Gemma, and you said you'd be comfortable leaving things to the FBI. And it's true, you have been busy."

He shook his head. "No, don't let me off the hook. I should have been beside you more through all of this. I sure didn't help when I came home to find you and Agent Hammersmith alone in the bedroom reading your grandfather's letters. That threw me, something I'm not proud of. I'm still embarrassed about the way I acted. But, Rebekah, you never even mentioned you had letters from your grandfather, and we've talked about him quite a bit. I knew him, too, not in the same way you did, of course, but still, in a way, he was part of what brought us together at first. I guess you could say he was our common root. I know how very important he was to you, so please, don't cut me out any longer. Let me help. Talk to me about your father."

She looked into the eyes of the man she'd fallen in love with, her husband of six months now, her life partner. She said slowly, "I never intended to cut you out, Rich. But you see, there were things my father asked me to keep secret, and I kept those secrets for over twenty years." She smiled up at him. "It seems silly not to tell you all about it now, about the poem. I already told it to Agent Savich." She didn't add in Agent Sherlock or Kit. He wouldn't understand.

"Poem? What poem?"

"A poem my father had me memorize when I was young, made me swear never to tell anyone else. It's part of the Big Take story I told you about after those men attacked me, the one Zoltan wanted me to talk about, the story she thought was real." She looked at him and said in a flat, singsong voice:

Don't let them know it's hidden inside
The key to what I wish to hide
It's in my head, already there
And no one else will guess or care
Remember these words when at last I sleep
And the Big Take will be yours to keep.

His hands tightened around hers. "In his head? The key is what he wants to hide? But it doesn't really say much of anything. Do you know what it means, Rebekah?"

"Nope. I haven't got a clue, and believe me, I've thought and thought about what that ridiculous poem could possibly mean. So it never really mattered that I didn't tell Zoltan or that Gemma never heard it."

He pulled away from her and began to pace. He paused, turned back, fanned his hands. "The poem says you know everything you need to find the Big Take even though the poem itself doesn't seem to be of any help at all."

"I told you, Rich, even if I knew where Father hid the Big Take, I wouldn't want it. I have no intention of becoming a criminal, no intention of letting the world find out what Grandfather—Father—and Nate may have done."

He searched her face a moment. "I tell you, Rebekah, this whole situation keeps escalating. There have been shootings now, violence, and I want to help put a stop to it, to protect you. And to be honest, protect myself. If the press were to get a whiff of what's happened already, my career could be in danger. I'm happy you trusted me and told me the poem. I wish you'd told me about it sooner, but I understand. It's a pity you don't know what it means. Maybe we can figure it out in time, and you'll change your mind about that money. Is there anything else important you've kept from me?"

Change her mind? She knew she shouldn't say the words, but they marched right out of her mouth. "After all that's happened, it's your career you're worried about, Rich? And finding the Big Take?"

He stopped cold, searched her face. He said slowly, "Why would you ask me that? Shouldn't my career concern you as well, Rebekah? I mean, we live in this fishbowl together. As for the Big Take, you can do with it as you wish if we find it."

The doorbell rang.

He gave her a long look. "Stay here, Rebekah. I'll see who that is. And then you and I need to get this straightened out."

60

I t was a professional messenger service with a package, asking for a signature.

When Rich returned to the living room, he handed Rebekah a heavy square box. He said, "It's addressed to you, from your father's lawyer, Mr. James Pearson at Pearson, Schultz and Meyers here in Washington. I signed for it."

Rebekah felt her heart pounding as she carried the box back into the living room and set it on an antique marquetry table. Rich handed her scissors, and she cut away the tape and opened the box, her hands unsteady. Taped on top of a thick bubble-wrapped package was a sealed envelope with REBEKAH written in black ink. Her breath caught at the sight of her father's distinctive sloping handwriting. She stood there a moment, holding the letter, wondering if her world was about to change.

Rich said, his voice gentle, "Do you want me to open the letter, Rebekah?"

"No, no, I will." She got it together and slowly opened the envelope to find six handwritten pages. Her heart pounded slow, deep strokes. The letter was dated four years before the strokes had plunged her father into a sixteen-year coma. She'd have been eight years old.

She stepped away, holding the letter close, and read:

> *My dearest Rebekah:*
>
> *As I write this letter, you are still my delightful girl, my Pumpkin. Since you are reading my letter, I've been dead for one month, and I hope you are at least twenty-one. Perhaps you are married, with children of your own. I hope you're happy, that your husband is, or will be, faithful and kind. Ah, isn't that what all of us wish for when we marry? I would have preferred to tell you this myself when you grew up, but it appears I never got the chance.*
>
> *There are so many things you don't know, things you wouldn't have understood as a child. Let me begin*

*with the most important, the truth
of who I really am to you. Perhaps
Gemma or Caitlin has already told you,
though they promised me they wouldn't,
and it wasn't in Gemma's interests that
you know. In any case, it's time you did
know, directly from me. My darling
girl, I am not your grandfather as you
were raised to believe. I am your father.
I met a young woman in Washington in
the late eighties, and we had an affair.
When she discovered she was pregnant,
she told me she simply couldn't keep
you, couldn't accommodate a baby in
her life. I wanted you very much, so I
paid her to carry you to term and sign
adoption papers to give you over to
me. No, she didn't extort me. She had
a very sick mother she cared for and
staggering medical bills, so she agreed.
You will want to know your birth
mother's maiden name was Constance
Riley. If you wish to find her, I can
tell you she moved back to England, to
Birmingham.*

*I was in public life, as you know, and
I couldn't let it be known I had adopted
my own child, born out of wedlock. I
didn't want Gemma to be your mother,
and I knew she would refuse in any*

case. So Caitlin and I decided she would be your mother and I would be your grandfather. I was certainly old enough. To be honest, Caitlin was hesitant, but once she saw you and held you as I had, she wanted you. Never doubt that, dearest.

Forgive me for the deception, but at the time I didn't feel I had a choice. Giving you over to Caitlin was the best way forward for all of us. It kept you close to me, and my love for you only blossomed as the years passed. It wasn't the same for Gemma, of course. She was against my plan, but I gave her no choice. If she wanted to keep running Clarkson United, she had to agree and accept being your grandmother. Our estrangement was complete from that point on.

Now let me tell you what happened in 1995. It has long since ceased to matter to most anyone, except maybe poor Miranda Elderby, but understanding it will soon matter a great deal to you. You see, for two years before Nate met and married Miranda, he and Gemma were lovers. Yes, I knew all about it but said nothing to either Gemma or Nate. Perhaps it's my own conceit, but I believed Gemma took Nate

as her lover to punish me for my own
betrayal. To be honest, I didn't care.
As I said, she and I shared a business
partnership by that time, nothing more.
And Nate? I'd loved Nate since we were
boys, loved him more than I'd ever loved
Gemma, truth be told, and I would have
forgiven him much more, and he me,
I suspect. Fact is, when I found out he
was sleeping with Gemma, I felt sorry
for him because I knew he had to feel
immense guilt, even though he knew
the only thing tying Gemma and me
together was the business. And yes, Nate
knew of my affair with Constance Riley
and about you

Nate broke off his affair with Gemma
when he married Miranda, a lovely young
woman you would have liked very much.
He fell in love, you see, for the first time
in his life, and I understood, maybe I was
even a bit jealous.

Then Nate's luck ran out. I
remember I warned him not to take
on a particular client being tried for
murder, told him it could end badly if
he lost because of his client's criminal
family, but he didn't listen. He lost
the case because the evidence was too
overwhelming. The family blamed him,

of course. It did end badly for him, but not in the way any of us could have imagined.

His client's family didn't murder Nate, Rebekah. Gemma murdered him that long-ago afternoon on Dawg Creek. I'm quite sure of it. It's true he'd been drinking, what with everything happening, and he told me he was going there to face off with Gemma, to tell her he was leaving the country with Miranda. Yes, he asked me for his share of a great deal of money due to him so he and Miranda could settle outside the country in lifelong comfort. I will tell you about that money in a moment, Rebekah.

Poor Nate didn't realize how vindictive Gemma could be, how quickly she could morph from pleasant and smiling to uncontrolled rage. I don't think she intended to murder Nate. I believe she went out to his boat hoping to convince him to come back to her, and when he told her he didn't want her, that he was leaving the country with Miranda, she lost it and killed him. As I said, I wasn't there, but I know that's what happened. You see, she came to me demanding Nate's share of the money, said she deserved it. He'd let our theft slip to her, but thank heaven he hadn't

told her where we were hiding it. I told
her I knew what she'd done, that she'd
killed him, and she threatened to tell the
world about how Nate and I had stolen
the money. So, we were deadlocked. I
agreed because I knew the consequences
of my telling the truth would have
been staggering. I've since regretted
that decision. Gemma deserved to be
punished, and Miranda deserved the
truth. But I kept silent, and Gemma did
as well. You need to know all this now
so you will understand what I've done
and what I plan to do.

It's time for you to claim your
inheritance. Yes, I left you a sizable
trust fund, but this is more, unbelievably
more. Ninety million dollars in bearer
bonds, bonds you can take to any bank
for payment. Nate and I hid the bonds
because we couldn't afford to draw
attention and agreed to wait until we
were sure no one would come looking for
the money or asking questions.

I've arranged to leave it all to you.
Only you will know how to find the
bonds, if you think and remember. I have
but one request: Gemma must never see a
cent of it.

Where the money is from is the last

secret I will tell you. As you know, I was
in Congress in the early nineties when
we were trying to steer our way through
the madness of Saddam Hussein's reign
in Iraq after Desert Storm. I served
on the House Intelligence Committee
when our government was involved in
clandestine efforts to topple Saddam or
at least sow trouble for him. We were
sending black-ops funds, off the books,
to support Shia clerics and warlords
militarily in the south of Iraq. It was a
gravely immoral act because they didn't
have a chance. I knew that money
would only lead to yet more chaos,
more unnecessary slaughter. But I
couldn't change enough minds, couldn't
stop it. It was Nate who suggested we
might be able to divert some of those
funds by leveraging my position on the
committee and my contacts in Iraq.
He arranged to pay off a key Iraqi
conduit to confirm to our government
that he'd received all the funds, rather
than only a part. All went as planned,
apparently business as usual in that
vicious sectarian war. I'm only sorry we
couldn't divert more of it.

I'm sure you remember the story
I told you when you were a child.

*So many versions of how Nate and
I managed to steal the evil sheikh's
treasure. I tried to make it more exciting
each time with ever more outrageous
adventures, so you would remember it.
The story was a tale for a child, but the
bearer bonds are real and will soon be
in your hands to do with as you wish.
What you already know, what you've
kept secret, will lead you to their hiding
place.*

*I have done what I can to be sure no
problems arise no matter how many years
pass before you read this letter. Surely
the bonds will have been forgotten, so you
needn't worry about cashing them. There
is so much good you can do with that
money, Rebekah. But in any case, it is your
decision.*

*I have loved you from the moment I
first saw you squalling in the nursery at
the hospital. I hope you will remember
me fondly despite what I felt I had to
keep from you. I've always thought life
is an incredible gift, regardless of its
unexpected tragedies. My life has been
blessed by a profound joy bestowed upon
me, namely you. Of course, I don't know
how or when I will die, but I will leave
this earth with only one regret—that I*

let down my friend Nate. I hope I have a
chance to ask him to forgive me.
　　Live happily, Rebekah, and try to
live honorably.

Your loving father,
John Clarkson

61

Rebekah blinked back tears and read the letter again, more slowly. All those wasted years when he was in the sanitarium, all the lies and deceptions that had molded her life. When she finished reading the second time, all she could think about was that her mother's name was Constance. She looked mutely up at her husband, unaware tears were slowly running down her face.

Rich pulled her against him, his voice warm against her cheek. "Don't cry, sweetheart. May I read it?"

She couldn't speak, only nodded and swiped her hands over her eyes. "What he wrote—I loved him so much, it got to me. Yes, read it, Rich, you'll see."

He hugged her again, took the pages from her

hands, and stepped away. She expected to see concern in his eyes as he read, and she did, but she saw something else, too. Eagerness? Barely banked excitement? She swiped her hand across her eyes, turned to the fireplace, and stuck out her hands to warm them, but there was little warmth, only her mother's name. Constance Riley. She felt like a blind person suddenly granted sight, but what she knew now gave her no comfort. Gemma had murdered Nate and gotten away with it. Her father and Nate had stolen ninety million dollars in bearer bonds. And her mother—no, not her mother; Caitlin was her half sister. Nothing she'd believed was real. She couldn't take it all in. No wonder Gemma had her attacked to get her hands on those bearer bonds. She was nothing to Gemma. She waited, watched her husband's face as he read the letter again, just as she'd done.

Rich looked up from the letter, and said, his voice gentle, honest, "Listen to me, Rebekah. John Clarkson loved you more than anyone in this world. Never forget that. And he tells you everything in this letter. He would have told you years ago if he could, when he thought you were old enough to know. He was trying to protect you."

"Yes," she said finally, her voice flat, "he would have told me himself. When I was eighteen? Twenty-one?"

Rich looked down at the pages again and slowly shook his head. "I never doubted he was brilliant at getting whatever he thought was right. He was a man I admired. What he writes, Rebekah, it's hard to take in, to believe. What he and Nate did, taking that money, he actually believed he'd done an honorable thing, the right thing. He thought it was justified."

She said in the same flat voice, "Even if that's true, he and Nate still stole a fortune in bearer bonds, and they kept it. He knew Gemma killed Nate and said nothing, hid the knowledge away. And he regrets Nate didn't get justice because of the agreement he made with Gemma? It was his doing, though Nate was the man he professed to love from boyhood. What kind of man was he, really?"

"I agree with you. There was no justice and never will be for Nate. Still, your father and Nate managed to steal ninety million dollars meant for Iraqi militias, and no one else was ever the wiser. Remember, Rebekah, he didn't spend the money; he hid it. He left it for you to decide what to do with it."

At her silence, he continued, "He gives you the name of your birth mother, Constance Riley." He smiled at her, stroked her arm. "Do you think you might be half Irish?"

What a thought for Rich to have, as if it were important. She looked up at him, saw his half smile. He was only trying to make her feel better. So she smiled back at him. "Maybe," she said.

He said thoughtfully, "I remember there were some rumors your father had killed his longtime friend, but very few believed them. But, Rebekah, that's all over, and he's left it up to you and me, sweetheart, to take the next step. Think, Rebekah, ninety million dollars in bearer bonds, hidden somewhere, and your father writes what you already know will lead you to where he and Nate hid them. It's the poem. I think if you and I go over the poem again—" He paused, studied her set face. "Rebekah, think of what good we could do with ninety million dollars. You and I can work on it together, leave the FBI out of it, just us."

She looked up at him for a moment, then turned away from him toward the sluggish flames. "Zoltan believed the poem was the key to finding the Big Take, but you've heard it now and you know as much as I do, which is nothing. And I've told you I don't want to pursue it." She looked back at his face, the lines softened in the firelight. Such a handsome face, she'd thought when she'd seen him that first time at Lincoln Center. She said slowly, "You really want to find those bearer bonds, don't you, Rich?"

He cocked his head at her. "Well, of course. It's an immense amount of money. As I said, there is so much good we could do with it, you and I. The letter points back to the poem, the answer's got to be there—" He broke off, stared at the bubble-wrapped package sitting on the coffee table where Rebekah had placed it. "We need to open the package, see what's inside, see if that key in the poem is in there."

"I told you, Rich, I want nothing to do with the bearer bonds." She picked up the bubble-wrapped package and held it to her chest. "Whatever is inside this Bubble Wrap is meant for me. Not you. Not us."

He grabbed her arm. "Rebekah, how can you think you still need to keep his secrets from me? That man lied to you your whole life, and I'm your husband. If you're concerned about ethics, what about our vows to each other? I hope you'll honor those, rather than a child's promise to a dead man. Give me the package, Rebekah."

She shook her head, held the package tighter.

"Give it to me, Rebekah."

She shook her head again. "No."

He moved fast, pulled the package out of her arms, and stepped back. He walked quickly to the marquetry table, picked a pair of scissors out of the drawer, and began cutting the Bubble Wrap, peeling it away. He said without looking up, "There's no need to get hysterical, Rebekah. We're only going to see what your dad sent you."

He lifted a plaster of paris bust of her father from its nest of padding, held it up to the light. "A bust of your father? Wait, I see now. The poem said the key is in his head."

Rebekah said quietly, "The bust is mine, Rich, not yours. Don't smash it."

"That's exactly what we need to do."

"Rich, no!"

He slammed the bust against the marble apron

in front of the fireplace. It shattered loud as a gunshot, spewing up shards of plaster.

Rebekah cried out, dropped to her knees, and began to pick through the plaster pieces. He saw the key first, leaned down, and grabbed it. "The key was in the old man's head. How very fitting. Without the poem, we would never have known it was there, and the bust might have stayed whole forever." He left her there, on her knees, her father's bust in pieces around her.

Slowly, Rebekah got to her feet. She watched him examine the key under a table lamp. He looked up, saw her, and smiled. "It's a small brass key, common, nothing on it, no indication what it's to, maybe a safe-deposit key, but there's no ID, no serial numbers." Still smiling, he carried the key to where she stood stiff, so angry she had no words. "Do you know what this key is to, Rebekah?"

She could make out two tiny wavy lines along the curved top of the key, one red, the other blue, barely visible to the naked eye. She felt her heart leap. She knew, yes, she knew exactly where those bearer bonds were hidden. She looked up at her husband, kept her voice calm, submissive. "It is what you see, Rich, a plain little brass key. I have no idea what it opens."

"Another secret inside a secret? That's a lot like him. Will they ever stop?" He paused a moment, studied her face, studied the key again. He said slowly, "But I don't believe you, Rebekah."

And suddenly she knew, knew it in her heart. "When did Gemma first talk to you, Rich, ask for your help? At the funeral?"

"What? Are you accusing me of something now? What's wrong with you, Rebekah?"

She looked up into his face. She saw impatience, calculation. She said slowly, "You and I talked much more about my father and his stories after he died. I thought you were being thoughtful and supportive, because I was grieving for him. I've been quite an idiot, haven't I? Gemma knew I would never tell her, but she knew you from way back in the nineties when you interned for my father. Did she see you as a kindred spirit, smart enough, sly enough, to help her find that money without my even knowing about it? Is that what you did to me, Rich?"

He fanned his hands in front of him, a gesture meant to reassure. "Whatever Gemma did, sweetheart, you mustn't ever doubt I love you. I asked you to marry me because I wanted you in my life forever, and I still do."

"You can't hide talking with her, Rich. There'll be phone records, emails."

"I'm not going to hide anything, Rebekah. Yes, Gemma did call me, told me about what one of the private duty nurses had told her about this poem you'd recited to your dad. Listen to me, Rebekah, Gemma knew you would never talk to her about it, and she doubted you'd say the poem again to anyone. And yes, she assured me a great deal of money was at stake. She didn't know how much, but she thought it was immense. Believe me, I thought long and hard about what to do, and in the end I decided it was in everyone's interest to find that money. It's meant for you, Rebekah, all of it."

She said dispassionately, "The séance with Zoltan, that would have been Gemma's idea. But I remember how supportive you were when Zoltan asked to see me. I was expecting you to resist my going, but you didn't; you encouraged me. You knew, didn't you? You knew Gemma hired Zoltan to try to manipulate me into believing I was speaking to my dead father, in her ridiculous living room."

"You never spoke of the poem, and Gemma believed Zoltan could convince anyone of anything. I saw no harm in it, though I warned her you have no belief in the occult, mediums in particular."

"Zoltan didn't believe I'd return, but I told you that, Rich, that same night. And the very next day, those two men tried to kidnap me. Was it you who hired those men so they could force me to tell them?"

He looked appalled, angry. "Listen to me, that's crazy. I love you. I'm your husband. I never hired anyone to kidnap you. I had nothing to do with that. I knew nothing about it, and after I found out what happened, I called Gemma. She denied it. All right, I didn't believe her. But you can believe this. I told her if anything like that ever happened again,

I'd tell you everything. You're my wife. I protected you."

"You said you didn't believe her, yet you still didn't tell me?"

He said nothing. Rebekah looked at the face of the man she thought she loved, and now that face was someone else entirely, a stranger, a lying stranger.

"And then Zoltan was attacked, after the FBI was onto her. Which of you arranged for her to be shot?"

Was that fear in his eyes? He was shaking his head at her, back and forth, thinking hard, she could see it, and when he finally spoke, he sounded horrified. "Not me! You must stop this now. I knew nothing about that Zoltan shooting. Nothing. What I've done, what I've tried to do, has only been in your own interest. All right, in both of our interests."

She marveled at him. Which were the truths, which were the lies? She no longer cared. He'd betrayed her, the man she'd given her love, her future. He'd betrayed her with Gemma. He'd betrayed her for money. There was simply nothing more left between them.

"Give me the key, Rich. It's mine, not yours. If you don't, I will tell Agent Savich what you've done, how you schemed to steal that money and failed. He's very good. He'll find a way to connect you to those crimes, you and Gemma both. Can you imagine the headlines when Congressman Manvers is indicted?"

"I want you to tell me what this key belongs to, Rebekah."

"What I know or don't know about that key is no longer any of your concern."

He cursed in a low voice, threw the key at her. It fell on the sofa beside her. "Keep the bloody thing. I don't care. I was an idiot to get involved in any of this with Gemma. An idiot. But if you accuse me to Savich, I will tell the world your father, the esteemed Congressman John Clarkson, stole ninety million dollars from the government. Your daddy doesn't deserve to be remembered as a criminal, does he?"

She saw the banked rage in his eyes fade the moment he realized they were deadlocked.

He gave a bitter laugh and shrugged. "You do know where the bonds are, don't you?"

She said, "I want you to leave the house now. No, I don't want your house. I'll move out tomorrow. But I want you to leave now."

"Rebekah, you have to believe me—"

"Do you know, I'm understanding Beck better with each passing minute in your company." She didn't look at him again, walked out of the living room, her head held high, carrying the small brass key and her father's letter, and climbed up the wide staircase.

She heard the front door slam. She slowly walked

back down the stairs and turned the dead bolt, remembered Beck, sighed, and flipped it off. It didn't matter if Rich came back. What could he do?

When she stepped into her bedroom, she looked toward the bed where she'd slept beside her husband for six months, a man she'd married and trusted, counted on. She looked at her father's letter again. *Life is an incredible gift, regardless of its unexpected tragedies.*

A gift. Perhaps someday she'd believe it. She looked down at the key and smiled.

62

Agent Dillon Savich, Agent Pippa Cinelli, Chief Matthew Wilde, and federal prosecutor Sonja Grayson sat in the small conference room and watched two guards bring in Marsia Gay, one holding each arm. Her wrists were pressed together with flex-cuffs. She stopped in the doorway and looked at each of them in turn. "What's all this? All the top guns here to visit me? To bring me news? Good news, I hope. And who are you?"

"I'm Chief Wilde of St. Lumis, Maryland. I believe you've visited my town."

She shook her head at him. "Sorry, never had the pleasure." Her smile stayed fixed as she turned to the prosecutor. "I suppose you're here, Ms. Grayson, to tell me I'm not going to trial? Not enough proof, is there? Poor Veronica. Does anyone know who attacked her? Such a pity. Of course, since I'm innocent, it will mean justice for me. When will I be released?"

Sonja said, "We'll talk about your legal status in a moment, Ms. Gay. First, Agent Savich wants to speak to you."

"Sit down, Marsia," Savich said.

The guards sat her down, placed her hands on the table in front of her. She said to Savich, "Isn't life strange, Agent Savich? You simply never know when misfortune will befall you. Me, being here, you, with that fire at your house? I have to say, in all fairness, what you did to me, putting me here, was worse."

Savich studied her face, saw the banked excitement in her eyes. Yes, Marsia thought she was about to waltz out of here. "I'd like you to hear what Agent Cinelli has to say. She was in St. Lumis to investigate the red boxes you had sent to me, the ones containing pieces of a puzzle depicting Major Trumbo hanging out of a burning hotel window."

"Sorry, Agent Savich, I don't know what you're talking about."

Savich continued over her, "Agent Cinelli worked with Chief of Police Matthew Wilde." He nodded to Pippa.

Pippa said without preamble, "Ronald Pomfrey and his mother, Lillian Trumbo, told us what happened that night in Ronald's cabin in the Poconos, where you witnessed Ronald stab Major Trumbo in the back. They're more than willing to testify against you."

There was not a single sign Marsia found this news upsetting. She even smiled. "Of course I know those people. I dated Ronald briefly when we were in school. But I have no idea what they've been saying to you." She tried to rise, but a guard pushed her back down. She smiled up at the guard. "Sorry."

Pippa said, "We know you dated Ronald Pomfrey in your first year at Maryland Institute College of Art. He thought you loved him, you were planning to move in together, but by the time you first showed him your black heart that night in the Poconos, it was too late for him.

"When Ronald and Mrs. Trumbo realized Major Trumbo was dead, you watched them try to figure out what they should do. You must have despised their shock, their dithering, their horror at what had happened. You bided your time, took pictures of his body without their knowing it, and you told them you knew exactly what they should do. You told them to bury the major's body where it wouldn't be found and forget him, go about their lives. They could say he died of a heart attack, pretend they'd had his body cremated. Otherwise who knew what would happen to them?

"You were careful not to help them bury the major's body. You stood back and filmed it all. After that, it would look like they'd simply murdered him, no matter what they claimed. You sent Ronald some of what you'd filmed, and they've been paying you ever since to keep it secret. You were careful not to empty the well. Besides, you thought you might need them, use them, someday. And you did."

Savich said, "You're smart, Marsia, loaded with talent, but you threw it all away because you're a psychopath without any sense of remorse to restrain you. You wanted your revenge on me and Sherlock, the other two witnesses against you. You picked my wife first because you wanted me to suffer losing her, losing my son.

"You're going to face attempted murder charges, namely of my wife and son, a conspiracy charge for arson, and, of course, charges for blackmail and extortion. I'm sure Ms. Grayson will tell you those are only a start."

Marsia drummed her fingers on the tabletop. She began humming under her breath, then sneered. "Is that your wish list, Savich? On the word of killers? And that's what they are."

Savich saw her pulse pounding in her throat. She hadn't expected this; she'd been simply too arrogant to believe Mrs. Trumbo and her son would ever confess to anything. Savich pulled Marsia's cell phone out of his pocket and placed it on the table. "Your first mistake was sending Ronald a sample."

Savich was pleased to see the sneer fall off her face. It was replaced not by rage, but by frenzied thought. She grew perfectly still, her hands fists in front of her. He said, "We located your old cell phone in a safe deposit box. If you've forgotten, take a look." Everyone crowded in close as he punched up the images. There were stills of Major Trumbo's body lying on a floor, a knife in his back.

"Now the burial." Snippets of video appeared, less than a minute long, but they showed both mother and son digging frantically into hard earth. When the hole was big enough, they rolled Major Trumbo into it and shoveled dirt over him, strewed dead leaves and branches over it all.

Pippa said, "Of course, you didn't film the major hitting his wife, trying to strangle her before Ronald stabbed him. That would have shouted self-defense. No close-ups of Mrs. Trumbo or Ronald, either, not a surprise, you would have edited them out, with all the bruises Ronald had from Major Trumbo's fists. And you made sure we don't see the bruises on Mrs. Trumbo's neck from the major trying to kill her. You're an artist, Ms. Gay. You know what has punch and what doesn't."

Savich switched off the cell phone, sat back, crossed his arms.

Marsia laughed. "That doesn't prove anything other than those two are murderers." She leaned back in the chair, raised her chin. "What I saw was cold-blooded murder, and now you've seen it, too. I documented what they did to protect myself so they wouldn't kill me, too, and bury me like they did Major Trumbo. I was grateful to leave that place alive. You should thank me for providing the proof. It's about time they go down for murdering her husband."

Wilde said, drawing her attention to him, "Blackmail only works so long as there is something left to hide, Ms. Gay. While there was, Mrs. Trumbo and Ronald did as you demanded, but then you asked too much of them. Ronald Pomfrey couldn't bring himself to torch the Savich house with Agent Savich's wife and son inside. He set a fire, yes, but only in the kitchen so he could show you he'd tried.

"It probably didn't matter to you whether he killed Agent Cinelli, but it did to him. And everything Lillian Trumbo did, she did to protect her son, from you."

Savich said, "I'll bet you were very angry at Ronald, Marsia, for failing at what you'd told him to do. Did it ever occur to you this man simply couldn't do it, couldn't kill two people?"

Marsia didn't move, didn't say a word. There was no expression on her face at all, but Savich knew she was hiding a deep black well of rage. She looked down at her fingernails, filed short. Finally she looked back at him. "As I said, Savich, it's my word against a couple of murderers trying for a lighter sentence, murderers you choose to believe." She looked at Wilde. "And you, the chief of police of that bum-crap little town, are you all aflutter the FBI is letting you play with them? You're a fool."

Wilde sat forward. "I guess you haven't figured out yet that Savich tracked down the IP address of the person who's been sending your instructions to the Trumbos. He didn't cover his tracks well enough. It doesn't matter you didn't put your name on them. We'll connect them to you, probably through your lawyer. You know what else? I can't tell you how pleased I am you're going to be in prison for the rest of your life, and how grateful I am for the small part I've played in saving all of us from having to deal with you again."

Sonja Grayson cleared her throat, bringing Marsia's eyes to her. "I'm here to inform you, Ms. Gay, that in addition to the charges we'll be bringing against you in the Trumbo case, the court is scheduling your trial for the attempted murder of Mrs. Venus Rasmussen."

Marsia sneered. "If you believe these FBI yahoos, you're not as bright as I thought you were. Without Veronica, you don't have enough evidence to convict me of anything."

"You'll be pleased to know your dear friend Veronica Lake is no longer in critical condition. Her condition is guarded, but it's likely she'll survive." Below the table, Sonja crossed her fingers, said a silent prayer.

Marsia Gay froze. She began shaking her head back and forth. Angela had promised her, right in the heart. She heard her mother's voice, booze-slurred and mean, *I told you Ronald was too weak, told you he'd fold, the little loser. But you never listen, and now it's all over for you, Daughter.*

"No, no, it can't be all over. No!" The drunk bitch was always telling her she was wrong, she was stupid. Marsia caught herself. She'd die before she showed these people any weakness. She looked at each of them in turn and said easily, "That's a line from a book. Unlike you Nazis, the book is fascinating."

Sonja rose and flattened her palms on the table. "Oh yes, Ms. Gay. Finally, I'll see you in court. Enjoy your book."

Marsia drew a deep breath and gave them a beautiful smile. "I'd like to see my lawyer now."

63

GEORGETOWN
M STREET
CLYDE'S OF GEORGETOWN
SATURDAY NIGHT

Savich, Sherlock, Pippa, and Wilde sat in a booth, a bit away from the happy laughter and conversation at Clyde's bar.

Chief Wilde said, waving a barbecue rib in his hand, "I'm asking for probation for Mrs. Trumbo, some community service, along with a stern lecture on her poor judgment in not reporting a death, self-defense or not. Of course, she would have done it if Marsia Gay hadn't extorted her. I can't see putting her in jail for helping her son, either, even after he attacked Cinelli. Mrs. Trumbo hugged me, and Ronald pumped my hand even though he knows he'll have to do some time, no way around it." He dabbed a bit of barbecue sauce off his chin. "Great ribs. I hear yours are even better, Sherlock, according to your husband."

Sherlock laughed. "What else could Dillon say? We'll have you over after New Year's when we have kitchen appliances again. Our logistics expert said something always goes wrong, in her experience. But Clyde's is always good. Glad you're enjoying it."

Wilde said, "Look at all the bones on my plate. Do you know, when Mrs. Trumbo hugged me, I smelled oatmeal cookies?"

Pippa grinned at him. "She hugged me, too. Alas, no oatmeal cookie smell. After Mrs. Trumbo and Ronald gave Sonja even more details of Marsia's extortion and blackmail scheme, she was so happy she'd have thrown the Trumbos a parade if she could. But what about us? We deserve a parade, too, don't you agree, Wilde?"

He laughed, patted her hand. "I gotta admit, Cinelli, when you showed up at my house all banged up, pathetic, really, you perked me right up. I've had as much fun these last few days as I ever had in Philadelphia." He paused a moment, fiddling with the final rib on his plate. "I'd forgotten the rush, the challenge. I'm thinking it's time I moved on, left St. Lumis, maybe moved here to Metro. What do you think, Savich?"

Savich said slowly, "St. Lumis was a good place to heal, Chief. You interested instead in the FBI?"

Wilde reared back in his chair. "Become a Fed? Like Cinelli here?"

Sherlock said, "You have excellent big-city police experience, Chief. Unless you stole coffee money from the homicide division pot in the Philadelphia PD, I think the FBI would be proud to have you, and very lucky. From what Pippa says, you have a good brain. Not as sharp and fast as hers, of course, but still."

"Something to think about," Wilde said, and wondered how Savich knew he'd had to leave Philadelphia to heal. He realized now he wanted to be back in the game, the real game. He said, "When does Marsia Gay go to trial, Savich?"

Savich took the last bite of his pesto pasta, chewed, and sighed with pleasure. "Sonja told me the first week of March. That will give Veronica Lake time to get well enough to take the stand and provide the testimony to nail the cell door on Marsia." He paused as he looked thoughtfully at his green beans. "I visited Veronica yesterday. She seemed different, more centered and self-aware, I guess you could say. Quite a thing to almost be murdered. When I left, she thanked me, told me her time with Marsia seemed like an ugly dream now, that she'd lost herself. She wants to make amends and wants to start in prison. She can teach, she said, she can listen. She's hoping she can heal herself."

Sherlock said, "We're endlessly grateful Veronica didn't die and is eager to put Marsia in jail for the rest of her life." She sat back, took a sip of wine, gave them a big smile. "It's all good."

"One less psychopath to sow misery and chaos in the world," Pippa said.

Sherlock turned to her. "The CAU will miss you, Pippa, but your unit chief was clicking her heels knowing you'll be back on Monday. Jessie told me she wasn't surprised you did a great job, because she'd trained you herself."

"I've learned a lot from her, of course, but—" Pippa took a sip of her rich cabernet, carefully set down her wineglass, and looked at Savich, who nodded. She said, excitement in her voice, "Yesterday I asked for a transfer to the CAU, with Dillon's permission and backing. I really did like bringing down white-collar slime in Financial Crimes, then again—" She shrugged. "I think the CAU is the best fit for me. Now I have to wait and see."

Savich raised his glass. "Let me announce, Agent Cinelli, despite your current boss's best efforts, you won't be returning to Financial Crimes. I talked to Mr. Maitland, and he's pleased to approve your transfer to the CAU. You're ours now."

"The fourth woman in the unit," Sherlock said, and squeezed her hand. "Welcome aboard."

Savich's cell phone vibrated. He looked down, then rose. "Excuse me a moment." He walked to the arch that led to the restrooms. "What's going on, Griffin?"

"Rebekah has asked me to accompany her and Kit to Amsterdam. They're on the trail of a forged van Gogh. Several days, maybe a week. Is this all right with you?"

Savich smiled. "I think it's a great idea. Take a week. Help them track down forgers, make the art world a better place. How is Rebekah doing?"

"Kit told me she's been on the quiet side, understandable with all that's happened in the past week and a half. She doesn't want to talk about it. We've both left her alone to sort through things herself.

"Rebekah did tell me she spoke to her half sister, Caitlin, and Rebekah has made plans for the three of us to fly to Spain after she and Kit finish in Amsterdam. On the way home Rebekah also asked Kit and me to stop with her in Birmingham, England, to meet her mother, Constance Riley." Griffin paused a moment, added, "I assume Caitlin told her all about her birth mother, since Gemma wouldn't give Rebekah the time of day, and there's no one else who knows. Rebekah's spoken on the phone to her mother, quite a thing for both of them. She said she's looking forward to meeting her daughter."

"You'll be a rock for her, Griffin, you and Kit both. And there's no reason for you all to stay here. Gemma refuses to see anyone again, Duvall would seriously like to pin someone to gain leniency but can't, and Zoltan has managed to disappear quite effectively, if she survived the gunshot. And I'll bet my Redskins tickets she did. But who knows, maybe something will turn up." Savich doubted it. He added, "You make Rebekah smile, Griffin, maybe tell her Congressman Manvers lost his greatest asset, namely her. I can understand her being private about their breakup. A great deal has happened for her to work through, but it came as a surprise."

Griffin said, "True enough. Kit will be a great support to her. She's got this wonderful smile, a really sly wit, and she loves Rebekah. And you wouldn't believe how smart she is, she—" Griffin coughed, shut up.

Savich was grinning into his cell, but his voice was matter-of-fact. "Yes, she is." He paused a moment, then said, "Do you know, Griffin, I find myself wondering whether Rebekah knows more than she shared with us about the Big Take. Do you think she might know where it's hidden?"

"I asked her, and she just gave me a look. Yes, she knows, but I doubt she'll ever tell a soul. She's only sorry Gemma won't ever pay for her crimes, especially for killing Nate."

As Savich walked back into Clyde's dining room, he thought, *Sometimes there isn't any justice even if you know the truth.* But acceptance was difficult. Still, Clyde's lights were soft, the conversation low and steady, the waiters were bringing plates, pouring drinks. He looked up to see Sherlock smiling toward him and let it go. He thought about Griffin and Kit Jarrett. You never knew. People were amazing.

EPILOGUE

Zoltan, who now called herself Sharma, hummed as she plaited cornrows in a young girl's long blond hair on her chosen beach in Montego Bay. Pretty girl, not more than sixteen, and spoiled rotten. It was easy enough for the teen to more or less order her mother to pay for the cornrows even though it was obvious Mrs. Grace Chivers, rich enough to own this five-star resort, didn't want cornrows on her daughter's head.

She hardly listened as the girl talked trash about her supposed best friend, her thoughts returning to the night that man had broken into her house to kill her. She had known it had to be Gemma Clarkson who'd hired him, and she'd called her, outraged. She should have thought it through, she'd realized once she'd calmed down, a big mistake on her part. She'd yelled at Clarkson for not having any faith she could coax Rebekah back, but now she was involving her in violence. Gemma hadn't even bothered to argue with her. It was clear she would stop at nothing. Zoltan had prayed she was wrong, but she'd realized she could be in danger. Agent Savich had brought that home to her.

And so she'd pulled out her small Colt buried in the back of her underwear drawer and carried it around in her pocket. It had saved her life. She'd shot him when he surprised her, a nice center shot, she hoped, after his bullet had only gone through the flesh of her arm. She lost lots of blood, of course, but that didn't stop her from grabbing what she needed and driving out of Washington. She'd stopped at an urgent care clinic in North Carolina, and then it was a straight shot to Miami.

Zoltan paused in plaiting a cornrow, raised her eyes to the awesome blue sky, and thanked Zoltan for teaching her to always keep a fake passport available. You never knew, he'd say, when it would be best to take your skills elsewhere. She did miss her beautiful old house outfitted with all the dramatic touches for her clients' benefit, but Jamaica had its own opportunities.

She thought about Rebekah Manvers, wondered if she knew where the Big Take was hidden.

A pity Rebekah never trusted her, never believed her grandfather had come to chat, even with her special tea. In the long run, though, would it have mattered? Maybe so, given what she'd read online yesterday. Clarkson United had been bought out. The financial analyst called it a merger, but between the lines, it was clear Clarkson United had been taken over, clear the old witch was no longer in the driver's seat. And that was the proof Gemma hadn't gotten her hands on the Big Take.

Zoltan studied the cornrow she'd just finished, saw it wasn't perfect, but it was good enough. She bet the teenager would notice and trash-talk her.

She looked out toward the incredible turquoise water at all the happy swimmers, the yelling children, the endless supply of Jamaican hawkers pushing their wares on the tourists. She loved Montego Bay. She couldn't say why she'd picked Jamaica, but it turned out she loved the heat and the fierce sun baking through her muscles, warming her very bones. She loved the sheer laziness of Jamaica, never hurrying or stressing about jobs or traffic jams, only an occasional small one if the goats hunkered down in the middle of the road. From what she'd seen, most of the men didn't work much, just lay about, literally, in the shade of blue mahoe trees, smoking ganja, the women steering the family's course. It was the tourists who were the manic ones, as if they'd been let out of jail for the first time and didn't know what to do with themselves. They seemed incapable of simply relaxing, which was good for her plaiting business and her other growing business as well.

She'd found a woman from the mountains to tutor her in obeah, the Jamaican version of Haitian voodoo. She practiced communicating with ancestors and spirits, and Zoltan certainly knew how to do that. It would be a hard sell to convince Jamaicans a woman from the United States could have any powers, and the fact was few of them had enough money to afford her in any case. Ah, but visitors to Jamaica were different. She'd already begun enticing tourists to let her guide them in obeah sessions. It gave them a chance to be a little wicked and use their money to wallow in a bit of the local shamanism, something to tell their friends when they got home. All seemed to like her name, Sharma. Maybe it gave them a little shudder, made them think of magic. And none of them realized how much you could find out about them in a minute on the web. Like Mrs. Grace Chivers. And after all, the Internet was a kind of magic, wasn't it?

She finished another cornrow, perfect, and she'd only learned two weeks ago. She laughed with pleasure, couldn't help herself. Miss Sixteen-Year-Old twisted around and said in a furious voice, "Why are you laughing? I know I'll look beautiful in cornrows. My mom's a cheapskate and doesn't like anything I do. If you're not doing them right—"

Zoltan leaned close to her ear. "Be quiet, or I'll speak with your grandfather, Phillip Arlington, tell him what a disrespectful brat you are."

"My grandfather? No, that's stupid. Grandpa's dead, two years ago. You can't—how do you know his name?"

Her voice wobbled a bit, and Zoltan saw alarm in those beautiful blue eyes. Good. "Hold still, I'm nearly done. I'm laughing because I'm happy. When your mother comes to pick you up, you will buy her a rum drink with one of those pink umbrellas and tell her she's beautiful and the greatest mom alive." Zoltan finished the last cornrow and held up a mirror.

"Wow, I look amazing." She fingered the cornrows, lifted them up and down, wrapped and unwrapped them around her fingers. And she started to laugh.

Zoltan saw the girl's mother coming, looking every bit as rich as Zoltan's Internet search suggested, a look of dawning horror on her face and cash in her hand. Zoltan leaned close to the girl's ear. "Don't forget to do what I told you. It's what your grandpa wants you to do. And tell your mother she might want to come back and see me. I'm Sharma, and I practice obeah. I can help her speak to your grandfather."

The mother pressed a twenty into her hand and walked away with her daughter. Zoltan saw the girl take her mother's arm, which surprised her mother, and heard the girl say, "Mama, you're so nice to let me experiment. Can I buy you a rum drink? Did I tell you? You're the prettiest mom on the beach."

Grandpa Phillip Arlington would be pleased when they talked to him, and she knew they would. Zoltan saw another customer walking toward her across the sugar sand, older, looking determined. A middle-aged tourist, good thick hair a pretty dark brown, wanting to try something outrageous. Yes, a little wicked. She'd look amazing when Zoltan was finished with her. She was wearing an expensive-looking cover-up. Zoltan gave her a little wave and nod. She felt a slight tug in her arm where she'd been shot. Almost well.

She smiled. Life was good.